What I Am Made Of

Nicole M. Ahles

This is a work of fiction. The characters, organizations, and events portrayed in this novel are either products of the author's imagination or are used fictitiously. Any resemblance to actual events, places, or persons, living or dead, is entirely coincidental.

What I Am Made Of
By: Nicole M. Ahles
Paperback – 2nd edition 2023

www.NicoleAhles.com

NAB Publication
Cover design © Copyright 2014 by Nicole M. Ahles
Interior design by Nicole Ahles
Printed by Ingram Spark

Second Edition
Paperback ISBN: 978-0-9911126-2-3

AUTHOR'S NOTE

The characters of this novel are fictitious. However, many of the described events and locations are not, especially those that occurred in Europe throughout World War II and the Holocaust.

This book is not a historical work, nor does it have the intention of being one. It was simply my goal to shed light on certain events, and to honor every life that was lost during this horrific time in our history. Every lost life, young and old, big and small, was a tragedy and as a world we still mourn. This is a tribute to everyone: to those we lost, those who survived, and those who fought so bravely to stare evil in the face. This is also a tribute to the generations that have since come from those survivors.

FOREWORD

People will not look forward to posterity, who do not look backward to their ancestors.
~Edmund Burke

Nicole Ahles is a wonderful contemporary author, but more importantly, she is also a very dear friend of mine. Not only do I get to work alongside her in the publishing industry, but we also coach a local winter guard team together. I was incredibly honored when she asked me to write this foreword for *What I Am Made Of.*

When Nicole was in the very early stages of the novel, she shared the premise of the story with me and I felt an immediate connection with this book. Like Rachel in *What I Am Made Of,* I have spent countless hours uncovering my family heritage and discovering my European Jewish roots. I learned through recorded interviews of my Great Grandmother Helen (Davidovic) Davis Ringer Greenblatt, that she had lost a couple of her brothers in the war, including her brother Adalbert, who perished in Auschwitz. I was thankful that I had the opportunity to share my family's story with Nicole, and was humbled when she chose to include our untold story in her novel. Like Rachel, my research has been an emotional, yet fulfilling journey.

What I Am Made Of brilliantly and ambitiously spans both decades and continents. It is a sweeping novel with an emotionally riveting and enthralling family saga that will keep readers turning the pages. I encourage people to research their ancestry because as we uncover our history, we reveal the true character of who we are.

Shoshannah R. Cobb
Senior Editor, Indigo Violet Publishing Co.

Do not remove the ancient landmark that your ancestors set up.
~Hebrew, Proverbs 22:28

In memory of *Adalbert Davidovic*

What I Am Made Of

ONE

Although it was technically daylight, it was still dark around the shop. The sun always took longer to rise around Lake Arrowhead. The towering coniferous pines were as much walls around the small village as the mountains were and they restricted the early morning rays of sunlight until late morning. However, the wide-open lake, beyond the north windows of the shop, was brightly lit. The sunlight flickered off of the pristine blue waters of the lake.

Rachel flipped on the lights in the drafty shop and shivered slightly. It would warm up as the morning pressed on. But this time of year was always brisk in the mornings and evenings. As the shop came to life around her, there was a jiggling of the front doorknob. Suddenly it burst open, and three children came traipsing inside, followed by their mother. Kristin was balancing two large boxes in her hands, most likely filled with some kind of pastry, while her children ran around her legs.

"Gracie, you need to finish your homework. Go sit at one of the tables and do that now, please," she told her oldest daughter.

"Morning," Rachel said as she scooped Parker, Kristin's youngest, up into her arms.

"Hi Ray-el" he said with a beaming grin, his dark brown eyes twinkling behind his long and envious eyelashes.

She kissed him lightly on the forehead and put him back down.

"Monday mornings aren't really my favorite," Kristin said as she set the boxes on the counter of the café. "But you've got to try these new cupcakes I made last night: white chocolate pumpkin cheesecake. They are to die for."

Rachel felt her stomach do a small flip. Despite the fact that they did sound absolutely delicious, the thought of eating something so sweet before her morning coffee was too much for her stomach.

Kristin slipped out of her jacket and hung it on the coat rack near the door, then stepped behind the café counter and went to work. She flipped on the coffee makers, which were already set to go from closing on Saturday. She turned on the cappuccino machine and then started bringing out her bakery items from the back kitchen.

A thud from overhead told Rachel that Aspen was finally awake. She glanced at the clock to see how much time she had before the bus came. Twenty minutes. Rachel rolled her eyes as she headed for the back staircase that took her up to their small apartment above the shop.

"Aspen!" she called when she stepped into the warm and cozy apartment.

Aspen came flying out of her room, fully dressed, and headed into the bathroom to brush her teeth.

"Nothing like cutting it close this morning," she said to her daughter.

Aspen turned to face her, her toothbrush sticking out of her mouth, bubbly toothpaste gathering at the corners of her lips while she ran a brush through her hair.

"Sorry. I just couldn't get up," she mumbled as she continued brushing her teeth.

"I think maybe you should go to bed a little earlier on Sunday nights. This seems to be a regular occurrence on Monday mornings," Rachel said with a sigh as she crossed her arms.

Aspen rolled her eyes and spit into the sink. "It's fine, Mom. Besides, I was doing homework. You can't really get mad that I stayed up late doing homework."

"When you spend all weekend with your friends rather than doing your homework, then I can be. I mean it. Next weekend, no friends until your homework is done," she said with finality so her daughter wouldn't keep arguing with her. "Now hurry up. I'll have a bagel ready for you when you come downstairs. You can eat it on the bus."

Back down in the shop, Rachel headed for the front door. It wasn't quite seven yet, but there was no point in keeping out paying customers on a twenty-minute technicality. Once she flipped the sign in the window from closed to open, she headed to the back storage room and pulled out a box of books that needed to be cataloged and added to the shelves.

Sinful Retreat was in a home that had been passed down through Rachel's family. Her grandfather had bought it after moving to California from New York in the forties. He and his wife Elaine raised their five children there. And after Elaine died of breast cancer and Aaron was no longer sound enough to take care of himself, Rachel's father, Joseph, moved his family from Los Angeles into the home to help care for his father.

After Aaron died in 2003, Joseph returned to Los Angeles and left the home to Rachel. A young, single mother, she opened Sinful Retreat with Kristin. It was a quaint, local bookstore and café perched along the banks of Lake Arrowhead.

Kristin put a paper baggie in front of Rachel. "For Aspen. It's breakfast," she said with a smile. "Parker, Kate," she called to her other children that had slipped into the children's nook to watch cartoons, "Come eat, please."

A moment later, Rachel heard the pounding of Aspen's footsteps coming down the back staircase into the shop.

"I mean what I said about next weekend," she said, handing her the toasted bagel.

"You're so unfair!" Aspen stomped as she snatched the food from her mom and headed out the front door. The roar of the approaching bus could be heard in the distance.

"Twelve going on twenty," Rachel said with a sigh and Kristin giggled.

"Mom, Parker's putting his food in my hair!" Kate called from a table near the window at the front of the shop.

"Parker…" Kristin called as she stepped out from behind the counter to discipline her youngest.

The front door of the shop opened, and the little ding of the bell rang through the shop. The heels of Tiff's boots clacked on the hard-wooden floors as she headed toward a table to drop her large tote bag.

"Morning sunshine," Rachel called to her friend from behind counter.

"Usual for you, Tiff?" Kristin asked.

"I need a double shot of espresso this morning," she said with a yawn. "Siena was up all night with a fever."

"Ooh, not good." Rachel stood up and set a stack of books on the counter. She reveled in the smell of new books. She grabbed a binder from the shelf behind her and flipped it open. "She at your mom's today?"

Tiff shook her head. "Mom has a doctor's appointment. Jake stayed home with her. I've got meetings almost all day."

"Here ya go," Kristin said, handing Tiff the hot to-go cup.

"Have either of you heard from AJ? How did her date go last night?"

"Don't know. Haven't talked to her," Kristin said slapping Parker's hand away from his sister.

"I'm telling you, I could use a date," Tiff said.

Rachel laughed.

"No, I take that back. *You* could use a date," she said with a nod toward Rachel as she wrote in the binder.

"That's not all she could use," Kristin called from the kitchen.

Tiff laughed as she eyed Rachel, who just rolled her eyes at her friends.

"Well ladies," Tiff said as she grabbed her tote, "as much fun as this is, I've got loans I need to write for people. Gracie? You ready to go?" The real estate office that Tiff owned was directly across the street from Gracie's elementary school and so she took Gracie every morning to help Kristin.

"Did you finish your work?" Kristin asked, looking over at her daughter.

The blonde child nodded as she stuffed papers into her pink backpack.

"Have your lunch?"

Gracie nodded again and Kristin kissed her on the top of her head.

"I'll see you later. Have a good day, sweetheart." Gracie smiled up at her mom and then followed Tiff out the front door.

The café grew busy around 7:30, with people coming in for their morning coffee and bagels. It always gave Rachel time to focus on the bookstore, inventorying her shelves and placing orders. Kristin and one of their clerks, Mark, bustled around the café, filling orders and meeting customer demands.

The smell of ground coffee beans and pumpkin bread wafted through the café. After Rachel completed her inventory for the week, she went to the computer to approve the designs for the posters and fliers for the upcoming book signing. Author Marissa Bristow was coming in a few weeks to promote her new novel, *My Mother's Mother*. The Tuesday afternoon book club, Kayscreek Club, was currently reading it, and Rachel was always so interested in it and their conversations about the book every week. She was meaning to read it herself but always had so much going on. It seemed that every night at bedtime, she would get only a few lines read before she fell asleep.

After the morning rush calmed down, Rachel's customers began trickling in. Many were tourists, as Lake Arrowhead Village was always filled with tourists. But some were also residents from the area. She knew nearly every local that came through her door.

"This sure puts a damper on my week." Mark explained as he looked up from his iPhone, "There's a storm coming in. Good chance we'll get some snow tomorrow night as low as 5,000 feet."

Rachel didn't mind the snow. Although it was kind of early in the year for snow, only late October, she knew any amount wouldn't stick around longer than a day. Winter was always a refreshing time of year for her. She loved snuggling up in a blanket near the fireplace and drinking one of Kristin's amazing hot cocoas.

"I've got to drop Kate off at preschool and I'm taking Parker to daycare. I'll be back in about an hour," Kristin said as she rounded up her kids and headed for the front door. "Mark, I need you to pull that Lemon Raspberry cake from the oven in seven minutes!" she yelled over her shoulder before she disappeared outside, her kids in tow.

The afternoon was quiet, and although there was plenty of work for Rachel to be doing, she decided to open *My Mother's Mother* instead. It wouldn't look too good as a bookstore owner to not have read the new release of the author she had coming in a couple weeks.

She quickly got lost in the book and barely even noticed Kristin return without her kids. Mark flitted between both the café and bookstore registers to help customers and Rachel was grateful to have him around.

A little after three o'clock Aspen returned from school. She helped herself to a cookie behind the bakery counter and Rachel put her book down. "How was school?"

"Fine."

"What did you do?"

Aspen shrugged her shoulders. "Nothing."

"Oh, well, isn't that great to hear."

"You're supposed to sign something so I can turn it back in to Mr. Crawford tomorrow," she said, reaching into her bag and digging around.

She pulled out a few stapled sheets of paper, tossed them on the counter and headed upstairs without another word.

Rachel reached for the papers and saw a large, bold red-letter F at the top of the front page. It was Aspen's science test. Rachel sighed loudly and felt her anger beginning to rise. One month into the school year and already Aspen had brought home two Ds and now an F.

"Mark, I need you to cover for me," she called over her shoulder as she headed up to the apartment above the shop.

"Aspen, what is this?" she called when she stepped inside.

"You need to sign it so I can hand it in."

"I realize that. But why did you get an F on this test?"

Aspen shrugged her shoulders while she finished the last of her cookie. She picked up the remote and sat down on the couch.

"No, I don't think so," Rachel said, ripping it from her daughter's hand. "And shrugging your shoulders isn't an answer. I want an answer. Why did you fail this test?"

"Mr. Crawford's a total jerk, Mom."

"Oh, I get it. He's a jerk so that's why you failed your test."

"Even Stacy Pennington, who is like the smartest girl in our class, only got a C on her test. It was so hard. Nothing that was on that test was talked about in class."

"I don't care what Stacy Pennington got on her test. She's not my concern. This is unacceptable. Where is your science book?"

Aspen shrugged her shoulders.

"That's part of your problem. Find it. Now."

Aspen rose from the couch and, dragging her feet with each step, she went into her room. A few minutes later she returned with the book.

Rachel seized it and turned to chapter two. Glancing back at the test, she skimmed for a few keywords and then looked back in the book. Within seconds she had found explanations for three of the four keywords from the test.

"You didn't even try to prepare for this test. All of the answers are right here in this book. So don't give me that crap about Mr. Crawford. It's been right under your nose this whole time. As far as I'm concerned, you're grounded. No phone, television, or Internet unless it's for school purposes."

"But Mom!"

"I don't want to hear it. And you can guarantee I'm calling your dad about this. Go get me your cell phone. Now."

"Ugh!" she gasped in frustration, and she made her way back to her bedroom, stomping her feet in exasperation with each step.

Reluctantly she put it in her mom's hand. "You're so unfair! None of my friends' moms treat their daughters like this."

"Well I'm sorry to hear I'm the only parent in the area. Deal with it."

Rachel put the phone on silent and put it in the top drawer of her dresser. Then, confiscating the remote controls and the laptop, she headed back downstairs to the shop.

"Umm, Rachel," Mark called over his shoulder from the Espresso maker, "there's a guy here looking for you." Mark nodded his head toward a man who stood at a nearby shelf of books, examining their titles.

Rachel put the things in her hands behind the counter and approached the man. "Can I help you?"

He turned around to face her. "Umm, yeah," he said, pulling a newspaper clipping from his pocket. "I'm inquiring about the apartment rental in the paper. Do I talk to you?"

She nodded. "Yes. It's not really an apartment, per se. It's a boathouse. It was remodeled into a small studio. One bedroom, a bathroom and a kitchen. No washer and dryer. $950 a month, utilities except phone and television included."

The man nodded his head. "Could I take a look at it?"

"Sure, give me a second." Rachel headed back to the counter where Mark was ringing up a customer who was buying some travel books for the area. "I'm going to step out back and show the boathouse. Let me know if you need any help. And if Aspen comes down here, the TV remotes and laptop are off limits."

Mark raised an eyebrow to her.

"I mean it."

Outside, the cool air on Rachel's skin was juxtaposed with the gentle heat from the sun's rays. The smell of the surrounding Sugar Pines was carried on the breeze as Rachel led the way to the old boathouse along the shores of the lake.

"This is a neat little place you've got here," the man said from behind her as he followed her.

"Thanks. It's been in my family for a few generations. Well, here we are," she said opening the door to the boathouse.

The smell of fresh paint met them in the entry as Rachel stepped in behind him. It was really the perfect space for one person. She stood near the door while he looked around. He tested the faucets in the kitchen and bathroom, glanced in the cupboards, fridge, oven, and closets and then nodded his head in approval.

"How do I go about getting this place?"

"I'll have you fill out an application form. And as long as your credit and background checks clear, the place is all yours. Nobody is really looking to rent around here this time of year."

He nodded his head.

"First and last month's rent upfront."

"Okay. Well, show me that paperwork and I'll get started on it."

They returned to the shop and he took a seat in the corner of the café with a coffee and the application. In the meantime, Rachel ran the information he gave her for his credit check and background check. In the poor economy, she was pleasantly surprised to see his credit score was above seven hundred. It was a hopeful sign that he wouldn't stiff her for the rent. The extra money would be nice to have with Christmas only a few months away. The background check also came back clean and just for precautionary measures, she called her brother, Ben, who was a police officer in Rancho Cucamonga, and he checked out the stranger as well.

"Ethan Kuhn, thirty-three, a fireman from Logan, Utah," she repeated into the phone.

"Yeah, I don't see anything on his record. He looks clean."

Rachel felt relief come over her. She didn't realize how much she had wanted to rent out the boathouse until just that moment.

"So what else is going on?"

"Oh the same old. Getting ready for a book signing in the store in a couple weeks. Aspen failed her science test."

"Oh really? Didn't you just say about a week ago or something that she had gotten a few Ds in her classes, too?"

"Sure did. I want to strangle her. It was so much easier when she was six."

Ben laughed. "I don't know about that. Chloe is six and there are many days I want to strangle her," he said about his oldest child.

"I'm gonna have to call Matt tonight and talk with him about all of this," she said with a sigh.

"And where is Matt these days?"

"Not sure," she said with a shrug. "I haven't talked to him since June. He was in Oklahoma then."

"He hasn't called since June?" Ben didn't mask his irritation with Aspen's dad.

"He has. But he's only talked to Aspen. I just get frustrated with him almost every time we talk and we just end up fighting. So I decided to stop talking to him unless I had to. He's been paying his child-support on time, so there really hasn't been any need to talk to him. Until now, that is. He's going to be pissed when he hears about this."

"As he should be," Ben said. "Hey, I hate to cut this short, but Emma just fell and is screaming. I've gotta go."

"That's fine. Send everyone my love. I'll talk to you soon."

"You too."

When she hung up the phone, Rachel felt a slight sting in her chest. She missed her brother. It wasn't like he was that far away. An hour, not even. But they were all so busy with their lives. She didn't see her parents as often as she would like, and they only lived in Orange County. Glancing at the clock, Rachel noticed it was almost five. Diane would be in any minute to take over for the last three hours and close up Sinful Retreat.

"So everything looks good on your background," she said as she approached Ethan.

"Perfect. And I just finished with this," he said, handing the application to her. "Can I just write you a check for the first and last month's rent?"

"That'll be fine. When do you want to move in?"

"Well, the sooner, the better. I'm just staying at my captain's house right now. I'm sure he's eager to get rid of me. Not a lot of room in that place."

"The place is empty, so as long as your check clears, you can move in this week if you want."

Ethan nodded. He handed the check to Rachel.

"Stop by on Wednesday and I'll give you a key to the place."

"Sounds good. Thanks. See you then," he said with a nod and a smile and then left the shop.

Within ten minutes of Diane's arrival, Rachel finished the last of her projects for the day and headed upstairs, leaving the shop in the hands of the sweet, old woman with glasses, much too large for her little head. Aspen was listening to her iPod from bed and didn't hear her mother come in.

Rachel went to the kitchen and grabbed the thawed chicken from the fridge. Putting it in a pot on the stove to boil, she headed to her bedroom to call Matt.

By the fourth ring, Rachel was ready to hang up, but he answered the phone at the last minute, sounding winded when he said, "Hello."

"Matt, hi. It's Rachel." She paused, waiting for him to respond.

Although he sounded slightly annoyed when he answered, she heard a smile come across his face as he spoke. "Hiiii," he said, drawing out the word. "It's been a while. How've you been?"

"I'm good, thanks," she said hoping to skip the small-talk. One of two things seemed to always happen when they talked: they would argue, surely about how little he'd been around and how annoying his mother could be with her, or he would pull out his charm, and inevitably get her hopes up about something. And getting her hopes up with Matt was always a mistake.

"And Aspy? How's she? I miss her so much."

"Where are you at these days?" she asked. Matt was a meteorologist and had a job with the National Weather Service. It always sounded impressive but what it boiled down to was that he was always on the road. He saw his daughter, maybe, twice a year. He did a better job of calling, but sometimes that could even be scarce, particularly during tornado season. He always spent his spring and summer somewhere in the Midwest in what was commonly known as Tornado Alley.

"I'm near Cape Canaveral, monitoring wind patterns with the approaching tropical storm. How's Aspen?" he asked again.

Rachel was suddenly aware that he noticed she was avoiding mentioning their daughter. But since she was indeed the reason for the phone call, there was no point in beating around the bush.

"We need to talk."

"Okay. Let me step inside the trailer. Hold on."

She heard the muffled sounds of multiple voices and then suddenly it went very quiet on the other end of the phone.

"Okay, that's better. So talk to me," he said. "What's going on? Is Aspen okay?"

"She brought home her science test to me today. Apparently, I need to sign it to show her teacher that I saw it."

"Well, that can't be a good thing."

"She failed, Matt. Thirty-three percent," she said bluntly.

There was silence on the other end. "Has this been a recurring pattern?"

"She's also gotten two Ds. One was in art and the other in English."

"How do you get a D in art? It's art!"

Rachel sighed.

"Sorry. What have you done about this?"

"Well, at the moment she's grounded. But I don't know what to do. She doesn't seem to give a damn about anything. It…" she paused for a moment before she said her next thought, "it would be nice if I didn't have to do this alone."

"Rachel, we've been over this. I'm sorry that I'm not there. But my job makes that impossible. You know that. And I always do what I need to do from wherever I am."

"Right. Because your job is your priority, not your family. Not your daughter. You know, if I were the one who up and left to pursue some career, then I would be labeled an abandoner. But no, I stayed and figured out what I could do with my life that not only paid the bills, but also took responsibility for my actions."

"What do you want me to do?"

"I want you to be a dad. I mean, maybe this would still be a problem if you were around, but maybe, just maybe, this is all because it's the only way to get some kind of response from you."

"So you're telling me I'm a terrible father. That's the reason my daughter's grades are slipping. You know, I don't have time to listen to this. I wasn't good enough for you; I'm not good enough for her… I'm not sure what you want me to do. I do this job because at least here, I'm good enough for someone."

"Look, I didn't call you to fight. But we are both her parents and right now this is a problem that both of her parents need to address," she said.

"Can you put her on the phone? Let me talk to her."

Rachel rose from her bed and headed across the hallway to Aspen's room. She knocked once on the open doorway and her daughter slipped off the headphones.

"It's your dad," she said, holding out the phone.

"Sorry. You'll have to tell him I'm grounded from the phone," Aspen said with a smirk on her face.

"Damn it, Aspen, take the phone. Or I'll ground you for a hell of a lot longer than you are now."

She sighed loudly to be extra dramatic and slid off her bed. She snapped the phone from her mother's hand.

"You better watch it. I am not kidding," Rachel told her as she pointed her finger at her. She watched as Aspen began talking to her dad and then headed into the kitchen to check on the boiling chicken.

The rest of the night was practically silent in the small upstairs apartment. Aspen was clearly mad at both of her parents, but since her dad was nowhere to be seen, the brunt of her attitude was taken out on Rachel. She simply ignored her daughter as she stomped around the apartment, closing doors louder than necessary, dropping books on the table a little too loudly and sighing randomly.

After Aspen finally went to bed for the rest of the night, Rachel slipped downstairs to double check that everything was shut off and locked up.

Upstairs she got into her pajamas and crawled into bed. Grabbing her book, she held it in her hands as she looked at the cover.

She began to think about her family lineage. After all, that was what the book was about, a woman tracing her family heritage and learning so much about her grandmother. Rachel knew her grandfather had immigrated to the United States when he was still young, before he had married Elaine. But she didn't know where he came from or why he came at all. She had a larger connection to him than to her other grandparents. Mostly because she lived and ran a business in what was once his home. But even her other grandparents she knew a little about. They had migrated to the United States from Sweden, generations ago, to become farmers. They first moved to the Midwest, Minnesota specifically, and then her great great grandfather broke off and moved to California. But what about her dad's side of the family, what about Aaron Taylor?

Curiosity began to burn inside of her and she reached for the laptop. She began with a simple Google search of his name. The first things to show up were a football player and a Disc Jockey. Further down the results list was a photographer and even a graphic artist. The list grew and grew and grew, but not one of them was her grandfather. She wondered where she could find anything out about him. Quickly she searched for her Aunt Sarah's phone number and typed it into her phone. She made a mental note to call her tomorrow. If anyone in her family knew anything about Grandpa Taylor, Sarah would be it.

TWO

Tuesday morning was uneventful. Aspen was up and out of the house on time, despite her *almost silent* silent-treatment for her mother. The shop opened as usual. Rachel spent her morning on marketing the bookstore's upcoming event. She did manage to slip away for about twenty minutes after Mark arrived in the late morning to get another chapter in her book read. She regretted having to go back to work after that, too. Her book was getting very interesting as the granddaughter was learning about her grandmother's role in women's suffrage. The more she read, however, the more unsettled she became about her own family's history. It had never occurred to her until now that she didn't know the real story.

At one o'clock, right on time, nearly a dozen women began to trickle into Sinful Retreat. They settled onto the chairs and sofas in the cozy corner near the bay window with warm sunlight spilling in from outside.

Sinful Retreat had four book clubs that met during the week. Tuesday belonged to the Kayscreek Book Club. Rachel secretly liked them the most. They were the most laid back and diverse group of them all. Not to mention, they all loved to spend their money at the shop. They all bought their books from Rachel and always bought drinks or something to snack on from Kristin. Today was certainly no exception.

Unfortunately, Rachel wasn't able to find work around the counter as much as she typically liked to. She wanted to listen to their discussion about *My Mother's Mother*, but she had an appointment with the newspaper and had arranged to hang posters around the village and in some local businesses. Mark eagerly took over the bookstore while she was gone.

Outside, the air was cool and refreshing. The sky was blue and cloudless and a light breeze was coming from the southwest. It was supposed to pick up later in the day as a storm rolled in, bringing the possibility of snow to the higher elevations, but for the moment it was a nice day.

The gentle waves in the lake lapped onto the shore and the ducks that swam in the chilly waters quacked and flapped their wings loudly.

There were few tourists out as Rachel made her way along the railing that edged the lake, her briefcase filled with posters and fliers.

Practically hidden in the trees near the grocery store and behind the McDonald's was a small press, The Village Gazette. Rachel stepped inside and smiled at Henry, the older man who had worked at the front desk nearly his entire life. Henry and his wife Aida ran the small press; together they started it over thirty years earlier. And despite limited resources in such a small community, it was highly regarded and carried a good reputation.

"Well hello there, Miss Taylor," Henry said as he stood up. He had been expecting her.

"I've got everything from the printer here. So it should be ready to go." She set the briefcase down on a vacant chair, opened it and took out the small replica of the poster advertising Marissa Bristow's book signing. She skimmed it one last time and then handed it to Henry.

"Oh! Aida just finished that new book of hers. She just loved it, you know. Aida!" he hollered to a room behind the front office.

Aida came in, her hands filled with papers. "Oh hello Rachel," she said, her eyes lighting up.

"Look at who is coming to Sinful Retreat," Henry said as he thrust the poster in his wife's face.

Aida squinted and then pulled the glasses that were perched on top of her head down onto her nose. "Oooh, I really love Marissa Bristow. I will definitely be there. How did you manage that one, Rachel?"

Rachel smiled proudly. "Fortunately, she's from southern California. And she is very adamant about supporting small businesses. I contacted her publicist a while ago."

"You're so good for this town. What would we ever do without you?" Aida asked with a wink. "Now please excuse me. I've got my hands full at the moment. Otherwise I'd love to chit-chat with you. Have a nice day, dear."

Rachel finished up a few minutes later with Henry and was on her way around the village to hang up posters.

With only two businesses left, Rachel's phone rang.

"Rachel, hi, it's Jody, from the bank. Just wanted to let you know that the check you brought in did clear. So you should be good to go."

"Oh good. Thanks for doing that for me. That was awfully fast."

Jody laughed. "Yeah well, that's what happens when you both bank here. Have a great day."

Rachel felt relief that Ethan's check cleared. So far, he appeared to be a stand-up guy. And she was pleasantly surprised to rent the boathouse out for the winter months. Typically, things like that were easier to rent out in the summer months, when there was a plethora of people looking to escape the city for a getaway in the mountains.

Glancing at her phone, she began a brisk walk back to the shop to get a car. She had a meeting with Aspen's science teacher in twenty minutes.

An hour later, Aspen sat in the front seat of the Corolla while Rachel drove along the windy Rim of the World Highway.

"You know, you're lucky Mr. Crawford is giving you the opportunity to make up some extra credit," she said over the quiet hum of the car. She made a mental note to get her radio fixed. It was painful riding with her almost-teenage daughter without the radio.

Aspen sighed with exaggerated volume. "Lucky? That's not how I'd describe having extra work to do."

"Well maybe if you had actually done the work in the first place to a satisfactory level, then you wouldn't be in this position. You've only got yourself to blame for it."

"Whatever," she said as she folded her arms forcefully across her chest and dramatically turned her body to look out the side window of the car.

"Just to give you a heads up, someone is moving into the boathouse. Probably this week, even."

"Who?" Aspen asked, turning back toward her mom.

"His name is Ethan. He's a fireman in town."

"Lame," she said as she crossed her arms again and assumed her previous position.

Rachel rolled her eyes and they finished the last few miles in silence.

"Thank God you're back," Mark said with wide eyes when he saw Rachel enter the shop. "It has been crazy in here this afternoon. I could barely keep up."

"It's true," Kristin said over her shoulder at the bakery counter. "Even I had to step in and help."

"That definitely isn't bad news," Rachel said as she made Aspen sit at a table and do her homework.

The late afternoon was a frenzy. So many people were in the shop. Rachel marveled at Mark's genius suggestion of making WiFi available for free at the store. It attracted so many customers. Rachel found over the years that once she got someone in the store, it was almost impossible for them to not buy something. And with the decadent smells that radiated through the place from of Kristin's baking, customers couldn't resist buying from the bakery.

By early evening, the wind had picked up significantly. It whistled past the old windowpanes of the shop and from the back, the sound of tree branches blowing against the building could be heard.

The front door swung open, the little bell ringing as a blonde woman stepped inside. Rachel glanced up from the counter and smiled.

"Well, well, I was wondering what happened to you!"

AJ sighed as she pulled her hands out from her pockets and tossed her handbag on the counter near the register.

"So? How was it?"

"I think I'm gonna give up on dating," she said seriously.

"That bad?"

AJ nodded. "He still lives with his parents. And not in a they-need-my-help-and-have-no-one kind of way. He asked if he could bring my leftovers home to his mom. Apparently, she loves grilled chicken."

Rachel laughed.

"Yeah, laugh all you want. But I officially give up. There are no good men up here. That aren't already married, anyway. And I already tried that route. It didn't pan out for me so well."

"I decided you either had such an amazing date with Mr. Running Springs that you were spending every moment with him possible or it was so bad that you had gone into hiding," Kristin said, coming out of the kitchen.

"The latter," Rachel said as AJ sighed.

"Oh, that's no good."

"Kristin, please tell your brother that I am never speaking to him again. If he thinks so lowly of me that his friend from Running Springs is who came to mind when you asked if he had any available friends, then clearly we aren't meant to be friends."

Kristin nodded with the curl of a smirk at the corner of her lips.

Diane stepped inside the shop, shaking off droplets of water as she made her way over to the register. "Starting to rain out there. And that wind is blasted cold," she said with a shudder.

"Well, I think I've got all my things finished for the day. However there is a box of some promotional items in the back on the floor by my desk. If you wouldn't mind taking them out and cataloging them, I would appreciate it," Rachel said as she grabbed a pile of things to bring upstairs with her.

"AJ, want to come up for dinner?" she asked as she glanced over her shoulder on the way to the staircase that went up to her second-floor apartment.

"Thought you'd never ask," AJ said, grabbing her bag and following after her. "See you later, Kristin!"

"Night ladies," Kristin said with a nod and a smile.

Upstairs, Aspen had turned the heat on and the apartment was cozy and warm.

"Where is my Goddaughter?" AJ asked as she kicked off her shoes and hung her jacket on the rack near the door.

"Avoiding me."

"Uh-oh. Another famous Mother-Aspen fight? What caused this one?"

"Her grades. I called Matt about it and now she's ticked at both of us."

AJ sighed, "It's a good thing you're meant to be her parents and not her friends, then. You're doing the right thing." AJ headed to the bedroom on the far side of the apartment. She knocked once on Aspen's door and then opened it, sticking her head inside.

"Hi-ya, Punk."

"AJ!" Aspen squealed in a way that only preteen adolescent girls could.

Aspen jumped off her bed and hurried to the door. She hugged AJ tightly and Rachel felt a knot form in the back of her throat. She tried to distract herself by sticking her head into the fridge looking for something to throw together for dinner.

"Heard you're giving your mom some trouble."

"Ugh. You heard her side of the story," Aspen said. Although Rachel was staring at a jug of milk, she could practically hear her daughter roll her eyes.

"And I'm sure yours is entertainingly dramatic; however, regardless of your argument, one thing is certain. You need to keep your grades up," AJ said.

"You too?" Aspen moaned.

"Yes, me too. You're a smart girl. If your grades were low because you were struggling, it would be one thing. But we both know that's not the case."

"Figures you'd take her side."

"Believe me, Aspen. In the end, we're all really on your side. Even if you can't see it."

AJ stood a moment longer in the doorway but Aspen was done responding to her. A minute later the door closed and AJ stepped back into the kitchen.

"So what will it be? I've got some of Kristin's homemade potpies in the freezer. I could put some of them in the oven."

"Mmm, that sounds good."

Two hours later, after they had all eaten and the kitchen was cleaned up, Aspen headed back into her bedroom and AJ and Rachel took a seat on the sofa, each with a glass of wine in their hands.

"So I've been thinking about looking into my family heritage," Rachel said as she sipped the Cabernet.

"Like on all those commercials for Ancestry or something?"

Rachel nodded. "Kind of. I've been reading *My Mother's Mother* and it's really sparked my interest. I don't know anything about my Grandpa Aaron. And I live in his house. I feel like I should know something about him."

"Everyone has a story. Where did you start?"

"I haven't yet. But I did find my aunt's phone number. Maybe I'll give her a call yet tonight. My dad won't be of any help, so I'm not going to start there."

AJ took a drink from her glass. "I can't say I know much about my ancestry either. Especially on my dad's side. My brother might know a little more since he is still in contact with him, but I doubt it."

"Oh, I forgot to mention, I rented the boathouse."

"Really? This time of year?" AJ asked.

She nodded. "I know. I was relieved. I hate having that place empty. It helps me so much financially when there is someone in it."

"So who's moving in?"

Rachel shrugged. "Some guy from Utah. Don't know too much about him. But he seemed to check out, so I'm not really worried."

AJ nodded. "I'd ask if he's good-looking, but I already told you that I was giving up on dating."

Rachel laughed. "Actually, he is pretty good-looking. More your type than mine. Tall, dark hair. He's thin but fit."

AJ smiled. "Hmm, maybe I need to rethink a few things. If he has muscular arms I might just melt on the spot. Does he?"

"No idea, I didn't look that hard."

"Of course you didn't. He's not Matt."

"What's that supposed to mean?"

"It means that you'll wait around for Matt forever."

"I'm not waiting for Matt," Rachel said. "I just don't have time to date. Besides, you've tested that water anyway and apparently there isn't anyone out there. So why would I put myself through that?"

"You need to at least have sex. It's been forever."

Rachel rolled her eyes. "It's not like it changed since the last time I slept with someone."

"How do you know? You haven't been with anyone in five years. And even that was Matt."

She shrugged her shoulders. "So I don't sleep around, so what?"

"I don't either. That's what Jack is for. You know, that once-in-a-while fix?"

"You sure are opinionated and full of attitude tonight. I think it's time you called Jack up and made a run down to Carlsbad."

AJ smiled as she took a drink from her glass. "I may just do that."

Rachel woke to a gray, cloudy sky, but when she peered out her window that overlooked the parking lot of the neighboring shopping plaza, she was surprised at the blanket of snow that covered everything. It was still early in the season, and all it would take was one nice day and all that white would be gone, but it was still a pleasant sight to wake up to.

Shivering in the cold room, Rachel slipped into an oversized sweatshirt and stepped into the living room. She bumped up the thermostat and a moment later the furnace came to life. She got ready for the day quickly and headed downstairs to the shop.

Kristin came in a minute later as Rachel flipped on all the lights and Sinful Retreat began to wake up for the day.

"The roads are awful," Kristin said, ushering her kids inside. "Wasn't sure how long it would take to get here and I slipped down Roger's Hill the entire way to the bottom."

"That pretty much means today will be a slow day," Rachel said, glancing over her shoulder and seeing that Diane did empty the box filled with all the promotional items.

"No sense in delaying our coffee any longer. Be back in a second. Kids, you go sit in the Children's Nook. And no biting, Parker!"

"Biting? That sounds rough," Rachel said.

"Painful, really."

Rachel put on a heavy pair of boots, some gloves and a thick jacket. She stepped out into the brisk morning and began clearing a pathway to the front of the shop. The air was cold in her lungs, but it felt fresh and clean.

"Good morning," a voice said from behind.

Rachel turned around to see Ethan headed toward the shop. She smiled as she scooped a pile of snow to the side.

"Everything looks good for you to move in," she said.

"Great. Would it be possible to get the key today even?"

"Today? I haven't cleaned it. It could use a good vacuuming and dusting."

Ethan shrugged. "Nothing I can't handle. I don't mind if you don't."

"I guess that's fine. If you really don't care."

"I don't. Let me help you with that," he said reaching for the shovel in her hands.

"Oh," she said, as he took it from her grip. "Thanks. I'm so used to doing this whenever it snows."

He laughed. "Well, I'm good at shoveling snow. I'm from Utah."

She nodded. "Since you seem to have this covered, I'm going to finish opening up. Come inside when you're done and get a cup of coffee."

Ethan nodded and took up scooping the snow where she left off.

Back inside, the smell of brewing coffee met Rachel at the door. Sinful Retreat was slowly waking up from the snowy night and the lights shone brightly around the shop. She stood at the door for a moment and took in the sight around her. Kristin was pulling desserts and treats out from the back and putting them in the display case, her kids watching morning cartoons while eating homemade sweet rolls. Kristin must have turned the fireplace on because it roared with red and orange flames that licked the ceramic logs framed inside the large stone mantle on the wall opposite the bookstore registers.

In a silent moment, gratitude washed over her as she looked at what she and Kristin had created: the colorful and inviting Children's Nook in the corner, the comfy chairs in front of the cozy fire and the hundreds of books piled on the shelves throughout the store. She smiled contently to herself and then crossed the shop to get a cup of coffee.

"Mom," Aspen said, coming out of the stairway.

"You're up. I didn't even hear you banging overhead."

"My homework is done," she said handing a small stack of papers to her mom.

Rachel took them and surveyed her daughter's work. "This looks good. Hopefully your teacher agrees and you can make up some credit from that test," she said, handing it back.

"Can I grab something to eat?"

Rachel nodded. "Go ask Kristin what she has."

Aspen shoved the papers into her backpack and trotted over to the bakery counter.

A few minutes later, Ethan stepped inside, his nose colored bright red from the chill in the air.

"That's some pretty wet snow. Sure makes it messy to clean up."

"Thank you so much for helping. That really wasn't necessary, but I wasn't going to turn down your offer," Rachel said with a smile. "Come, get some coffee."

Ethan accepted her offer and sat at a nearby table while Rachel checked her emails for the day and went through the financial papers from closing the night before.

When the shop opened, a few regulars popped in for their morning coffees but otherwise the shop was quiet. The snow wasn't so inviting for people to be wandering around the village, especially with the nip in the air, and thus, no one was wandering into the shop.

Rachel took advantage of having Mark around in case anyone did come in and slipped into her office and closed the door.

She reached for her phone and dialed Aunt Sarah. It rang three times and just before Rachel hung up, someone on the other end picked up. Her hello sounded winded as Rachel smiled.

"Aunt Sarah, it's Rachel. How are you?"

"Hi darling. I almost missed your call. Was throwing in some laundry. What a pleasant surprise to hear your voice. I was just talking to your mom the other day."

"I was wondering if this is a good time for you? I have some questions and I'm hoping that maybe you can help me. Or at least point me in some direction."

"Sure. I've got some time. What are you up to?"

"I've been reading this book about a woman who is discovering her family lineage, and it got me thinking that I don't know much about Grandpa Aaron at all. I haven't asked my dad anything yet, but I don't imagine he will be much help. I was hoping maybe you had some insight?"

"Oh," Sarah said with a loud sigh. "My dad was pretty quiet about his upbringing. He never really did say much. I'm not even sure where in Europe he came from, to be honest. He was always quite vague. Eventually I stopped asking questions. It wasn't as popular to know these things back then."

"I understand," Rachel said, feeling her disappointment.

"But let's see here. I did a paper a long time ago on the family name, Taylor, and I know for certain that's English."

Rachel reached for a pen and began scribbling down what Sarah was saying.

"I'm not sure that's where he came to the United States from, of course, but I know that about the name. My dad did have family, some siblings. I'm pretty sure he was the oldest. I remember him once talking about New York City. It was brief, but I remember thinking that maybe he lived there. But oh, I don't know. I could be completely wrong, too."

"So you think he's English?" Rachel asked.

"Not really sure. Come to think of it, I know my mom had been to London as a girl and one night over dinner she told us about her trip. He seemed as interested as the rest of us, so I really don't think he'd ever been to London, at least."

"Interesting," Rachel mumbled.

"Sorry I'm not much more help than that. If I think of anything I will certainly give you a call. Maybe I'll go through some of my old albums. Hopefully it can trigger something for you."

Rachel felt the disappointment as she finished her conversation with Aunt Sarah. She pondered the few scribbles she had made on her notepad from their conversation. Then with a sigh, she put down her pen and pulled up the payroll documents on the computer. Getting back to work, she didn't have a spare minute to think about her and Sarah's conversation for the rest of the day.

The rest of the week passed in a blurry frenzy. Rachel was looking ahead to the upcoming year and scheduled meetings for events that Sinful Retreat would be hosting. She updated the store's blog, posted promotional sales on the Facebook page, linked some articles to her Twitter, inventoried and ordered office supplies, finished the sales reports from the first half of October, approved the radio advertisement for Marissa Bristow's upcoming book signing, and began planning Sinful Retreat's Annual Children's Christmas Reading Event.

By Saturday, the weather had warmed back up into the seventies, and business was steady. The last week of Oktoberfest always brought crowds to Lake Arrowhead Village. With Diane managing the counter, Rachel was able to pull from storage the Halloween decorations and began preparing the store for the holiday that was only days away.

Kristin was always able to come to work childless on Saturday mornings and Rachel always noticed the ease about her as she went about her business without refereeing her children.

"Because of the snow earlier this week, we sold a record amount of coffee for this month. I need to put in an order already. I can hardly believe it," she gasped as she filed through her reports on a laptop below Rachel stringing decorative cobwebs through the open, wooden rafters near the ceiling.

"That's not such a bad thing."

"Indeed it's not," Kristin mumbled as she studied the numbers on her screen. "Oh, I've been meaning to ask you, is Aspen busy tonight?"

"Not that she and I have discussed, no. Need a sitter?" Rachel climbed down from the ladder for a moment to grab a large, fuzzy spider. She climbed back up and wove his eight long legs through the cobwebs and secured him to the ceiling.

"Darren decided last night while lying in bed that he wanted to head down into the valley for dinner and a movie," Kristin said.

"That sounds nice, actually." The single life didn't usually bother Rachel. In fact, she found it easier to set her own rules than have to work with someone else's schedule. But every now and then, she found herself wishing she had someone to flit off to the valley with, just for a few hours reprieve from life. "Yeah, she can babysit."

"I'll just keep her for the night if that's okay."

Rachel nodded. "Sure."

After the decorations were hung, Rachel stepped onto the back deck that overlooked both the boathouse and Lake Arrowhead. Despite the snow earlier in the week, there were boats on the lake frolicking in the warm sunshine overhead. She took a moment to take in the sight around her. The trees had begun to change colors and the large maple that grew near the corner of the store was already dropping its brightly colored red leaves to the ground.

"Hey there," a voice called.

Rachel jumped and caught her breath.

"Sorry, didn't mean to scare you," Ethan said from below the deck.

"I didn't realize I was so jumpy. Just getting off work?" she asked, noting his fireman uniform.

"Yeah. Just spent forty-eight hours on duty. It's a great day, though. I was thinking of maybe exploring a little. Any suggestions?"

"Well," she said, "there's the obvious Oktoberfest that's going on. There are beer gardens and stuff if that interests you. There's also the yacht club and the golf course, or you could take a ride on the Queen Paddleboat."

"Hmmm."

"None of that sounds interesting?" she laughed.

He smiled and for a brief moment she couldn't help but feel a sense of familiarity with him. She quickly dismissed her foolishness and continued to rattle off ideas. "There's hiking, rock climbing, and mountain biking, if you're into any of that."

"That's more my personality. Know any good hiking spots?"

"The Crab Creek Trail is my favorite. The scenery is incredible. It's not too difficult either. It's a little over two miles."

"That sounds good. Crab Creek, huh?" he asked.

She nodded.

"I'll check it out, thanks."

"How's the boathouse been?" she asked, unsure of why she wanted to keep him there to continue talking to him.

"It's good. I didn't have much so I'm pretty much settled in."

"Already? Wow. That was fast."

He laughed. "I can be a bit of a minimalist at times. This being one of those times."

"Rach," Kristin called from the doorway.

"One sec," she said. "Looks like that's my cue. Enjoy your hike."

"I'm gonna take off. Diane's going to head over to the bakery counter."

Rachel nodded. "Sounds good."

"I'll pick up Aspen around six. Maybe tomorrow evening we can have some wine or something."

"That'd be great. I'll let Tiff and AJ know. Have fun tonight."

"I plan to. Later," she called over her shoulder with a quick wave and then disappeared out the front door.

As the afternoon passed and evening came, the number of customers was small, but they were at least steady. A few asked Rachel for her opinions on books, which was one of her favorite parts of the job. She maintained a book review column on the store's website simply because she loved to go into detail about books and explore underlying meanings and sub-stories disguised among the plots of books. Books were her passion. And whenever a customer asked for her thoughts, it was always very obvious to anyone around that she was doing what she loved.

Kristin was true to her word and picked up Aspen right on time. She showed up in a gray pencil skirt and bright, multi-colored sleeveless top and the cutest flats. Another moment of brief jealousy: someone to dress up for.

"You look incredible," Rachel said. She rarely saw Kristin with her hair down and straightened. It had gotten so long since the last time she saw her wear it like that.

"Thanks," she said with a happy grin.

Aspen appeared in the doorway with a bag over her shoulder. "Sorry I was late. I was on the phone with Dad."

"You're right on time. The girls are looking forward to spending time with you tonight," Kristin said.

Aspen smiled and then hugged her mom.

Rachel was surprised to find no animosity in the hug and smiled to herself. She knew that if Aspen were to see her smile, the moment would quickly come to a screeching halt. It was just better to appreciate those moments internally.

"See you tomorrow."

Shortly after eight, with the store officially closed for the night, Rachel stepped out front to lock up. Since she had no one to make dinner for upstairs, she decided to lock up and take a stroll down by the water. It was a perfect evening. A cool breeze rustled the leaves of the trees and a subtle scent from the pine trees wafted through the air. Most shops were closed for the day but a few restaurants were open, with strings of golden lights illuminating their outdoor patios and the soft tunes of music carrying through the open doors and windows.

She passed an older woman walking her dog; the schnauzer tried desperately to stop and sniff around a light post. A young couple that were holding hands, and a family that reminded her very much of Kristin and Darren's.

It was a calm and peaceful night and Rachel stopped at the railing along the water. Without the sun high in the sky, the water was shadowed and the weeds, rocks, and fish that were visible during the day were all hidden beneath the cover of darkness. The sun had already dropped below the wall of pines that surrounded the lake, but in the distance the orange glow still rose just slightly above the tree line.

With the sound of footsteps approaching, Rachel looked over her shoulder. She smiled as she saw Ethan approaching her. He must have taken her suggestion and gone for a hike, as he was dressed in gym shorts, a long-sleeve t-shirt and sneakers. And his face was flushed pink.

"It's a nice night," he said as he came to a halt a few feet from her along the railing.

"It is. I was just reveling in it myself."

"Thanks for the hike suggestion. It was great to get out and see the area a bit," he said as he wiped his brow with the sleeve of his shirt.

"Good, I'm glad you liked it." Suddenly her book came to mind and Rachel glanced down at her watch. "My daughter's gone for the night, so I'm thinking I'm going to take advantage of the quiet and start working on a project I've had on my mind."

"Well, since we're both headed in the same direction, I'll walk with you."

Together they walked along the water back in the direction she had come from. It was nice to have him near her, even though he was almost a complete stranger to her.

"So what's this project you're going to work on?" he asked.

"I want to trace my ancestry."

Ethan nodded his head. "That sounds interesting."

"Yeah. Sinful Retreat used to be my grandfather's home, actually."

"Really? And you turned it into the bookstore?"

She nodded. "Shortly after my daughter was born, I needed an income," she said, chuckling slightly.

"Well hats off to you for making it work."

She couldn't help but look at him. The evening darkness shadowed his face, but she finally let herself actually look at him. He looked older up close than she initially thought. The lines near his eyes and mouth offered a sense of maturity to him. But his eyes were gentle, youthful looking, and she took comfort in his presence.

"Thank you," she finally managed to say, hoping she hadn't lingered too long.

"How old is your daughter?" he asked as they rounded a corner and Sinful Retreat came into view across the parking lot.

"Aspen is twelve. And growing up too fast. I miss the days I could hold her on my lap."

"Yeah, kids have a way of growing up without parents even noticing."

"You talk like you have experience," she said.

Ethan shook his head. "Not personally. My sister has kids. Five to be exact, and they've all done that to her."

"Wow, five kids. I can't even imagine. Some days Aspen is too much for me to handle."

He laughed quietly. "My sister feels that way about hers most days."

Once they reached the store, they rounded to the back. Saying goodbye, they parted, and Ethan walked off to the boathouse while Rachel ascended the back staircase to her second-story apartment.

THREE

Rachel sat on a barstool at the counter and opened her laptop. Her fingers were tingling with excitement as she headed straight for the Ancestry website. She had seen the commercials a million times. It was strange how it had never occurred to her that she too had a family history. Something inside of her pulsed with assurance that she would find the answers she was looking for.

After setting up a new account, she got straight to work. Recalling her conversation with Sarah, she decided to begin her search in England. She had a name and a birthdate. A disheartening feeling flooded through her body as the results listed before her. There were over ten million record listings that could be a possible match. But what stood out even more were the birth years listed beside each search result. None of them were for 1924.

She began to scroll down the screen. It was possible that the birth year was recorded incorrectly. After all, archives from that time were written by hand. There were so many factors that could have created errors in recording information. With this in mind, the marriage records seemed the most plausible place to search next. Somewhere out there was a legal record of Aaron's marriage to Elaine Thompson. Searching for this, along with Aaron's birth year, or something in close proximity, she was bound to turn up something.

Rachel took her search back to the United States. A search of the U.S. Census Bureau came up empty. Census records were only released seventy-two years after the census date. Aaron would have been only seventeen at the date of the most recently released census, but without knowing whose household he lived in at the time, there was no way of finding him listed as a dependent.

After nearly two hours of searching in circles, Rachel closed the laptop. With a heavy sigh, she moved to the couch, a glass of red wine in her hand. Lying back on the sofa she closed her eyes and memories of Grandpa Aaron rushed back to her. She had so adored him as a young girl. He smelled of Old Spice and coffee and never missed an opportunity to slip her a piece of candy, usually an orange slice. Her summers with Grandpa Aaron were spent fishing on Lake Arrowhead, playing Yahtzee on the back deck that overlooked the water, eating French fries, pancakes and his favorite, ice cream. He was happy, full of jokes, most of which were inappropriate for children, but that never stopped him. He never yelled at the grandkids, offered knuckle sandwiches to be funny, and whenever Rachel and her brother were headed for a day at Disneyland, he would slip each of them a hundred dollars.

Her heart grew heavy as she thought of life without him. He had died of a heart attack before Aspen was born. She had been four months pregnant at the time and found comfort in hoping that he and the baby inside her had passed each other along their journeys of coming and going.

Rachel swallowed a rising lump in her throat and taking a drink of her wine, tried to push the emotion away. After a decade had passed, it was still difficult to take. She tried to live in their happy memories, but the end of their story always seemed to creep into her thoughts.

Just after midnight Rachel locked up the house, rinsed the wine glass and set it on the counter and then retired to bed. Her night was restless. She had strange dreams that woke her several times but as soon as she awoke, she could no longer remember anything she had just been dreaming about. The only thing she knew was they left her feeling highly unsettled.

By morning, once the sun was peering through the tiny cracks of her blinds, she kicked off her blankets and decided to get up. She felt heavy, sluggish, and tired but was unable to sleep. She made her way to the kitchen and started the coffee.

She spent her morning cleaning the house. She vacuumed, scrubbed the floors and dusted all the ledges. Aspen returned home around eleven with more money than Kristin should have paid her for the night. But she was happy, and Rachel wasn't going to cause waves.

"Want to grab lunch somewhere?" she asked her daughter, as a sort of peace offering for their conflicted week.

"The Malt Shop?" she asked, her eyes lighting up with excitement. Rachel just laughed.

An hour later they were in the car, winding through the forest trees, the lake off to their left as they made their way to the Cedar Glen Malt Shop. It was Aspen's favorite place to eat. When Matt was in town, he sometimes took her there every day for a malt or shake. And Aspen couldn't get enough of it.

After lunch they continued their way down Hook Creek Road. There was a newer development going up all around for a few miles. Then they entered the forest and all the homes disappeared. Rachel slowed the car and opened the windows. Quiet drives through the forest were a favorite for her. But Rachel hadn't done this with Aspen since the week she brought her home from the hospital. Something about the serenity of the open wilderness around them and all the fresh air was calming for her.

Rachel couldn't help but smile at her daughter beside her in the front seat of the car.

Shortly after Aspen was born, the area they drove through now had been devastated by fire. So many homes had been lost. Rachel's parents took Aspen while she came up into the mountains with Tiff and her husband, who lived in Cedar Glen, to see what remained of their home. They were some of the lucky ones. Both their garage and shed were gone, consumed by fire, and all that remained were the charred skeletal remains of their possessions. The house had gone untouched. In the last ten years, however, Mother Nature did what she did best. She thrived. And although remnants of the fire could still be found, new trees grew, fresh leaves sprouted from surviving branches and wild grasses and flowers flourished along the hillsides. It was a beautiful thing to see the forest come back to life.

By evening, the temperature had dropped ten degrees. Rachel sat on the deck that overlooked the lake with AJ, Tiff and Kristin, the red and white wine pouring freely among the four of them.

Kristin and Tiff could always relate well because their kids were the same ages. Those two always seemed to understand best why the other wanted to pull out their hair because of their children, all the while gushing about the cute things they did that day. Rachel had known AJ since childhood. They grew up across the street from one another and although they could be polar opposites on most days, there weren't many people out there who understood each other the way they did.

"The lights are on in the boathouse," Tiff said, pointing across the rocky beach.

"I rented it out. Just this week," Rachel said, topping off her glass of wine.

"A guy, too," AJ added with a smirk across her face.

Tiff raised a curious eyebrow.

"You guys are terrible," Rachel gasped.

"Oh whatever," Kristin said with a flip of her hand. "He's hot. You're single."

"Not to mention a few clicks shy of becoming a virgin again," AJ added.

Tiff and Kristin laughed loudly.

"His windows are open!" Rachel buried her face in her hands. "There are clear disadvantages to having friends who know practically everything about you."

The others laughed.

"Lighten up, Rach. I'm sure Matt will show his face around here sooner or later," Tiff said.

Rachel rolled her eyes. Sometimes the Matt innuendos got really old.

"So, speaking of sex," AJ chimed in, noticing Rachel needed a new direction for the conversation, "guess who I'm meeting in the valley tomorrow?"

"Jack," Kristin said bluntly.

Rachel and Tiff both smiled.

"Yes, Jack. What's wrong with that?"

"Nothing. Just answering your question," Kristin said with a smirk.

"Well, for your information, he asked me to be his date to a dinner function his office his hosting."

"Ah, so you're actually going on a date, then?" Tiff asked.

AJ nodded. "I think it'll be kind of nice."

"Where's this dinner at?" Rachel asked, setting an empty wine bottle on the floor of the deck. She pulled her legs up to her chest in the chill of the evening air.

"Dana Point."

"Ahh, that's too bad. Unless of course you guys want to shack up in the back of a car," Kristin said with a giggle.

"Okay, okay, I get your point. But just to prove to all of you that I don't have to sleep with Jack, tomorrow I won't," she said with finality.

Rachel's eyes widened. "Wow, guys, this is serious."

The others laughed loudly while AJ rolled her eyes and sat back in her chair.

The four of them sat on the deck until well after dark. The air had grown quite cool and in the distance, they could hear the subtle and gentle lapping of the waves on the lake. Aspen stepped outside around 9:30 and sat for a moment on the side arm of the chair Rachel was in. But after a few minutes she said goodnight to them all and disappeared to their upstairs apartment for bed.

"Heard she's giving you a run for your money," Tiff said, keeping her voice low.

Rachel nodded.

"What did Matt say when you talked to him?" Kristin asked.

"Oh, you know, the same thing he always does. 'Let me talk to Aspen… I can be hero dad over the telephone.'" She shook her head. "And then we got into a fight about how he's never here. I don't even know why we still fight about it. It's been the same thing for twelve years. Nothing changes."

"He's a typical guy," Tiff said with a sigh as she glanced down at her cell phone for the time.

"I don't know how you put up with it," AJ said.

"What choice do I have? He's her dad. There's nothing I can do to change that, and God knows I've tried everything I can to make him want to move home."

"It'll never be about anything you do, you realize that, right?" Kristin asked.

Rachel sighed and nodded her head. "I do."

Monday morning was like any other for Rachel. She woke up early, opened the store and went right to work. The following day was Halloween and they had big things planned. Spooky children's stories began at 5:00 and then they would spend their evening passing out treats to the children. She always spent a little extra money to get the alphabet gummies to hand out to her Trick-or-Treaters. It was worth it.

Shortly before lunch Ethan came into the store. He bought a coffee and deli sandwich from Kristin and then made his way over to Rachel at the book counter.

"You look nice today," he said when their eyes met.

She felt herself blush and could feel Kristin's eyes on her from the bakery counter. She smiled, "Oh, um, thanks."

"I'm assuming you have travel books on southern California."

"I do," she said.

"How about the local area?"

"I have those, too." She leaned forward on the counter. "This is a bookstore, you know," she whispered with a grin. "They're right over here," she said, stepping around the counter. She led him to a shelf near the large fireplace.

"These two shelves, right here," she said pointing. "This one," she grabbed one from a shelf just taller than her, "is really good for this area."

Ethan took the book and turned it over in his hands a few times. "Great. I appreciate this."

"I'll be up at the counter if you need anything else."

"You look nice today, Rachel," Kristin whispered from behind.

Rachel jabbed her elbow forcefully into Kristin's arm and rubbing the tender spot on her arm, Kristin giggled quietly.

"Hey, Rachel," Ethan called from the bookshelf. "Do you ski?"

"You'd think so considering where I live, but no, not really."

"This winter, I'll take you."

"Umm, okay," she said, again feeling Kristin's eyes on her.

After helping two other customers and ringing up a third, Ethan came to the counter with three books in his arms. Two were about southern California and the third was about the San Bernardino Mountains, where Lake Arrowhead rest.

"This is a really great area," he said, setting the books onto the counter.

"I love it here. I know some people don't do the small-town thing, but I can't imagine living anywhere else."

"I can see that."

"$56.98," she said, suddenly feeling awkward standing so close to him, despite the counter that separated them.

"I really hope this isn't inappropriate, considering you're my landlady and all, but umm, I'm wondering if you want to grab something to eat some time?" he asked as he handed his credit card to her.

Rachel felt her body momentarily freeze. It had been three years since someone other than Matt had asked her out. If that was, of course, what he was actually doing.

She forced herself to relax as she took the card quickly from his hands, hoping he wouldn't notice her quiver.

"Like dinner or something?" she asked.

"Well, yeah. Like a date or something," he said, a smile curling at the corners of his mouth.

"Uh, sure. I guess that would be fine. When did you have in mind?"

"I have to work for the next 48 hours, so how does Thursday night sound?"

"Good," she said, feeling herself fumble over her words.

"Meet you here at 6:30?"

She nodded with a grin and stood there in slight disbelief. Then she realized she hadn't swiped his card yet and felt like an idiot. She quickly ran his card and finished his transaction and then slipped his books into a bag and they said their goodbyes.

"That was painful, even to witness," Kristin said after he stepped out of the store.

"Oh my God," she gasped. "What just happened?"

Kristin laughed. "Umm, you got yourself a date, sweetie."

Rachel felt her stomach tighten.

Mondays were her late nights at the store. She worked until close at 8:00 on those evenings and tonight was quiet in the store. Leaving the door open to listen for any customers who came in, Rachel slipped into her office behind the counter and opened up her laptop. She stared blankly at the screen in front of her for a while before finally opening her Internet browser. As the search window stared back at her, she wondered how to begin to search for Grandpa Aaron.

With her mind coming up blank, her eyes began to wander around the small office. Then something caught her eye; near the corner, on a small shelf, was a photo of her grandparents from their wedding. An idea came to mind. If she was able to track down her grandmother, then maybe there would somehow be a link to her grandfather.

She logged back into Ancestry.com and began her search for Elaine Thompson, born June 12, 1928 in Temecula, California. To her surprise the 1940-1959 California, Marriage Index appeared before her. She clicked on the document and began looking for her grandmother. And then, about half way down on the second page, she found it: "Name of Bride, Elaine Thompson, Name of Groom, Abarron Taylor, married August 2, 1949."

Rachel stared at the names before her. Abarron? Who was that? Clearly it was her grandfather, but she had never heard that name before.

The front door to the store chimed and Rachel quickly got up to welcome her guest. She was surprised to see Matt's mom, Linda.

"It's quiet in here tonight," she said with a smile. Their relationship was always a bit strained, but Linda usually tried to be civil.

"Yeah, it is. Not so good for business, but I don't mind so much," Rachel said.

"Matt told me Aspen is acting up."

Rachel felt her chest tighten. Where was this going? "Yeah. Her grades. And not because she really is struggling but rather, she doesn't want to do the work."

Linda made her way over to the fiction bookshelves and started scanning. "I told Matt he needed to step up. He couldn't expect you to do all the heavy lifting."

Rachel felt her mouth drop slightly but quickly closed it before Linda saw her.

Linda grabbed a book from the shelf and skimmed the back. Then she looked up at Rachel. "Anyway, you shouldn't be so hard on him. I heard you two got into another fight. He is a very good dad. He's just a dad with a career."

There it was. At least now that Linda was showing her true colors, Rachel didn't feel the need to wonder if she should be concerned for the woman.

"I'll take this one. Decided I needed a new read," Linda said as she set the book on the counter.

Rachel forced herself to be pleasant even though she really just wanted to strangle the woman. She rang her up and listened to her go on a while longer about how much Aspen was growing up. Rachel smiled and nodded. And when Linda finally left, she felt herself exhale for the first time since Linda had been in the store.

After the store was closed, Rachel brought the laptop up to her apartment. Aspen had made homemade pizza and they sat down for a quiet, late night dinner. Rachel's head was swirling with the marriage records she saw. Was Abarron her grandfather's real name? It was similar to Aaron. Too bad there were no censuses available yet that would have both her grandparents on it. Those seemed to always supply each person's birthplace. She sighed, at least she had made some progress.

"Mom, you okay?"

Rachel's ears heard her daughter, but her mind was far away and she didn't answer.

"Mom?" Aspen asked, waving her hand inches from Rachel's face.

"Oh, sorry," she said, snapping out of her trance.

"What's on your mind?"

"Just some stuff with Grandpa Aaron."

"Whose house this was?" she asked.

Rachel nodded. "I'll clean up. Just leave this mess. I need to make a few phone calls, okay?"

"Sure. I'm going to watch some TV and then go to bed."

Rachel grabbed her phone and headed to her bedroom. She shut the door and called Aunt Sarah.

Sarah answered after only the second ring and Rachel immediately filled her in with her discovery.

"And you're sure it was the right Elaine?" Sarah asked.

"Yeah. There was a link to her birth certificate that showed Great Grandpa and Grandma Thompson. I saw it with my own eyes. And the marriage record was for August, 1949. It's them, Sarah."

"Hmm. I've never heard anything about his name being Abarron. This is news to me," Sarah said.

"Would any of your siblings know?" Rachel asked, thinking of her other aunts and uncles.

"I would assume if they had, they would have told us. But maybe not. I'm going to ask them about this. It is sort of strange."

Rachel felt slightly relieved that she wasn't the only one who felt unsettled with the discovery of her grandpa's name. "I'll change up my searches and see if I can find anything. I just wanted to ask you first."

"I'm glad you called, really," Sarah said.

"And you know nothing about your grandparents?"

"Nothing. Not even a name. My dad told me once they were dead and never spoke of it again. They were never a part of our lives."

"Hmm." Rachel was baffled. None of this seemed to reflect the man she knew. She remembered a man who was gentle and kind. Someone who liked to tell stores and share jokes. He knew everyone in town, seemed to be friends with everyone. How could someone with so many friends not have any family? "I'll call you in a few days."

Rachel spent another night tossing and turning. The name Abarron kept coming back to her as she slept. She woke several times and each time took her a while to fall back to sleep. She finally got up for the day before even the sun was up and went straight for the computer.

Researching the onomastics of the name was unhelpful. Her searches revealed it was Hebrew but they gave no specificity to geographic locations or regions where the name was common or popular. Another dead end.

A search on Ancestry for Abarron Taylor, England yielded nothing as well. Rachel's frustration was rampantly growing. Maybe he didn't come from England at all. Widening her search, Rachel searched his name internationally. Nothing was found. There were tens of thousands of A. Taylors, many that matched the birth year of her grandfather's, but they too appeared to be dead ends.

Sinful Retreat was busy on Halloween day. Mark was working between both the bakery and bookstore and Kristin's employee, Becky, was also working the bakery counter. Kristin was back in the kitchen finishing some Halloween treats they had run short of the day before. Feeling a bit disgruntled, Rachel slipped into her office and shut the door.

"San Bernardino County Recorder's Office, Phoebe speaking."

"Hi. My name's Rachel and I'm trying to trace my ancestry. I'm wondering if it's possible to get a copy of a marriage certificate?"

"Anyone may obtain a certified copy of a public, declared or non-clergy marriage certificate," Phoebe said.

"Well, I'm assuming this one falls in the category of a public marriage. But I don't need a certified copy. Do you do photocopies?" Rachel asked.

"Per California Health and Safety Code, that can only be released to an authorized person and there is a fee of $14. What is the nature of your relationship to the persons to which you are trying to obtain this document?"

Rachel couldn't help but think that the woman on the other line, in a way, had too much power. "I'm their granddaughter. Does that qualify as an authorized person?"

"Yes, ma'am," said Phoebe. "If you go to our website, you will find a marriage certificate application form. Print that out, fill it in and bring it in to my office. I'm here until 4:00 during the week. You are required to provide a valid photo ID and if for some reason the record you are looking for cannot be found, the fee will still be retained for searching and you will then be issued a Certification of Search."

"Wow. This is more intense than I thought. I'll go print off that application. Thanks for your help," Rachel said, in slight disbelief. All of that for a copy of a marriage certificate? She just had enough time to print the application and fill it out before Mark came knocking.

"Sorry to bug you, boss. Need your help out here."

"I'm coming," she said with a sigh as she put the application aside and headed out of her office.

The rest of the day's activities for the holiday consumed Rachel. Just before the book reading began, she slipped upstairs to put on her witch costume. She couldn't help but notice her white and black streaked wig was beginning to look a little tattered. She ran her fingers through the faux hair and slipped it on her head. She was kind of grateful that Ethan wouldn't be walking in to see her dressed like this. Obviously, she had a pass considering it was Halloween, but that wasn't really how she needed him to see her.

Kristin was dressed in a witch costume as well and together they stood at the door and welcomed all the children who had come for the spooky stories. Aspen, also dressed as a witch, guided the families and herds of children around to the Children's Nook. It had been carefully decorated with pumpkins and ghosts, bats that hung from the ceiling and spiders that dangled from their webs.

Sinful Retreat was bursting at the seams, filled with moms and dads, superheroes, princesses, lions and tigers and bears, witches, and bugs and goblins and ghosts. The walls echoed with the sounds of children's squeals of delight and laughter.

Rachel was an animated reader. Kristin's youngest, Parker, dressed as Superman, made sure to get a spot right up front as close to Rachel as possible. And at 5:00 on the dot, they began story time.

They started with one of her favorites, *Room on the Broom* by Julia Donaldson followed by *Bats at the Library* by Brian Lies and *Big Pumpkin* by Erica Silverman. Then Kristin took over for a few more books. After an hour their spooky stories were over and all the children lined up to collect their treat.

The remainder of the night was filled with the ebb and flow of Trick-or-Treaters coming in and out of the store and after they closed up for the night, Rachel was exhausted.

Upstairs in her apartment she realized she had missed a call on her cell from Sarah. She dialed into her voicemail to hear the message:

"Rach, it's Sarah. I talked to Leah, Mike, Max, and Joe today and the news of Dad's name being Abarron came as a shock to all of us. None of us have ever heard him go by anything else. But I got to thinking, since it was on their marriage certificate as Abarron, maybe my aunt Ruth heard it. I am planning to call her tomorrow and will let you know what she says. Happy Halloween!"

That was a good idea. In the meantime, she thought about the application on her desk down in her office. She thought about going to retrieve it, but there was nothing she actually needed it for tonight, so she left it alone and headed to bed.

That night, she finally slept.

FOUR

At noon on Wednesday, with Mark covering the counter, Rachel drove down into the valley to the San Bernardino County offices. Her heart pounded with anticipation as she made the windy trek down the mountains. She was confident this would be the break she was looking for. A birthplace would go a long way in her search.

She was slightly irritated once she arrived to learn that Phoebe, the woman who could assist her with these records, was out to lunch. She sat on an uncomfortable chair in a small waiting room that was blowing cold air conditioning from a large overhead vent. She tried to escape the power and chill of the blowing air, but it was impossible, so she moved to a chair in the corner and wrapped her arms around herself tightly.

She grabbed her cell and called back to Sinful Retreat.

"Looks like it will be a little bit longer than I thought it would be," she said to Mark.

"Marissa Bristow's publicist called to go over a few things for the book signing. Do you want me to text you the number she left?"

Rachel sighed. "Yes, please. I'll call her on my drive back up the mountains."

"Also, Heather from Pubnet's Rapid Response Ordering called about an hour ago. She said there was something wrong with your SAN number on the purchase order you submitted this morning."

Rachel felt her tension growing. Apparently it was the wrong day to take a drive down to the valley. And to just sit in a cold and windy waiting room, no less.

"Okay. Kristin can handle that. Tell her the invoice is filed in my office and she can find the SAN number on that to confirm it. If there's a problem, have her give me a call."

"Will do. I'll let you know if anything else comes up," Mark said before hanging up.

Barely a second passed after hanging up with the store when her phone began ringing. "Hello?"

"Ms. Taylor?"

"Yes," she said with hesitation.

"This is Principal Robinson, I'm calling about Aspen."

Rachel felt her heart drop.

"We will need someone to pick her up. She's been suspended for three days. We caught her and two other classmates smoking in one of the girls' bathrooms."

Anger began soaring through her body. "Are you serious?"

"I'm sorry to break the news to you. She will be waiting in the academic office."

"No, I'm sorry. I really am. I have no idea what's gotten into her. Okay. Someone, or I, will be there to pick her up. Thank you."

Rachel hung up and quickly started making another call. "AJ, I'm so glad you answered. Can you do me a huge favor?"

"Sure, what's up?"

"I just got a called from Mr. Robinson. Aspen is in the academic office right now, and I know this is your prep hour, could you bring her home?"

"Home? What happened?"

Rachel sighed loudly as she gripped the phone with frustration. "She was busted smoking in the bathroom."

"Good grief. Are you serious?"

"Yes. And I'm down in San Bernardino at the moment."

"Yeah, I can bring her home. I've got about forty minutes left of my prep, so that will give me plenty of time. What do you want me to do with her once she gets home?"

"Tell her to park her butt in my office and not to move a muscle until I get there."

"Sure thing. And Rach, good luck."

"Thanks," she said with another sigh and hung up.

Just as she stood to leave the county office, the door to the waiting room opened and a woman appeared. "Rachel Taylor?"

"That's me. Are you Phoebe?"

The woman nodded. "Come on back to my office and I'll see what I can do for you."

Maybe something would finally go right. She followed the stocky woman through a long corridor and then they sat down in a small, minimalistic office.

"Do you have the application?" Phoebe asked.

Rachel nodded and pulled the paper from her bag.

"And photo ID?"

She opened her wallet and handed that to the woman also.

Phoebe began typing away at her computer, glancing periodically at the application and the driver's license Rachel had handed to her.

"How do you want to pay for this today?" Phoebe asked.

Rachel handed her credit card over, and Phoebe went right back to typing. She swiped the card and handed it back. A few moments later the printer fired to life and spit out a sheet of paper. Phoebe grabbed it and handed it, along with the driver's license, to Rachel. "Here you go."

"Thanks," Rachel said, folding the document before she even had a chance to look at it. She slipped it into her bag and got back on the road as quickly as possible. Glancing at the time, she called AJ.

"I think she's scared for you to come home," AJ said.

"She better be. What am I going to do with her?"

"Well, I think you should probably calm down a little before you actually talk to her. Not that I know anything about parenting."

"Seriously AJ, I could kill her. I just want to strangle that girl."

"I know, Rach. I know."

"Anyway, I'm going to try to reach Matt before I get into the canyon. My reception gets kind of sketchy there. Thanks for bringing her home for me."

Rachel was surprised when Matt answered. When she told him what happened he grew instantly silent on the phone.

"Hello?" she asked after a few minutes of silence.

"I'm still here."

"Matt, I don't know what to do. Help me. You're her dad."

"Oh Aspen…" His anger was almost tangible through the phone. "I don't even know what to tell you."

"Gee, that's helpful."

"Don't get that way with me. She wasn't under my control when she did this."

"Are you kidding me?" she gasped. "First of all, my *control?* If I could control her this wouldn't be a problem! Second of all, she wasn't with me, she was at school. And third, she's never under your supervision, or *control,* as you put it, because you're never around!"

Rachel had to tell herself to calm down. Her screaming into the phone had resulted in a thin film of spit all over her steering wheel.

"I can't talk to you when you're like this. I get it, you're pissed at me. You think this is all my fault. Fine. Maybe it is."

"I'm sorry, I didn't mean to yell like that. I've just had it. And it's hard doing this alone."

Matt took a few moments before finally responding. "I'm sorry. I'm sorry for the way things are and I'm sorry you don't feel like you can depend on me."

"Matt, that isn't why I called. I want your input on this."

"I say ground her until she's eighteen."

"Oh yes, that's realistic. I'm serious."

"Rach, I don't know what to tell you. You're better at this stuff than I am. Look, they're calling me back into the control room. I've got to go. I will call you later tonight to talk."

She hated Matt for how easy it was to bow out of his parental responsibilities. But even more so, she hated that she still let him disappoint her.

Rachel pulled up in front of Sinful Retreat and took a moment after she turned off the car to gather her thoughts. She had contemplated a whole range of disciplinary actions the rest of her drive home, none of which she had actually narrowed down to use. Of all the books in her store, why wasn't there one to give clear cut directions on how exactly to handle this situation.

"Time to step up, Rach," she said to herself as she stepped out of the car. When she walked into Sinful Retreat, Mark looked up nervously from the counter and Kristin mouthed, "Good luck," from the bakery counter.

Rachel stepped into her office and shut the door behind her.

"Mom, I'm sorry, I—"

Rachel put her hand up to stop Aspen. She took a seat in her desk chair. "First I want to know why."

"What?" Aspen asked, looking confused.

"Tell me why you wanted to do this. Why you decided the school bathroom was the place to have a cigarette."

"Umm, well, I don't know. Kasey brought them to school and Breanne was laughing at us that we had never tried them before," Aspen was timid when she talked and avoided eye contact with Rachel.

"Where did Kasey get them?"

Aspen shrugged. "I don't know. I think from her older sister."

"Okay. So you decided to smoke to prove something to Breanne?" Rachel asked, folding her arms across her chest and reminding herself to keep her cool.

Aspen shrugged her shoulders.

"You'll need to do better than a shrug. Come on, I want an answer. You were suspended from school for this. You better have a better reason than a shoulder shrug."

"I don't know. I didn't want her to laugh at me. And I was curious anyway."

"Was it good?"

"Huh?" Aspen asked, her head snapping up quickly to look at her mom.

"Was it?"

"No. I guess. It was kind of gross. And I'm all shaky and itchy right now."

"From where I'm sitting, this was pretty stupid. Not only did you get yourself kicked out of school, but all your teachers are going to know why. You got yourself in trouble at home, and for what? A gross cigarette? A friend, who sounds to me like she isn't much of a friend to begin with? If it were up to your dad, you'd be grounded until you're eighteen."

Aspen's eyes grew wide and her shoulders dropped.

"And although I've entertained that possibility, I don't think it will really solve anything. But you are grounded. For two weeks. No friends. No phone with the exception of talking to me or your dad, no computer, iPod, iPad or television."

"What!" she gasped.

"I'm not done yet," Rachel said, taking pleasure in Aspen's distress. "For the next three days, while you're on suspension, you will be working in the bookstore, doing whatever it is that we need you to be doing."

"Does it pay?"

Rachel laughed loudly. "It most certainly does not. You can start down here today. But first, head upstairs and collect your electronic devices for me."

"Mom, this is so unfair—"

"No. What's unfair was having my day interrupted by a phone call from your principal. What's unfair is having AJ use her prep hour to drive you home. What's unfair is getting news that my daughter was doing something that, in this day and age, is completely nonsensical and just plain stupid. That's what's unfair. Go get your stuff. Now."

After Aspen left her office, Rachel felt herself begin to shake. She was proud that she had managed to keep her cool, but she was infused with anger and it was manifesting in the form of a quiver. She took in a deep breath and closed her eyes. After a minute she stood up and left her office.

"I'm proud of you," Kristin whispered under her breath as she stepped up behind Rachel.

She could only shake her head.

"I'm serious. You handled a tough situation well."

"You think so?" she asked, turning to face her friend.

"I'm sure," she said with a nod. "I talked to Heather at Pubnet and we got everything fixed. There was just a typo on the purchase order. But everything went through just fine," Kristin said.

"Thank you for doing that."

"No prob."

"Rachel," Mark said from behind the counter, "did you call Marissa Bristow's publicist back?"

"Damn it. No. I forgot. I will do that right now. Aspen is coming down to relinquish her electronics. Have her put them in the box under the register. And then, give her something to work on. She's our newest employee for the next three and a half days."

Kristin smiled in understanding and gave Rachel a nod. "I think we can handle that."

Rachel stepped back into her office and skimmed her papers for Joann Walker's number.

By that evening, Rachel wanted nothing more than to collapse onto her bed. But just after Aspen headed to bed for the night, she remembered the marriage certificate folded up in her bag. Rachel went to retrieve it, not feeling quite as tired as she was only moments earlier. Rachel read through the document. It listed the county her grandparents were married in, the date, the city and the officiant. Rachel's excitement grew when she saw her grandparents' full names listed beside their dates of birth: "Abarron Alter Taylor, 4th of April, 1924." The certificate went on to list their witnesses and information of the officiant but Rachel's eyes looked only at her grandfather's name. Who was Abarron Alter? She quickly pulled out her computer to search the middle name, but like before, the results yielded nothing helpful. It was almost as if Abarron Alter Taylor existed nowhere outside of San Bernardino County.

In that moment, Rachel wasn't sure if the newest discovery was helpful or just more frustrating. She was hoping she would have heard from Sarah, but she didn't.

Pouring herself a glass of Cabernet, Rachel called AJ.

"Your daughter still alive?"

"Barely. By her account, of course," Rachel said. She brought the wine glass to her face, letting the aroma fill her nostrils before taking a drink.

"Let me guess, you took away her electronics?"

"Of course. They're a tween's lifeline, aren't they?"

AJ laughed. "They sure are. So, not to trivialize your drama with your daughter, but when were you planning to tell me you have a date tomorrow?"

"Oh, Kristin," Rachel said with an eye roll.

"Yes, Kristin. Thank God for Kristin."

"It's nothing. He asked if I wanted dinner. I was a little blindsided, to be honest. If I would've known it was coming and I could've mentally prepared, I would have turned him down," Rachel said.

"Why is that? Because dating is against your religion?"

"Speaking of dating. How was Dana Point?"

AJ laughed. "Well, I didn't sleep with him, if that's what you're asking. Actually, it was nice. Really nice. He was sweet and, oh I don't know… I sound like a schoolgirl right now."

"Hardly."

"Well, I expect you to call me tomorrow night after your date and I'm hoping you sound a little like a schoolgirl yourself."

"Yeah, well, don't hold your breath. I've got a million irons in the fire at the moment and there just isn't a lot of room for dating."

"Well, maybe this one will be different."

"Maybe," Rachel said.

Thursday morning, when Rachel went to open the store, it was pouring rain outside. The rain was always their biggest customer deterrent. But like most mornings, Tiff and AJ came in for coffee.

"I'm thinking of heading down to Ontario Mills this weekend to get some new shoes," Tiff said as she sipped her coffee. "Anyone want to join me?"

"Mom, Parker is trying to bite me," Kate yelled from the Children's Nook around the corner.

"Parker!" Kristin yelled as she made her way around the counter. A minute later she came back, Parker in tow, and plopped him on a chair near the bakery counter. "You sit there for two minutes."

"I'll come with you," AJ said. She noticed Aspen dusting the top of the fireplace mantle. "How's the new intern?" she asked Rachel.

Rachel glanced over her shoulder at her daughter who seemed to have a permanent scowl across her face. "Cheap labor is hard to come by these days. But free is even better," she said with a smile.

The front door chimed and the four of them glanced at the entrance as Ethan walked into the store.

"That's Rach's date," Kristin quickly mumbled to the others. "Morning, Ethan," she said turning to face him with a welcoming smile on her face. "I've got to check my muffins in the oven."

As Kristin walked away, AJ gave Rachel a conspicuous wink. "Stop it," she whispered forcefully to her as she discreetly elbowed her.

AJ and Tiff both laughed.

"Well, I've got to get going. You know how these corners can be slick in the rain," Tiff said as she reached for her briefcase. "Gracie, sweetie, let's go." She turned toward Rachel, "I'll be here in the morning for details." She winked before her and the child stepped outside.

"You guys are killing me," Rachel said to AJ.

"Rachel," Mark called from the counter, "you have a phone call. Sarah?"

"Oh, great. I'll take this in my office. See you later," she said with a wave to AJ and slipped into her office and closed the door.

"I got a hold of my Ruth; she's my mom's youngest sister. Now granted her memory isn't as sharp as it once was. She said that my mom met my dad shortly after he moved to southern California from New York City. Legally his name was Abarron, but he preferred to go by Aaron. And shortly after they were married, he legally changed it. She also said that she thought he came from somewhere in central Europe, not England."

Rachel took notes on the things Sarah was telling her.

"So I got to thinking, I know many people changed spellings of their names when they moved to the U.S. in an effort to assimilate, so maybe there is another spelling of Taylor that you could try. I'm guessing that's why he changed his first name. This is just assuming his last name was different."

"Central Europe? I got their marriage certificate and on there is his middle name, Alter. Have you ever heard that?"

"Yes. I knew that was his middle name. Sorry. I should've given that to you," Sarah said.

Rachel rolled her eyes. "When I looked up the genealogy of Alter, I found that it's a Yiddish name."

"Yiddish?" Sarah asked. "I have no clue where that would have come from. Maybe there is some German in the family line. That's central Europe."

"That's true," she said with a nod. Although this, of course, was all speculation. There was nothing scientific, in the slightest, about their conversation. "Did Ruth mention when Grandma and Grandpa met? That could help narrow down a time frame for when he came to the U.S."

"He was young. I think she said they met when he was only nineteen."

"Okay. Well, thanks for calling me back. I appreciate your help."

"Rachel? Just so you know, I did tell Ruth and my siblings, including your dad, that you were working on this project. So if any of them think of anything or find anything, they will be calling you."

"Thanks Aunt Sarah."

When Rachel stepped out of her office, she noticed Aspen sitting at a table with Ethan over an open book. Curious, she asked Kristin about it.

"Well, she finished dusting everything and I asked if she had homework. She was having problems with the math stuff and Ethan said he was able to help her. So I introduced them and they've been working on it since. Who were you on the phone with?" Kristin asked.

Rachel noticed the relaxed look about Aspen and the smile on her face. She smiled to herself, then turned to look at Kristin. "That was my aunt, Sarah."

"Was she helpful?"

"Well," she said, pondering how to answer that question. "Yes and no. I mean, she doesn't know much. No one seems to. And I thought maybe she was helpful with the things that she did know, but come to find out she knew Aaron's middle name this entire time and never mentioned it. So basically I paid the county $14.00 to tell me something my aunt could have told me."

"Ugh. That kind of sucks. It's weird to me that no one seems to know anything. I mean, I don't know a ton about my ancestry, but way more than this. I can't imagine having a dad and not knowing where he was from or even my grandparents' names."

Rachel nodded. "I agree. It is weird. And I'm kind of embarrassed that I never even thought about this all until now."

"Well," she said, looking at Aspen, "I'd say you've had a lot on your plate the last twelve years."

Rachel smiled, "Yeah. Guess I have."

As Kristin headed to the bakery counter to help a customer who had come in the store, Rachel had thought about going over to talk with Aspen and Ethan. But she quickly changed her mind. Maybe it was best to give Aspen her space. Besides, it was kind of nice to watch them together, which was weird maybe, since she hardly knew him, but there was something almost endearing about the sight of them together.

Instead, Rachel made her way to the counter.

"I took an order from The Haven book club while you were on the other line. They need you to order nineteen copies of *Children of the Jacaranda Tree* by Sahar Delijani," Mark said as he handed her a note with the information on it.

"Great. I need to order some other things from one of our publishers and this should help me meet the freight requirements," she said taking the paper and stepping into her office. She rarely closed the door and while she worked on her purchase order, she could hear Ethan and Aspen laughing together. She couldn't help but smile at the sound of them.

After placing her orders, Rachel inventoried a delivery of new titles; she loved getting new books into the store. Then she set up a new display to feature four of them. Mid-afternoon another shipment arrived and when Aspen and Ethan had finished with her math assignment, she put Aspen to work calling their customers to let them know their order was in.

"Is there anything you're in the mood for tonight? You do know the area far better than I do," Ethan said as he approached Rachel at one of the book displays.

She felt herself blush and immediately became irritated with herself. "Uh, well, that depends. I'm open to pretty much anything. What are you thinking? I could make some suggestions." She felt herself smiling and her effort to take it down a level failed miserably.

"Italian?" he asked, raising an eyebrow.

"I like Italian. Pazzo's in Crestline is good."

"Let's do that, then. I'll see you in a few hours," he said with a grin and a nod before he left the store.

"You can't wipe that smile off your face," Tiff said.

Rachel felt her face go bright red. "I, uh, didn't realize you came in."

"You wouldn't have realized a freight train come through here talking to him. Look at her, Kristin, she can't stop smiling."

"I know," Kristin called over. "She's a smitten kitten."

"You like him Mom?" Aspen asked.

Rachel's stomach dropped. "I don't even know him. He asked me to dinner. That's all."

"Well, I think he's kind of cool. Although I'm not sure why he'd ask you out, then."

Rachel's smile was gone now.

"Are you kidding? Your mom's a catch," Tiff said.

"Whatever."

"Get back to your phone calls or you'll be working overtime," Rachel said.

"I'm not even getting paid," she said in a whiny voice.

"That's why I can authorize the overtime. Now get back to work."

At five, when Diane came in, Rachel was a ball of nerves. She headed upstairs, leaving Aspen in the store to do the receiving on a third shipment. She didn't need her in the house criticizing her every move.

She showered, did her hair and make-up and then standing in the doorway of her closest felt completely ill-prepared for the evening. She should've had Tiff come over and help her figure out what to wear. She glanced at the clock. It was ten after six. No way Tiff could get here, from Cedar Glen, with enough time to spare to pick out an outfit by the time she needed to head downstairs.

A few minutes before it was time to meet Ethan, Rachel had decided on an outfit: a pink V-neck top, with a three-quarter sleeve black blazer, a bib necklace and a pair of jeans that Tiff always complimented her in. As a result of this outfit, however, most of the items that once hung neatly in rows in her closet were now strewn about the room. Some on piles on the bed, a few on a chair in the corner and several more on a few piles on the floor. She felt like a teenager. She slipped into a pair of shoes with a thick heel, as opposed to a thin one in hopes this would reduce her chances of tripping and falling during the night, and headed downstairs.

Ethan was standing near the fireplace, perusing the travel bookshelf, in a pair of jeans and a slightly fitted button-up shirt. She couldn't help but think how sexy he looked standing there, unaware of her, skimming the book titles and all dressed up for an evening with her.

A moment later he turned to see her standing in the doorway of the stairway and a large smile broke out across his face. In an instant, her stomach swarmed with butterflies and excitement came over her. Then, off to her right, she noticed some movement and turned to see AJ, Kristin and Tiff hunkered behind the bakery counter and watching all of this unfold.

Rachel wanted to elbow each of them, but instead she chose to ignore them, despite their giggling.

"You look so great," Ethan said as they walked closer to each other. "I mean, you look great all the time, but right now you do, too."

She smiled at him. "Thanks. You look nice, too. You clean up well," she said, not really thinking he ever looked bad.

He smiled as he looked over her head to her friends behind them. "I think we have an audience."

"Ignore them, please."

"Want to get out of here then?"

"Absolutely."

He offered his arm and without a thought, she slipped hers through it, and then realized that they were indeed touching. She grew self-conscious but tried desperately not to show it as they walked out of the store to his 4-Runner in the parking lot.

As Rachel gave him directions to Crestline, Ethan told her about his transition to California. He had been a firefighter in Logan but had always known he would eventually leave Utah. The move was hardest on his mom, who seemed to call him nearly every other day. And although he was slightly embarrassed to share that part, Rachel found it endearing that he was close with his family.

As they passed Lake Gregory, Ethan asked Rachel about her family and she shared with him the journey she was currently on.

"That sounds fascinating. I can't imagine living in a house with so much history."

"Yeah, but it's discovering that history that's been much harder than I thought it would be," she said. "They make it look so easy on TV."

He laughed. "That's true. Everything usually looks easier on TV."

"My mom's aunt did this very same thing for their family. My family is mostly Italian and German. Apparently we have some douchebag German relatives who were persecuted for war crimes during World War II."

"Seriously?"

He nodded his head. "Yeah, it's pretty crazy."

"That is crazy. I mean, you hear about that kind of thing, but I've never met anyone who knew of relatives that played a role," she said.

"When you consider the numbers, it was bound to happen."

She nodded her head in disbelief.

"So, on that cheery note, want to have dinner?" he asked as he pulled the vehicle into a parking space at Pazzo's.

Inside, they were seated in a booth in the corner of the small restaurant while quiet Italian music played throughout. They were each handed menus and waters and their waiter said she'd be back in a few minutes.

"So, do you want to do pizza or pasta?" she asked, skimming through the menu.

"Any suggestions?"

"I like their pizza. But maybe pizza is too corny for date food."

Ethan laughed. "Not for me, it's not. Let's do pizza."

After their pizza was ordered, their wine was brought out to them and then they were left to themselves for a while.

"Your daughter seems pretty great," he said.

"She usually is. She's been on my short list as of lately."

"How come?"

Rachel rattled off the short version of the last few weeks with Aspen. "Sounds like my sister at that age."

Rachel shook her head. "Sometimes I don't know how our parents didn't kill us."

He laughed. "I have to say, I'm glad you agreed to come out tonight. I don't usually ask women out when I barely know them. This was a little out of character for me, and well, I'm relieved you said yes."

Rachel felt her cheeks grow warm. "It was a little out of character for me to say yes, so, I'm kind of relieved that this is new territory for you as well."

"You don't date much?"

"That would be a no," she said.

"Wow. I mean, that just shocks me. You're gorgeous. And I'm not just saying that. I really think so. I can't imagine guys not lining up to ask you out."

"I'm flattered, but I live in a small town. Most men around here know me and not all of them are okay with a woman who has a child."

"Their loss, my gain."

Rachel couldn't help but become completely enamored with Ethan as they talked. He was easy to talk with, seemed genuine in everything he said and made her laugh like no one had in a long, long time.

Long after they finished their dinner, they continued to sit at their corner table talking, laughing, telling stories. He shared with her about his childhood, his hobbies, the things he liked and the things he didn't, such as basketball. He was terrible at basketball but loved to golf.

Rachel told him how she and Kristin opened Sinful Retreat and how she had gotten the house from her grandfather after he passed away.

"It was the best way I could think of to make a living. And people told me I was crazy. More people sell books than buy them. And with the digital market what it is, I was nervous. But Lake Arrowhead Village isn't a metropolis. It sets its own rules. It's a tourist's haven and my place does well. I mean, I'm far from rich or anything, but I can pay my bills and I have all the things I need."

"I'm impressed. Really, I am."

Rachel couldn't help but smile when she looked at Ethan. And despite how nervous she had been at the beginning of the night, looking into those dark brown eyes now, she felt nothing but calm.

"How about, since I'm walking in the same direction, I walk you to your door?" he asked as they got out of his vehicle back at Sinful Retreat.

"How about my stairs?"

He smiled and together they walked side by side around to the lake side of the building. At the bottom of the stairs that took her to her deck and apartment, they stood for a moment in the darkness.

The large, white moon shone on the still waters about forty yards away from them, and in the distance Rachel could hear the sounds of crickets. "I had fun tonight," she said.

"I'm glad. I did too. And thanks for the recommendation. The food was good."

"Do you want to do this again sometime?" she asked.

"I do. Sooner, rather than later."

She smiled. "Okay. When do you want to do this again?"

"Is Saturday too soon?" he asked.

She was thankful for the cover of night because she knew her face was burning red. "That sounds good."

"Well, goodnight, Rachel."

"Goodnight," she said. She lingered at the bottom of the steps for a moment as he turned and headed toward the boathouse.

Inside her apartment, Aspen had left a lamp on in the living room but had already gone to bed. Rachel peeked into her room and saw her daughter fast asleep, an upside-down open book across her chest.

She crept across the room and gently slid the book out from under her loose grip. She folded a corner page, closed it and set it on the nightstand. She brought Aspen's blankets up and covered her and then gently kissed her forehead before slipping out of the room.

In the confines of her own room, she picked up the telephone and dialed. When AJ answered, Rachel gave her a long, high pitched and drawn out 'Hi'.

"Well," AJ said, "that was definitely a schoolgirl hello."

FIVE

Rachel woke before her alarm on Friday morning. With the extra time before she had to head down to the store, she decided to make breakfast for her and Aspen. She whipped up some pancake mix, sliced up strawberries and fried a few sausage links. Just before it was ready, Aspen's door opened, revealing a yawning, messy-haired girl.

"What's gotten into you?" she asked as she rubbed her eyes and took a seat on the barstool at the counter.

"Just in a good mood," Rachel said.

"So your date was good then, huh?"

Rachel turned quickly to face her daughter. "It was good. Does that bother you?" she asked, setting down the plate of pancakes and taking a step closer to Aspen.

She shrugged her shoulder. "Not really. Why?"

"Well, I just don't do this very much and I didn't know what you thought about it."

"Mom, seriously, I don't really care. I guess I feel like, if you have someone else in your life, maybe you won't worry so much about me."

Rachel rolled her eyes and picked the plate of food back up. "You're so insightful. Grab that plate of sausage," she said with a nod over her shoulder.

After breakfast, Rachel got dressed and headed down to the store.

"Hi Ray-el," Parker yelled with a beaming smile from a table near the bakery counter. His face was covered with jam as he stuffed his mouth with a pastry.

"Not too often I beat you here," Kristin said as she popped her head out of the kitchen. "I want details."

Rachel blushed but she didn't care. She made her way to the counter, a smile across her face.

"That good, huh?"

She laughed. "It was good. So good. And it felt good just being there, with him."

Kristin smiled.

"I like him. I think I like him a lot. Oh my God," she said, "this is crazy. I barely know the guy. I need to calm down."

"Don't be ridiculous. It was a date. It's not like you're getting married. Enjoy this. Are you going out again?"

Rachel nodded, a sheepish grin curling at the corners of her mouth. "Tomorrow."

"Good," Kristin said with a nod. "Stop being overly analytical and let it just be whatever it's going to be or not be."

"You're right."

"I know. Now turn on the register. It's time to open."

The first few customers of the day kept Rachel busy. One, who was clearly not much of a reader, insisted on giving Rachel obscure details of an unknown book expecting her to instantly summon the name and author. Another was on a hunt for a good romance novel, even though she had read practically everything in the section and the third was placing an order for several books Sinful Retreat didn't stock, but had the ability to purchase.

By midmorning, the store began to fill up as people from The Haven book club filtered in. The Haven was the largest book club that met at Sinful Retreat and was also the only coed one. They were often the noisiest group to meet there, but they only met once a month, so Rachel was able to tolerate the headache for the business.

"Do something different with your hair this morning, Rach?" Tom asked. Tom was a local accountant whom she had made the bad decision of agreeing to let take her to dinner years ago. He still hadn't given up on her yet.

"Just washed it," she said, not lifting her eyes from the computer screen in front of her. She knew he would back off as soon as the book club began discussing their latest read, but in the meantime, she always had to keep herself busy to avoid him.

Aspen, who had been filing papers in Rachel's office all morning peeked her head out the door to see what all commotion was from. A few people who knew her nodded or said hello and about ten minutes after they began coming in, they all sat down around the roaring fire and began their book discussion.

Mark arrived for his shift halfway through The Haven's meeting. He rolled his eyes when he spotted Tom, who had carefully chosen a spot to sit where he could both participate in his book discussion as well as watch Rachel at work.

"I see Lover Boy is here," he mumbled under his breath as he clocked in on the computer.

"And that's why I am going into my office to pay bills," she said. "Convenient."

She laughed as she stepped into her office and closed the door.

"Why don't you go see what kind of help you can give Kristin," she said to Aspen. "She just got an order of supplies and it will probably need to be inventoried."

"Jobs are so overrated," Aspen said as she got to her feet.

"Hmm, well, considering the hurry you're in to grow up, you'll be needing one sooner than you think. Maybe it's not such a bad thing, this whole still-being-a-kid thing, huh?"

Aspen gave Rachel her famous eye roll, and with a hand on her hip, she left the office.

Before getting to the store's bills, Rachel thought again about her grandpa. She knew that ships were a common form of transportation for many people who had migrated to the U.S. and wondered if that could be how Aaron had come. Without much hope, Rachel pulled open the website for the United States' National Archives. Immigration and Naturalization Service records revealed a New York passenger list microfilm from 1897 through 1957. But the INS records yielded nothing helpful.

She didn't feel incredibly disheartened when her search came up empty this time as she knew it was a shot in the dark. She had nothing to even indicate Aaron had come via ship. Nearly everything she and Sarah discussed was speculation. Rachel couldn't help but feel that she had come as far as she could in the search for Aaron Taylor without having any more information.

She sighed and pulled up her accounting forms on the computer and began paying the store's bills.

Rachel emerged from her office at lunchtime with all her accounts current and the weekly payroll completed. She felt proud of her progress until she noticed Tom sitting in the bakery, reading a book and sipping a coffee. He gave her a large, toothy grin when he saw her step behind the counter and immediately closed his book and made his way toward her.

"Thought maybe you were avoiding me," he said with a laugh.

"Working, Tom. Always working. What can I do for you?"

The bell at the front door chimed and a cool draft came in with a customer. Rachel looked up to see Ethan as he stepped inside. She smiled at him as her stomach gave a flutter.

"So, do you?" Tom asked.

She quickly looked back at Tom with a blank look across her face. "I'm sorry, what?"

"I said there's a book trade show in San Diego next month and I was hoping you'd want to go with me," he said, a hopeful expression on his face.

From the corner of her eye, Rachel watched Ethan move to a chair near the fireplace. "What interest do you have going to a book trade show?"

Tom shrugged. "I don't know. I mean, it's something you're into, so I figured I could be into it, too."

"Tom, no, I'm sorry. I won't be going to any trade show with you."

"Well how about dinner then? I mean, how many times can you say no?"

She sighed. "I'm sorry, but we won't be having dinner, either. You've asked me once a month for almost four years now and you've gotten the same response each time. I think the better question to ask is, how many times can you listen to the answer no?"

"You'll say yes. Some time, you'll say yes."

"I need to get back to work now," she said, leaving the counter and making her way toward Ethan.

"Hey," he said, a knowing look on his face.

She couldn't help but smile. She sat down on a chair next to him. "Thanks again, for last night," she said, leaning closer to him.

"I've got big plans for you tomorrow night," he said.

Rachel glanced up to see Tom watching them from the counter. "Big plans?"

"Just dress up."

"How dressy?"

"Not black tie or anything, but dressy. That okay?"

She nodded. She couldn't remember the last time she had gotten dressed up for someone and eagerness for being able to do it for him warmed her inside.

"Rachel, phone call," Mark called to her.

"Well, it's back to work for me," she said as she stepped into her office.

The rest of the day went by in a hectic blur. Shortly after lunch, a shipment arrived and as Aspen was checking-in the new inventory, she noticed a large error. The order was missing over two dozen books and another two dozen were incorrect titles. Rachel spent much of the afternoon going through purchase orders and making phone calls to her wholesale suppliers to straighten out the mistakes.

By 5:00, she was relieved to see Diane and gave her surprisingly few tasks for the evening. She was too exhausted to think anymore and retiring upstairs, she collapsed onto the sofa.

Her relaxation was quickly interrupted by the phone ringing. And she didn't feel any relief when she answered to hear Matt's voice on the other end.

"How did you handle it with Aspen?" he asked.

Her frustration began building instantly. "How nice of you to call, *Dad*."

"I'm sorry. First, I was too mad to talk to her and then I got busy with work."

"Oh right, because you're the only one with responsibilities…"

"Rach, I said I'm sorry. I am. Now just tell me how you decided to handle this so I can support you."

"Ask your daughter. Because, quite frankly, I don't want to talk to you." She covered the mouthpiece of the phone and called for Aspen. "Your dad's on the phone."

Aspen contorted her face. "Does he know?"

"Of course he knows. I talked to him before I even talked to you."

"You know, most of my friends' parents that aren't together don't talk to each other as much as you two do. You don't have to tell him everything."

"Aspen. Don't start with me. Take the phone. If you didn't want to deal with the consequences of your stupidity, then you should've made better choices. Now take the phone!"

She snapped the phone from Rachel's hand and retreated to her bedroom to talk to Matt.

Rachel didn't have the energy to listen to their conversation. She closed her eyes and in moments she drifted off to sleep.

◆◆◆

Rachel's eyes snapped open to the sound of Aspen's sniffles. Through blurry eyes, she saw her daughter sitting on the coffee table beside her, the phone in her lap.

She rubbed her eyes and sat up, the room coming into focus. Aspen's face was wet with tears. "He is so unfair sometimes. I wish he wasn't even my dad."

"What did he have to say?" Rachel asked as she reached her hand out and stroked Aspen's soft brown hair.

"He said I was being a hellion. And that he was tired of getting calls hearing about what a selfish brat I was being."

Rachel sighed.

"I don't get it. Why does he think he can have a say when I'm misbehaving but he isn't ever around for any of the other stuff. He's not once been to one of my track meets."

"Your dad has an important job. If he could be here, he would." Defending him and his actions to Aspen made Rachel furious. But she also refused to be the parent who bashed the other parent to their child. Her issues with Matt were hers and she didn't think they needed to be Aspen's as well.

"No, he could be here. He just chooses not to be. He chooses to have that job. I hate him. And I even told him that," she said, tears streaming down her face.

"Come here," she said, taking her daughter into her arms. Aspen curled into the fetal position on her lap and buried her face in the crook of Rachel's neck.

"Just know that I love you. Whatever things are between you and your dad, always know that I love you."

Aspen sobbed for almost a half hour before she finally pulled away from Rachel. "I'm sorry, Mom," she said. "About the smoking thing. It was stupid and I'm sorry."

"Sometimes we have to learn the hard way in life, but I set rules for a reason. And I do expect you to follow them."

"I know. I really am sorry."

"I know you are," Rachel said with a nod.

Sinful Retreat was busy Saturday morning. Both Mark and Diane had to work the book counter while Kristin and Becky worked the bakery and Aspen flitted between the two as needed. Rachel hibernated in her office going through proofs that the printer had dropped by that morning. November and December were the store's busiest months. The following Saturday was the book signing event with Marissa Bristow, and Rachel hadn't even picked up the book in weeks. The week after that was the release of the newest thriller by author David Sharpe and then the following Saturday kicked off Sinful Retreat's pre-Black Friday sale. All hell broke loose after that with Black Friday and Christmas shortly after.

Rachel's proofs were covered in sticky notes that were filled with comments for the printer.

There was a slight knock at the door and Diane popped her head into the office. "The promo materials just arrived from Bristow's publicist."

"Just put them by the door," she nodded to her office door.

"Also, a shipment of *Children of the Jacaranda Tree* arrived. I've got them all checked in and put in the system," Diane said.

"I need to create invoices for all of them, so you can put that box in the back room and bring me the inventory record. Oh, and send Aspen in, will you?"

Diane nodded and left the office and a few minutes later Aspen appeared in the doorway. "What's up?"

"The magazine rack by the counter needs all of the October issues pulled and the new December issues put out."

"Uh, I think you're losing your mind. It's November, Mom."

"Yeah, those were put out last month. December issues can be found in the storage room in the back."

The day went by in a blur. Ethan came in shortly after lunch to check his emails and read from his travel guide, but Rachel only had time for a smile and a wave from afar.

Shortly after lunch, something went wrong with the register and while Mark sat on the phone with tech-support, Rachel redirected all book sales to the bakery counter.

Kristin put a freshly made batch of crullers up front and the store was flooded with the delightful aroma of the sweet pastry. Rachel's stomach growled and she glanced at the clock. She needed to finish her invoices before the end of the day, but with the register down, she was also needed up front. Her shoulders tightened with stress. A reprieve from customers allowed her to get an update from Mark, whose head was buried beneath the counter so he could access the register's wiring.

He didn't have any good news, so Rachel took the opportunity to slip back into her office to finish invoices. She told Aspen to grab her if things started getting busy again.

An hour later she emerged from her office, all the invoices completed and ready for her customers. Mark had gotten the register working again and another hour later it was time to call it a day and head up to shower for her date.

"Mark," she said before locking up her office for the day, "don't forget to reconcile all of the e-commerce transactions tonight before you leave."

He nodded his head. "Sure thing."

Tiff walked through the front door of the store, a tote looped over her arm, and instantly made eye-contact with Rachel.

She smiled as she approached her. "Kristin might have mentioned you were going on another date, so I thought I would offer my services while you're getting ready," Tiff said.

Rachel glanced over her shoulder at Kristin who stood behind the bakery counter giggling.

"Besides, I needed to get out of my house. The girls terrorized the downstairs and while they were supposed to be cleaning, they found everything in the world to bicker about. And Jake is no help because he is glued to the PlayStation."

Rachel laughed. "Men. And why is it you're all encouraging me to find one of them?"

Tiff shrugged. "Despite their many shortcomings, they still have their perks."

The two headed upstairs and Rachel jumped in the shower. Fifteen minutes later, her hair wrapped up above her head in a towel, she stood in front of her closet, a defeated look on her face already.

"Where are you guys going?" Tiff asked.

"Don't know. He said to get dressed up."

"That sounds fun!"

"Yeah, if I had something to get dressed up in. I don't do this kind of stuff very often."

"Oh relax," Tiff said with a wave of her arm. "We'll find something. I brought over a few pieces of jewelry, too. It's amazing what a nice necklace or earrings will do to an outfit."

Tiff stepped into the closet and began rummaging through the articles of clothing. "You like him?" she asked, her voice was muffled with her head buried in clothing.

"Yeah," she said, feeling the heat rise to her face.

"He's pretty nice to look at. Not going to lie to you. That dark hair and even the little scruff on his face."

Rachel laughed. "You could be describing Jake. Guess you *do* have a type."

Tiff stepped out of the closet, a knowing smile on her face, carrying a few hangers in her hands.

"This dress still has the tags on it," Tiff gasped as she held out a coral belted waist A-line dress.

"Miranda gave it to me. She didn't like the cap-sleeves on her."

Tiff nodded. "Sounds like her. She and your brother haven't been up here in months."

"I know. He's been pretty swamped with work. I think the girls are keeping him busy, too," Rachel said as she took the dress and stepped into the bathroom to slip it on.

"Three daughters will do that to you," Tiff called through the cracked door. "Braelyn and Siena keep me flying by the seat of my pants usually."

Rachel stepped back into her bedroom in the dress. She rarely wore dresses and felt slightly uncomfortable in it.

"You look gorgeous," Tiff exclaimed followed with an audible exhale.

"Really?" Rachel contorted her face as she turned to look in the full-length mirror.

"Your dark hair makes that color just pop on you."

Rachel stared at her reflection. She saw pasty legs, the bump on her belly from having Aspen, which she vowed to get rid of and never did, and bony shoulders.

"This is the dress. Now take it off before your hair soaks it. I'm going to open a bottle of your wine."

"I only have white left. But pour me a glass. I'm going to blow dry my hair."

With a few minutes to spare, Rachel stepped into the living room, wobbling slightly on the carpeting in the heeled sling-backs on her feet. Dresses weren't the only thing she wasn't used to wearing.

Tiff stood, a glass of wine in her hand, and silently nodded her head. "You are beautiful."

"Are you sure?"

"I'm so sure."

There was a knock at the door and Rachel's heart jumped.

AJ and Aspen stepped into the apartment and Rachel felt her shoulder drop in relief at the sight of them.

"Wow, Mom. You look hot."

The three women laughed.

"Thanks," Rachel said with a smile as she slipped her arm around her daughter.

"It's true. You do," AJ said as she picked up Rachel's glass of wine from the coffee table and drained it in one swallow.

"Where are you guys going?" Aspen asked.

"No idea."

There was another knock on the door and Rachel exchanged glances with Tiff.

"Have fun," Tiff said with a smile.

"Aspen and I will be having girl's night here. So don't worry about us," AJ said with a nod as Rachel made her way to the door.

"Wow," Ethan said when she opened it.

"Hi," was all she could manage from her mouth at the sight of him. Tiff was right. His slightly scruffy face, even when shaved, brought a rugged sexiness to him. But his eyes were gentle, lending an almost boyish appearance to him.

"Just out of curiosity," he said as he glanced behind her, "will your friends be here every time I take you out?"

"Just think of them as an over-protective father."

He nodded with a smile. "All right, well you ladies have a good night," he said to them.

The evening air was cool, but Rachel hardly noticed as they made their way down the back steps of her apartment and around to the front of the store where Ethan was parked.

"So are you going to tell me where we're headed?" she asked as she slid into the car.

"We're driving down into the valley. Hope that's okay?"

She nodded. "You're not going to tell me any more than that, are you?"

He smiled. "You'll find out soon enough."

Winding their way down the San Bernardino Mountains and into the valley, Ethan told Rachel about his week at work. She found his job fascinating.

"I know so many kids say they want to be a fireman when they grow up, but when did you know that's what you really wanted to do?" she asked.

"Where I'm from, in Utah, is a heavily forested area. When I was in college a pretty serious wildfire broke out and my family was evacuated from their home, along with all of our neighbors. We didn't lose the house or anything, but it was inspiring to me how in such dangerous conditions, there were people willing to sacrifice everything to keep it safe for everyone else," he paused. "Wow, that was probably pretty cheesy."

Rachel noticed his cheeks redden slightly and couldn't help but grin. "Not at all. It's kind of impressive actually."

As they wound through the streets of Riverside, the Mission Inn came into view.

"Is this where we're going?" she asked, anticipation building.

He nodded. "I was told it was a great place. Especially if I was trying to impress someone."

His eyes caught hers and they lingered for a moment before he looked back to the road ahead of them.

Rachel caught a brief glance at the magnificent and chromatic Amistad Dome before they turned into a parking lot.

Walking alongside one another, Ethan slipped his hand into hers. It was warm and soft and her stomach fluttered with nerves.

They stepped through the wrought iron gates of Duane's Prime Steaks and Seafood and were welcomed with the redolence of pepper, garlic and Sherry. The soft amber hues and dimmed lighting transported them into a world of elegance.

Ethan stepped forward to talk with the hostess and a few moments later they were being quietly ushered through the restaurant, passing timeless art and tables of patrons enjoying their dinner.

They were seated at a small table along a wall which boasted a brilliant painting of Teddy Roosevelt and the Rough Riders that stretched nearly eight feet above their heads.

Sitting beside him, Rachel felt at ease and her nerves dissipated into the air around them. He took her hand from across the table, and she didn't drop her gaze from his eyes.

"This is really above and beyond," she said quietly.

He smiled. "Don't expect things like this on a regular basis."

"You say that like you have some longevity in mind."

"Would that be such a bad thing?" he asked.

Rachel felt her head slowly shaking from side to side.

After they ordered their food, he took her hand once again. For a moment they sat in silence and Rachel wondered what a future with him could be like. She had never thought like that about anyone other than Matt before and the idea was both exhilarating and frightening.

Ethan broke the silence first. "Can I ask you about Aspen's dad?" There was hesitation when he spoke.

"Of course," she said with a reassuring nod.

"I've not heard him mentioned and I wondered if he was in the picture."

"He's kind of in the picture. Matt travels around the country for his job and even though we rarely see him, we stay in touch through phone calls and emails. He and Aspen Skype occasionally, too."

"Were you guys married?"

Rachel shook her head. "I was only twenty when I got pregnant. Both of us were in college and I knew from the beginning that his priorities would be his career and that I would always come second. So would the baby. But I wanted to have her. When I was only a few months pregnant my Grandpa Aaron died and left his house to our family. My parents own a place in Newport, so when I proposed my idea of Sinful Retreat, they let me have the house."

"Did you love him?"

"I did. Probably more than I should've. I held out for him for a long time. But nowadays he tends to infuriate me more than anything else."

He smiled.

A server appeared and placed their food in front of them. Rachel reveled in the heavenly smells before her, and her stomach rumbled with anticipation.

Their dinner was quiet and peaceful. Ethan didn't ask any more questions about Matt and Rachel shared stories about Aspen that made him laugh. She told him about her brother Ben, his wife, and their daughters, and she told him a few stories about Aaron.

"Have you made any progress in your search?" he asked.

"No," she said with a shake of her head. "I'm pretty sure I've hit a dead end."

"Maybe something will show up."

After dinner, they walked hand in hand through the arched walkways of The Mission Inn along Sixth Street. The overhead lights illuminated the surrounding brick walls with a tawny glow.

"Can I confess something to you?" she asked keeping her eyes focused straight ahead.

"Absolutely."

"It's been three years since I've been on a date. And even longer since I've been on a second date."

He stopped walking and pulled Rachel toward him. Reluctantly she looked up at him.

"And how long has it been since you were last kissed?" he asked, his voice barely above a whisper.

She swallowed hard as her body went warm all over. She felt his hand slide up to the middle of her back as he pulled her in closer and kissed her tenderly on the lips. When he pulled away slightly a moment later, she pulled him back into her and slid her arms over his shoulders.

SIX

Rachel spent Sunday morning reliving the night before. She found joy in the realization that regardless of age, a first kiss could still be a magical moment. Lying in bed, she relived the feeling of his lips against hers and it made her body tingle deep inside. If she knew he hadn't left for the fire station early that morning she may have headed down to the boathouse just to kiss him again. But alas, he wouldn't be there and instead she tossed and turned beneath the blankets of her bed until AJ interrupted her thoughts.

"Are you still sleeping?" she whispered from the doorway.

"No," she said, her head buried beneath a pillow.

"Oh good. I have a ton of work to get done today, but I wanted the scoop from last night."

Rachel rolled over as AJ took a seat beside her on the bed. She described their night together, again feeling her body come alive deep within.

"Is he a good kisser?"

Rachel's sigh was tangible. "Oh, hell yes."

AJ laughed. "I'd really love to stay longer, but I have grades due tomorrow and a ton of papers to finish correcting."

Rachel glanced over her shoulder at the clock and in an instant, reality set in and her stomach dropped. "I've got a ton of work to do as well."

"That's right, the book signing is Saturday. Well, good luck this week. Let me know if you need any help. Jack is coming up on Tuesday," she said with a grin.

Rachel raised an eyebrow. "He is? Do I get to meet him?"

"It's possible," AJ said as she stood. "Later."

The rest of the day went by in a flash. Rachel, Aspen, and Kristin spent all of Sunday cleaning Sinful Retreat from top to bottom. Despite all of the dusting she had Aspen do the week before, the place was in desperate need of a deep clean. And it took them all day. Come night fall, Darren arrived with the kids, who were eager to help. Kristin gave each of them a wet wipe and put them to work on the tables in the bakery. Darren was good at lifting heavy things and moving shelves around, and well after ten, they finally retired for the night.

Rachel was up early the next day and found herself back in the store preparing for the book signing. There were so many promotional items to organize, and she was thankful that the sleet outside kept the customer traffic to a minimum, allowing her time to run errands for the store. She spent all of Monday and Tuesday preparing for the book signing and was on the phone with a vendor looking for a missing order of books by Marissa Bristow when AJ came into the store, a guy following closely behind her.

"Well, I need that order. I don't care if you have to send an entirely new one, get me my order!" she yelled into the phone, feeling spit fly from her mouth as she spoke.

After hanging up, Rachel stepped out of her office and put a forced smile across her face.

"Whoa, someone's having a stressful day," AJ said.

Rachel sighed.

"Rach, this is Jack," she said, stepping aside and letting a tall man with sandy blonde hair come into view. He was dressed in a designer suit that was custom tailored and Rachel couldn't help but nod in approval at his appearance. "Jack, this is Rachel."

"Nice to finally meet you," he said extending his hand out to her.

"Oh," she said, not expecting the handshake, "you too."

The three of them made their way to the vacant sofas near the fireplace. "It's colder up here than I expected it to be," he said when they sat down.

"We're supposed to get snow tonight," AJ said.

"I've been so swamped that I haven't even listened to a weather report," Rachel said. "So I hear you're a finance manager?" she asked.

Jack nodded his head. "For the Mercedes-Benz dealership in Carlsbad."

Rachel recalled that AJ had met him on a cruise to Ensenada while he was in the middle of a divorce. "And what do you think of Lake Arrowhead?"

"It's nice. I've only ever been to Big Bear. I usually do some skiing up there every year, so I'm kind of shocked I've never been here until now," he said.

"You know she doesn't ski, at all, right?" Rachel asked with a nod toward AJ.

"I told him," AJ said.

He laughed. "I have plans to change that."

"Rach," Mark called from the counter, "phone call."

"Sorry guys. Gotta run."

"It's Matt," Mark said as she passed him and walked toward her office door.

"What's up, Matt?"

"Sorry to bug you at work. But I can't get a hold of Aspen," he said.

"What do you mean?"

"I mean, she says she doesn't want to talk to me and hangs up on me."

Rachel sighed. "What do you want me to do about it?"

"I want you to talk to her. Make her take my phone calls."

"Matt, I can't do that. If she doesn't want to talk to you, that's between you guys. And honestly, I can't say I blame her after what you said to her."

"I lost my temper. But it's not like she didn't have it coming."

"I'm not getting in the middle of this. You need to figure out how to be her dad. I won't have any part in that."

"This is exactly what you've been waiting for, since the day I took this job. You've been waiting for the moment that you could drive a wedge between Aspen and I because you're mad at me. Don't take your anger out on her."

"Are you kidding me right now? That's what you think I'm doing? If there is a wedge between you and your daughter, it's because you put it there. And every time you talk to her the way you do and every year that goes by that you're not a physical part of her life, you're your own hammer pounding that wedge in further. Don't put this on me. Now I've got to go. I've got a job to do," she said and placed the phone on the receiver.

Rachel felt anger surging inside. She wanted to scream but knew her office wasn't the place to do that. It was times like these that she wondered how she could've been so blind and naïve to have ever been so head over heels for him.

There was a slight knock on the door and Kristin popped her head in. "You okay?"

Rachel, startled, looked over her shoulder.

"I could, kind of hear you."

Her heart sank and she felt embarrassed.

"Don't worry about it," she said, slipping into the office and closing the door behind her.

"That's *super* professional of me."

"For all anyone else knows you were straightening out a messed-up order."

Rachel gave a weak laugh. "Some days I just want to pull my hair out."

"To be honest, and as your friend, I don't think you could pull off the bald look. But, if it will help, my pumpkin roll will be ready in about ten minutes."

Rachel nodded her head. "Yeah, I think that may help." A smile curled at the corner or the mouth.

"By the way, something came while you were on the phone. It might help, too."

"What?"

"Come look," Kristin said with the wave of her hand as she left the office, Rachel following behind her.

On the book counter, near the register, was a vase filled with bright pink daisies. Rachel felt her breath catch.

"Ethan dropped them off a few minutes ago," Kristin said, a smile on her face.

Saturday came quickly. Despite all of Rachel and Kristin's preparations, come that morning, they both still felt incredibly unprepared. A large sign with the book cover was placed outside to greet people as they entered Sinful Retreat and tables were set up around the store, each featuring a book by author Marissa Bristow. A large table replaced the seating area in front of the fireplace for Marissa to sit at. There was another large poster with her photo and the cover of *My Mother's Mother* on the front that was displayed there, along with a few copies of her books.

Kristin was frantic in the kitchen. She had far outdone herself for this event. The savory aroma of her foods filled the store, and one by one she filled the display counter with French chocolate bread, prosciutto and gruyere croissants, Swedish cinnamon buns, homemade pretzel rolls, and so much more.

"Where do you want the ad for the Pre-Black Friday Sale?" Mark asked.

"What's the discount for the featured book today?" Diane asked.

"Mom, where do you want the box of extra books?"

She took a breath. "Mark, put that on the counter so all the customers can see it when they check out. Make a note on the register so we can remind them about it as well. Anyone who buys *My Mother's Mother* today gets it twenty percent off. Aspen, put that box behind the counter beneath the register."

Rachel felt sheer relief when the store finally opened at ten. A flood of people who had been lined up outside stepped in from the cold and the sounds of conversation and laughter took over. Rachel flitted between Marissa, her publicist Joann, the front counter, and customers. Darren and Becky helped Kristin in the bakery, Diane exclusively worked the book register, Mark helped customers and Aspen was the gopher for everyone, helping with random tasks here and there. The crowds didn't seem to end. Or thin out. People had come from all over to meet Marissa and Rachel was beaming with pride, all while trying to keep calm as she kept the event running smoothly, answered questions for customers, and put out a few small fires at the register.

When Ethan came in, Rachel brought him a cup of Kristin's famous homemade caramel apple cider and they slipped out of the chaotic crowd and into her office. She left the door slightly ajar and welcomed the drastic drop in volume.

"I've been watching you work for a little while now," he said with a smile.

"Really? You didn't just get here?"

"You should be proud of yourself. Few people could pull this off like you have."

She felt herself blush.

Ethan took a sip of the cider. "This is incredible."

"I know, huh? Kristin is amazing in the kitchen."

"I won't keep you too long. But I wanted to tell you that you look amazing."

"I look frantic."

"True. But beautiful, too."

She smiled as she looked up into the richness of his dark brown eyes. She leaned into him and gently pressed her lips against his. She felt his hand slide up her back as he kissed her back. But a moment later their kiss was interrupted by a knock on the door.

"I need a manager override on the register," Diane called in from the cracked doorway.

"Coming," she said and gave Ethan a half-hearted grin before she stepped back into the store.

A few minutes later, Ethan slipped a piece of paper in Rachel's hand as he passed her on his way to the door. She looked at it after he was already gone, and smiled at the words on the paper:

"Drinks. My place. After closing tonight."

"Rach, I see in the system there's an inventoried box of *The Casual Encounter*, but I can't find it in the storage closet," Mark said coming up from behind her.

"All additional copies of Marissa's books are in my office."

"Gotcha. Thanks."

Marissa Bristow was finished by two that afternoon, and although the crowds died down drastically, they didn't completely disappear altogether. Many customers still came to buy the featured book at the sale price, and lots came because of Kristin's amazing food, which after more than ten years, certainly had a reputation, especially during an event. Others meandered into the store to see what the hype was all about. Rachel felt a respite at the end of the day at the loss of the significant weight that had been on her shoulders for weeks now. She knew it was short-lived, and that come Monday, as preparations for Black Friday and Cyber Monday would begin, her anxiety would reach new levels. But for now, she decided to just breathe.

As a reward for all of her help, Rachel let Aspen invite her friend Olivia over to spend the night. She also granted her access to the DVD player. As the girls popped popcorn and made themselves comfortable on the sofa in the living room, Rachel stepped into her bedroom and slipped into a pair of jeans and a sweater. The temps had dropped that week and the snow they got on Tuesday night was still on the ground in a few places.

She ran a brush through her hair, refreshed her face with some make-up, and then slipped out of the apartment and headed across the yard to the boathouse.

The lights from inside reflected through the windows onto the still lake, and for the first time, Rachel didn't feel nervous as she approach Ethan's door.

Inside, his apartment was warm and cozy and she took a seat on a small sofa near a window. He poured each of them a glass of wine and joined her on the sofa, their legs pushed up against one another.

Rachel took the glass and took a drink, feeling the red wine travel down to her stomach and warm her on the inside. She looked over at Ethan and smiled.

"How did the rest of your day go?" he asked.

She nodded slowly, taking another drink. "It went well. It was so busy. But that's always a good thing."

He reached out and brushed a stray hair behind her ear and the soft touch of his finger along the side of her face raised goose bumps on her arms.

"I wanted to stay longer but didn't want to get in your way," he said.

"It was probably a good thing that you left. You did kind of distract me," she said with a grin.

Ethan leaned into her and pressed his lips against hers. Rachel felt her heart begin to pound in her chest as she kissed him back. A moment later he took her wine glass and set it down, along with his, on a nearby table. With both hands free, she pulled him closer to her.

He tasted sweet and heavenly in her mouth: the weight of his body, the firmness of his chest pressing down against her. His hands roamed her body and caressed the tops of her thighs, and she ran her fingers through his thick hair.

His lips traveled to her jawline and then to her neck, leaving a faint trail of moisture behind, and she took the moment to catch her breath before his lips were pressed back against hers, her tongue circling around his.

Her heart raced as they continued to kiss, and his hands slid under the bottom of her sweater. He hesitated slightly and when she didn't protest, he migrated up her back, his fingers caressing her skin along the way. She felt him hard and firm as he pressed against her, and she couldn't help but feel joy inside for being able to turn him on. It had been so long since she had been kissed like this by anyone and didn't even know until now that she was craving it.

After a while, things slowed between them and as he wrapped his arms around her and pulled her against him, she rested her head on his chest and closed her eyes. As she lay there in the silence, she took him in: the smell of his body, his clothing, his shampoo, the sound of his breathing, the rise and fall of his chest. A joy that had been so long absent now pulsated through her veins with every breath that she took.

"You're going to fall asleep," he whispered. His lips delicately brushed her ear when he spoke.

"Mmm," she groaned.

"What about Aspen?" His breath was warm on the side of her face.

Slowly she opened her eyes. "What're you doing tomorrow?"

"Something with you, hopefully."

She smiled. "Want to have dinner with Aspen and I at my place?"

"I'd love to," he said with a nod. He leaned in and firmly pressed his mouth against hers. "Good night," he said with a wink at the door.

As she walked toward the house, Rachel felt him watching her from his doorway and she couldn't help but smile to herself.

Rachel spent Sunday frantically cleaning the apartment. Aspen, amused with her mother's stress, read a book on the couch.

"You know, if you're not going to help me then you could at least go somewhere else," she yelled over the roar of the vacuum.

"Where am I supposed to go? It's creepy in the store all by myself and I'm sick of hanging out in my bedroom," she whined.

"Then go unload the dishwasher."

"What?"

"You heard me. Unless you want me to extend your lack of technology another week?"

Rachel heard her daughter's sigh over the vacuum as she zoomed in front of the couch and Aspen stomped into the kitchen, one hand on her hip.

After vacuuming, Rachel dusted the entertainment center, tossed a stack of outdated magazines in the recycling, pulled some excess books that were exploding off the bookshelf and tossed them on the top shelf of her closet, watered the plants, and fluffed the pillows.

"I've never seen you like this, Mom," Aspen observed from the kitchen as Rachel went through a stack of mail on the counter.

"Thanks for the observation. Now get to work."

Aspen laughed. "Slow your roll. It's going to be fine. I highly doubt he's going to care what our house looks like anyway."

"It's not that. I just—I just haven't had someone up here in a long time."

"Whatever, AJ was just up here last weekend."

She sighed. "That's not what I meant."

"You mean a *guy*?"

"Aspen…"

"Oh relax. It's no big deal."

"Are you sure you're okay with this?"

"Yes. For the millionth time. I'm fine. I like Ethan. He's pretty cool. Although I don't know if cooking for him is the best way to impress him."

"You're not helping me."

"I'm just saying—"

"I'm baking one of Kristin's frozen lasagnas."

"Oh good," Aspen said with a nod.

Rachel frowned. "Is your room picked up?"

"It doesn't matter. It's not like you're going to be in there at all," Aspen said, shutting the dishwasher.

"Get in there and pick it up. Now."

"You're no fun."

"Sorry to hear that."

Just after six, there was a knock on the door and Aspen leapt from the couch to answer it. Rachel heard her greet Ethan as she was bent over, sliding a loaf of garlic bread into the oven beside the lasagna.

"She's been a nervous wreck all day," Aspen mumbled.

Rachel felt her heart drop. "Thank you, Aspen," she called over her shoulder as she shut the oven door. Grabbing her glass of wine and a second, untouched glass, she headed around the corner into the living room.

"Hi," she said, a grin on her face.

"Your place looks nice," he said, glancing around him. He slipped off his shoes and took the glass of wine.

"I, umm, am finishing dinner. If you want, you can come into the kitchen." Rachel felt ridiculous and she knew her face was an obnoxious shade of red. She quickly turned her back to him. Why was she such a raveled ball of emotions around him?

She motioned for him to take a seat at the counter between the kitchen and dining room while she stepped into the kitchen to wash the lettuce for their salads; she welcomed the distance between them.

"Mom, can I watch TV?"

"Sure. Whatever."

The television came to life in the other room and Rachel appreciated the noise it spread throughout the apartment.

"Smells awesome. What're you making?" Ethan asked. He was calm and collected as he took a drink of wine.

"Lasagna." She couldn't bring herself to look at him. Suddenly she was acutely aware that there was a man in her home. That Aspen was in the next room. And that he was studying her every move; she could feel his eyes on her as she willed herself to focus on each task, as miniscule as each seemed.

She began thinking about the night before, about his lips, the way he tasted, the feeling of his hands against her bare skin, the pressure of his body against hers. Her mouth went dry and she suddenly realized that she had been standing at the sink holding a head of lettuce, the water running from the faucet, without doing anything for nearly a minute.

"Are you okay?" he asked.

"Yes. Yes, I am." She shoved the lettuce beneath the cold water, the chill bringing her back to reality and she willed herself to again focus on the task at hand.

Rachel went through two glasses of wine as she prepared dinner and was relieved to finally sit down and eat. Not only was the pressure of cooking off, but she was beginning to feel a little tipsy and that, paired with her complete foolishness, was a recipe for disaster.

Ethan did most of the talking during dinner. He grabbed Aspen's attention immediately when he told her he owned a boat that he left in Utah and that he was a skilled water skier and wake boarder.

"I am dying to learn how. You'd think that since I live on a lake I would know how, but I don't. I've only ever gone tubing and I did try knee boarding for the first time this summer. That was pretty swag."

Rachel rolled her eyes.

"Are there even lakes in Utah?" Aspen asked.

"A few. Mostly reservoirs. Bear Lake is not too far from where I'm from. It's pretty big," he said.

"I can't wait to tell Kasey, Breanne, and Olivia." Aspen squealed in delight.

Rachel looked up from her plate of food and her eyes met Ethan's. They locked and she felt her body go limp. God, he was sexy. Her pulse quickened and she silently prayed that he couldn't hear her heart pounding beneath her chest. Actually, she prayed Aspen couldn't hear it because she would never let her live it down.

There was something about him that got both her heart and mind racing like never before. Not only could he make her squirm in her seat just by sitting across from her, but there was something in the way that he sat there and so easily carried on a conversation with her daughter. The way he made her smile and laugh and was able to draw her out of her shell brought a lump to the back of her throat that barely allowed her to take a breath. She silently watched them banter back and forth, and for a brief moment she wondered if this was what a family was like. She quickly forced the thoughts from her mind. They were foolish. They were hasty and they would inevitably set her up for major heartache.

When they finished with dinner, Aspen retreated to her bedroom and Ethan took the initiative to help clean up the kitchen. Rachel couldn't help but notice his physical proximity to her as they wound around the small kitchen, and she continually caught whiffs of his cologne; a woody aromatic scent that almost had a hint of a Gin and Tonic.

As she stood at the sink and rinsed the dinner plates, he approached her from behind, the heat from his body radiating against her back, and gently his lips brushed the outer ridge of her exposed ear. She reeled on the inside as her heart raced and she turned her body slightly to let her lips meet his.

Rachel braced herself against the counter, reaching behind her with a free arm and turning the faucet on high, the water running loudly into the sink, splashing against the dishes piled inside and spraying cool droplets of water onto the bare skin of her arms.

Ethan's arms slipped around her waist, and he pulled her body into his. He was strong and firm around her and she let him consume her smaller frame as she backed herself against the counter.

"Your kitchen will never get clean," he mumbled between kisses.

"I'll hire someone," she said as she pulled him tighter against him and kissed him harder, not letting another word escape his mouth.

"Mom, I have a—"

Ethan pulled away from Rachel faster than a lightning bolt shot from the sky.

"Oh, sorry!" Aspen spun quickly on her heel and ran back to her bedroom.

"Give me a sec," Rachel said, feeling as embarrassed as Ethan looked.

Rachel knocked slightly on Aspen's door before stepping inside. "Mom, I'm so sorry. I didn't mean to—"

"It's fine. Really. I'm sorry. You probably didn't need to see that," Rachel said as she sat on the edge of the bed near the desk where Aspen sat.

"I just, I just had a question about my homework."

Five minutes later, Rachel emerged from the bedroom, closing the door behind her. Ethan had finished loading the dishwasher, refilled both of their glasses of wine and was sitting in the living room waiting for her.

"I am so, *so* sorry," he said quickly.

She shook her head. "It's fine. Really. But, since we're on the subject, kind of," she said as she sat down beside him, "can I ask where this is headed? I mean, not to put pressure on you or anything. I just have someone else—"

"To think about," he said, finishing her sentence.

Rachel nodded. "Yeah. I do."

"Uh, well. I've never dated anyone who had kids before, but I'm certainly not opposed to it. Besides, I think Aspen's pretty great."

She couldn't help but smile. "So, it doesn't bother you?"

"No. Besides, I was aware of her when I asked you out the first time."

Rachel nodded her head. "This is all new territory for me, so please, bear with me while I navigate these uncharted waters."

"Absolutely," he said as he grabbed her wine glass and handed it to her. He held his out in front of him and said, "To trying new things."

She smiled and gave a small nod of her head. They lightly tapped glasses and each took a drink.

Sometime after they put in *Forrest Gump*, Aspen emerged from her bedroom, dressed for bed, to brush her teeth. She hugged her mom and then disappeared once again, this time for the rest of the night.

With Aspen in her room for the night, Rachel felt her nerves returning. She was curled into the side of Ethan, his arm draped around her body, and every now and then his thumb would lightly stroke the back side of her arm. She thought about kissing him, and despite her loathing internal self-lecture, she looked up at him. His eyes met hers when he felt her move against him.

For a moment they just looked at one another and a sense of calm washed over her. Then in another moment their lips were against one another, her hands beneath his shirt, gripping at the bare skin of his back as his tongue pushed hard into her mouth.

In a swift, seamless movement, he pulled her up and then lowered her back down on top of him, her legs straddling his thighs. She felt a heavy pressure between her legs as she pressed him into the back of her couch.

Ethan was in no hurry as his lips and tongue explored the nape of her neck, her collarbone and the open V of her shirt. His hands wandered tenderly around her body, lingering on her breasts, cupping them fondly. Exhilaration charged through her body and Rachel felt an overwhelming sense of both excitement and fear.

Suddenly she became very aware of how long it had been since she'd been with someone and in an instant, doubt began to plague her. She no longer was sure of where to put her hands, how to turn her tongue against his, or how to glide her pelvis in rhythm with his.

She tried to force the thoughts from her head.

New thoughts crept in. What if he thought she was bad? What if he was thinking about how he'd had better?

Rachel slowed the rolling movement of her hips; she decreased the force behind her mouth when she kissed him and a few moments later, detecting the change from her, Ethan pulled away all together.

"Are you okay?"

Sitting up straight she suddenly became very aware that she was straddling him. Rachel slid to the side and back onto the sofa next to him.

"I'm sorry. I uh— Oh my God, I feel like an idiot." She rose from the couch and began pacing the room.

Ethan stood to his feet and approached her. Grabbing hold of her on the arms with both hands he was able to stop her pacing. "What's wrong?"

"I just… Oh, I'm nervous. I'm out of practice. I'm… maybe this is moving too fast," she said feeling the panic across her face.

"Hey, that's fine," he said. "If you're not ready for anything, that's okay."

She looked up from the floor. "Really? You're not mad?"

He laughed. "Really. We've only been seeing each other for a couple weeks. It is moving a little fast. If you're not ready, that's okay."

Rachel was embarrassed. She did want him. How could she not? He got her excited in all the right places. So why couldn't she go through with any of it? She bit the corner of her bottom lip as she gave him an uncertain look.

"Really. It's okay. Besides, your daughter's in the next room. Probably a good idea you stopped things when you did."

She felt her shoulders come down a level in relief, but she was still far from relaxed. Suddenly she felt like a fifteen-year-old girl all over again.

"Not because of this," he said, "but I should probably get going. It's getting late. And we both have to work tomorrow."

"Ethan, I'm—"

"Stop," he said, placing a solitary finger over her lips to silence them. "Tonight was great. Let's leave it at that."

SEVEN

"So you just rolled off of him?" Tiff asked in disbelief.

Still mortified, Rachel buried her face behind her wine glass as she nodded her head.

"You might just be a lost cause after all."

"Is it really that bad?" Rachel asked, feeling her face redden by the minute.

"Well, let's just say it's a good thing we don't live down in L.A. or he would've found some chick willing to put out far more than you do, Rach," Jake said over his shoulder, Siena on his hip and a sippy cup in his hand.

Rachel groaned and took a large gulp of red wine.

"You're so not helpful. Put our daughter to bed and go play your PlayStation," Tiff said with a flippant wave of her hand. "Ignore him," she said turning back to Rachel.

"He's right. He's so right."

"He's an idiot," Tiff said with a nod.

"Well, idiot or not, he's still right. How am I going to recover? I'm going to die a virgin."

Tiff laughed. "You're not a virgin. You have a twelve-year-old daughter to prove that."

"Yeah, well, I'm fairly certain that if virginity could grow back, mine has."

"You didn't see Ethan at all today?"

Rachel shook her head. "No, he is at the station for the next couple days. I won't see him until Wednesday night. At the earliest."

"Don't be too hard on yourself, Rach. So you've been out of the dating circle for a while. If he doesn't like it, then he's not worth your time."

Sinful Retreat had a busy week. They survived the busy and highly anticipated new release of *The English Graveyard* by bestselling author David Sharpe and Rachel quickly moved on to preparations for Saturday's big Pre-Black Friday Sales Event. It was an event she and Kristin had thought up eight years ago and every year seemed to be bigger than the last. The Saturday before the infamous Black Friday was always Sinful Retreat's Pre-Black Friday Sales Event. And for every twenty-five dollars spent, every customer received a five-dollar coupon to spend on Black Friday in addition to the already discounted merchandise.

"Rachel, Matt's on line one," Mark called across the store as Rachel signed for a large shipment from the UPS man at the door.

"Please take a message." It was the third time he had called the store that week and she had given the same response each time. After the delivery man left, Rachel grabbed the dolly from the back storage closet and moved the boxes to her office where she began to inventory all of them.

"He doesn't sound happy," Mark said, leaning into her office.

"He'll get over it."

"He told me he has something important to talk to you about, so call him as soon as you can."

"Sure," she said with a nod.

Mark laughed and stepped back behind the counter to help a customer.

By the time Diane arrived at five for her shift, it was dark outside. Rachel was still in her office, buried in boxes of books she was inventorying and on the phone with a vendor correcting an order error. Feeling her temper beginning to rise, she reached out and kicked the door shut with her free leg as to not disturb the customers outside her office.

Nearly ten minutes later, when she emerged from her office, she pasted a smile across her face. Mark had already left and Diane was helping a customer in the science fiction section. Darren, holding Parker in his arms, had come into the shop with the kids and stood talking to Kristin at the bakery counter. Rachel made her way toward them.

"Boy, I'd say if stressed had an expression, that would be it," Darren said with a nod.

Rachel sighed, dropping the fake smile. She knew she didn't need to pretend around them.

"Rough day?" he asked.

"Rough week," Kristin answered.

"You could say that again," Rachel said with a nod as she leaned back against the counter.

"Hi Ray-el," Parker said as he perked up in his dad's arms.

"Hi Park," she said with a genuine smile. She always had real smiles for him. His big brown eyes and long, fluttery eye lashes would make any girl smile at him.

"My mom's coming up tomorrow to take the kids for the weekend. I've got Darren helping in here on Saturday," Kristin said as Darren put Park down and they watched him run off with his sisters.

"Susie's taking all three?"

"Big step, huh?" Kristin said with a smile and a nod.

"I thought she had a not-in-diapers rule?"

"She's making an exception this once. Parker is almost three. Just refuses to potty train. She's going to take all three after Thanksgiving next weekend for the Black Friday sale too. I can hardly believe it."

"Wow. I think this officially thrusts her into sainthood."

Darren nodded. "That's what I said. I can barely handle them some days. And they're my own kids!"

The three of them laughed.

"Umm, Mom," Grace said, stepping in the middle of the three adults, "Kate took a marker and drew on her face."

"Katie," Kristin called across the store as she headed through the bakery and toward the children's section. She appeared a moment later, the brown-haired child reluctantly in tow by the arm, her bottom lip heavy and her brows furrowed. Blue marker was streaked across her cheeks, over her nose, between her eyes and across her forehead.

"Katie Faye," Darren said as the attitude-filled girl came to a halt at his feet, "what were you thinking?"

Kate crossed her arms.

"Kate..." Darren said as he crouched down to his daughter's level.

"I didn't do anything," she said.

"That's not true. I can see it all over your face. Now explain," Kristin demanded with the impatient tapping of her toes.

"It wasn't me. It was the marker. It just started writing on my face."

Rachel quickly turned her back to Kate to stifle her laugh and Kristin forcefully elbowed her in the side.

"You're kidding me, right?" Darren said as he glanced up at Kristin.

"Get your butt in the bathroom and wash it off. All of it. And get back out here when you're done. And when you're clean, you better be prepared to talk about what really happened," Kristin said. "Now go!"

"Oh my goodness!" She gasped after the child was out of earshot. "She's lucky she's leaving for the weekend. I'm gonna strangle her. Actually strangle. Does she think I'm going to believe some crap story like that?" Kristin began pacing the bakery.

"She's going to be just like Aspen when she gets older. You realize that, right?" Rachel laughed at the realization, feeling relief in knowing she wouldn't be alone. "Speaking of, where is that child? I'll be right back."

Rachel crossed through the bookstore and headed up the stairs to the apartment above. Panic began to fill her chest when she realized that it was well after six and she hadn't seen her daughter come home from school yet. In between the horrible thoughts that were suddenly racing through her head, she was also berating herself for not even noticing she hadn't seen her daughter. *What kind of mother am I?*

Taking the stairs two at a time, she reached the second floor in no time and when she opened the door into her apartment, relief flooded her when she found Aspen on the couch. But as quick as she was relieved, she was shocked to see Ethan sitting beside her daughter, tears in Aspen's eyes and her cheeks soaked from crying. Rachel rushed to her.

"What's wrong?"

Aspen was crying so hard she could barely get any words out. Her whole chest shook and when she tried to speak, she coughed and cried harder.

"I found her like this on the back steps," Ethan said. Aspen was curled into the crook of his arm and despite having Rachel there, she still clung to him. "Her dad called her at school."

"He what?" Rachel said, sitting up straight on the couch.

Ethan nodded. "I didn't get all the details. Just that he called the office and they got her out of class toward the end of her last class of the day. I don't know what he said to her though. She just keeps saying how much she hates him."

"I do hate him," she mumbled. Her face was half buried in Ethan's chest and Rachel could see all the places where her daughter's tears had soaked the front of his shirt. She suddenly felt torn between feeling badly that she hadn't been there for her daughter and relief that this man, who was so new to their lives, had let her daughter unload on him.

"Asp," Rachel said as she reached forward and stroked her daughter's hair. At Rachel's touch Aspen's body began to relax and within minutes she grew incredibly exhausted from crying so hard for so long. "How about you lie down in your bed?" she whispered to her daughter, the same way she did when she was a baby.

Aspen gently nodded her head.

With his arms around her, Ethan scooped up the girl and carried her into her bedroom. Rachel took the lead and pulled the blankets back on the bed and he gently slid her down onto it. Rachel took a few moments to quietly cover up her daughter, who was nearly asleep and didn't stir. She ran her fingers through her silky brown hair, and then turning out the lights, she shut the door and stepped back into the living room where Ethan had retreated.

"I'm so sorry about that. And thank you, for everything. I'm sorry to do this to you, but would you mind staying up here a little while longer? I have to run back downstairs and wrap up a few things and I don't want her to wake up and be alone up here and—"

"It's fine. Go. Take care of what you need to. I'll be just fine up here."

"Are you sure?"

"Rachel, yes," he said with an assuring nod and smile.

She turned and headed for the door.

"Wait. You forgot something."

"Oh." She turned quickly around to see him approaching her. "What?" A few inches from her, he gently leaned in and kissed her. She felt herself relax and smile.

"I'll be back."

Downstairs Kristin and Darren had hung around the store to make sure everything was okay with Aspen. But then they became a different kind of worried when Rachel told them what happened when she found her upstairs. Diane and Becky were managing the store after Kristin and Darren left. Rachel stepped into her office and grabbed a list of books that were missing from her orders that she needed to call about. She also needed to reconcile the e-commerce transactions from the previous day, but she could do all that from upstairs.

Rachel gave Diane a quick list of things she needed to finish before the end of the night and then headed back upstairs. When she stepped into her apartment, she was overcome by the aroma of tomatoes and spices and stepped into the kitchen where she found Ethan at work over the stove.

"I figured you might not have eaten yet. And I was starving. And on the off chance that you did eat, well, I would just have a lot of food. I hope you like spaghetti."

Rachel smiled as she set her work and laptop down on the counter. "I don't even know what to say to you right now."

He looked over at her. "Well, thank you is always appropriate."

She shook her head. "No. That just doesn't seem to be enough at the moment." She made her way around the counter toward him at the stove. Sliding her arms around him from behind, she rested her chin on his shoulder. "But it's something to start with. So thank you," she whispered into his ear.

"I'm glad I was there to help," he said. He leaned his head back and kissed her forehead. "Dinner will be ready in about fifteen minutes."

"If you don't mind, I've got some things to do for work."

"Go for it."

Rachel opened up her laptop at the table and set straight to work. Fortunately, it didn't take long to resolve the ordering issues with the errors from that shipment. However, there were some problems with the computer system which complicated the e-commerce reconciliation. But just as Ethan was about to serve dinner, Rachel wrapped up her work for the night.

Right before sitting down to eat, Rachel peeked in on Aspen, who hadn't moved since being laid in her bed. Rachel felt a pull on her heart as she looked down at her daughter. Although she was now twelve years old, she often still looked down and saw the tiny and helpless newborn she brought home from the hospital. Today was one of those days. And like she did then, Rachel wanted to crawl in beside her sleeping baby, curl up around her, and protect her from everything that could cause her harm. She took in a deep breath and slowly retreated from the dark room.

Rachel was relieved to have some laughter in her day while she and Ethan ate their dinner and drank some wine. He told her stories of his week at the fire station and the couple strange calls he had been called out on. After a while it grew quiet and the only noise was that of the wind, growing stronger and stronger outside.

"What's Aspen's relationship like with her dad?" he finally asked.

"Oh," she said with a sigh. "How do I characterize that? Well, generally speaking, it's fine. She wants, he gives. That's pretty much how it's been with them since the beginning. And usually, as long as the status quo isn't messed with, things are fine."

"The status quo?"

"Yeah, you know? The fact that each of them really wants something more. Like Aspen, for example. She wants a dad. It kills her in the spring, when she's at her meets for track and field and she sees her friends, or even people she doesn't know, there with their dads and hers is never there. And not necessarily because he can't be, but mostly because he chooses not be. He, on the other hand, expects a daughter who comes to him with problems, one who calls him to tell him about a test or the school dance or if a boy likes her. She of course discusses none of these things with him because she just doesn't know him like that. So when one of them pushes too hard for either of these things, the other one gets mad. The system breaks down. Aspen is stubborn, and when her feelings are hurt, she shuts down. Matt, because he's 3,000 miles away, who doesn't see her shut down, he thinks she is pushing and fighting him. So he fights back. He forgets that he's the adult here."

"And meanwhile, you get stuck being the mediator in all of this."

She nodded her head. "I used to, more often than now. But now, as hard as it is to not intervene, because, believe me, all I want to do is call him and cuss his ass out, I just try to be here for her. I can't change him. That I've tried. Too many times. And failed every single time. And I absolutely hate that he hurts her and breaks her heart, but it's not between me and her. I've paid a lot of money in both therapy and wine to learn to say that."

He smiled.

"So now I just try to be here for her. To be a pillar of strength and show her a better road. Because the truth is, he's hurt me too. And he won't be the last person to ever break her heart. And we all have to learn how to get up and keep going."

Ethan was silent as he cocked his head to the side. She watched him swallow hard, but still he said nothing. His eyes remained steady, locked on hers and she couldn't help but wonder what was going through his head.

"You're making me nervous," she finally admitted after a few quiet minutes.

"I've never met anyone like you before."

Rachel's brow furrowed and suddenly she wished she had magical powers to teleport out of her chair. At that very moment, anywhere else in the world would do.

"No, no! It's a good thing. Great, really. You just amaze me. Every time I'm with you I just can't seem to wrap my head around you. And I like it. It keeps me on my toes."

Rachel felt her face turn blazing red.

"And now I've embarrassed you," he said with a smile.

"Uh, ah, uhh…" she began tripping over her words. With no clear English coming out of her mouth, she opted for a nod of her head instead.

He laughed. "Another fine example. Just a moment ago you were so confident in how you were leading your daughter and now you're so embarrassed you can't even speak."

Rachel stood, her heart racing in her chest, and feeling overwhelmingly self-conscious she excused herself while she stepped into her bedroom.

Behind the privacy of her closed door, she finally took a breath. Her palms and armpits were profusely sweaty, and she stepped into the bathroom to dry herself off and quickly reapply deodorant. She grabbed a magazine from the toilet and fanned herself down and willed herself to take deep breaths.

"Pull it together you buffoon!" she demanded of herself.

She turned to look in the mirror. Her face was indeed a shade of pink, but fortunately not an unbearable one. There was nothing she could do about it, so it would just have to work.

She recalled what Tiff had said earlier in the week and then realized that he had been complimenting her before she grew strangely embarrassed and left the kitchen table. It was time to pull it together and put aside her insecurities. She was a grown woman and clearly, he liked her or he wouldn't still be around.

Feeling calmer, a bit more collected and slightly confident, albeit annoyed with herself, she stepped out of her bedroom and forced the insecure version of herself into hiding for the rest of the night. She crossed the living room to the kitchen and dining room where Ethan was still sitting at the table and took her seat beside him.

"I'm sorry about that. I seriously have no idea what just came over me."

He smiled. "Well, you did warn me you were out of practice."

Rachel smiled, suppressing the part of her that would have turned red in the face. "How about I open another bottle of wine and we go sit on the couch? I'll clean this up later," she said.

"Okay."

In the living room, Rachel turned off the overhead lights and left on the corner lamp. She sat beside him on the sofa and Ethan slipped his arm around her and pulled her close to him.

"Saturday is going to be a busy day for me at work, but Aspen is spending the weekend in Orange County at my parents', so maybe I could make dinner for you up here that night," she said, as she leaned into him.

Both of his arms wrapped around her body, and they held her close. His face was so close to hers that she could almost taste the delicious zing from the pasta sauce that lingered in his mouth. She began to feel a tingle in the back of her throat that radiated through the core of her body and as he gently pulled her body close to his. It sent her reeling from the inside out.

"Saturday night. Just you and I?"

She nodded her head.

"I think that sounds like it could be a good time."

She smiled as she reached up. Her fingers laced through his hair. She could feel the thick muscles in his neck as she pulled him into her and kissed him. With his arms wrapped around her, he gently picked her up and swiftly swung her body across his lap. He lowered her with a leg on each side and she clenched him between her thighs.

His hands caressed up and down her back, his fingers gliding firmly between the lines of her muscle. He kissed the side of her neck, his tongue circling her collarbone and sending goose bumps across her body.

She laced her fingers through his hair, dragging her nails gently along his scalp and he let out a soft moan that excited her. She kissed along his jaw line and back to his earlobe, which he must have liked because he clenched her tighter.

She felt him hard and firm between her legs and he felt so good. She wanted in the worst way to take him back to her bedroom and let him have his way with her. But even he seemed to sense her hesitation.

At one point Rachel laid back on the couch and Ethan wedged half on top of her and half on the back of the sofa. He slid his hand under the hem of Rachel's shirt and caressed the soft and smooth skin on her belly. Lifting it slightly, he kissed around her belly button and smiled when she giggled from her ticklishness.

Lying beside her, an orange glow coming from the corner of the room, he propped his head up on his fist and looked down onto her. Carefully he ran his fingers through her dark brown hair, his eyes locked steadily with hers.

"I like this," she said. "Lying here with you."

He gave her a soft smile. "Me too."

The room was still and quiet. Rachel could hear the steady ticking from the miniature version of a grandfather clock Grandpa Aaron had handcrafted for her years earlier and outside she could hear the howl of the wind. Aspen still hadn't stirred.

"You are the most beautiful woman I've ever met."

For a moment Rachel wanted to dispute his comment, but as she looked into his eyes, she saw something that stopped her; she saw conviction. Suddenly, lying in his arms, she knew something greater brought this man into her life. If she tried to explain it, she knew she would sound ridiculous. But she was sure of it. Quietly, she closed her eyes and pulled him down toward her. Wrapped together on her couch, they fell asleep.

"Mom, Mom… Mom, wake up. You're gonna be late for work."

Rachel's eyes fluttered open. Daylight stretched through a window that was not her bedroom one and confusion began to trickle in. Suddenly she sat up in a panic. As her eyes opened fully, she realized she was on her couch, Ethan beside her. It was indeed morning. Aspen stood over her. Her eyes wandered around the apartment and paused briefly at the dinner mess that never was cleaned up from the night before.

"How do you feel?" she asked, standing up and pulling her daughter in for a hug.

"Ugh. I feel like crap. Look at my face."

Rachel stepped back to look at Aspen. Her daughter's eyes were large and swollen with small, red dots from broken capillaries surrounding them.

"Aspen!" she gasped. "Let me quickly call Kristin and have her open for me and tell her I'll be a little late. Go sit in my room and wait for me. I want to talk to you."

Aspen did as she was told, and Rachel called Kristin who was happy to help out. "How's she doing?"

"I'm not sure. She's not in tears. I'm going to keep her home from school today. Maybe my mom can pick her up earlier or something."

"Okay. Well, come down when you can," Kristin said.

"I'll let you guys talk. I'll see you later?" Ethan said.

"Sounds good."

He kissed her and then headed out the door.

Rachel found Aspen curled up under her blankets in her bed.

"Ethan spent the night?"

"It wasn't anything like that."

"Clearly. Considering how I found you both this morning," she said with a laugh.

"You ready to talk about what happened?"

Aspen grew quiet as she shrugged her shoulders. "I hate dad. It's simple. I'm joining your club."

"I don't hate your dad. You know that."

"Well you probably should after everything he's put you through."

"Aspen. This isn't about me right now. And you're probably right. But hating him would be the easier choice. And in the long run I'm the one who has to live with those feelings. It never feels good to hate someone," Rachel said.

"That makes no sense Mom."

"Well, maybe someday it will. Come now, sit up and talk to me."

Aspen sighed as she sat up.

Rachel could see the hurt still in her daughter's eyes.

"I was in history and an office runner came down and said I had a phone call. I figured it was you. So I went to the office. And when I picked it up, it was Dad."

"Okay. So what did he say?"

"He said he's been trying to get a hold of me. And I said that I didn't want to talk to him because I was mad at him. Then he started yelling at me, telling me I had no right to be mad at him. And that if anything, he had a right to be mad at me because I was the one who was caught smoking in the first place. And that I was just a spoiled and ungrateful child who didn't deserve anything that I had. And so I hung up on him."

"You hung up on him"?

"Yes. And I was in the office, so like everyone heard him yelling at me and they all turned and were like watching me and I was trying to not let them see that I was crying, so I ran out of there as fast as possible. I just got my stuff and ran out to wait for the buses."

"Asp, you could've gone to AJ's room. She would've taken you home."

"I didn't want you to know. I was just so embarrassed, but the longer I sat, the angrier I got and the next thing I knew, I was talking to Ethan. I… I just don't understand why he thinks he gets to talk to me like that. Like, is that how he talks to people in every-day life? How does he even have friends? Or a job?" Tears were streaming down Aspen's face once again and Rachel pulled her into her arms.

"Why can't it just be you and me Mom? Why does he have to be in the picture at all?" she asked.

"I know sweets, I know." The two sat in silence together, Rachel holding Aspen to her chest, rocking her.

EIGHT

Rachel made it down to Sinful Retreat shortly after nine. She called her mom, who was more than thrilled to pick up Aspen early, and helped Aspen pack for the weekend in Newport.

Kristin looked slightly frantic when Rachel appeared and was relieved to have her back to work. She had called Mark in early, which was a smart thing to do, as Friday mornings were usually busy ones.

"AJ and Tiff both send their love. I can't talk though, I've got so much to finish before tomorrow," Kristin said, bounding her way from the book counter back to the bakery counter.

"Anything I can help with?" Rachel called.

Kristin couldn't contain herself with laughter. "I'm never that desperate!"

"Thanks!" she called back.

Mark stood at the counter giggling to himself as he helped a customer.

Rachel went to work in her office and about an hour and a half later heard the unmistakable laugh of her mom coming from the store. Jenn Taylor was a beautiful and bold woman. Her heels clacked against the wooden floors of Sinful Retreat as she made her way toward Rachel's office door.

"Knock, knock," she called out before stepping into the office. "Look at you, hard at work. How's my daughter?"

Rachel stood up, a smile across her face. "Hey, Mom."

They embraced and Jenn took a seat across from Rachel. "It's been too long since I've talked with you. I assume this means you've been busy. So tell me, what have you been up to?"

"Oh, you know me. Work, work, work."

Jenn nodded. "I do know you. And that's what I was afraid of. Although, your Aunt Sarah told me you haven't *just* been up to work; you've been on a genealogy hunt into your Grandpa Aaron's past?"

Rachel nodded. "Guilty. Dad didn't say anything?"

Jenn waved her hand dismissively. "Are you kidding? Unless it has to do with motorcycles or deep-sea fishing, he rarely talks about anything these days," she said with a laugh. "Besides, that kind of stuff never interested him in the slightest. Now I, on the other hand, would be quite interested in anything you might unearth."

"Well, that's been the problem. I can't seem to unearth anything. Other than the fact that his birth name was Abarron Alter Taylor."

"Hmm, well, Taylor is English. Maybe there is something that can help there," she suggested.

"I thought about that. But it's a common English name. I would need something to narrow it down. And aside from marriage records and the birth records of his children, Abarron Taylor didn't seem to exist prior to 1949 in California."

"Well, Rachel, I don't have any suggestions for you. But you've always been an incredibly smart woman and you've never failed at anything you've put your mind to. So I have no doubt that you'll somehow figure this out too. Just remember, history didn't happen overnight. So maybe there's a reason these answers aren't presenting themselves to you all at once."

"No offense Mom, but that sounds a little ominous."

Jenn smiled as she stood. "Now, as much as I love sitting here chatting with you, because believe me, I really do, I know you have work to get back to, and I have a granddaughter that I am dying to spend my weekend with."

"What are you guys planning?" Rachel asked, following her mom out of the office and into the store.

"Oh, I don't know. Maybe a movie, shopping, dinner, the beach, boardwalk, boat ride, hang out by the pool. Who really knows?"

"Mark, I'm going to run upstairs for a few minutes."

"Sure thing," he said with a nod.

Jenn followed closely behind Rachel as they ascended the stairs to find Aspen. They were greeted at the door with loud music ringing through the apartment.

"Aspen!" Rachel yelled through the noise.

A few moments later, the music instantly turned off and was replaced by silence as Jenn and Rachel stepped into the living room. Aspen came out of her bedroom, her suitcase in tow.

"Oh my goodness, Aspen, I think you've grown nearly six inches since I've seen you last! And that was only two months ago. And oh, look at how long your hair has gotten. I love all that blonde. Really, I am so envious."

"Hi Gram," Aspen said, her face beaming with joy. Rachel's mom and Aspen had a special connection since the day they met in the hospital when Aspen was born. As a newborn there was no one that could calm Aspen down like her Gram could.

"Are you ready for a top weekend? Grandpa is headed to Palm Springs on the bike for the weekend, so it is just you and me, girlfriend. And we are going to live it up."

"Okay, well, don't live it up too much," Rachel said as she grabbed Aspen's suitcase.

Jenn put her arm around Aspen and they walked toward the stairs that took them to the bookstore.

Rachel followed behind, bag in tow, to the car that was waiting outside. The fresh air was refreshing when they stepped into the parking lot. The sunshine felt warm against her skin, and she pulled the bag around to the trunk. Aspen stepped up beside her.

"Thanks Mom, for everything. And good luck tomorrow. I know it's a busy day for you. Sorry I won't be around to help."

"Nonsense. You go have fun. Forget about the other stuff that happened. This weekend is about you, okay? I'll call and check on you tomorrow night sometime, after the store closes, okay?"

Aspen nodded. "Love you."

"Love you more." Rachel pulled her in and hugged her tightly.

After Aspen got in the car, Rachel stood by her mom on the driver side of the car. "Keep her distracted this weekend."

"I will. I'm good at that sort of thing."

Rachel smiled.

"Good luck with your weekend. We'll talk. But I'll probably have her home by dinner time on Sunday."

"Sounds good. Thanks Mom."

Jenn leaned in and hugged her daughter. "Love you."

"You too. You guys have fun."

Rachel watched them pull away before stepping back inside Sinful Retreat. It was always a little bittersweet for her whenever Aspen left.

"Hey Rach," Kristin called from the bakery counter. "Douchebag called. I told him you weren't taking personal calls at work."

"Really, you said that?"

Kristin nodded.

"You really said that?"

Kristin nodded again.

"This coming from someone who wouldn't even growl at someone who cut you off on the freeway?"

"Aren't you proud of me?" Kristin beamed.

"Hell yes I am!"

She laughed. "Yeah, and now I can't stop shaking. So I think I'll go back to never being confrontational again. Ever."

"Just for the record, I didn't ask you to do that."

"Oh I know. But Aspen is like another child to me. I had to defend her honor. And well, now that the honor is defended, my part is done. Forever."

Rachel laughed as she made her way around the bakery counter. She reached out her arms and hugged Kristin from the side, leaning her head against her arm. "You're really the best."

"I'm glad you see it, too. Now, I have sweet rolls to pull from the oven."

Rachel laughed as she made her way to the book counter.

By mid-afternoon, Rachel was feeling confident and prepared for the sales event that started the next morning. Kristin, on the other hand, was beginning to panic. And when Darren arrived with the three kids after school, Rachel thought she might drop to the floor from a pulmonary embolism. It was always slightly amusing to Rachel when Kristin became frantic like this, because usually she was so level-headed, calm and collected. It was partly why she made such a great business partner for Rachel, who was rarely any of those things.

"Oh man, I think I came at a bad time," Darren said after Kristin snapped at him when she told him not to touch something and to get out of her kitchen and to keep the kids far away from her.

"Yeah, I think so. I'll put in a new movie one of my vendors sent me. It should keep them semi-entertained," Rachel said.

Darren hauled in the kids' roller bags from the van, each brightly colored with a different character on the front, their own Pillow Pet secured around the handle. Next came the sleeping bags. He took all the weekend gear, piled it neatly in the corner and took a seat at a table and waited for his mother-in-law.

"Hey Mark, I'm going to be in my office doing this week's bookkeeping. I put your paycheck under the tray in the register. But tell me when Susie gets here, I'd like to say hi to her."

"All right. Thanks."

"And let me know if it gets busy and you need help out here."

"Will do."

Rachel took a seat in her office and as she sat down at her desk, she glanced at a photograph of her and Aspen in a frame near her phone. She thought about Matt and she felt her anger return. He infuriated her so much. She wanted to pick up the phone and scream at him. Tell him all the things he just yelled at their daughter. But then who would she be? Him. Maybe not him, exactly. But she would be no better than he was. And she would accomplish nothing and it would be that much more difficult to get him to listen to her the next time they did talk. She witnessed it all the time between him and Aspen. She just wanted so badly to get through to him. That's really what it came down to. In fact, that's what it came down to for him, as well: he wanted to get through to Aspen. But what he didn't realize was that she wanted to get through to him as well. They were spinning in circles and going nowhere, and Rachel felt guilty for putting her daughter in this position in the first place. When she had first learned she was pregnant, many people had suggested she get rid of the pregnancy. Grandpa Aaron was the only one adamantly opposed to her aborting the child. He suggested that if she didn't want the baby, that she give it up. But neither of those seemed realistic for Rachel. Sitting at her desk now, considering her daughter's heartbreak, she felt selfish for thinking so much about herself back then.

A knock at the door interrupted her thoughts. "Susie's here," Mark said.

"Oh. Oh, good," Rachel said, relieved to not think about that anymore. She quickly rose from her desk and stepped out of her office.

"Susie, you made it up here!" Rachel said.

"Oh goodness, yes! And every time I do I swear to myself I won't do it again. Either my fear just intensifies or those mountains get steeper. I'm convinced it's the latter."

Rachel laughed.

"Goodness Kristin, I don't think I've ever seen you look so panicked. Do you need a Xanax?" she asked when she saw her daughter step out of the kitchen.

"Probably wouldn't be the end of the world," Darren said from behind Kristin. He started rubbing her shoulders to help her relax. "Gracie, Kate, Parker, your grandma's here," he called over his shoulder back to the Children's Nook.

Only seconds later, a thin blonde came bouncing around the corner, followed by a shorter skipping brunette, and a little boy running so eagerly that he tripped and slid across the floor on his belly. But in his excitement, Parker immediately got to his feet, grabbed his navy baseball cap that came off during his fall and resumed his run to Grandma.

The three children bombarded their grandma, tackling her to the ground, giggling and squealing in delight. She lay beneath them, laughing loudly as the patrons of Sinful Retreat turned to watch the spectacle. They couldn't help but laugh at the folly before them.

A few minutes later, the children had calmed down. Kristin a bit, too.

"Your first overnight with Parker? You're brave," Rachel said with a laugh.

"Oh I know I am. But I figure, I know CPR. And anything I'm not certified or trained to do as a nurse practitioner, I know someone who is. So we'll all at least survive the weekend. That's all Kristin and Darren really need, is their kids to come back alive."

Kristin rolled her eyes. "You've inspired a lot of faith in me, Mom."

Darren shrugged his shoulders. "Sounds fine to me."

"Oh don't give me that, Miss," Susie said, pointing a finger at Kristin. "I raised you and your three brothers just fine."

"Yeah, and look at my brothers," Kristin said with a smile.

"Well. Most of that happened after they were out of my control. Besides, they're not all my DNA. Your dad's family plays a role, too."

Kristin laughed. "I've gotta get back to work. I have so much left to do. At this rate Darren and I will be here until midnight."

"We will?" he asked, his eyes growing wide.

"All right kids, let's load your stuff in Grandma's car. We've got to switch your car seats over," Kristin said.

"Why doesn't your mom just take our van down to the valley with her for the weekend?"

"That's probably a good idea. Especially since it's got all the car seats in it already," Susie said.

"Okay."

Kristin and Darren said their goodbyes to the kids. Rachel said goodbye to each of them too. It was the first time they left Parker overnight and it was a tearful goodbye. He screamed for his mama as long as he could. Rachel eventually had to step back inside the store as it was too sad to watch any longer. She immediately went back to work in her office but after she heard Darren and Kristin come back into the store, she could tell they, too, were having a hard time with it.

By five, when Kristin and Rachel usually packed up and headed home, both stayed in the store working. Kristin was still baking for the sales event the following day and Rachel was inventorying boxes that came in for Black Friday. Sideline items were always a crucial part of Sinful Retreat's success. And this time of year Rachel and Kristin liked to work with their local community. Lisa Lee designed and handcrafted Christmas ornaments, Maria Zavala made the most gorgeous scarves, Pilar and Hector Bardem made custom jewelry, all of which was sold in the store.

"Kristin, I have no idea how to inventory these mugs and thermoses," Darren called into the kitchen.

"I showed you how! Follow the instructions on the paper. Unless you think you can perfect this Brown-Bottom Butterscotch Cashew Cream Pie!"

"Here," Mark said, setting down his sweatshirt and keys on a nearby table, "I'll do it."

"Aren't you done for the day?" Darren asked.

"It's no big deal. Hand me the computer. We'll do this box together. Then you can probably handle that box. Besides, there's no way I want to deal with her like that," he said as the tip of his head nodded toward the kitchen.

Darren chuckled. "You're telling me."

It took him about twenty minutes to get a strong hold on the inventory system and then Mark left. Any questions after that he directed to Rachel. Becky ran the bakery counter, while Diane ran the book counter. Rachel helped customers in both the bakery and the bookstore, finished the weekly bookkeeping and nearly finished setting up the bakery and bookstore feature stands for the following day. Nothing was actually on sale for the event, but there were items being promoted and special advertisement boards hung from the ceiling, in front of the counters, behind the counters, in front of the registers, and in the windows, along with little table tents that advertised that for every $25 spent, tomorrow only, everyone received $5 to spend on Black Friday in addition to whatever discounts already applied. Also applicable to online sales and gift cards. By closing, Rachel was almost finished filling a shelf of bagged coffees and tea infusers in the bakery when Ethan came into the store.

Darren decided to take a break and poured both himself and Ethan a cup of coffee and the two sat down near the fireplace.

Rachel observed inconspicuously from behind the bakery counter and jumped as Kristin crept up behind her. "Who're you spying on?"

"Seriously, are you trying to give me a heart attack?"

"Oh, look at our boys, making friends over there," Kristin smiled. "That is what you're looking at, right?"

"Yes, that's what I'm looking at. Well, Ethan really. He just seems to be assimilating into my life lately. Last night was Aspen, right now it's Darren."

"That's a good thing, though. Right?"

"Yeah. I think so. It's just different. I'm not used to this. And it totally took me by surprise with Aspen. She's just so full of attitude. I always thought if I was ever going to have a guy in my life, I would have to practically bribe her to get her to like him."

"I think you're forgetting that Aspen sort of met Ethan on her own, though."

"What do mean?" Rachel asked.

"It's not like you introduced him as the guy were dating."

Rachel paused to think about that for a moment. "That's true. I never thought of that."

"So she got to pass her own judgment before you even came into the picture."

"Hmm." Rachel watched the two men together. She couldn't hear anything they were saying, but from afar they seemed to carry on as if they had known each other for years. "I slept with him last night."

"You what?" Kristin blurted out.

Across the store both men looked up toward the bakery counter and Rachel quickly pulled Kristin back and out of sight.

"Not like *that*. I mean we slept. Literally slept. On my couch. Fully clothed. Nothing happened."

"Oh my goodness. For a second there I thought, 'The world just came to an end; Rachel had sex.'"

Rachel elbowed her and Kristin laughed. "Does anybody know?"

"Aspen knows. She woke us up this morning."

"Okay, anyone other than your daughter? This is juicy stuff. I mean not really. Like no one would watch a soap opera if this was as good as it gets, but really in your life, this is pretty juicy. I've gotta call AJ and Tiff."

"Kristin."

"Oh, I'll be right back. It won't take me long."

Rachel sighed.

Ten minutes later Kristin emerged from the kitchen, a satisfied grin on her face. "Come on back here. I've got a cranberry sauce to put on these cheesecakes."

"So you want the dirt?" Rachel asked as she grabbed a stool. Typically, she took a seat on the counter, but at the moment there wasn't an open inch of counter to be found. Every surface was covered with the most decadent treats and desserts Rachel had ever seen. "Oh my God," she said as she looked around the kitchen. "You've seriously outdone yourself. You should be in a book or on television. Or both."

"Why thank you. And I quite agree. I did do some nice work. And the best part? It all tastes even better than it looks."

Rachel felt her stomach rumble. "It's seriously no wonder that I've put on weight that I just can't lose since we became business partners."

Kristin laughed. "Now you sound like my husband."

"But seriously, do you want the dirt?"

"Not yet."

Rachel raised an eyebrow. "What?" Then it hit her. "Are you kidding me? When are they coming? You do realize he's here right now?"

Kristin grinned as she averted her eyes from Rachel and drizzled cranberry sauce, sugared cranberries and mint leaves over a dozen cheesecakes. Just as she finished, a timer made a loud ding and Kristin crossed the kitchen to the ovens where she pulled out oversized loaves of bread and a sweetened aroma of gingerbread flooded the room.

"What is that?" AJ asked as she stepped into the kitchen, a bottle of wine in each hand.

"That would be Earl Grey-Maple Gingerbread," Kristin said.

"Smells heavenly," AJ said as she crossed the room. "Hey there, Sleepy. Or maybe it was that you didn't get much sleep. I'm not sure. I guess that's why I'm here, to get filled in on the details," she said with a smirk as she hugged Rachel.

"I think I need new friends."

"Nonsense. You'll never find any as awesome as us," Tiff said as she stepped into the kitchen, her heels clacking on the tiled floor, the necks of two wine bottles sticking out of her oversized Vuitton.

"You guys are killing me. He is in the next room. And if you haven't noticed, this kitchen doesn't have a door on it," Rachel said, growing frantic.

"I'll take care of this," Kristin said. "Besides, I need to keep working anyway, so whatever pow-wow we do has to be back here." She made her way to the doorway. "Darren, honey, could you come here for a second?"

It took Darren a minute to get to the doorway, there was some quiet chattering that Rachel couldn't hear, some nodding and a minute later he was gone, and Kristin was walking back toward them with a grin as wide as Lake Arrowhead itself across her face.

"What did you—"

She held up her finger, "Wait for it… wait for it…" A moment later the front door of Sinful Retreat opened, there was the sound of feet shuffling out the door, the door closed and then there was silence. "And they're gone," Kristin said.

"Where did they go?"

"Oh just to have a beer or two. They'll be back later. Now, I've got to get these cheesecakes in the fridge, so don't get started until I get back."

Rachel slumped over on the stool she sat on, feeling utterly defeated.

"Hey Kristin," AJ called across the kitchen, "did you make those cranberry cream tartlets again this year?"

"Sure did. Why do you ask? You hate cooked fruit."

"I know. I'm just wondering," she said, a smirk on her face.

Tiff gasped. "It's Jack. He likes that kind of stuff, doesn't he? Spill it."

AJ couldn't hide anything, and her face turned red as she lit up ear to ear in a smile.

"Oh shoot!" Kristin yelled loudly from the freezer. The other three went running.

"What happened? What's wrong?" Rachel asked, getting there first.

"I forgot to take out that box of Asiago Bagels. How am I supposed to sell them if they're frozen?"

Rachel saw the stress across Kristin's face. "It'll be fine. We'll take them out now and put them in my office. We can turn the heat up in there and they'll be just fine."

"Okay but not too high, because if they thaw too quickly the condensation will make them soggy," Kristin said as she pulled the box from the freezer.

"They have all night to thaw. Just don't sell these first thing during the day," AJ suggested.

"I need tomorrow over with. Where is that wine?"

"You want a drink? Even though you're still baking?" Tiff asked.

"One drink isn't going to hurt me."

"One drink it is," Tiff said, handing her bag over to Kristin.

Tiff sat Kristin down with a glass of wine and the other three took over bagging the chocolate Babka for the next day. As Rachel told her story from the night before, she started with what had happened with Aspen first and then rolled into what happened with Ethan. The whole time she told the story, her brain switched back and forth between wanting to kiss Ethan and wanting to eat the fresh chocolate Babka she was bagging.

"I think you need to sleep with him," Tiff blurted out.

"What?" Rachel said.

"I agree," AJ said.

"This snuggling on the couch stuff is really sweet and all, but really, Rach, sixteen-year-olds do that kind of stuff," Tiff said.

"Sadly, they don't stop there," AJ said.

"That's even sadder for you, Rachel."

"But I see where Tiff is going with this. You're building this up too much. It's not like this needs to be a huge deal. He's clearly into you, so you don't have to be afraid that he's just using you for one night and then he's out of there," AJ said.

"He did let your daughter cry all over him," Kristin said.

"Rip his shirt off, throw him down on your bed and have your way with him. He won't complain," Tiff said.

"What am I? A puma?"

"Not yet," AJ said.

"I'm just…what if—"

"What if what?" Kristin asked.

"What if I'm not any good?"

"Well, then you'll get good, I guess," AJ said.

"Gee, that's helpful."

"Okay, so you've only ever been with Matt. And Matt's arrogant as hell," Tiff said.

"What's your point?" Rachel asked.

"My point is," Tiff said, "that you must be better than you think because Matt, arrogant as he is, would never sleep with someone, ever, more than once, if they weren't better than good."

Kristin and AJ simultaneously nodded their heads.

"She makes a strong argument," Kristin said.

"You know, we have Cosmos out front, I could read one of those," Rachel said.

"No!" AJ said. "That will only confuse you. Just be yourself. That clearly has been working for you. Don't change it up now. It's crucial, especially in the bedroom, that you don't change it up."

"I agree," said Tiff.

The front door of Sinful Retreat jiggled for a moment and then opened. "Kristin? We're back."

"Still back here," she called.

"End of discussion," Rachel said.

"That means I've gotta run. I told Jake I wouldn't be late. But I'll be here tomorrow, spending lots of money," Tiff said, a smile on her face. "Rach, good luck tonight. Love you all, see you in the morning."

"How long do you think you'll be down here?" Rachel asked Kristin.

"Well, let's see. I'm waiting on the last of the Italian Bread to finish, I need to frost the last six dozen or so cupcakes and put sticks in the cake pops. But the frosting won't take long, the bread is almost done, and I'm going to put Darren to work on the cake pops. Go home."

"Are you sure?"

"Very sure."

"Well, that's my cue as well. See you both tomorrow," AJ said as she hugged both and headed out into the cool night.

Rachel headed out of the kitchen and grabbed Ethan's hand. She locked up her office and together they made their way upstairs.

She was pleasantly surprised to see that Aspen had cleaned up the kitchen that morning from the spaghetti mess. She hoped her daughter was having fun with Grandma. Peeking at the answering machine, Rachel saw the blinking light, but rather than listening to the messages, she scrolled through the caller ID. A few were telemarketers and four calls that day were from Matt. No doubt the messages on the machine were from him, too. She was glad she didn't play them. She gently slid the phonebook over the machine to cover up the nuisance of the blinking light.

"You've got a big day ahead of you tomorrow," Ethan said as he took a seat beside her on the couch and pulled her into his arms.

"I do. But I feel ready. And it's nice, we open an hour later and close an hour earlier because it's madness all day."

"Ahh. Look at you, big business owner."

"Actually, it's a rather small business."

"Yeah, well, you're a successful business owner. So that makes you big in my eyes," he said with a smile.

"It's so quiet in here tonight," she said. He seemed content on holding her in his arms. Which was great. But after her talk with her friends, she suddenly was feeling a little courageous.

"It's always quiet in here."

"I don't know. With Aspen not here, it just seems empty," she said.

He hugged her tighter, sighed and sank deeper into the couch. "Speaking of Aspen, you don't think she was mad that I stayed here all night last night, do you? I was a little worried this morning when she woke us up. I didn't mean to fall asleep."

"No. She wasn't mad. She seemed unbothered by it completely."

"Are you sure?" he asked.

"Yes, I'm sure."

"Good. I'll tell you one thing, you've got one comfortable couch. I could fall asleep on this thing any time."

Rachel felt her heart sink.

"Oh you could huh?"

"Mmm hmm," he mumbled.

"Well," she said, rolling out of his arms to her knees on the floor. "I've got something better in mind for you and I. But I'm going to change out of my work clothes. Think you can manage to wait and see what I've got in mind?" she asked as she leaned in toward his ear and let her tongue lightly graze his lobe.

He smiled. "Absolutely."

"Good." She kissed his lips and headed into her bedroom. She slipped out of her slacks and headed for her closet. Suddenly she was drawing a blank about what to wear. She slipped on one of her two thong panties and her black yoga pants and then was at a loss as what to do next. She briefly thought about calling Tiff, but it was after midnight and even if Tiff didn't mind, either the girls would wake up or Jake would. And, rightfully so, they would be mad.

Realizing how long she was taking, Rachel began to frantically peruse through the tops in her closet. Suddenly she grabbed a cream thin sweater that hung low, to the middle of her butt, so it would show just enough of her in the tight pants to keep up curiosity. It was a wide and deep V-neck, and she always wore a shirt under it, but for tonight she opted against it. Slipping into it, she felt sexy as the one side draped loosely off her shoulder, revealing her collar bone. She took off her socks and pulled her hair down. Quickly spritzing her mouth, she stepped back into the living room. She turned off the overhead light and quickly turned on the lamp in the corner as she passed by and made her way to the couch. As she knelt down beside Ethan on the sofa her heart dropped.

He was asleep.

Rachel sat beside him on the floor for a few minutes and watched him as he slept. His thick five o'clock shadow looked darker than usual from the shadowed living room, making him also look sexier than normal. With his right arm stretched up behind his head, his shirt was lifted slightly at the waist, revealing a small amount of his refined V muscle that led to the waist of his jeans.

Rachel bit the corner of her bottom lip to keep from waking him up. A minute later she rose, covered him with a blanket, checked that all the doors were locked and crawled into her own bed for the night.

NINE

Rachel was groggy when her alarm woke her up on Saturday morning.

Ethan heard her alarm from the living room, and quickly rose from the couch and came into Rachel's room. "Morning," he said as he slid in behind her on the bed.

The night before played back to her like a movie and Rachel felt her disappointment all over again. "Morning," she said. She slipped out of bed, still wearing the yoga pants and sweater she had slipped into for him the night before. She made her way to the kitchen, grabbed a bagel and glass of water and started to get ready. She felt him come up behind her and slide his hands beneath the sweater as she was putting on some make-up at the mirror.

"Do you really have to go in right away?" he asked. He kissed her neck and exposed collar bone.

"I'm not sure I follow," she said, gently brushing him off. "I'll be right back. I've got to change," she said glibly.

"Are you sure? I mean, I think you look pretty fine in what you were wearing," he called through the bathroom door.

She emerged a few minutes later in black slacks and an abstract printed chiffon ruffled top.

"Okay, something is off with you today," Ethan said as she walked coolly past him.

"Well, why don't you sleep on it for a while? Tell me what you come up with. In the meantime, I've got a busy day ahead of me at work. See you later?" Rachel opened the door to head down to the store.

"Shit. Sleep. I fell asleep."

As she tried to pull the door closed behind her, Ethan grabbed it but Rachel continued heading down the stairs. "It's fine. Have a good day."

"Rach, I'm an ass. Worse than an ass. I'm…"

"Bye, Ethan," she said when she reached the bottom and stepped into Sinful Retreat.

Kristin and Darren were already there. The place smelled magnificent. And all of the Asiago Bagels were thawed and ready for sale.

"What time did you go home last night?" Rachel asked.

"Don't ask," Darren said.

"Darren, would you please grab that last box of blueberry muffins and fill that tray in the display case?" Kristin asked as she stepped out of the kitchen with a tray of holiday decorated cake pops.

"Did you take a bottle of Prozac?"

"Oh, I wish."

A knock at the door indicated Mark was there and as Rachel went to let him in, Becky arrived as well.

"Perfect. Now remember, Darren will be running the register, nearly exclusively because that's what he's best at. Okay?" Kristin asked as she looked at them all.

Rachel's eyes widened as she tried to figure out if Kristin indeed did take a whole bottle of Prozac, was drunk or abducted by aliens and cloned during the night. This version just didn't seem real. She glanced at the clock on the wall. Five minutes until opening, and there was already a gathering of people outside the store. Rachel was growing excited. It was the days like these that she lived for as a business owner.

Finally Sinful Retreat opened, and a steady flow of people filled the store all morning. Rachel was bombarded with customers, old and new, asking questions and looking for recommendations.

The local vendors that sold things in Sinful Retreat also came to represent their items, which was helpful and meant that Rachel and Kristin didn't have to learn how to answer questions about those items. The line to the registers stayed consistently long and the complaints were minimal. Rachel was pulled in every direction across the store to help with one thing or another.

Mark grabbed Rachel from behind as she made her way to her office. "Sorry, need to borrow you for a moment."

"Sure, what's up?" she asked, noticing the incredibly large man standing beside him. He was so tall she feared he might actually get a paper cut on his bald head from their ads that hung from the ceiling.

"This is Mr. Woken. Mr. Woken, this is Rachel Taylor, owner of Sinful Retreat. Perhaps she can better help you find what you're looking for today, sir."

"Yes, I'd be happy to help. And what is it that you're looking for?" Rachel asked.

"Mr. Woken is interested in historical fiction, although there seemed to be nothing in our classics section that appealed to him," Mark said with a glare that only Rachel would understand.

"Ahh, yes. Tell me, Mr. Woken, how do you feel about the *Lonely Lords, Speak Easy,* or *Children of the Moon*?" Rachel asked.

Mr. Woken's eyes lit up as a smile crept across his face. "I just finished *Dragon's Moon*."

"Well, you're in luck. We have *Warrior's Moon*. Follow me," she said.

Mark stood in disbelief as he watched them make their way through the crowd.

"Did you read *Speak Easy*? Oh Melanie Harlow is such a gifted writer. She really toes the line with her characters and steps outside the box. I really admire that one," he said with a distant look in his eye.

Rachel tried to hide the strange look she couldn't help but give him. She pulled *Warrior's Moon* from the shelf. "You know, there are some other great ones here by Lucy Monroe if you like her. Here's *The Sheikh's Bartered Bride* and following that one is *Wedding Vow of Revenge*." She pulled both of those from the shelf and handed them to him. "I've heard excellent things about them," she said with a nod of her head. From the corner of her eye she saw Mark nearby, listening intently to their conversation.

"Really? I haven't read any of these. To be honest the *Children of the Moon* series is the first by Lucy Monroe I've ever read. But I do really like her," Mr. Woken said, a giddy smile on his face and he held the books.

"Well, it really is your lucky day," Rachel said. "Come on, I'll ring you up in my office. I won't make you stand in that line. It'll be our secret," she said with a wink.

Five minutes and over forty dollars later, a very happy Mr. Woken was walking out the door, three books richer.

"You're terrible," Mark said.

"No. I'm good. And he's a bit of a perv," she said.

"Clearly. And how did you know all that stuff about romance novels?"

She shrugged. "I memorize the titles and authors. Maybe a character here and there. It's one of the things that makes me good at my job."

"I'm speechless. Really."

"Well, Speechless, get back to work."

"Sure thing, boss."

The day pushed on and a slight lull mid-morning gave them just enough time to restock where needed and prepare for a heavy crowd around lunch time. People flocked into Sinful Retreat around the noon hour to get their fill of things to eat. Although Kristin didn't serve actual lunch food on days like this, people didn't care. They were more than content filling up on her delicious muffins, breads, pastries and desserts. Tiff arrived just after noon with her girls and Jake. It took them nearly forty-five minutes, but they managed to sit down at a table. While the girls inhaled their yummy, sweet treats, Tiff perused the bookstore.

She was planning an anniversary trip to Italy in early summer, so the first place she went was the travel section.

"Hey girl," Rachel said as she stepped up from behind her.

"Hey you. So," she said, her eyes quickly darting around them, "how was last night?"

"Don't. Ask."

"Uh oh. That bad?"

"It didn't happen."

"What? Really? I thought you were all primed and ready to go?"

"Wow. Now I really sound like a puma all ready to be grilled," Rachel said. "Apparently he's so used to not getting any that he just fell asleep on *my oh so comfortable couch*. I'm going to throw that sucker out and burn it. And in its place, I'm going to put a rock. Damn!"

A small, older woman standing only feet away from them quickly looked in their direction.

"The *Hoover* Dam. It's such an amazing feat of engineering," Rachel said loudly, enunciating carefully. Her eyes darted carefully back at Tiff as she twisted her mouth.

"Well, I say you turn it up, all the way tonight. Don't even give him the chance to fall asleep. Or, on the off chance that your couch really is that comfortable and he does fall asleep again, men don't ever protest to being woken up in certain ways."

"Okay I get that, Tiff, but the point is not to get him to fall asleep in the first place."

"When I don't want Donny to fall asleep yet, I just crush up a couple Excedrin and slip it into his water. You could always try that," the old lady said before she moved through the crowd.

Their eyes wide, mouths open, Rachel and Tiff looked at each other.

"I'm gonna go die now." Rachel spun on her heel and headed toward her office. She could hear Tiff laughing as she walked away.

"Rachel, there you are. I've been looking all over this place for you." Rachel turned to see Matt's mom headed straight for her. Of course this is who she would see at this moment.

"Linda," she said, forcing a smile across her face. "So nice to see you, how are you?"

Linda pulled Rachel into a firm hug and over her shoulder she saw Ethan walk in the front door. She hoped he wouldn't come over to talk to her. The last thing Linda needed to know was that she was seeing anyone. That would go over terribly.

"Have you talked to Matthew?" she asked.

"Umm, no. I've been so busy with work, actually."

"I can see why," she said as she looked around at the bustling crowds. "No matter. You'll find out soon enough. Has he got a surprise for Aspen. Oh, I cannot wait. And look at you, aren't you looking darling as ever? How on earth did my boy ever let you go? Well, guess he's not totally perfect, huh?" she asked, laughing loudly at herself. "So, tell me what's good to read these days. I haven't picked up a book in ages. Tell me, who really has time to read anymore?"

"Uh, well, Linda, what do you think you'd be into?"

"Well, let's see here, I really like that *Yes, Dear*. Oh and *Wendell and Vinnie* makes me laugh. Jeff always liked that *King of Queens*. And *King of the Hill*."

"When you go to the movies, what do you like to see? Drama, science fiction, thriller?"

"Anything with Will Ferrell in it. That guy just cracks us up."

"Of course he does. Who doesn't he, right?" Rachel said. "Why don't you get a seat in the bakery? I'll get you something to eat. You still drink coffee, right?"

"Oh you better believe I'll never give that up."

"Right," she said. "And I will have a book sent over that will be so perfect for you."

"Aren't you just the sweetest? You know, if you find two, make it two. I'm all for supporting the locals, especially when it's my granddaughter. And after all, if I support you, I support her, now don't I?"

Rachel forced that smile across her face so big that her cheeks began to burn. She watched as Linda made her way through the crowd, smiling and waving at as many people as she knew.

She made her way over to Mark. "Do me a favor to make up for the pervy giant."

"Anything."

"Matt's mom is here. In three minutes, I want you to bring her some dessert thing, make sure it has nuts, the more the better, and a coffee. Caffeinated. Also, pull two James Patterson books from the shelf."

"Which two?"

"Any two."

"What if she already has them?" he asked.

"She's never going to glance at the titles again after she walks out of here today, let alone pick them up to read them. I assure you, you'll be fine. Just give her the total, she'll give you her card, run it and be done with her."

"Okay. I can handle that."

"Thank you."

Linda gushed over Mark when he brought her things and Rachel laughed under her breath from the counter as she rang up customers.

"Hi Jody," Rachel said as the woman she frequently worked with from the bank stepped up next in line.

"You guys are so busy in here today. This is great. I'm always so happy to see things like this for local businesses."

"This is kind of our kick-off event for the holidays. We'll be busy like this again next Friday for Black Friday of course, but we stay pretty steady through all of December. It's nice. Although January is nice too, when it slows down a bit. $106.33 is your total today. And you get four coupons that are good next Friday only."

"Great. And what time do you open Black Friday?" Jody asked.

"We open an hour early, at six."

Mark returned to the register. He was the quickest of them all at it, and it freed Rachel up to help customers on the floor, which she preferred anyway. She was happy when AJ came in. Jack came in a few minutes later when he finally found a parking spot for the car.

"This place is crazy busy," he said. "Way to go Rachel," he said proudly. "I'm going to look around, AJ."

"How goes your busy day?" she asked.

"It's been good. Minimal complaints. A few fires to put out. So far it's been running pretty smoothly. Kristin's sales have been phenomenal. She sold out of her white sandwich bread by 10:30 this morning and the honey wheat by one this afternoon."

"Didn't she double the amount she made last year, too?"

Rachel nodded.

"Dang. Way to go."

"I know, right?"

"I talked to Tiff," AJ said, a wince on her face.

"Yes, so now I don't have to explain it to you."

"How about that little old lady and the Excedrin? How random is that?"

"I'm still a bit in shock about that one."

AJ laughed. "Oh come on. That's funny. You can't seriously tell me you didn't laugh."

"Speaking of. I saw Ethan come in here. But I haven't seen him since." Rachel looked around but didn't see him anywhere. She shrugged her shoulders.

"Well, if you don't mind, *Miss*, I came here to do some shopping. I've got books to buy and Black Friday cash to earn," AJ said.

"Shop away my friend. Don't let me stand in your way."

Diane arrived around four to help with the last few hours of the night. Becky left, but Mark, who didn't mind the extra hours, stayed the full day to continue working until the store closed at eight. Ethan showed his face again around seven. When Rachel asked what he'd done all day, he said he had helped his chief with a few things, cleaned his apartment and just hung out. He and Darren did whatever Kristin and Rachel asked to help clean up the shop and disassemble from the day's event. And by 8:30, everyone was ready to go home for the evening.

Rachel was exhausted. Her feet were tired and sore. She learned years and years ago never to wear heels to events like this. But before she stepped upstairs, she wanted to quickly step inside her office and call Aspen.

"Do you mind?" she asked Ethan. "I know I promised I'd make dinner. I still will. It'll just be a late one. Or we can order in. Whatever you prefer," she said.

"You should call her. I don't care about dinner. I'll just be upstairs. Take your time," he said.

She smiled. "Thanks."

Rachel stepped into her office; it was quiet, and she paused a moment to take in the peacefulness around her. After a moment, she sat down at her desk and picked up the phone. It was answered after the first ring. "Hey Asp. How are things with Gram?"

"Oh Mom, they're so good! We went shopping yesterday and I got the cutest pair of shoes ever. I can't wait to show you. Then we went to a movie last night. Today was nice out so we just stayed by the pool and I worked on my tan. We went to Benihana for dinner tonight and I think we're going to head over to the boardwalk tomorrow just to walk around."

"That sounds like a great weekend. I'm jealous. I want to work on my tan."

"Mom, you're never tan."

"That's because I never get to work on it," she said.

"You sound tired. How was your event today?"

"It was good. Which is why I'm so tired."

"Did Kristin save me anything good?"

Rachel laughed. "I'm sure she did. She always does."

"I know. She's the best. She's like a second mom."

Rachel smiled. "I'm glad you're having fun. Is Gram there?"

"Yeah, hold on, I'll grab her for you."

"Hey Rach. How was your event?" Jenn asked, taking the phone from Aspen.

"It was good. Really good. I'm too tired to really go over any numbers. Plus I have no idea what our online records look like. I'll know in the next couple days or so."

"Okay. Well, that's still good to hear, though. For tomorrow Aspen and I were planning to head down to the boardwalk and then I think I'll bring her back for dinner. Your dad wants to have dinner with the Kleinmen's in Riverside on his way back through from Palm Springs so I figured that would be perfect if I'm coming down from the mountains. So, six okay?"

"Yeah, that's great."

"All right. I'll see you tomorrow. You enjoy your evening."

"Tell Aspen I love her."

"Of course I will. Night."

Rachel hung up the phone and headed upstairs. When she opened the door to her apartment she was greeted with a faint, orange glow and a faint, flickering light. She stepped into the warm room, a few candles on each flat surface around the living and dining rooms.

"Oh my God," she whispered to herself as her bag slipped off her shoulder, down her arm and to the floor.

Ethan emerged from the kitchen. "I felt really bad about last night. And I wanted to make it up to you."

"Is this what you were up to all day?"

He nodded, a boyish smile across his face. "I hope I don't burn your apartment down."

"I hope so, too," she said. She couldn't hide the smile on her face.

They walked closer to each other. "I still meant what I said, about taking things slow and going at whatever pace you want and so if this isn't what you're ready for—"

Rachel reached her arms around his neck and pulled his mouth against hers. "This is exactly what I want," she said a moment later.

With both arms around his neck, she pulled herself against his body. His hands untucked her shirt from her slacks and slid beneath the fabric against her soft skin. She felt him instantly grow hard as he pulled her tightly against her body.

His lips were soft and tender against hers as his tongue explored the inside of her mouth; slowly they moved their way down her neck to the center of her collarbone. She tugged at her shirt and released the top few buttons, and he buried his face into her neck, kissing her, sending chills along her spine.

His mouth returned to hers and his hands were in her hair. Her fingers traced the lines of muscle along his back and as she worked her way up, she removed his shirt from his body altogether. For a moment they stood still, looking at one another, excitement building inside of her. She grabbed his hand and led him across the room to her bedroom. When she turned back around to face him, she had unbuttoned her shirt fully and he willingly and with eagerness took her into his arms, sliding the chiffon material down her arms to the floor.

Gently he kissed her as he pulled her into him. She reveled in the tenderness of his touch and reeled in eagerness for his next one. Her body tingled and ached in the same places, and she couldn't seem to kiss him hard enough or pull him close enough. He left her breathless and wanting more at the same time.

Afterward, she lay atop him, afraid to move, too weak and frightened that moving would break the spell and she would wake from her dream. She was thankful her face was turned away from his, afraid he would see the emotion she knew was blatantly written all over her. She was overwhelmed with an excited happiness that was contradicted by confusion and fear. She wasn't sure what to make of her feelings and she felt ridiculous. Why did she have an overwhelming urge to cry? This wasn't like her. Ever. Had it really been that long since she'd had sex? Maybe it was just that good. After all, even her hands had tingled. In fact, they were still tingling. And she had peaked well over a half hour ago.

Someone finally spoke. "I think you killed me," he said.

"I hope that's a good thing."

"Are you kidding? That's an a-freaking-mazing thing. In a you-killed-me kind of way."

She laughed. Rachel rolled off of him, and feigning composure, looked over at him. The moonlight coming in through the curtains cast a white glow across his face making him look sexy as hell. She couldn't help but feel turned on all over again.

"I need some food," he said, getting out of bed, but not bothering with clothing. Naked, he walked to the kitchen. Moonlight bounced through the open paned windows into the house.

In the kitchen, Ethan stuck his head in the fridge, careful to keep his body back a little way. Rachel followed closely behind. "Do you have any bread?"

She grabbed a loaf off the counter and handed it to him. He retreated from the fridge with turkey, cheese, lettuce, tomato, mayo and mustard.

"Wow. You are hungry," she said with a smile. She hoisted herself up onto the counter. It was so out of character to do anything around her place naked. Especially with anyone else. She felt exhilarated. She felt free.

"You want a sandwich? I can make you one?" He offered.

"I'm fine, thanks."

"Suit yourself. But I've got to build up my energy because as soon as I'm done eating, we are going to do that all over again. As many times as we can."

Rachel laughed.

Ethan set down the condiments and slid over to where Rachel sat on the counter. Pulling her to the edge of the counter, he stood between her legs and looked up at her. "I'm quite serious."

She smiled down at him. "I know you are." She leaned in and kissed him. "So hurry up with that sandwich already."

After he ate, they headed back to bed and made love two more times before finally falling asleep. At some point during the night, Rachel awoke with a start. She had a heavy feeling in her chest that left her feeling strangely unsettled.

She looked over at Ethan who was sleeping soundly beside her. He was content and peaceful looking, but she couldn't shake the feeling that something was wrong.

She crawled out of bed and paced around the apartment. She got a drink of water hoping that would settle her, but something had her rattled and she didn't know what.

Stepping outside, the cool nighttime air helped a bit. It at least helped her feel sleepy again. She gazed out over the placid waters before her, its darkness running deep.

Taking a few deep breaths, she returned inside the house.

Quietly she crawled back in bed beside Ethan. He stirred slightly but only to wrap an arm around her. She felt safe in his arms. She closed her eyes and willed herself to think of other things. She thought about Aspen, happy in Newport with Gram. Somehow Rachel managed to drift off to sleep.

Rachel woke in the morning to the slight and rhythmic sound of Ethan's snoring. As she opened her eyes and realized what it was, she couldn't help but giggle. She'd never woken up to anyone this way before. Well, except for AJ, but there was nothing slight, or rhythmic, about her snoring. When AJ snored, it was like alarming the entire U.S. of a pending terrorist attack. Kristin sometimes complained of Darren's snoring, too. She always kept a pair of earplugs on hand. But this didn't bother Rachel. Something about this, on this morning, made her happy. She rolled to her side and watched him.

His chest would rise and fall in connection with the rhythmic sound of snoring. His bottom jaw always dropped slightly farther open on the exhale and his eyes raced from behind his eyelids.

Rachel watched him silently. She knew to anyone looking in on them it would probably seem incredibly weird. But she didn't care. In that moment she was happy. So happy. Happier than she had been in so long. And it was her life and all that mattered was how she felt.

She didn't know how long she watched him like that. It was a while. Finally, he stirred. His eyes fluttered open a bit and then closed again. Then they shot open quickly. "Were you watching me?" he asked.

She backed up from him. "Sorry. Was that creepy?"

"No. I just wasn't expecting it, that's all," he said. He relaxed and a smile crossed his face. "Man, I am in big trouble."

"Why is that?" she asked as she cocked a brow.

"Because you're even sexy in the morning."

She laughed loudly.

"Like so sexy that I think I should get to have my way with you," he said as he pulled her on top of him. He was firm as a rock.

"One rule."

"You're making rules?" he said.

She nodded as she placed her hand in between their mouths and noses. "No kissing. I haven't brushed my teeth yet."

"I haven't brushed my teeth yet either. We'd both have bad breath."

"Yeah, I'm still not into that. No kissing. I don't even like talking to you with our faces this close."

"Is that why your hand is between our faces like a mask?" he asked.

She nodded.

"Can I kiss your neck or other things?"

"Yes. But not the mouth."

"Okay. Deal."

A moment later Rachel was once again reveling in his touch. She could totally get used to waking up beside him if this was how he did it. She couldn't believe how amazing he felt.

Afterward, she felt depleted, like she'd done both a morning workout and a morning run, and she'd never even left her bed. Yes, she decided, she could definitely get used to this.

"Ugh," she sighed, loudly.

"Did I lose my touch?" he asked.

She laughed. "Not even close. No, I was thinking how it will be awfully hard to do this in the mornings when Aspen's back in the house."

"Ahh. Yes. We'll have to learn how to be very quiet. And install locks on your doors."

"I don't think I can be that quiet."

He laughed. "Yeah, sorry about that. It's my fault really."

Rachel heard her doorbell ring from the next room.

"Was that your doorbell?" Ethan asked.

"Sure was. Who's bugging me on a Sunday morning?" Rachel crawled out of bed and went in search for clothing to put on. After searching nearly a minute for underwear, she gave up entirely on those and slipped on the yoga pants on her chair from the other day. She grabbed Ethan's shirt, pulled it on and headed for her door.

Realizing she wasn't wearing a bra, she folded her arms firmly across her chest for protection and opened the front door. Her body nearly froze in an instant.

"Hey Rach!"

At first, she couldn't say anything. She just stood there, dumbfounded.

"Rachel?"

"Matt?"

TEN

"**W**ow, I never knew you as the type to sleep in," Matt said with a laugh. "Is Aspy around?"

"Actually, she's not," she said curtly. She couldn't hide the shock on her face to see him standing on her doorstep. Never in twelve years had he ever shown up unannounced.

He looked taken back. "I thought she was grounded."

"I'm sorry, why are you here?" she asked, blocking him from the doorway, silently praying Ethan wouldn't emerge from her bedroom. And that if he absolutely had to, that he would be clothed.

"Where is she?" He asked trying to peek over her shoulder into the house. He could sense she was hiding something.

"She's in Orange County."

"Ah. At your parents'. When's she going to be back? I've got something I want to talk to her about. You too, actually. I can talk to you right now, if you want."

"Now isn't a good time for me. Aspen will be home around dinner. Why don't you call later, and we'll set something up for you guys to get together?" she suggested.

"Okay."

"How long are you in town? A few days, the whole week?" she asked.

"Uh, at least the week," he said. He gave her a smile. "It's nice to see you. It's been a while."

She forced a smile onto her face, hoping it didn't look too frantic, before she closed the door on him.

With the door separating them, she felt herself take a breath and relax slightly. She heard Ethan emerge from her bedroom and looked up to see him walking toward her in his jeans, bare feet and no shirt. Then she realized she was wearing his shirt.

"You look like you've seen a ghost," he said.

"About as close to one as possible. That was Matt."

"Aspen's dad?"

She nodded. A large knot tightened in her stomach. "Oh God. He's probably here because she's been avoiding his calls. Well, if she didn't want to talk to him on the phone, I can guarantee that seeing him won't go over well. Oh God. Oh God." She began pacing the living room. "Is it too early to drink?" she asked.

"I think so. But maybe let's start with coffee. We'll make it black. How about we get dressed?"

An hour later, they were sitting at a small table in the corner of The Belgian Waffle Works down by the water of the lake. They missed the breakfast rush for a Sunday morning, and it was rather quiet.

The hot coffee was good at calming Rachel's nerves. But when she began to think too hard about Matt being in town, that overgrown knot in her stomach began to tighten once again.

"Rachel, there's nothing you can do about him being here. Just go on about your lives. I mean, surely he's shown up before and it's never been a problem," Matt said.

"Yeah, but never unannounced. This can't mean anything good."

"But maybe the only reason it was unannounced was because neither of you were taking phone calls from him. Did you consider that?"

Rachel felt her shoulders drop. She hadn't considered that. How could he have told either of them when, it's true, they were avoiding his calls? "You're so smart Mr. Ethan Kuhn."

He smiled. "Now can you finally relax?"

She nodded her head.

"Good, because there was something else I wanted to talk to you about," he said, his face becoming a little serious as he pushed his plate back slightly to make room for his arms on the table. "We've been seeing each other for a few weeks now. About a month. And then last night, of course," he began to trip slightly over his words. "And I'm not seeing anyone else. And I don't think you're seeing anyone else, and well, I was thinking maybe we should make this official, between us."

Rachel set down her fork, a smile across her face. She leaned in closer to him. "If I thought there was a chance that you were seeing someone else, I promise, I wouldn't have slept with you last night. I've kind of been operating under the assumption that we've been together for a little bit now."

"Really?" he asked with a grin. "Since when?"

"Probably since the night I had you over to have dinner with my daughter and me."

He nodded. "That makes sense. I like your line of thinking." He leaned in closer and sweetly kissed her before returning to his breakfast.

After breakfast they walked hand in hand along the water of Village Bay. The late fall air was cool, but the uninhibited sunshine that beat down from high in the sky was warm on their skin. Rachel pulled up the sleeves of her sweatshirt to let it kiss the bareness of her forearms.

The smell of fresh cedar wafted through the trees and the sound of the water lapping on the shore blended with people's conversations and laugher in the distance. Rachel pulled herself up closely to Ethan, the warmth of his body against hers and she felt at peace.

Together they wound through the trees and the maze that was Lake Arrowhead Village. They passed a quiet Lollipop Park, closed on Sundays, a shoe store and dog bakery. They passed the fountain and the Mexican Restaurant and made their way to the oversized parking lot. Across the distance, in the far eastern corner, Rachel spotted Sinful Retreat.

Parked out front was Susie's car. The front door of the store was unlocked and she and Ethan stepped inside to see Darren and Kristin.

"Hey guys," Rachel said.

"Hey!" Kristin said as she popped up from behind the counter. She finally looked rested and like herself. "Thought I would utilize my time while my monsters were still at my parents'. What were you guys up to?"

"Had breakfast. Came back here to get some work done as well," Rachel said.

"Ethan, could you give me a hand with these signs?" Darren asked as he grabbed a ladder from the storage room.

He nodded and followed Darren.

"First, we need to talk about who showed up on my doorstep this morning," Rachel said, as she grabbed Kristin, and they took a seat at a table. Rachel quickly filled her in about her night with Ethan and then about her morning when Matt showed up.

"Noooo."

She nodded.

"Aspen's going to freak."

"Tell me about it," Rachel said.

"And what are the chances that he would show up like that the morning after you, *you know*, with someone else?" Kristin said.

"Trust me, that thought hasn't escaped my mind, either."

Kristin laughed as she rose to her feet. "I can't believe how much stuff we sold yesterday. I thought I was going overboard by doubling my breads from last year. Nope. I could have doubled what I doubled. I have less than one Brown-Bottom Butterscotch Cashew Cream Pie left and about nine Italian Bread loaves; I have a few tartlets, shortbread bars, and cupcakes left over. Oh, and a few bagels. Otherwise, I am cleaned out. Tomorrow is going to be sparse in the bakery until I whip some things up."

"Dang. I know I sold out of David Sharpe's new book. And I have a ton on back order. Off the top of my head, that's all I can think of though," she said.

Rachel unlocked her office and sat down at her computer. She pulled up all the sales records from the previous day and began to run an e-commerce reconciliation report.

"Why don't we have Darren and Ethan grab the Christmas décor out of your attic since they're here to help," Kristin said, popping her head into the office.

"Great idea. I'll call AJ and see if she can help," Rachel said.

A minute later AJ was on the phone. "What are you up to today?" Rachel asked.

"Just hanging out. I have papers to grade. But it's not imperative, so I'm sure I won't do it. Why, what' s up?"

"Want to decorate the store for Christmas? Please?"

She groaned. "You guys and your holiday décor. You're lucky I'm just good at things like that. Sure. I'll be over in a little while. Tell Kristin I better get some food out of the deal."

Rachel laughed. "I'm sure she knows."

Rachel's computer was running slowly. It's like it knew it was Sunday and it was supposed to be its day off and was fighting her. She stepped out to the register to reconcile the credit card machine. She typed in a few numbers, hit a few buttons, and reports began printing from the receipt tape. While she stood waiting for those reports to finish, she heard the printer in her office fire up. The computer had reluctantly given in and yielded the reports she had requested and was now printing those too. Now to combine everything.

Back in her office, as she sat down and began combing through sales numbers, she heard the guys return to the store with the

Christmas tree. They disappeared for a few minutes and then returned with more boxes of décor. This pattern continued for nearly twenty minutes, but Rachel tuned them out while she continued to input numbers, adding and subtracting, trying to figure out the overall sales from the day before.

When Rachel emerged an hour later from her office, there was a large faux Christmas tree near the fireplace, half strung with lights. Darren was high on a ladder, his head buried in the open rafters of the ceiling and garland wrapped in deco mesh as AJ stood with her feet planted firmly on the ground.

"A little left. Oh, too far. Nope, now more left. Oh, just a hair more. Oh stop! Right there. Perfect. Nail it in, Darren," she said.

"Why does Ethan get to string the lights and I have this job?" he asked as he peeked around the green and red glittering deco mesh.

"Because," AJ said nicely, "he's new to the family. I'm not about to scare him away, yet. Now, next rafter set."

Darren sighed as he climbed down the ladder, grabbed the next collection of rolled garland, moved two rafters over and ascended the ladder once again.

"Kristin," AJ called to the kitchen, "you've got yourself a good man here. He's complaining, but not arguing."

"I know," she called back.

Rachel perused the boxes of ornaments. "There's one missing," she said, as she looked around.

"I grabbed everything I found in the attic," Darren called down from the ladder.

"No, I'm pretty sure there's one missing," she said.

"Well, I can go look in a minute," Ethan said, his head buried between branches of the tree as he tried to get the lights to reach the trunk of the tree.

"I'll go look. I've got to use the bathroom anyway," Darren said, coming back down the ladder. "AJ, sit tight. Or climb the ladder and hang that stuff yourself."

"Whatever, I'll find something else to do. Have you seen how much stuff these two have?"

"Seen it?" Darren scoffed. "Are you kidding me?"

Rachel rolled her eyes as she stepped back into her office. "Well, you guys seem to have that all under control. I've got a new sales catalog and some sales history I've got to take a look at. You know where you can find me if you need me."

A few minutes after sitting down at her desk, Darren's head popped through the open doorway. "Found that box you were talking about. Was this it?" he asked as he thrust a box just larger than a shoebox through the doorway.

"You did find it! Great. Thank you," she said.

"Just out of curiosity, what's in that old rickety trunk up there in the corner?" he asked.

"What trunk?"

"The one that's in that little nook area way back in the corner," he said.

"I haven't the slightest clue what you're talking about."

He sighed. "You know how on the one side of the attic, where there aren't any floorboards and you have to walk on the beams, there's that cove-like thing that goes around the corner?"

Rachel shrugged her shoulders. "Never been back there. I didn't know there was a cove. I never go over there because there is no floor. What were you doing over there?"

"Uh, looking for your ornament box," he said.

"Why would it be over there?"

"I don't know. I wasn't sure where it was. Anyway. Around that corner, way in the back, is a really old looking, rickety trunk. It's super dusty, and thick with cobwebs. Doesn't look like anyone's been back there in decades."

"Probably because no one has. But good to know that it's there. Someday, when I have all this time on my hands, maybe I'll put in a floor on that side of the attic, go back there and clean that all out and see what the heck is up with the old trunk. In the meantime, I've got work to do. But thank you for finding the box. I do appreciate it."

"Women," Darren said with a sigh as he left the office. "Get out while you still can, man," he said to Ethan as he set the box down with the others.

Rachel rolled her eyes and went back to the catalog in front of her.

A little after five, everyone who was working at Sinful Retreat retired for the day. Rachel and Ethan headed upstairs and began dinner and waited for Aspen to return home.

Shortly before six, her daughter came bouncing through the door, her mom following behind her, both with smiles on their faces.

"Wow, looks like you guys had a good weekend," Rachel said. She noticed right away the sun-kissed glow on Aspen's face from lying poolside in Gram's backyard.

"Can I do that every weekend?" Aspen asked as she dropped her bags and jumped on the couch.

Jenn was shocked to see a man standing in her daughter's apartment. "Hello," she said, not hiding her approval. "I'm Jenn, Rachel's mother."

"Ethan," he said as he reached out his hand to shake hers.

She eagerly shook it and glanced over at Rachel with a smirk on her face.

"Yes, Mom, it's exactly what you think."

"I feel so out of the loop. You didn't say anything to me."

Rachel rolled her eyes. "Aspen, go put your bags in your room. Dinner will be ready in about fifteen minutes."

"Well, as much as I would love to stay and chat, and *believe* me, I really do, I've got to go meet your dad. But rest assured, I will be calling. Love you, Aspen. Thanks for a great weekend. See you later." And as quickly as she had arrived, she was gone.

The room grew quiet for a moment. And then Aspen reappeared with a box of shoes in hand. "Mom, look at these," she said, lifting the lid as if she were revealing gold inside. Her face lit up with excitement as she showed her mom the strappy shoes inside.

"Adorable," Rachel said with a smile to appease her daughter.

"I know, right?" she said with a high-pitched squeal before running back into her room.

"Girls," Ethan said with an eye roll. He stepped back into the kitchen to check on their dinner and Rachel followed him to grab the plates to set the table.

As Rachel and Ethan worked in the kitchen, Aspen tried on her new shoes in the living room. A knock on the door interrupted the three of them and Aspen was the first to reach it.

"Dad? What're you doing here?" she asked.

Rachel felt her chest tighten as she realized who was at the apartment.

"Hey kiddo. How long did you think you'd be able to avoid me?" he asked as he stepped into the house and pulled Aspen into his arms. He embraced her firmly, tucking his head low into her neck. "I've missed you Aspy," he mumbled through her hair. When they separated, Rachel distinctly saw tears in his eyes.

Matt slipped off his shoes and stepped into the living room.

"When did you get to California? How long are you here?" Aspen asked as they sat down beside each other on the couch.

"I got in yesterday. And well, there are some things I want to talk to you about. You and your mom," he said glancing over his shoulder. "Hey Rach."

"Matt," she said, standing between the dining and living rooms, "we were about to have dinner."

"Oh, well, sure. I'll join you," he said, standing up and heading into the dining room. He took a seat at one of the dinner plates.

Rachel lost the will to argue with him and went into the kitchen to retrieve another plate from the cupboard. Ethan looked at her wide-eyed and in disbelief by Matt's brazen and bold behavior. She shrugged her shoulder at him as she reached for another fork and knife.

Ethan sighed loudly, venting his irritation, grabbed the dish of Thai pasta and brought it into the dining room. Matt looked up in shock at the presence of another man.

"Oh, I wasn't expecting someone else to be here," he said.

"Matt," Rachel said, knowing the bitter tone his name took when she spoke, "this is Ethan."

Ethan simply gave him a single nod and took a seat beside Rachel.

"Dad was in Cape Canaveral working for the National Weather Service," Aspen beamed proudly.

Matt laughed, a bit arrogantly. "It's a great place. Ever been there?" he asked.

"No. I don't care too much for Florida. It's the humidity I don't like," Ethan said.

Rachel took a breath as she felt the tension in the room close in around them.

"So Dad, how long are you in town?"

"Well, Aspy, that's what I wanted to talk to you guys about. I guess now's as good a time as any," he said, briefly making eye contact with Ethan before looking back and forth between Rachel and Aspen. "I'm staying here. Permanently."

"What?" Aspen gasped.

Rachel's fork slipped through her fingers and made a loud clanking noise as it hit her plate.

"Really? What about your job?" Aspen asked.

"I decided it was time I stepped up to the plate. Take responsibility for the family I have right here." His eyes fluttered back and forth between Rachel and Aspen again.

Rachel grew uncomfortable and Ethan readjusted in his chair.

"Which brings me to the next thing I wanted to discuss with you, Rachel. The boathouse. I want to rent it from you."

"Oh, well, that's not possible," she said.

"I live there," Ethan said bluntly.

"Oh I see!" Matt exclaimed with excitement. "This makes sense now. I was trying to— I get it now. You rent the boathouse."

"Actually—"

Rachel elbowed him from under the table and he abruptly turned to look at her, his eyebrows cocked in curiosity.

She ignored him as she looked at Aspen.

"I guess that rules that out," he said with disappointment.

After dinner, Matt didn't bother to help clean up. He sat in the living room with Aspen while Rachel and Ethan cleaned up their dishes.

"Why wouldn't you say anything to him about us?" he asked.

"It had nothing to do with Matt," she mumbled under her breath near the running water so that they wouldn't overhear them from the living room. "I just didn't think Aspen should find out the same time he did."

"Oh. That makes sense. And I'm an ass," he said.

She giggled. "You're not an ass." She leaned forward and kissed him briefly on the lips. "But I do want to talk with Aspen."

"Fair enough."

By nine, both Ethan and Matt were long gone and only Rachel and Aspen remained in the apartment.

Rachel sat on the couch in silence, listening to the running water of the faucet as Aspen brushed her teeth for bed.

"Hey Aspen," she called when she stepped out of the bathroom. Rachel waved her over to the couch.

Aspen took a seat beside her.

"Are you excited about your dad moving back?" Rachel asked.

She shrugged her shoulders. "I guess. I mean, it'll be nice having a dad around."

Rachel nodded. "Sure. I can understand that. I wanted to talk to you about something."

"About Dad?"

"No. About Ethan."

"Okay?"

"Well, this weekend, when you were at Gram's, Ethan and I decided that we were only going to date each other."

"So, like, be boyfriend and girlfriend?" Aspen asked.

"You could call it that," Rachel said. "I just wanted to tell you so that you knew we were together."

"I kind of assumed that already. I mean, you did sleep on the couch together."

Rachel laughed. "That's true."

"I just have one thing I'm kind of worried about," she said.

"Tell me. Anything."

"I won't have to see him in like his underwear or anything, will I?"

"Aspen!"

"What? I just don't want to see him like that."

"Oh my God. No. Why would you see him in his underwear?"

"Well, from when he spends the night and stuff."

"What is it that you think Ethan and I are going to be doing?" Rachel asked.

Aspen sighed and rolled her eyes. "Oh Mom, pu-lease. I am not dumb. You guys act like we don't know what goes on, but we so do."

"I am trying to be a responsible role model for you," Rachel said, sitting up straighter, trying to act innocent and pretending that what happened this weekend in her bed didn't happen at all.

"Oh Mom. It's not 1950 anymore. It's not like you bring guys home every week. Heck, you've never brought home a guy. I'd hardly classify you as an irresponsible parent."

"Well, I will still be making the rules around here, and the rules are still the same. No boys in bedrooms. That includes mine."

"Whatever you say," Aspen said with a smirk.

"Stop it. And go to bed."

Rachel had a difficult time dragging herself from bed on Monday morning. Her eyelids refused to open. Some days it defied nature to rise before the sun. This was certainly one of those days.

Hitting her snooze repeatedly was counterproductive. As soon as she fell back asleep, the alarm would startle her awake, louder than the time before, leaving her more agitated than before. Finally, she conceded. She turned off the persistent machine, rolled out of bed and started the shower. She dreaded the day ahead of her.

It must have gotten colder than usual that night because Sinful Retreat was freezing. There was a thin layer of frost on the inside of the windows and the heater clinked and clanked angrily before it finally roared to life. Rachel then turned on the fireplace. That too didn't seem to want to get going for the day. She understood all too well. But alas, she only had so much sympathy to offer before growing frustrated.

"Hi Ray-el," Parker said as Kristin opened the front door of the store and her kids trickled in one-by-one. She followed behind them with three boxes stacked on top of one another.

"Morning sweeties," she said to the kids as they passed her on their way to the Children's Nook. "Still managed to make some goodies?"

"Of course," Kristin said as she crossed the store and set the boxes down in the bakery. "Muffins, sweet rolls and more Babka."

"Sounds delicious. I see the kids survived the weekend with your mom."

"They had a great time. They're so excited to go back this weekend, too. Even Park."

Rachel nodded, impressed. "That's good news."

"Speaking of news, I've got some of my own."

Kristin flipped on the lights in the kitchen and under the display counter. Gently she pulled the treats from the boxes and set them in the display.

"Matt quit his job."

"He what?" Kristin looked up abruptly from her task. "Does that mean he's…" She let her sentence trail off when she saw the affirming nod of Rachel's head. "Oh no."

"Twelve years ago, I would have done anything to make this happen. And now I'd to anything to keep this from happening. How selfish am I? Please don't really answer that."

"Rach," Kristin said with a sigh. "I know this sucks, yeah. But really, this doesn't have anything to do with you. I mean, it affects you, indirectly, but think of all the good this could do for Aspen."

"I know. I know. I'm an awful person for thinking it. I'm an awful mother, too." She buried her face in her hands, ashamed of herself.

"You're not awful. He's put you through a lot. He's put you both through a lot. You have every right to feel this way. But just think, he doesn't hold all the cards anymore. He doesn't get to just bat his eyes and make you go weak in the knees. You've moved on. So what if he moved back. That ship has sailed," Kristin said.

Between the tears gathering in her eyes Rachel blurted out a laugh. "You just compared me to a ship?"

"It's a legitimate metaphor."

They both began to laugh at the ridiculous comparison.

"Okay, yeah, it's kind of lousy now that I think about it," Kristin said. "This doesn't have to change that much. You don't have to let it."

Rachel nodded. "I hope you're right," she said. She took in a deep breath and glanced at the time. "I've got to turn on my register. We open in a few minutes."

"It's finally warming up in here."

Fifteen minutes later and the store was open. A few people stepped inside from the brisk morning to start their day off with coffee. As Rachel sat in her office she heard the thud overhead of Aspen getting out of bed for the morning. At least she knew one of them was having no problems getting up. She heard the front doorbell chime, indicating another customer. She peeked her head out the doorway and saw Matt headed toward the bakery counter.

"Look what that cat dragged in," she heard Kristin say.

Rachel smiled to herself as she finalized the orders she was placing and then headed out of her office.

"You have more attitude than I ever remember," Matt said to her as he approached the counter. "Can I have a regular coffee? Medium," he said laying a five on the counter.

"What brings you in so early?" Rachel asked as she approached from the side.

"Thought I'd bring Aspen to school. If that's all right with you, of course," he said.

"I'm sure she'd prefer that over the bus. Be my guest."

"Wow," he said.

"Wow what?"

"You can talk to me without being hostile."

She sighed. "Sorry. I'm just shocked and a little confused to see you here. Back in Lake Arrowhead."

"Do you have a minute to talk? I mean, I know you don't take personal calls at work, but maybe you can make an exception and have a personal conversation," he said eyeing Kristin from the corner of his eye.

"Mark will be here any minute, I'll grab you if I need back up," Kristin said, nervousness in her eyes.

Rachel led the way to her office and they each took a seat.

"I didn't come here to fight with you, Rach," he said. He took the defensive tone out of his voice.

"I don't understand what you came here for, though. Why are you suddenly moving back here after all these years?"

"I guess maybe I took your advice. I decided to listen to you."

"That would be a first."

He smiled. "Kind of is, huh?"

She smiled back.

"I know you've been saying since day one to get my act together. I've got a family and responsibilities and those responsibilities extend beyond mailing a check once a month."

"Yeah," she said with a nod. "Yeah, they do."

"And I know I'm probably twelve years too late, but I hope it's better late than never. I'm here. And I'm ready to stand up and fight for my family. You and Aspen are my family, Rach, and somehow I'm going to make this all work."

Rachel took a deep breath. "Matt, I'm so glad to hear that you want to step up. And you're right, Aspen is your family. But I'm not. I never have been. There was a time when there was a possibility of that, but you left, and I never became that person. And I'm not her today."

"What are you talking about? You're my Rachel. You're my daughter's mother. You will always be my family."

She shook her head. "I will always be Aspen's mother. And our history will never change, but I'm not your family. And you should probably know that I'm with someone."

"It's that guy from last night, isn't it? That silent, broody, *I-live-in-the-boathouse* guy. No wonder he was so arrogant. I'm sitting there like some ignorant, blind idiot and he's all, 'Florida is too humid for me.' What the hell is this, Rachel? Joke's on Matt?"

"It is not like that. Would you please sit down?" she said.

"No. I won't sit down. In fact, I'm out of here. Where's Aspen? She and I are out of here. I'm taking her to school. You and hunky doesn't-like-Florida can chum it up or do whatever after we're gone," he said, storming out of her office.

Rachel felt eyes on her from the few customers that were in the bookstore that early in the morning. She willed her pounding heart to slow down and within thirty seconds Kristin was at her doorway, pushing her back into her office and closing the door.

"Very quietly, let it out," she said as Rachel began pacing the small space behind her desk. It was only big enough to allow two steps in one direction before needing to turn and go the opposite direction.

Her fists were balled tightly as she punched the air down by her hips and she grunted quietly to herself. "Is Mark here?"

"Yes, he's got things under control out there."

ELEVEN

The week went by in a blur. Rachel and Matt avoided each other, both with equal measure. Rachel was swamped in the three days the store was open. She was incredibly glad she was spending Thanksgiving at Tiff and Jake's and didn't need to be preparing for that as well. Getting the store ready for Black Friday was enough to make her hair turn gray. Kristin's as well.

Every year they went a little bigger than that year before, but they were both in agreement that this year they overdid it. Rachel was hoping this wasn't indicative of their future events.

By closing on Wednesday, she wasn't feeling confident, but rather very nervous for their re-open on Friday morning. Fortunately, she had a day in between to distract herself.

"Mom," Aspen said coming from her bedroom, "Grandma Linda is making me feel guilty that I'm not coming to her house tomorrow for Thanksgiving. I told her that I've had plans to go to Tiff and Jake's for months now."

"Yeah. And that's where you'll be."

"She says they're not even family."

"Well, I'm your mother and you'll be with me. That's about as family as it gets. Besides, my parents will be there, so will your uncle Ben, Aunt Miranda, and the girls. They're family, too. Just because your dad showed up in town last weekend doesn't mean everyone's plans change. Besides, I've got it written by the court that you're with me."

"Well, can't you tell them that? It sounds better when you say it."

"Sure. I'd be happy to tell Grandma Linda that you're staying with me. Hand me the phone," Rachel said, reaching out her palm to accept the phone.

"Never mind. I don't think we should make enemies."

Rachel laughed as Aspen disappeared back into her bedroom.

There was a knock on the door and Rachel eagerly went to answer it. She smiled when she saw Ethan standing on the other side of her door.

"So glad to have you back after your three days at work," she said as she wrapped her arms around him and pulled him into her.

"I think she's mad at me," Aspen said coming out of her bedroom, a depressed look on her face. "Which I don't understand. It's not like I get to make the decision for myself anyway. She should be mad at you."

"She's using you as a pawn. By making you feel guilty, she's hoping I will feel bad, thus, letting you join their Thanksgiving."

"But you're cold hearted."

Rachel nodded her head.

Long after Aspen had gone to bed, Rachel and Ethan sat in the darkness in the living room, nursing a bottle of red wine. She had told him briefly of her encounter with Matt on Monday over the telephone, but since he was at the fire station, she hadn't gone into depth. She filled him in on the details she had left out then.

"And you haven't spoken to him since then?" he asked.

"Other than hello or good-bye when he picks up Aspen and drops her off, no. And I try to stay busy at work around those times to avoid even that."

"His pride's hurt. He basically told you he still loved you, you rejected him and then said you were with someone else."

"That is not what happened," she said defensively.

"Sure, it is."

"No, it's not."

"Then what do you think happened? Why do you think he got so mad?" he asked.

"Because we weren't forthright with who you really were when he was here."

Ethan nodded. "Yeah, that probably doesn't help. But that's not all of it. He came back here thinking he was going to get his family. Think about it. This whole time you haven't had any serious relationships. In his head he's thinking that you've been waiting for him. Not to mention that occasionally as he's shown up over the years things have happened between you guys. So, to his chagrin, things didn't play out the way he was expecting them to. Now, clearly, I'm not complaining. I'm just saying that's why he's pissed."

"Whatever. I disagree. If he had still felt that way about me, he wouldn't have left in the first place. Now can we please change the subject?"

"Happily," he said, setting down his glass of wine. "I was hoping for a conversation with a little less talking." He grabbed the fabric near the neck of her shirt and guided her toward him.

"You know," she said as she took breaths of air between kisses, "I know…of a…a better…and safer…place to do…this."

His hands slid beneath her butt and he hoisted her up, her legs straddling his hips as he carried her across the living room to her bedroom.

Rachel woke Thanksgiving morning to an empty bed. Her outstretched hand patted a vacant spot beside her and when she realized it wasn't going to find anyone, she opened her eyes and sat up. Looking around her room, Ethan was nowhere to be found.

She slipped out of bed and glancing into the living room, she spotted his foot sticking up above the back of her sofa. Then it came back to her. He must have moved from her bed to the couch in the middle of the night so Aspen wouldn't find him in her room. She exhaled and collapsed her body against her door frame as she watched him. The blanket was barely covering his body, with most of it piled on the floor; his mouth was hanging open and all his dark hair was tousled, sticking up in every which direction. She smiled.

Aspen opened her bedroom door and headed for the bathroom. Glancing into the living room, she saw Ethan. "That looks uncomfortable," she said with a contorted look on her face.

At the sound of her voice, Ethan stirred. His eyes fluttered open, and he saw Rachel standing in the doorway of her room. "Morning," he said as he rubbed his eyes and sat up.

Aspen disappeared into the bathroom.

"What time are we leaving for Tiff and Jake's?"

Rachel glanced over her shoulder at the clock on her nightstand. "Probably not for an hour or so. When we're all ready."

"Can I hop in your shower?"

"Absolutely," she said.

He stood up from the couch and walked toward her. "Want to join me?" he whispered in her ear.

She laughed. "Badly. Now get in there before the temptation is too much to handle."

◆ ◆ ◆

An hour and twenty minutes later, the three of them were in the car and driving down the road for their Thanksgiving Day at Tiff's house.

"Where're we headed?" Ethan asked as he glanced out the passenger window at the trees as they whirred by.

"Cedar Glen," Rachel said, turning the car sharply around a bend. She loved living in the mountains.

"They don't live right on the lake?"

"Nope. They live just outside of town."

"In, like, the nicest house ever," Aspen added from the backseat.

Rachel rolled her eyes. "Far from it," she said, glancing into her rearview mirror. "But it is nice," she said looking over at Ethan.

They drove for a few minutes in quiet, enjoying the beautiful scenery around them. Ethan cracked his window to let in some fresh air. It was a warm Thanksgiving Day, almost sixty degrees.

Rachel slowed her speed as they drove through the quaint town of Cedar Glen and Aspen pointed out the Malt Shop to Ethan as they passed it. "It's my fave," she said.

"I haven't met Tiff's husband, right?" Ethan asked.

Rachel shook her head. "No, I don't think so. Let's see here. Jake is a military veteran. Air Force. He was honorably discharged after an IED explosion in Iraq, and he had to have his spine stabilized. Since then, he doesn't really work, except he loves to do woodworking, so he does custom stuff from home and sells it and makes some money on the side of what Tiff does."

"And Tiff is a realtor?"

"She owns North Shore Realty."

"Don't they do all the high-end property sales around here?"

Rachel nodded her head. "They sure do."

"All right then."

As they approached the house, Aspen eagerly pointed out which one was Tiff's to Ethan. He looked around to the new and open development around him. It wasn't what he had pictured and seemed out of place to him, so high in the mountains. It was unlike most of the other areas around there.

"Was this a burn scar?" he asked Rachel as she parallel parked the car along the road.

She nodded her head. "Yup. The vegetation has really filled in during the last few years."

"If this is Cedar Glen, was this from the infamous Old Fire?"

As a fireman, he clearly knew his stuff.

Again, she nodded. "Jake and Tiff were lucky, they only lost their shed and garage. For some reason the house was spared. From the flames, at least. There was still enough damage from the smoke and stuff though. Then they built this house."

As Ethan stepped out of the car he looked up at the house. "You've got to be kidding me. Rach, it's got turrets."

She laughed. "They're not really turrets."

"Then what would you call them?"

She shrugged her shoulders. "Well, I don't know. I don't know all the words. Bay windows that extend to all the floors?"

"And create separate peaks of their own?"

"Just come inside," she said grabbing his hand.

At the door, Tiff greeted them with a happy smile and a glass of wine in her hand. "Come in, come in! I'm so happy you're here. We have so much food. Nora will take your bags and things and Javier will get you anything you want to drink. All the food is in the kitchen, please help yourselves to whatever. Oh, and let me grab Jake. He's on the deck."

"Javier?" he asked, leaning into Rachel.

"The bartender," she whispered. "It's a holiday thing."

Tiff returned with a very tall, dark-haired man with a matching goatee in tow. "Jake, meet Ethan."

"Hey man, what's up? Welcome to our chaotic Thanksgiving. Have a drink, it makes it easier."

Both guys laughed as they shook hands.

"What do you drink?" Jake asked.

"Ahh, what have you got?" Ethan asked.

"You drink scotch?"

"Sure, I'll drink a scotch. On the rocks."

Jake gave him a nod. "Javier, get the man a Buchanan's Red Seal scotch on the rocks." He gave Ethan a pat on the shoulder. "We'll get you feeling good here in a sec and then I'll take you out back and show you my nice twenty-eight-pound turkey I've got in the smoker."

"You've got a twenty-eight-pound turkey in a smoker?"

Jake nodded proudly. "I sure do. Tiff didn't think I could do it. Had to prove her wrong."

"Yeah well, we haven't eaten it yet," she said as she walked past.

"So if we're supposed to eat around one this afternoon, when did you start smoking that thing?" Ethan asked.

"I put it on about five last night," Jake said proudly.

Javier handed Ethan his drink. "Oh, thank you," he said.

"All right, let's head outside. Tiff, send Ben out when he gets here," he called over his shoulder.

Rachel took a drink of wine as she sat down in an oversized chair near the front windows. The sun shining in was warm on her skin. Somewhere else in the house she could hear Aspen playing with the children; their squeals of delight brought a smile to her face as Tiff sat down beside her.

"What're you thinking about?" she asked.

Rachel sighed. "How nice it is to be here." She looked around at the busy room. Tiff's family was here: her mother and her boyfriend, her dad and stepmother, her brother and his wife. Rachel was sure their three boys and daughter were somewhere around the house, too. Her brother was talking with the husbands of Tiff's two sisters who were both with newborns in the other room, their other children also running around the house. The only people missing from the chaos were her family. But the knock on the door suggested that was about to change.

Rachel followed Tiff to the front door. She smiled when she saw her family on the other side. Her nieces looked so much bigger than the last time she had seen them, which was only been a few months ago.

Ben set Emma down, who was now able to stand on her own, but was reluctant to enter the house. Her sisters, Riley and Chloe, were far more eager, and ran in without inhibition.

"Take your shoes off," Joseph, Rachel's dad, yelled from behind them.

Miranda picked up Emma and carried her into the house. Everyone took turns hugging, excited to see one another.

"Sorry we're late," Jenn whispered to Rachel. "Thanksgiving Day traffic was a nightmare on the 210."

"It's no problem," she said.

"Mrs. Taylor," Javier said with a smile as he handed Jenn a Merlot.

"Oh Javier, you are too much. Every year you remember. You're such a dream," she said with her best smile.

He blushed and smiled back before asking the others what they would like.

"Cognac," Joseph said firmly as he slipped out of his blazer and handed it to Nora.

The doors from the back deck opened and Jake stepped inside with Ethan. "Hey, you made it," Jake said when he saw the rest of his guests had arrived.

"And this must be the new guy my wife keeps telling me about," Joseph said, looking over at Ethan.

"Ethan Kuhn," he said, stretching his hand out to shake Joseph's.

"Ethan, this is my dad, Joseph," Rachel said, stepping up beside him. She eyed her dad carefully, reminding him to be on his best behavior.

After a moment he shook Ethan's hand. "You can call me Joe. Nice to meet you. Where's that cognac?" he asked looking around for Javier.

"Right here, sir," Javier said quickly, stepping up immediately beside him and handing him his drink.

"Thanks kid." He took the drink and took a swig. "All right. Where's Jake. Jake? Let's go see what you're smoking up this year. Come on Ben. You, too Ethan," he said with a wave of his hand. "Where's Hank and Pete?" he asked, looking for Tiff's dad and her mom's boyfriend.

"Tiff, could you have any more people in your house?" Miranda asked as she looked around, Emma on her hip, her other two girls off running around with the other children.

"There's a reason we hired a bartender. And it had nothing to do with all of you," she replied.

"Speaking of which," Rachel said, "your glass is empty. Let me get you a refill."

A moment later, Rachel was back with a fresh glass of wine for each of them.

"Where are Kristin and Darren? And how about AJ? What are they all up to today?" Jenn asked.

"Kristin and her family are in Malibu at Susie's place. They're leaving the kids there for the big sale tomorrow and AJ is in Carlsbad with a guy she's been seeing. It's where he lives."

"Really?" Jenn asked, her eyes widening. "That's terrific. What's he like?"

"Dreamy," Tiff said.

Rachel nodded. "A little bit, yeah."

"I bet they spend all weekend in bed," Tiff said.

"I would if I could," Rachel said with a laugh.

"Really?" Jenn said, turning to face her daughter.

"Uh," she said. She handed her glass to Tiff. "Suddenly I've got to use the bathroom. I'll be back." She walked away from them quickly and rounded the corner toward the bathroom. From the corner of her eye, she could see the guys through a back window ,and she paused to watch them. Whatever they were doing, it looked like they were enjoying themselves. And just like that day she watched Ethan and Darren together, Ethan once again seemed like a natural fit with this crowd. A warm sensation came over her as she watched them for a few more seconds, a smile on her face. Ethan seemed completely comfortable with both her brother and her dad. But when Tiff's brother and brothers-in-law joined the rest of the group outside, Rachel moved on, as to not be seen watching them.

By the time the giant turkey was ready to be carved, everyone had made their way downstairs. The pool table, leather sectional sofa, and ping pong table had been taken out of the great room for the day and in their places were large tables pushed together and covered to make one enormous table with thirty chairs surrounding it. Two large cornucopias filled with flowers, squash, gourds, and pumpkins served as centerpieces on the tables and the rich array of food was strategically spread around them. Glorious aromas, the sweetness of the yams and cranberries and the spices from the stuffing and pumpkin pies, wafted through the room. Each family grouped together so they could sit near one another and then, with Jake making the first carve of the meal, they indulged in their giant feast.

"So, my sister told me what you've been up to these days," Joe said, looking over Aspen to Rachel as he shoved a piece of dark meat into his mouth.

"You mean about Grandpa?" she asked.

He nodded. "What's wrong with just leaving things the way they are?" His mouth was a straight line.

"I don't see what's wrong with wanting to know where he comes from. We don't know anything about him," she said.

"If my dad wanted us to know those things, he would've told us," he said sternly. He took a bite of stuffing.

"I don't know Dad," Ben said, stepping in. "I agree with Rach. It would be nice to know. Why did it have to be some big secret anyway?"

"That was Dad's business. Not yours."

Everyone else around the table fell silent as they exchanged coy glances with each other.

"Joe, leave them alone," Jenn finally said.

"It's not like I've found anything anyways," Rachel said, feeling defensive.

"There's nothing to find," Joe said flatly.

"I'm not surprised," said Ben. "Remember what some of those rooms looked like when you took over the house? There was so much junk. We didn't know what we were looking at."

"Oh yeah," Jenn said with a nod.

"We went through everything though. There wasn't anything in that to provide any hints into Grandpa's past," Rachel said. Suddenly she didn't have much of an appetite left. She felt Ethan's hand slip onto the top of her thigh from under the table. He gave her a gentle squeeze to let her know he was there for her. She smiled at him.

"If my dad wanted you guys to know all this stuff, he would've told you. End of discussion."

"Oh come on, you don't think it's at all strange that you never knew your grandparents? Not even their names?" Ben asked his dad.

Joe shook his head. "No. I asked once as a child and my dad said that they had died a long time ago. Since they were dead, he said there was no point in talking about them. End of story."

"And that was that?" Rachel asked.

"Yes, that was that," he said matter-of-factly. "Why do you all think you need to know where you come from these days? What's the big deal? England, Estonia, Zimbabwe, Russia, South Korea… we're all just people. Now, I said end of discussion."

Rachel sighed. There was no point in getting into an argument over it and he clearly wasn't going to see their point in one afternoon. She decided to drop the subject. Looking around the table, she saw the tension their dispute had created and suddenly she felt guilty. She knew she had to make this up to Tiff.

"Who has plans to Black Friday shop?" she asked the rest of the group.

Most of the women responded with yes. The men all scowled with disgust, and she couldn't help but laugh. "Where is everyone going? Tiff, I assume you're headed to Orange County?"

She sighed. "Last year traffic almost killed me. So I think this year, I'll stay local."

Jake let out a loud laugh that no one in the room could miss.

"Okay, relatively local. Probably Ontario Mills," she said.

"That's where I'm headed," Miranda said. "We should meet up."

"Absolutely. I'm headed out early. Probably around 2 A.M."

"Perfect."

"They're all crazy," Ben said, and Jake nodded in agreement.

It didn't take long for everyone to forget the argument and then it was time for dessert. Kristin, despite her absence, had still thought of everyone and baked for their Thanksgiving dessert. There were mouthwatering homemade pumpkin pies, a triple-layer chocolate pumpkin pie, a pumpkin roll, two succulent pear frangipane tarts, and then there was Darren's favorite, a cranberry upside-down cake.

By the end of the meal, no one could move. They had stuffed every limb to its fullest. Ethan turned his head toward Rachel. "That was the best meal I think I've ever had," he said.

"I concur."

Nora came and collected the dessert dishes that sat in front of everyone and the only people who had it in them to move were the children. Javier reappeared to top off any drinks, but there were few takers. The adults sat around the table in a Thanksgiving Day stupor until slowly, beginning first with Marcy, Tiff's mother, they began to thank Tiff and Jake for being such incredible hosts.

Tiff's dad Hank slowly rose to his feet. "Pete, Joe, any of you other gentlemen care to join me out back for a cigar?"

Joe wasn't going to miss out on that and got up from that table with surprising speed. Ben, Tiff's brother, and one of her brothers-in-law joined as well, but Jake and Ethan, as well as Tiff's sister's husband, Brian, all stayed at the table.

"You know," said Ethan, leaning closer to Rachel, "Darren had mentioned something that day we were decorating the store for Christmas. About a trunk in your attic."

"What about it?" she asked.

"Think about it. It's not yours. And it's old and hidden in some corner you didn't even know was there. Who knows how long it's been there. What if it was Aaron's? Might be worth taking a look, at least. Don't you think?"

Rachel thought about that for a moment. She couldn't believe she hadn't considered that. *Why hadn't she?* "Yeah, definitely. When we get back, we'll go up there."

There was silence between them.

"Wow," she said. "Now I'm excited. I kind of want to leave right now."

"I'm sure that would go over really well with your dad."

She raised her eyebrows and gave him a knowing nod with a laugh.

As the afternoon passed, the group migrated out of the house into the beautiful afternoon weather. With winter fast approaching in the mountains, days like this would be few and far between and they took the time to enjoy it. The trees that weren't pines, the maples and oaks and the wild brush, were in the middle of changing colors. They were full of fierce shades of orange, yellow and reds outside of their usual seasonal colors.

The kids laughed and chased one another down the hillside. Fortunately, Tiff's yard wasn't as steep as many around it were, and the turf lawn was so green and inviting that the children couldn't help but run around on it.

Rachel tried to stay as invested in their conversations as possible, but she was distracted. She kept imagining what she might find buried in the trunk in her attic back home. Letters to the family revealing some deep dark past. Millions of dollars or investments that meant nothing back then but would be life changing today.

Ethan would gently tap the underside of her palm to remind her to step back out of the attic and back onto the deck in Cedar Glen.

Rachel felt relieved when nightfall came. The cooler temperatures drove people inside and also reminded them of the time. Everyone began gathering their things and their children to head back home.

"Don't worry about your dad," Jenn said to Rachel as they gathered near the door.

"If I do find anything, I won't be saying anything to him."

"I think he's scared. It's weird and he knows it. He just doesn't want to admit that he's wrong. He's stubborn. Where he got that from is anyone's guess," she said with a flick of her eyebrows.

Rachel gave her a half smile. "I'll keep you posted. Thanks Mom."

Twenty minutes later and everyone was cleared out of Tiff's house with the exception of Rachel, Ethan and Aspen.

"Want Aspen to stay here tonight with your sale tomorrow? She can come shopping with me in the morning." Tiff said.

"Oh can I?" Aspen chimed in without hesitation.

Rachel sighed. "You don't have any clothes here."

"I can give her something to sleep in and we'll swing by before we head down the mountain in the morning and she can grab something to wear."

"Whatever," Rachel said with a shrug. "If that's what you want to do."

Aspen was nodding her head before she had gotten her sentence out.

"Don't bug Tiff about buying things for you. It's not her job," she said, eyeing Tiff more than Aspen.

"Oh stop it," Tiff said with the wave of her hand.

Another few minutes later, after their goodbyes, Rachel and Ethan were on their way back to Lake Arrowhead Village.

"That may have been the craziest Thanksgiving I've ever been to," he admitted as they pulled away from the house.

She laughed. "It does get pretty chaotic with that many people," she agreed.

They took their time winding their way home. It looked darker than it was, the tall pine trees blocking the last daytime remnants of sunlight. Tiff didn't mind. The drive was peaceful. She cracked her window and the let cool air flood the car, along with the scent of pine. All too early in the morning, more chaos would come into her life: Black Friday chaos. She took a deep breath and felt Ethan slip his hand into hers.

"I'm glad you brought me, today," he said, interrupting her thoughts.

She glanced over at him. "Yeah? I thought it was crazy?"

"Oh, it was. But I'm still glad I was there. And that I got to meet your family."

"And witness my dad's outburst at dinner?"

"I agree that was awkward, but I figure it wouldn't be a true family event without something like that, now would it? I mean, my family inevitably has something dramatic happen."

She laughed. "Touché."

When they arrived back at the house, a knot began to form in Rachel's stomach. She thought about the trunk hidden up in the attic. Suddenly, despite all her daydreaming, she decided not to get her hopes up. What if it was just like everything else in the journey, simply another dead end?

Ethan went back to the boathouse, and she went to the apartment, each to change, and they met ten minutes later in her living room. To say she was nervous was an understatement and she couldn't even understand why. It was a trunk.

Rachel opened the door to the attic. It stuck a little, per usual, and she gave it an extra hard pull. They headed up the narrow stairs. Only part of the attic was accessible like a regular room. The other half was more like a crawl space and it didn't have a floor, just exposed beams and the ceiling from the rooms below. Rachel stayed away from that side of the attic out of the fear of falling off a beam or dropping something and going through the ceiling below. That was a mess she didn't want on her hands. She stayed in the half of the attic where she could stand up and that had a floor.

It was dark and dingy, like most attics. There was a layer of dust nearly an inch thick that covered everything, except where Ethan and Darren had walked to come retrieve the Christmas decorations the week before. Their footprints were nicely preserved marks on the floor.

"He said it was where the exposed beams are," she said with a nod to where the ceiling dropped low, and they had to squat to avoid hitting their heads. She led the way and braced herself with the ceiling above her.

Slowly, she took one step at a time on the narrow beam, treating it like a tapered balance beam. When she started to wobble, she stopped to steady herself, Ethan helping from behind, before moving forward again. When she breathed, she could feel the dust in the air, and she coughed.

"I think my attic could use a good cleaning."

"It's an attic," he said.

She kept walking, Ethan right behind her. Soon she reached the back wall. She stuck her right foot out to another beam for extra balance and turned her head left and right and then she saw what Darren had been talking.

It looked as though a small wall had been removed long ago, and the insulation pulled out from behind it. It created an L-shape that ran along the back side of the house that wasn't discernable from the rest of the attic. It was dark back there, very dark, but even from where she hunched over, Rachel could make out the shape of something: something large and bulky.

Keeping her balance with the wall, she used the beams like steppingstones, and one step at a time, she made her way across the crawlspace toward the darkened alcove. She pulled out her flashlight, and to her chagrin, saw that it was filled with spider webs. But Darren was right, it was unmistakably a trunk.

"Look at that," Ethan said from beside her. He looked around them and grabbed a loose board on the wall. With a slight tug it broke free, and he used it to clear the cobwebs. Rachel lit up the alcove as he stepped in the small chamber-like area toward the trunk that nearly took up the entire space. He gently brushed his hand over the top and chunks of dust, dead bugs and even flecks of the outer covering of the trunk flaked off.

Rachel distorted her face as she watched, thankful she didn't have to touch anything. Her back was beginning to ache in her hunched-over position.

"There's something inscribed on the top here, but I can't make it out," he said brushing at it and blowing at the dust. "We've got to get it out of here."

"And how do you suggest doing that?"

"You're going to have to do more than stand there and shine a light," he said.

"And by do more, you mean call Jake, right?"

He sighed. "Whatever. Tell him to bring some two by fours or some two by sixes or something. Anything, really."

Rachel nodded and headed back toward the other side of the attic, Ethan following behind her.

Within the hour, Jake had arrived with everything that Ethan had mentioned and the two set to work lying down a makeshift floor in the attic to drag the trunk out on. In the meantime, Rachel packed an overnight bag for Jake to take back to Aspen.

"That sucker's old," Jake proclaimed, stepping out of the attic behind Ethan. Both men were covered in dust.

"You got it out of that spot?" she asked.

"Yeah, but it's still up in the attic," Ethan said, dangling a piece of metal. "A handle fell off of it. We pulled it out into the open area, so that's where you'll have to go through it. I sure hope you can find something, because that thing is a beast."

Jake laughed. "No kidding."

"Thanks for doing that. Here's a bag for Aspen," she said.

"All right, well, I'm out. Take it easy," he said with a nod and then left.

Rachel looked up the stairway to the attic and took a breath. Slowly she began to climb the stairs, reminding herself not to get her hopes up. She'd been down this road before. There could be a million different things in the trunk.

Ethan followed behind her with a tube of Clorox wipes. But in the light of the attic, she could read the inscription he had mentioned before when it was in the corner. The lid of the trunk clearly read "Schneider". She wasn't sure what that meant.

Lifting the lid was like opening a time capsule. Everything before her eyes was a shade of brown or beige or in black and white. Rachel took a breath as she lifted out a photograph and immediately recognized the two people in it. It was Aaron and Elaine, on their wedding day.

Tears sprang to her eyes in an instant as she gently began to leaf through the papers. But a few papers in, and she realized something was off. Something didn't seem right. She stopped to examine them further, and then she realized what it was. She wasn't able to read anything. All of the documents in front of her were in another language.

TWELVE

Sinful Retreat's Black Friday Sale's Event went by in a haze. A haze that Rachel felt had no end. She found herself distracted and unusually impatient with some of her customers. And this was the absolute wrong day of the entire year for both of those things. Yet she couldn't get her mind out of that trunk in her attic.

She stayed up most of the night rummaging through it. Layer by layer, she tried to piece together what she was looking at, all while trying not to disrupt it too much on the off chance that there was some kind of order to it. She was able to determine some of the foreign language was German. But there was another language on some of the documents that she could not identify. It looked similar to German, but even Ethan agreed that it didn't seem to be German.

The other things she couldn't get out of her mind were the photographs. Those images seemed to be burned into her memory, and the unknown faces, the stories of the people she didn't know, haunted her while she tried to work. Who were these strangers?

"Earth to Rachel!" Mark said, waving his hand in front of her face.

It startled her and snapped her out of a trance.

"This customer is looking for some materials on Rheumatoid Arthritis. I told her we don't carry anything like that in the store," Mark said.

Rachel nodded. "He's right, we don't. I'm sorry."

"Why wouldn't you carry that? I mean, you can carry trashy romance novels and murder stories, but not this? This is real stuff," the woman complained.

"I couldn't agree more. Unfortunately, we just don't sell enough medical literature. But I'd be more than happy to order something and have it sent to the store for you. That would save you the hassle of shipping costs."

The woman still didn't look happy that she wouldn't be leaving with what she came for, but she looked slightly more satisfied. "I guess that will have to do."

"Let's step into my office and see what would be the best book for you and what you're in need of," she said, motioning toward the closed door.

The crowds had died down after lunch, which gave Kristin and Rachel and the rest of the staff a welcomed reprieve. Black Friday shoppers were always more rushed, greedy, and impatient than shoppers any other day.

Rachel was happy to see Ethan come in and signaled to Mark to help with a customer while she went to talk to him.

"What did you find?" she asked eagerly. She knew he'd been going through the trunk for her while she was working.

"Well, you were right. Some of those papers were definitely German. And I think, *I think*, some of the others are Yiddish," he said. "But that's just a guess."

"Why Yiddish?"

"Well, because I tried translating them online and I can't find anything that will translate them. They look a lot like the German documents, but they clearly have their differences. And since I can't seem to find anything to translate them, well, it leads me to think they might be Yiddish."

Rachel nodded. "That might make sense, actually. When I found out his middle name was Alter, I looked it up and found that it was Yiddish. So maybe not a coincidence?" she asked with a shrug.

"Are you saying your grandpa was Jewish?"

"I doubt it. I mean, he wasn't really into practicing any religion, but I think it would've come up. Don't you think?"

"Probably," he said. "Also, I found this." He handed her a photograph of a family at the ocean. The water stretched on forever in the background, three pilings standing strong and erect amidst the waves as seven people sat on a sandy beach. They were all in swimsuits, modest suits compared with today's. Some wore swim caps on their heads, squinted in the sun and wore solemn expressions on their faces. But still something about them said they were happy.

She turned the old photograph over in her hands and saw the delicate writing on the back:

Die familie Schneider, Juni 1935
Ostsee, Deutschland
Vater Otto und Mami Lena, Hanna 10 jahre alt, Ephraim 15 jahre alt, Isak und Rachel, Abarron 11 jahre alt

Rachel looked up. "Abarron? Is this?"

Ethan handed her another document. It was thin and yellowed and also in German. Paper-clipped to the document was a small piece of paper with a translation on it.

She took them carefully in her hands. First, she looked at the German document.

Zertifizierung der Geburt
Abarron Alter Schneider
Geboren 4. April 1924
die Eltern Isak Schneider und Rachel Schulz Schneider, Dresden Deutschland

With her eyes welling at the sight of Abarron's name, she read Ethan's translation:

Certification of Birth, Abarron Alter Schneider, born 4 April 1924 to the parents Isak Schneider and Rachel Schulz Schneider, Dresden, Germany. It continued to list a hospital and a witness, but Rachel stood mesmerized. She clasped the document in her hands as if it were gold. She was not sure why his last name had gone from Schneider to Taylor, but of one thing she was certain, this was her grandfather. The birthdays were a match.

She went back to the photograph and found Abarron, furthest to the right on the photo. He squinted the most in the sunlight, which made sense to Rachel. As an adult, he even made sure that his glasses where the photochromatic transitions so that he didn't have to bother with sunglasses when he went outside. She smiled and giggled to herself as a tear released from her eye and slid down her face.

"You okay, Rach?" Ethan asked.

"This is him," she said, a smile stretching across her face. "I don't know yet why he changed his name, but this is him." She began to laugh at the revelation. How ironic that the truth had been buried in her attic the entire time. An overwhelming relief came over her that juxtaposed the sudden weight that settled upon her as the new discovery inevitably meant she was to set forth on a new journey. She felt hesitant to take those steps and couldn't explain to even herself why she felt that way. She dismissed the ominous feeling and instead decided to rejoice in her findings. She felt closer to Aaron than she had in years.

◆◆◆

The rest of her day dragged on. But Rachel found herself in a good mood with all of her customers. She was excited about her discovery. She wanted to share it with the world. And she would have, too, if she thought any of them would have listened. When AJ came into the store near closing, she was thankful to finally tell someone. She told her and Kristin who were both very excited for her. But AJ, always the realist, cautioned her for what she might find.

"Not that I'm not excited for you, because really, I am, but there's a reason he changed his name and didn't talk about any of his past. So before you get too far in, just make sure you've prepared yourself, at least knowing that it's probably something tragic," she said.

"She's right, Rach," Kristin agreed. "Not to rain on your parade or anything."

Rachel sighed. It was true. She knew it which was why deep, deep, deep down, a part of her was terrified. But she still felt she had to know. Somehow it was her duty. "I know guys."

Matt came into the store, angry and not hiding any of it. "Where's Aspen?"

"What do you mean?"

"You were supposed to bring her to my mom's at noon today," he said.

Rachel grabbed his arm and pulled him into her office. "I don't have a clue what you're talking about."

"Oh don't give me that. Where is she?"

"Seriously, Matt, I don't know what you're talking about. She spent the night at Tiff's to go shopping with her today."

"That's just perfect, isn't it? You wouldn't let me have her on Thanksgiving, so I told her to have you drop her off today and then you can't even do that. No, it's more important that she spend the day with your friends. Are you trying to ostracize me from her life completely? What the hell is this? My mom was right, I need to go back to court and get custody since I'm back because clearly, you're not willing to work with me."

"Whoa, slow down," she said, trying to keep her voice down. "First of all, she never said anything to me about going with you for today. I had no idea. So when *she* asked to stay at Tiff's to go shopping, I had no idea there was a conflict. And no, we do not need to go back to court. Your mom needs to stay out of this. I'm sorry, but this is between you and me. And you need to stop barging into my workplace and yelling at me. I know we can have a civilized conversation; we've done it many times before. But when your mom starts dictating procedure, I get pissed. Now, if you're willing to have a conversation, without yelling, I'm willing to do that. But you're going to have to give me twenty minutes while I close down the store. And then you'll have to meet me upstairs. Can you do that?"

He took a breath. "Fine. Yes, I can do that. I'll see you up there."

Back in the store, with Matt up in her apartment, Rachel began shutting down for the night. She felt exhausted. Not just physically, but emotionally drained. In reality, she didn't want to go upstairs and deal with Matt. A small part of her didn't want to continue going through the trunk, either. She was afraid of what she was finding. Why would there be things in Yiddish in the trunk? Not that there was something to fear there, it just opened doors to something she knew nothing about.

"Are you okay?" AJ asked from a chair near the fireplace.

Rachel wasn't aware she was being watched. She looked up, trying to act nonchalant, but knowing it was too late. "I'm fine. Just tired."

"No," AJ said, rising from the chair. She walked toward Rachel at the counter. "There's more to it than that. What's going on with you? Is it this stuff with Aaron? Is everything okay with Ethan?"

"I'm fine, really," she said, looking up from a stack of papers that needed to go into her office.

"I don't believe you, but clearly you don't want to talk about it."

Rachel gave her a half smile before walking away. She set the papers down on her desk, took one look around her office and decided to finish her reconciliation reports from home. She wanted to head upstairs.

Kristin said she'd lock up the place, so Rachel said good night and disappeared up the stairway.

Matt didn't look pleased to be sitting in the company of Ethan, who clearly treated the place like his own and Matt was just a guest there. Rachel couldn't help but smile to herself as she set the computer down on the table.

"I offered him a bottle of water or something, but he didn't want anything," Ethan said. "And I've found a few more things in the trunk you might find interesting when you've got a chance," he said.

"You're the best. Have you been at this all day?" she asked as Matt sat impatiently on the couch.

"Well, that and the translation stuff," he said.

"I got thinking about the Yiddish," Rachel said. "I was good friends with someone in college named Rose. She was only in school with me for two years before she joined the military, but she was Jewish, and I know she spent all of her elementary school years for sure in a Hebrew Day school. I was thinking of emailing her. Maybe she could help me out."

Ethan nodded. "That could be helpful."

She smiled. "Anyway." She walked into the living room and sat down across from Matt. "Sorry about that."

"When is Aspen getting back?" Matt asked.

"She texted me an hour ago and said she was on her way home, so she should be here any minute," Ethan said called over his shoulder into the living room.

Rachel could see Matt's shoulders tighten.

"I'm sorry about today," she started. "I was completely unaware that you had made arrangements with her for the day, so when Tiff offered to take her and Aspen wanted to go, I didn't see the big deal. Of course, had I known you had made plans with her, I never would've agreed to it."

"Really?" he asked mockingly.

"Really. Why don't you believe me?"

"It just seems convenient is all," he said.

"I want you to have a relationship with your daughter just as much as you do. So don't give me that. The only reason I wouldn't let her spend Thanksgiving Day with you is because we already had plans. You had just shown up in town. You can't just show up on a whim and expect all of our plans to change to accommodate you."

The front door opened, and Aspen came bouncing in, a wide smile across her face. "I had the best day ever!"

"Well I sure hope it was worth standing me up for," Matt said, rising to his feet.

Aspen stopped dead in her tracks, dropping her shopping bags at her feet, her smile washing from her face in an instant.

Rachel rose to her feet. "Matt, sit back down. Aspen, come over here. We need to talk." In the background, she saw Ethan watching them as Aspen came and sat beside her.

"Dad, I totally forgot I said I would come spend the day with you and Linda—"

"You call her Grandma," he corrected her in an instant.

Rachel felt Aspen stiffen beside her.

"I am tired of trying and trying to be a good dad and it just never being enough. I just quit my damn job and moved back here for you and you still don't want to spent time with me. Hell, I find out you'll text Mr. New-Dad in the hallway back here, but you can't even pick up the phone to call me," he said with a nod of his head toward Ethan.

"That's not fair," Aspen shouted across the room to him. "You've never been around and suddenly you show up one day and in one instant you think everything is going to be different? Well, it's not. You don't even know me!"

"I'm trying to get to know you. But it's kind of hard to do that when I make plans with you and you don't show up. Like today," Matt said.

"That's enough yelling from both of you," Rachel said. "Matt, I agree with you that since you're back here, you should have more time with Aspen. And we're adults and I'm confident we can make this decision without having to go to court."

"What about me? Don't I get a say in this?" Aspen chimed in.

"Yes, you should get a say, too," Rachel agreed.

"Well, I would like to keep bringing her to school every day. And until I get things squared away with a new job, I'd also like to continue picking her up."

"I think that's fair," Rachel said.

"And I want every other weekend with her. And every Tuesday and Thursday, too."

"Done," Rachel said. She wasn't eager to give up Aspen that frequently, but she knew Matt deserved just as much time with her that she did. And she really didn't want to go to court and fight him about it. Besides, she didn't have any reason to hold her from him.

Aspen sighed loudly, crossed her arms and threw herself against the back of the loveseat. "I thought I got a say in this."

"So say something," Rachel said.

Aspen eyed her with a glare from the corner of her eye. "Whatever. It's not like it would make a difference. You guys clearly have made up your minds."

"Can I have Aspen next weekend?" he asked.

"Sure. But anything going on in her life, like prior engagements and responsibilities, still apply even, if they fall on your weekend," she said.

"Understood."

"And it might be advisable if you moved out of your mom and dad's place."

"Oh, I did. I didn't mention that?" he asked. "I'm renting a place near Running Springs. Aspy, you can decorate your room this weekend. No paint, though. Sorry kiddo."

After Matt had left and Aspen had gone to bed, Rachel sat on the dusty floor of her attic, slowly leafing through the finds in the trunk. Most of the time she didn't have a clue what she held in her hand. But one thing she was certain of, this did belong to her grandfather.

Ethan appeared with the laptop and a bottle of wine. "Figured it might be a long night," he said, sitting down beside her.

"Suddenly I wish I would've taken German in high school rather than Spanish," she said.

"I'm sure that would've done you so much good up until now," he said with a laugh. "I did find a good translation site."

"Can you look up *Ostsee*? It's on the back of so many of these beach photos."

Ethan typed it into the computer. "It's German for Baltic Sea."

"Hmm," she said, turning the photos back around in her hands to look at the faces on the front. She couldn't help but wonder about the strangers she looked at.

"Look at this," Ethan said as he opened a shallow and worn box. Inside was what appeared to be a military medal. He slowly lifted it from the cotton swaddling and laid it gently in his palm. It was a black iron cross with a wreath that circled the arms of the cross. The center bore the insignia FA and it was attached at the top to a blue ribbon with vertical red stripes along the edges.

Rachel looked over the medal in awe and curiosity. It clearly looked meritorious, but for what she was unsure. Ethan handed her the medal and she turned it over in her hands, scrutinizing its every angle. "This 1914, is this the year, you think?" she asked about the numbers on the bottom arm of the cross.

Ethan shrugged. "Could be. Let's see what Google thinks," he said, grabbing the computer and setting it on his lap. "Here we go," he said with excitement. "Germany World War I military medals," he said and clicked on a website. "This is it. It's the Friedrich-August Cross, 1914. Dang. So whoever this belonged to served on behalf of Germany in the First World War"

"And they must have done a good job," she said, gazing down at the medal. A chill ran down her spine as she realized what she was holding in her hands: an award to one of her family members for their service to Germany in World War I. The world as she had always known it suddenly didn't seem so big to her anymore. And the things she had grown up learning about in her history books didn't seem so disconnected from her at that moment.

Rachel put the medal back into its swaddling in the box and replaced the cover. In the corner of the cover, she saw the scribbling of the name Isak Schneider. Carefully she set the box aside and picked up a small pamphlet, the words *Reichsvertretung der Juden in Deutschland* boldly across the front. An ominous feeling came over Rachel and this time she took the laptop to translate it herself.

Reich Association of Jews in Germany.

Technically it meant nothing to her. But she couldn't rid the feeling in her gut.

"What's wrong?" Ethan asked.

"I'm not sure exactly. I found this," she said, showing him the pamphlet and telling him the translation. "So either my family was Jewish or they had a strong connection to Judaism. I don't think this much crossover is a coincidence anymore. Aaron was born in Germany in 1924 and this pamphlet clearly has Nazi affiliation and well, I guess I'm just feeling a little anxious about all of this. You know, the Jews, Germany, the Nazis, it's an equation that doesn't have a good outcome."

"Rach, relax. Clearly Aaron wasn't killed by any Nazis. So take a breath. We'll get this figured out."

She nodded, feeling herself calm down. It was true, he had lived to be an old man, after all. But why hadn't he told any of them that he was Jewish? Was he Jewish? Her head spun with confusion.

"It's late, let's go to bed," Ethan said.

Rachel nodded and rose to her feet. She took his hand and followed him down from the attic. Her apartment was quiet and still, and she yawned. Glancing at the clock, she was shocked to see that it was well after one. Her shoulders dropped at the thought of getting up early for work. She headed into her bedroom to get ready for bed.

A few minutes after crawling beneath her cozy blankets, Ethan slipped in behind her, his arm looping around her waist and pulling her body into his. She relaxed instantly in his warmth, and he sweetly kissed the nape of her neck.

"You shouldn't let this stuff stress you out so much," he whispered between kisses. "You can't rewrite history."

She sighed and took a loud breath, inhaling through her nose. "I know I can't."

Rachel woke to a dusting of snow on the ground. And despite the little amount of sleep she had gotten the night before, she felt well rested and was ready for work that Saturday.

Sinful Retreat had opened, and the holiday season had begun. Saturday mornings were typically slow, but not during the holidays. People were eager to do their shopping, and any place that sold coffee was always the best place to start. Although the bookstore was a little slower than the bakery, Rachel always had customers that made their way over. There was something about customers who bought coffee on the go rather than brewing it in their homes that also made them predisposed to liking books. Rachel was always in a good mood when she began her morning with sales.

AJ came into the store, a large tote hung over her shoulder and her computer tucked under one arm. She took a seat at a table, set her things down and proceeded to the counter where Rachel was standing.

"You're in here early for a Saturday. No Jack?" Rachel asked.

"He had to work this weekend and I'm getting neighbors who apparently couldn't wait to move in all their bulky, heavy furniture until later today. I couldn't sleep through the banging and pounding, not to mention all the 'it's slipping,' 'pivot,' and 'come my way,' yelling that they're doing. I hope this isn't any inclination as to what type of neighbor's they're going to be. I'm moving if that's the case," AJ said.

Rachel laughed. "Wow, you're cheery this morning."

"Whatever," she scoffed. "You lived with me in college. You know I'm not a morning person. I figured I'd come here, get some coffee and do some grading."

Rachel gave an unconvinced nod and a smile as AJ made her way toward Kristin. At that moment, the front door opened, bringing a cool draft in with it, and Tom stepped into Sinful Retreat. Rachel felt her heart drop with a lack of enthusiasm to talk to him. She instantly grabbed a stack of papers that needed to go into her office, but without Mark in the store until ten, she would be out of luck. There was no one to run the register or to help with customers.

"You're looking more beautiful than usual," he said in a particularly sly manner as he approached her.

"Is there something you need Tom? I'm kind of busy this morning." Rachel said. She noticed another customer come in from outside and head straight to a bookshelf near the fireplace. This would be her chance to escape.

"Just wanted to see you," he said, a boyish grin on his face.

"Well, you'll have to excuse me. I've got a customer," she said, slipping out from behind the counter and heading toward the woman at the bookshelf. "Morning," she said cheerfully as she approached her. "I'm Rachel, is there anything in particular you're looking for this morning?"

"Actually, yes. I'm kind of embarrassed to admit this," the woman said, a shy smile on her face. She spoke kind of quietly and looked briefly at the ground. "I have been working on establishing my family lineage, you know, where we come from, things like that, and someone mentioned a book to me, but for the life of me I can't remember the name of it."

"How funny, I've been working on the exact same thing," Rachel said.

"You have? Oh what a relief. So many people think it's kind of strange. But I've thought it's been such a fascinating journey," the woman said.

"I couldn't agree more. This book you're looking for, do you know anything about it?" Rachel asked.

"Something about a mother, maybe? Does that sound familiar?" The woman's face contorted.

"*My Mother's Mother*?"

"Yes! That's the one! How did you know that?"

Rachel laughed. "I've been doing this for a long time. I've got that one right over here," she said, waving the woman over as she led the way across the store. Rachel pulled the book off the shelf and handed it to her. "Have you had much luck in your search?" she asked.

"Some. I've really just begun. My neighbor told me about this book. She said it would really inspire me to keep searching, even through the dry spells that I'll inevitably encounter."

Rachel nodded. "It's true."

"And how about your search?" the woman asked as she clutched the new book in her hands with eagerness.

"Well, let's just say that if I could read German, I'd be much better off," she said with a laugh.

"German? I'm a German Linguistics Professor at USC," she said, her face lighting up.

"Are you kidding me?" Rachel asked, feeling dumbfounded.

The woman laughed. "I'm not. I'm staying at my friend's cabin for the weekend. Dana Albrecht," she said as she thrust her free hand out to Rachel who took it enthusiastically. "If you want some help, I would be more than willing to translate for you."

Rachel felt overwhelmed. She couldn't help but feel like this woman was a gift to her. Like fate had known she would need her and dropped her off at her door that very morning. "I don't even know where to begin to… are you kidding me? Are you really willing to…"

Dana laughed. "Absolutely. I don't really have much planned while I'm up here. I mean, I'm not a hiker or anything like that. I was going to walk around the village today. But maybe after you're done working, we could get together."

Rachel began nodding her head profusely. "Yes, that would be incredible. I would love that," she said, a smile so wide she was sure all of her teeth were showing.

"Well, how about we go ring up the book," Dana said, partly laughing at Rachel.

Still nodding her head, Rachel walked to the counter. She rang up the book, giving the woman a discount on her purchase. "I live just upstairs. And I'm done at two."

"Perfect. I'll just meet you back here," Dana said.

Rachel couldn't contain her excitement after Dana left the store. She blew Tom off completely, who had waited for her at the register, and headed directly over to AJ at her table.

"You are never going to believe what just happened," she gasped as she sat down. Rachel unloaded everything in two breaths.

"Whoa. Umm, first of all, breathe," AJ instructed. "That's great, but you're never going to make it until two o'clock if you stop breathing before then. And secondly, wow. Are you kidding me? What are the chances that this even happens?"

"I know, right?"

The rest of Rachel's day dragged on minute by minute. Tom was like a pesky fly that she couldn't shake. He didn't seem to want anything other than to hang around and simply annoy her. She was thankful when Mark came in, but she couldn't hide in her office for long bouts of time because there were too many customers to tend to. Tom had nothing better to do than read at an empty table or chair until Rach had surfaced from her office again.

Ethan was running errands and helping a friend of his that also worked at the fire station move. He stopped in around lunch time and Rachel was relieved to see him. She enthusiastically shared her news about Professor Albrecht. Tom, on the other hand, wasn't thrilled to see that Rachel was clearly involved with someone. He even had the audacity to corner Ethan as he was leaving the store to ask him about his relationship with her.

Embarrassed, Rachel intervened and explained to Tom, yet again, that she was not interested in dating him. She didn't understand his genuine shock when she introduced Ethan as the man she was seeing. She was thankful when he finally left.

Shortly after one, AJ packed up her things and vacated Sinful Retreat. Rachel stepped into her office to finish up some last-minute Rapid Response Ordering before Dana came back.

Finally, when two o'clock came, Rachel was relieved to leave for the day. And right on time, Dana came waltzing through the front door of Sinful Retreat, as promised.

"This is quite the quaint little village up here. I really enjoy it," Dana said, kicking the water from the melted snow off her boots. The dusting of snow that had come during the night had long since melted in the sun.

"I couldn't agree more. Follow me upstairs," she said. With Ethan gone and Aspen with her friends for the day, it would just be the two of them and Rachel was eager to see what Dana would have to say about the things in Aaron's trunk. She briefly gave her an overview of what the situation was and how she had found the trunk. Dana seemed genuinely interested.

"Looks like you've made good progress up until now," she said.

"My problem," Rachel said, hesitant to admit to Dana because of her collegiate status, "is even what I can translate, thanks to almighty Google, I still don't have much frame of reference for. Take for example, this," she said, grabbing the pamphlet she had translated late the previous night.

Dana took it into her hands. "The direct translation of this is Reich Association of Jews in Germany."

"Right. I actually managed to figure that much out on my own. But like I said, I have no frame of reference for it. What is it, exactly?"

Dana nodded toward the couch in the living room. "Come sit," she said. "Not to give you an extensive history lesson here, but when the Nazi's took power in Germany in 1933, the Jewish community banded together and established organizations. Now, I don't know lots about them, my area of study doesn't focus on that. However, I can tell you that one of them was this organization here," she said, holding up the pamphlet, " the *Reichsvertretung der Juden in Deutschland.* It was essentially a representation, nationally, of the German Jews."

"What was its purpose?" Rachel asked.

Dana shrugged. "Most likely to address important national issues at the time. No one could anticipate what was to come, or at that point in the early thirties, perceive the Nazis' uncompromisingly anti-Semitic sentiment and the pogroms that would stem from it. So organizations such as this one would most likely address Jewish needs like education, welfare and possibly even emigration assistance."

"Okay, you probably can't answer this, but why would someone have this pamphlet then? Would that mean they're Jewish?"

"It's probable. Or they have some ties to the Jewish community. Either way, they would've recognized at the time that the Jewish community would have been in need of assistance. But it is most likely that they would be Jewish since this was at the very beginning of the Nazi regime. The Third Reich hadn't had the chance to put into place a ton of what was to come. For the outside community, there wouldn't have been a large understanding that there was a need to protect much of anything at that point," Dana said bluntly.

Rachel sat silently while she digested what the woman had just said to her. She took the pamphlet back into her hands and read the words across the front once again. That's when she spotted a small stack of papers on her coffee table with a note attached to the top in Ethan's handwriting.

Rach,
Found these. I think they'll be helpful.
E

Below the folded sheet of paper was the faded blue cover and binding of a passport. She opened it to see the black and white photo of a boy's face looking back at her. The name beside it read: Abarron Alter Schneider. Her eyes reverted back to the photo. She stared at it for a moment and suddenly she saw them: the same eyes she had known her whole life. There they were in that small and foreign booklet, youthful and looking up at her. She took a breath.

"It's his passport," she mumbled under her breath. How had she missed this?

"May I see it?" Dana asked quietly, almost as though she were trying to not interrupt Rachel's thoughts.

She handed her the small booklet and Dana carefully leafed through it. "The decree requiring all Jewish passports to be stamped with a J was passed in 1938, so he emigrated before then, he wasn't Jewish, or somehow, he managed to evade the law and avoided it. Do you know when he left Germany?"

Rachel shook her head as Dana continued to page through the passport.

"Well, it looks here, like he left Berlin on a train for Paris on Monday, September 30th, 1935. He departed three days later on October 3rd from Le Havre, France, aboard the *Rochester* and arrived in New York City a week later. Look here," she said, showing Rachel the pages in the passport that would indicate Abarron's travel dates.

She took the passport back and looked at them. She flipped between the pages Dana held her fingers between. Finally, she found something in English, Abarron's arrival in the United States, marked and stamped October 10, 1935.

For a moment she stopped breathing altogether as she stared down at the date. It was the date that forever changed the course of history for her family. Because of that one day, everything was different for Abarron and thus giving her father Joe, Abarron's son, and herself, a completely different life than Rachel imagined her grandfather once had.

Her eyes welled with tears as the numbers before her eyes began to blur.

"Rachel, are you okay?" Dana asked.

She nodded slightly and a tear came loose and ran down her cheek, stinging along her skin as it slid down her face. She looked up, overwhelmed with emotion. "I never knew about any of this. None of us did. He never told anyone."

"It's been my experience over the years," Dana said, lowering her voice and speaking softly, "that many people didn't talk about the things the war took from them."

"I don't get it, though," she said shaking her head and biting back her tears. "He was just a boy. He was eleven years old. He couldn't have come alone. He would've come with his family. Right?"

Dana's shoulders dropped. "Sadly, many families were divided during this time. I mean, it's possible that he emigrated here with his family. But there is a chance that he didn't come with anyone at all. I would suggest the National Archives. Find the passenger manifest for the Rochester and see who was on that ship with him. It'll be listed."

"The National Archives?" she asked.

Dana nodded. "I caution you though. This was a time of unrest. And when it comes to protecting our families and our children, we will go to great measures."

Rachel furrowed her brow.

"It's just a caution. Be careful what you wish for."

THIRTEEN

Rachel continued to flip through the stack that Ethan had left on the coffee table for her. Below the passport was a professional family photo. She recognized the faces, although they looked a few years younger than they did from the photo along the Baltic. "This is his family," she said. "I have another photo with their names on the back. Let me grab it," she said as she went to her room to grab it from her dresser. She returned to the couch with the beach photo in hand to reference it.

"So this one must be Isak," she said pointing to the father in the photo. He stood tall and proud in the back center of the photo, wearing a suit and tie, his family positioned around him. "And his wife is Rachel. Kind of coincidental. This one," she said pointing to Aaron, "is my grandfather. I'd recognize those eyes anywhere. So this must be his brother Ephraim and his sister Hanna."

"He never mentioned any of them?" Dana asked.

Rachel shook her head. "Never. My dad and his brothers and sisters never met their grandparents. Never even knew their names. Just that they were dead." She grabbed the next item from the stack. "We translated pieces of this. I'm pretty sure this is Isak's diploma."

Dana nodded her head. "It is. From *Koniglich-Sachsisches Polytechnikum*, the Royal Saxon Polytechnic Institute."

"Wow. How incredible that even back then, in 1916, he had a college degree."

"It was rare. And impressive. It speaks to the social standing of his family, certainly. It's evident in this later photo when Isak has children. It's a professional photograph, not a snapshot. They're all well-dressed; he is in a suit and tie. And even this photo here, where they are vacationing along the Baltic. Again, it suggests a certain comfort in their living, at least. And when he was attending university, it was during a time of war. Which is something to consider, as well. This would have been during the First World War."

"I found, among all these things, a Friedrich-August Cross, which I learned was from World War I."

"So he did serve, then, at some point. I'm not familiar with military awards and rankings or anything of that ilk. But that's certainly what that would be indicative of," she said with a nod.

Rachel was feeling proud in that moment. She wasn't quite sure who Isak really was. She was certain he was her great grandfather, but beyond that, she wasn't sure of much. But of the little she did know, she found him to be an impressive man.

"It's probably not a coincidence or anything, but did you look up the meaning of the name Schneider?" Dana asked.

"Actually, no, I haven't. I looked up Taylor, which is English. But when I discovered he had changed his name, I never thought to look up Schneider."

"Well, Schneider is German for the occupation of a tailor. And Taylor is English of that occupation, of course. So, like I said, I'm sure it's no coincidence that Taylor is your surname."

Rachel felt her mouth fall open but wasn't able to bring herself to close it. She sat in disbelief on her couch beside Dana. "Are you kidding me?"

She chuckled. "Not at all."

"So, Schneider is just the German form of Taylor, that's what you're saying?"

She nodded. "That's what I'm saying."

"This makes sense. I mean, kind of. I mean, at least, where Taylor came from. Why, though, would he change his name in the first place?"

"Assimilation, most likely. But there could be a dozen reasons he changed his name. I think we should get onto Ancestry.com and see what we can find there. What are the other names in the photo from the Baltic Sea?"

Rachel grabbed it off the coffee table. "Otto and Lena Schulz are the others that were on the beach with them."

Rachel signed into her Ancestry account and was thankful when Dana instructed her on where to go and what to put in her search fields. In only a matter of minutes, a German birth certificate that matched the one she had found in the trunk for Abarron was yielded from their search. From there, Dana was able to guide Rachel back further where they found a muster roll for Otto Schulz.

"He was military. Could the medal be his?" Rachel asked.

"Could be." Dana skimmed the document in its original German language. "Looks like he served in the Wehrmacht. According to this muster roll, he was conscripted in 1935 as a *Feldwebel*."

Rachel opened a new browser to look up the word. "Basically, he was platoon leader."

"For the Nazis," Dana added.

"So his daughter's husband was possibly Jewish, but he was a Nazi?"

"It would appear so," Dana said with a slow nod. "What's also interesting is the date on this. Because the war didn't officially begin until 1939. Now granted, the Wehrmacht was around well before then, and although, like I said earlier, my military knowledge is limited, it would be my guess that Otto had prior military experience. I doubt anyone would be conscripted into a platoon leadership role without experience. I'm willing to bet that whatever his experience was, he had a good name for himself, which was why he was conscripted early on. Hitler had only reinstated the conscription in early 1935. Prior to that, the Versailles Treaty prohibited it."

"I don't know what I'd do without you," Rachel said with a smile. "It's like you're my personal history book."

Dana laughed. "Well, most of that was conjecture."

"Still, what are the chances that you are exactly what I need and you came into my store right when I needed you?"

She laughed again. "I have to admit, it's nice to feel needed. The only times I'm usually listened to is when my students are being tested on what's coming out of my mouth."

"I'm just finding it hard to wrap my mind around any of this. And to think it was all right here, under my nose. Well, above my head literally and beneath my fingertips, this entire time."

The door opened and Aspen came in and Rachel realized that it was dark out.

"Hey Mom. What's for dinner?"

"Umm, there's cash on my nightstand, order some pizza."

"Really?" Aspen stopped dead in her tracks.

"Do you want something?" Rachel asked Dana.

"Whatever is fine."

"Whatever you order, Asp."

Aspen gave her mom a strange look and Rachel waved her off.

"Oh, here's another muster roll," Dana said. "This one is dated for 1942, so well into the war by now. Again, Otto Schulz, umm… rank *Unterfeldwebel*. That's weird. That would suggest a demotion."

"In seven years, wouldn't you think he'd have been promoted?"

"You'd think," Dana said. "Maybe it's a mistake. Here's one muster roll." She clicked on the third and final image and skimmed it.

This one was the hardest to see. Either it didn't scan well when it had been digitized or the document had been in poor condition to begin with. "This seems to say the same thing. *Unterfeldwebel*. It would appear Otto was demoted at one point for something."

Rachel felt confused. Not only could she not understand how her family had a Jewish connection, but where did the Nazi tie suddenly come in? And from the grandfather of her grandfather? And why, if he was good in the military, which would make sense if the Friedrich-August Cross had been awarded to him, would he eventually have been demoted during service?

"I found what Ethan believes to be Yiddish text in my grandfather's trunk. Are you able to read that at all?" she asked Dana.

"Yiddish? Oh no. Not in the least. That's a difficult language."

"Really? It looks so similar to German."

"A common misconception. In reality it's comprised of so many languages, mostly German and Hebrew, but there is even some Polish and Russian mixed in as well. So unless you know all of the above, really, it's pretty impossible to actually translate."

"That's why Ethan couldn't find anything online to translate it."

Dana nodded. "Yeah, that'd be why. It's an amazing language, really. And even in English today we use phrases from the Yiddish language that we don't even realize, but it's unique and I couldn't help you with that one." Dana glanced at the time on her phone. "Let's search for a few more things and then I think I'm going to head out."

Rachel agreed as Dana looked at their notes and typed a few things into the computer for her.

"Here is a death record for Rachel Schneider. Let's take a look at this," she said, clicking on it and pulling up the image of the German document.

Rachel hovered over Dana's shoulder as she translated. "Rachel Schneider. Hmm, this doesn't give an actual date. Just says December 1937 in Leipzig, Germany. Interestingly, it says that she is unmarried, but lists her married name."

"I wonder if that means she was a widow."

"Good question," Dana agreed. "Oh," she said in excitement and then paused while she skimmed what appeared to be a news article.

"Oh? Oh, what?" Rachel asked feeling anxious.

"There was an article published in the *Volkischer Beobachter*, a newspaper, about Rachel Schulz, daughter of *Fedwebel* Otto Schulz and wife Lena of Leipzig who was found killed by a Jewish man. He was unidentified."

Rachel felt her stomach tighten as Dana loosely translated the article for her.

"He was spotted by the *Schutzstaffel*, the police, long after curfew, near the edge of the woods. He was digging a grave for a woman. When he was spotted, he picked up her lifeless body, and weeping profusely, refused to put her down until she could be buried. The young woman's body was confiscated, and the Jewish criminal was immediately detained by the *Schutzstaffel*. It appeared she had been dead for several hours as her body was cold and stiff, and she appeared to have been pregnant." Dana took a breath before she continued. "It continues on from there with a bunch anti-Semitic propaganda and why they should continue their efforts in finding a solution to the Jewish Question."

Everything went quiet around Rachel and all she could hear was the pounding of her heart. She had never been aware of it like she was in that moment. Maybe it was because she had pictured the lifeless body of Rachel Schulz Schneider, in the arms of a stranger, with no heart pounding in her chest.

She felt cold and numb and no longer recognized the room around her.

Dana was quiet and still beside her, letting Rachel process the article.

Rachel closed her eyes for a minute. And instantly that was a mistake. The image, an image she had never seen but only heard, of pregnant Rachel in the arms of a man on the edge of the woods came to her mind. She swallowed hard and suddenly it became difficult to breathe. Without a thought she rose to her feet and raced to the door. The next thing she knew she was standing on the small deck outside her apartment door.

The night air was cold, but it felt good. It seemed to ground Rachel back in reality. She took a breath and felt the icy air inside her lungs. It felt fresh and alive. She looked into the darkness around her. She saw Dana approaching.

"I'm so sorry. I didn't mean to upset you."

"No, it wasn't you. I just wasn't… I wasn't expecting that. I wasn't expecting any of this, to be honest. And it's all—" she wracked her brain for words, "it's heavier than I thought it could ever be."

Dana nodded sympathetically.

"How do I tell my family any of this?" she asked, feeling the cold bite on the bare skin of her arms.

"Maybe now you'll begin to understand why Aaron kept the secrets that he did."

That thought had never occurred to Rachel before. An overwhelming weight settled over her chest and once again she found it difficult to breathe. This entire time she had found herself frustrated with him that he never shared any of his past with them and here she was, barely having scratched the surface and already she was questioning how to tell her family. She felt like a coward and a hypocrite. She felt ashamed of herself.

Footsteps from behind her interrupted her thoughts and Rachel turned to see the pizza deliveryman walking toward the apartment door. She sighed and hollered in through the open doorway to Aspen.

"I think we should call it a night," she said, looking to Dana and trying to hide her face from the deliveryman.

"I agree," she said with an exhale. "I did write down my number and my email on a piece of paper on the coffee table. I really would like to help you some more. And it's no trouble, at all. You've definitely stumbled into something here and if I can be of any help to you through this, I would really love to be a part of that, however I can be."

Rachel felt truly grateful for this woman and the gift that she was for her on this day. "I can't thank you enough," she said.

"You can thank me by finishing this. See it through."

Rachel took a deep breath, wondering where she would find the courage to do that. Strangely, she nodded her head. She wasn't even sure why or where the nod came from, but she nodded, and Dana smiled.

Ethan returned to the apartment about an hour after Dana left and was acutely aware of Rachel's somber mood from the moment he walked in the door. But she refused to discuss anything while Aspen was awake and instead tried her best to put on a happy face.

But inside she was haunted. Her mind couldn't escape the image it had conjured while Dana had translated the newspaper article. It left her unsettled and yet she had a burning urge to know more. She couldn't shake the sensation that she knew only part of the story. And it was significant to remind herself of the source of her information, an Aryan newspaper.

"Mom?"

Rachel looked up. Aspen was standing in front of her in her pajamas. "Tomorrow is your day off. I was wondering if we could go to the beach or something?"

"The beach? In December?"

Aspen nodded with a grin on her face. "Not to swim or anything. I just want to get out of the mountains and do something. Besides, we haven't had a family day in forever. And Ethan's never had one with us," she said with a smile as she eyed him next to Rachel on the couch.

"A family day with Ethan?" Rachel asked.

Aspen nodded. "Yeah. We could go to Newport Beach. And stop at Gram's after."

"I'd be game for something like that," he said.

"Sure. That sounds fun."

"Great!" she said with a nod, and she jumped to her feet. "Okay, well, I'm supposed to call Breanne back. Then I'm going to watch a movie until I fall asleep. Good night, guys. Oh," she said, pausing and spinning around as she was halfway to her bedroom, "Ethan, you really can stop setting your alarm and moving to the couch early in the morning. I mean, unless you really like waking up there, you don't have to keep it up because of me." She turned and disappeared into her room.

Rachel and Ethan's eyes met and a moment later they began laughing.

"That lasted longer than I really thought it would," she admitted.

"I feel like an idiot right about now," he said with a nod of his head.

"I guess that's that."

Ethan slid his arm around her and pulled her into him. He kissed her on the top of her head. "Are you finally going to tell me what happened to upset you?"

She sighed and began from the beginning when she and Dana first got up to the apartment.

Ethan sensed her emotion when she began to tell him about the newspaper and he clutched her tighter. She felt safe in his arms as she retold him about the news article.

When she finished, she surprised herself with how together she had remained and instead of pouring out words of condolences, he simply held her in his arms.

Rachel breathed him in and felt her tension dissipate. She felt her pounding heart calm and her breathing slow to a normal pace. She rested her face against his chest and closed her eyes. With her arms wrapped around him, she remained there, focused only on her breathing. This kept the haunting image of the man carrying Rachel Schneider at bay.

She wasn't sure how long she had rested against his chest, but when she sat up, she looked him in the eyes. They were calm and content and something about them told her she was safe with him.

"I love you," she said. She wasn't sure where the words had come from. She had thought them before. Many times, actually. But she had never considered saying them aloud. Saying them meant exposing a part of her that she wasn't ready to show yet. It meant laying a part of herself bare and vulnerable to someone she wasn't completely confident would return the sentiment. But in that moment as she said the words, none of that seemed to matter. It was all just doubt. As she looked into those dark brown eyes, she was certain of something, that love wasn't about doubt and uncertainty, and what she so had mistook for vulnerability was in fact something more than that. It was something stronger. It took a lot to love a person, to really, actually and truly love a person. And she did love him. If she learned anything from the things she'd been going through all day was that life was short. Those words needed to be spoken.

He lifted his hand and caressed the side of her face. It was warm and soft as it smoothed her cheek and jawline. His eyes met hers and they seemed to smile. "I love you, Rachel."

Her heart swelled and emotion pricked at the back of her eyes. She smiled as she leaned in to kiss him. As his arms wrapped around her and embraced her, she felt protected and rejuvenated and suddenly she understood where the nod she had given Dana had come from. Ethan wasn't her strength, but he was undoubtedly a pillar of support.

Newport Beach was nearly vacant. With the exception of a few scattered people, the beach was wide open, the sky blue and nearly cloudless; the marine layer had lifted and the waves were crashing into the shore. The air was cool. It was in the low sixties and a breeze that carried a chill with it came in from the ocean.

Rachel slipped off her shoes and rolled the cuffs of her pants to expose her bare ankles. She pulled her sweater tighter around her body and Ethan slid his hand into hers. They walked just inches above the water that crept up into the sand, but it still could not catch them. Aspen was just a few strides in front of them. She kicked at hardened clumps of sand, busting them open and reaching for the tiny seashells that broke free from them.

The wind whipped Aspen's hair around her face, and she turned the front of her body toward her mom, her face hiding beneath her mane of blonde hair. Rachel and Ethan laughed.

"I told you to bring a ponytail holder," Rachel said.

"Did you? I forgot."

Rachel stuck her hand out and Aspen grabbed at the band around her wrist.

"I've never been to a beach in the winter," Ethan said as he looked around. "I kind of like it. It's completely different than a beach in the summer."

Rachel nuzzled up next to him. "It's my favorite time to come. The only people around are a few locals and some crazy tourists who insist on trying to swim in the freezing water."

He slid his arm around her and pulled her into him. "Nothing about today screams swimming weather," he said and laughed.

"Look," Aspen said, pointing across the beach. Near the bluffs a crowd of colorful kites had taken to the sky. They drifted freely in the wind and Rachel watched them as they soared, higher and higher, carefully dodging one another in the breeze.

A seagull swooped low, and Rachel ducked, her arms going instantly over her head in protection as Ethan laughed. "Are you seriously afraid of a bird?"

"I don't want to get pooped on."

Aspen laughed loudly. "He almost got you Mom. Look, his pile is right behind you." She was unable to contain her burst of laughter.

"That's funny?" Rachel asked, looking over her shoulder to make sure the bird had missed her entirely.

Ethan joined Aspen in the laughter.

"Now you, too? Glad I could be the entertainment for the day."

As they began to calm their laughing, Ethan put his arm around Aspen. "I've got a question for you," he said looking down at her.

"Hmm?"

"What's wet, covered in sand and screams while it runs?" he asked.

Aspen shrugged her shoulders. "No idea. What?"

Ethan gave a sly smile. "You will be."

Aspen looked at him for a brief moment and then in an instant, she took off running down the beach, laughing and squealing while she tried to get away. Ethan was quickly running after her. Rachel stayed where she was, laughing as her daughter ran farther and farther down the beach, Ethan only strides behind her.

Once he caught up to her, he scooped her into his arms and walked her into the oncoming tide. Aspen kicked and screamed, her legs and arms flailing wildly about, as she tried to break free, but it was futile. The spray from the crashing waves got both of them and Ethan laughed as he hung her body over the water. He had all the control and Aspen was completely at his mercy. She had given up fighting and instead looked into the cold water, waiting for it. Just before meeting it, he pulled her back and retreated to the shore, setting her back into the dry sand just as Rachel caught up with them.

"That was so uncalled for," Aspen said, a smile still across her face.

Rachel was laughing as she slid an arm around Ethan.

"Well that was fun," he said, straightening out his shirt. The three of them resumed their walk along the shore, but not before Aspen gave him a playful smack on the arm.

After walking for a while, they picked a quiet spot away from any tourists and sat down in the sand. The sun was warm on their skin, but the breeze was cool. Aspen pulled her iPad from her bag and Rachel, her head in Ethan's lap, took the opportunity for a nap while Ethan put in some earphones and listened to music on his phone.

Rachel, her eyes hidden behind her sunglasses, was in and out of consciousness, the waves roaring in the background and seagulls cawing overhead. The sound of Aspen's voice jarred her slightly.

"Ethan, can I ask you a question?" she said.

Rachel felt his body shift slightly beneath her head and she closed her eyes once again.

"It's kind of a weird one," Aspen said.

"Okay. Anything," he told her.

"Do you love my mom?"

Rachel's eyes opened. She wasn't expecting that. She was careful not to move and was thankful the sunglasses shielded her face from both of them.

She felt slight movements in his body again. "I do, Aspen. I really do."

There was silence for a moment.

"Is that hard for you?" he asked.

"No," she said matter-of-factly. "People think that because I'm just a kid that I don't know much, but I know my mom and dad shouldn't be together. They drive each other crazy."

Ethan laughed a little.

"Besides, I don't think my dad deserved my mom. I mean, I love him and all. He's my dad. But my mom does everything for me and my dad really only thinks about himself. She deserves someone better than that."

Rachel felt emotion rising inside of her and she struggled to maintain her composure as she lay across Ethan's lap, feigning sleep. She'd never heard Aspen talk like that before. She never knew she'd recognized some of her sacrifices for her. She felt the sting of tears as they pressed behind her eyes, and she willed herself to calm down.

"Your mom loves you more than anyone else in the world. And you're right, everything she does is for you," Ethan said. "You're a good kid, Aspen. And even if your dad doesn't always get it right, he loves you, too."

"I'm glad she has you," she said.

"Thanks," he said.

There was another silence between them and then Rachel felt his body adjust again. A moment later she heard the muffled sound of his music playing again and she heard the faint sounds of the game from Aspen's iPad resume. She took a breath.

They pulled up to Joe and Jenn's house in Newport by mid-afternoon. Jenn answered the door, their Welsh Corgi named Dee-o-jee, in tow. He became instantly excited at the sight of Aspen, his docked tail waving eagerly from side to side before he dropped his butt to the floor and panted until she squatted to his level to pet him.

"You made it," Jenn said, a smile on her face. "How was the beach? Anyone swimming?"

"There always is," Rachel said as she leaned in and hugged her mom. She smelled of Chanel perfume and was instantly brought back to her childhood. "Where's Dad?"

"Where's my granddaughter?" Joe asked with eagerness as he stepped into the large and open foyer of his home. He pulled Aspen into his arms and kissed her on the top of her head. "And of course, my daughter," he said, and pulled Rachel in for a hug next.

As she hugged her dad, she saw her Aunt Sarah come around the corner next. "Hi," she said, shocked to see her.

Sarah smiled at them. "Your mom called me and said you would be coming. Hope you don't mind that I'm crashing your party."

After everyone finished exchanging hellos and hugs and introductions to Sarah, they made their way to the patio around the pool out back. Jenn poured wine for them, and Aspen opened a soda while she sat on a lounge chair with Dee-o-jee on her lap. He curled into a ball and fell asleep while she pet his long, soft coat of fur and lost herself on her iPad.

"I'm just telling you, it's a great new set of golf clubs. The best I've ever had," Joe said with a nod.

"He hasn't stopped talking about those new golf clubs since he got them a week ago," Jenn said, leaning toward Sarah and Rachel.

Rachel laughed.

"Can't a man be pleased with his purchase?" Joe asked defensively.

"I agree," Ethan said with a nod.

"Oh, you don't need to do that to be on his good side," Sarah said with a smile and the others laughed.

Joe rolled his eyes.

"So Rachel," Sarah said, changing the subject, "how is your search on my dad coming along? Find anything new?"

Rachel felt her body tense up and her face grow warm. This definitely wasn't a conversation she wanted to have with her father yet.

"Yeah, how's that all going anyway? Did Dad head up the Mafia? The Yakuza?" Joe asked and then laughed at his jokes.

Rachel readjusted awkwardly in her chair. "Uh, well, I learned a few things," she said, dancing around the subject.

"Like what?" Sarah asked eagerly.

"Aaron's birth name is Abarron Alter Schneider."

"Schneider? What the heck's that?" Joe blurted out.

"Joe, shut up, I want to hear what she says," Sarah said.

Joe looked taken aback. Only his older sister could get away with telling him to shut up.

"Schneider is the German form of the English surname Taylor," Rachel said, ignoring her dad.

"Really?" Jenn said, sitting up straighter. "How interesting. So he changed his name, but not really. He kept the literal meaning of his surname, just used a different language. How fascinating," she said.

Rachel nodded. "I know, right?" She glanced at her dad who had sat back in his chair, a staid expression on his face. "His parents were Isak Schneider of Dresden, Germany and Rachel Schulz of Leipzig, Germany."

"Rachel, huh?" her mom asked. "What are the chances that your great grandmother and you share the same name?"

"Small world," Sarah said.

"Rachel's father, Otto, served on behalf of Germany in World War I."

"Wow," Sarah said, dragging the word out. "How did you learn all of this?"

"I met a German Linguistics professor from USC, and we went through Ancestry.com together. It was quite amazing the things we could find when I had some help and understood the parameters a little better."

"How did you find Schneider?" Joe asked from his corner on the patio. Everyone turned to look in his direction.

"What?" she asked.

"Schneider. How did you find it? It's not like Ancestry would have yielded that information for you. You would have had to find something to directly link Abarron Alter Taylor to Abarron Alter Schneider. What was it?" he asked.

Rachel felt her mouth go dry. She hadn't anticipated this.

"What, do you think she's lying about all of this? Why would she lie about this, Joseph?" Sarah asked.

He shook his head. "No. No, I don't think she's lying about anything. But I do think she's hiding something. Tell me Rachel. How did you make that connection?"

Rachel looked at Ethan who seemed to be at a loss. Her heart pounded, making it harder to focus. "I found a birth certificate," she finally said.

"Whose? My dad's?" he asked.

She nodded.

"What else aren't you telling me?"

Rachel swallowed hard.

"Rachel, you're my daughter. I've been able to read you like a book your entire life. I know when you're hiding something. Out with it."

"Joseph, leave her alone," Jenn said, rising from her chair.

"This is my dad. I told her to leave it alone. But she couldn't. And now she insists on keeping something from me and I have a right to know what it is. Tell me, Rachel. What do you know?" His voice was stern but he did not yell.

Jenn and Sarah exchanged glances beside Rachel.

"I don't know anything for certain," she finally said.

He sighed. "Then what do you suspect?"

Rachel looked over at Ethan who gave her a sympathetic looked. Then she looked at her mom and Sarah, and finally back to her dad. "I'm fairly certain," she said, "that the Schneider family was Jewish."

"That's not possible," Joe said, rising to his feet.

Rachel stood. "Why not?"

"I would've known if my dad was Jewish," he said.

Sarah and Ethan now stood as well. "Dad didn't really practice anything," Sarah said. "What makes you think that?"

"I found things in Yiddish. Papers. I haven't been able to translate them, so I have no idea what they say."

"Then how do you even know that they're Yiddish?" Joe said.

"I've had other people take a look at them. To an untrained eye they look German. But nothing can translate them because Yiddish is a compilation of mostly German and Hebrew, but also other languages. You'd have to know all of them to translate it. I also found pamphlets from just before the outbreak World War II, promoting Jewish rights in Germany. The professor I've been working with told me that most German citizens wouldn't have had things like that because at the time they weren't aware of the real situation for the Jews. Hitler's real plans hadn't been fully revealed yet. I found the *Haggagdah*, the *Tanakh*, and the *Talmud*. Why would Grandpa Aaron have these books in his possession if they didn't mean something to him? Those are all Jewish religious books, Dad."

"Where are you getting all this stuff?" he asked incredulously.

"From a trunk," she said quietly.

"What trunk?" Sarah asked.

"The trunk I found hidden in my attic."

"You found a trunk up there?" Sarah said.

Rachel nodded. "With the name Schneider on the top. There are photos, a military award, letters, and birth certificates in it. The list goes on. It's full. I even found his passport. I know when and how he came to this country." She took a breath. "I think, I think something terrible happened during World War II to his family and that he came to California and changed his name for a clean start."

FOURTEEN

"I can't believe he just walked out on me. Like I made this up or something!" Rachel stormed into her living room, pacing back and forth through any open space, throwing her hands up in the air.

"Rach, calm down," Ethan said. "It's just a big shock to him. That's all."

"What did Sarah mean when she said that she and Grandpa and their brothers and sisters had Jewish names? I didn't realize there were such things," Aspen said as she took a seat on a chair in the living room. "And what's the big deal about being Jewish, anyway?"

"Nothing is the big deal about it. It's just not what my dad… it's just not what Grandpa thought. He's making a huge deal out of nothing," Rachel said, still pacing the living room.

Ethan stood up and cut her off. "Why don't you go to your room and just have some time for yourself. Whatever you need. Aspen and I will be fine out here," he suggested.

She sighed loudly and glanced over her shoulder at her daughter. "It's not such a bad idea Mom."

She grabbed the laptop from the coffee table and disappeared into bedroom, locking the door behind her. Sprawling out on her bed, she opened her email. She was surprised to see a response from her old college friend, Rose. She opened the email.

> Rach, nice to hear from you stranger. Sounds like life in the mountains is keeping you awfully busy. My three kids, Celia, David and Micah keep me on my toes. We are planning a family trip to Israel in a few weeks, and I am very excited. My husband's brother, Teyve, lives there with his family and we will be staying with them. Anyway, enough of that. I looked at the letters you scanned to me and emailed me. Yes, you're right that they are Yiddish. My Yiddish isn't too good, as I'm not fluent in either German or Hebrew but I can get by in both. Thank the military for posting me in Germany for four years and thank my parents for sending me to Hebrew Day School when I was a kid. With that said, what you sent didn't

appear to be letters like you thought, but instead they are *derashot*. They are the equivalent in Judaism to sermons or homilies in Christianity. So, perhaps you have a Rabbi in your family line? I did find a name scribbled on one. Perhaps it means something to you. Alter Schneider of Plauen. Hope this helps. Wish I could give you more. If anything else comes up, don't hesitate. If you're ever in Santa Barbara, let's do lunch.
-Rose

Rachel's pulse quickened as she pulled up her Google Maps and searched for Plauen. She found it on a map, nearly equidistant from Leipzig and Dresden, near the Czech border in Germany. She took notes so that she could send them in an email to Dana. Even if she could find any documentation of Alter, it would futile; they would almost certainly be in German.

This information now gave her something she hadn't had before. She had certainty. She had proof. Whether Aaron had been Jewish, she didn't know, but her suspicions were now confirmed; her family, at some point, was Jewish.

That night, with Ethan lying next to her, his breathing shallow and loud, Rachel lay awake in her bed. Sleep was the last thing on her mind. So many thoughts and images raced through her brain. All of it was like a puzzle that she was trying to piece together, but she couldn't seem to find all the pieces. Every time she felt she was getting a little bit closer, she realized how much bigger the puzzle really was.

She tossed and turned, rolled her body from side to side, trying desperately to find a comfortable position. A little after three, she finally got up and went into her living room, bringing the photo of Aaron and his family from the beach along with her. She flipped on the small lamp on her end table, its soft glow illuminating the corner of the room as she took a seat in the chair and studied the photo.

No one smiled, but they seemed to still be enjoying themselves. They seemed to be comfortable, at peace and relaxed. She glanced at the year on the back: 1935. So much would change so quickly after this photo was taken. Was it one of the last happy times they were all together? A chill ran through her body.

Rachel wasn't sure how long she had sat in her chair looking at that photo in her hands. But the next thing she knew, Ethan was shaking her awake.

"Rach, you're going to be late for work." Groggily she pried her eyes open. They were heavy and resisted her. "Why are you out here?" he asked.

"I couldn't sleep," she said, yawning.

"You what?"

"I couldn't sleep," she repeated. "What time is it?"

"The store opens in twenty minutes," he said. "And I'm going to be late for the station. I'll see you in a few days when my shift is over. Love you," he said kissing her and then disappearing out the door.

Rachel flew from the chair into her bedroom and dressed in a hurry. She was downstairs in no time where Kristin and the kids were already opening the store.

"I was wondering what happened to you," she said. "I ran into Darlene at the grocery store yesterday and she said she was looking for some part-time work. I told her to stop in here mid-morning, after I had a chance to talk to you."

"I think that's a fantastic idea," Rachel said as she rushed to power on the register, credit card machine, her computer and printer. "Our Twenty-Five Days of Christmas begins today at four. I don't even have the books picked out yet."

Kristin laughed. "Sounds about right. Why are you more frantic than usual?" she asked.

"It's been a crazy weekend," she said with a sigh.

"Care to share?" Kristin asked as she pulled a tray of mini peach turnovers out of the back and set them in the display case.

"Not at the moment."

"Hi Ray-el," Parker said, coming up and squeezing her leg.

She patted him gently on the head. "Hey handsome," she said.

"I not hamsom. I Parker," he said with a definitive nod.

"Oh. Sorry, bud."

"I not bud. I Parker."

"Oh. Parker. I'm sorry," she said.

"Park, go play," Kristin called over her shoulder. "Gracie, come get your brother. So you're really on board with hiring Darlene again? Just for the holidays?"

Rachel nodded. "Yes, absolutely. She's worked here before, so she should get the hang of things relatively quickly, not to mention we could use the help. We say that every year at this time."

"I agree. I just thought it would take a little more persuading on your part."

"No persuading needed. I'm on board," she said as she went to unlock the front door. She was surprised to see Tiff headed straight for her as she opened it.

"Morning ladies. Kristin, I need a large latte," she said, dropping her bag onto a nearby table.

"You're earlier than normal," Rachel said.

"You'd think I just came from my house. Oh no. I was at the office. Submitting an offer on a house that a couple insisted they couldn't wait on until morning." She sighed as she took a seat.

"Wow. They must really want that house," Kristin said setting the latte in front of Tiff.

She groaned under her breath. "It's a good thing it will be a pretty commission if it's accepted. And it better be accepted. That's all I have to say."

A few minutes later the front door opened again as AJ stepped inside. "Well good morning," Kristin said.

"Coffee. Black."

Kristin giggled as she stepped behind the bakery counter and AJ took a seat beside Tiff.

"Well, you look like you're having a morning about as great at Tiff here. Happy Monday to you," Rachel said.

"Like you can talk," Kristin called over the counter.

"Jack had to work all weekend. Apparently, people buy lots of cars during the holidays. Which is odd because, well, no one has ever bought me a Mercedes for Christmas, but that's beside the point. Anyway, so I've been grading all weekend and sitting in my apartment all by myself and then during a break, when I was standing in my kitchen, I got to thinking, why do I keep my wine glasses up on the third shelf in my cupboard? I mean, I'm not a short woman, but I'm certainly not tall. And let's be real here, I use those glasses at least at frequently as I do the water glasses."

"If not more," Tiff added.

"Right," AJ nodded. "So I decided to move the coffee cups that I never use because I always come here from the first shelf to the third shelf and take the wine glasses from their spot on the third shelf and put them on the first shelf. And then, well, they were just so accessible," she said.

"And you're hung over today," Rachel said, motioning toward the black coffee.

"Not terribly. But enough so that I'll want to strangle any kid who steps out of line with me in any of my classes."

"And that's our public school system, folks," Kristin said with a smirk.

AJ elbowed her in the side and Kristin bent over in laughing pain. "That one actually hurt."

"Good," AJ said as she took a sip of the coffee.

A few customers came into the store. Two of them went straight to the bakery counter but the third went to the bookshelves and Rachel followed to see if there was anything she could do for them.

After AJ and Tiff left, business began to pick up, and as Kristin had said earlier, Darlene showed up around ten, just before Mark came in for the day. She was excited to start working again.

Customers were in and out of the store all morning in a steady rhythm. And while Rachel had a pile of work on her desk, she wasn't able to slip into her office for even ten minutes to tackle any of it.

"I can't believe it's this busy for a Monday," Mark said after finally clearing the line at the register.

Rachel sighed as she received a shipment from a vendor and quickly began to inventory the items. "Fortunately Kristin, and I decided to hire Darlene back for the holidays."

"Darlene? Tall, brunette?" he asked, helping her with the second box.

She nodded.

"That will be helpful," he agreed as he stood to his feet to help a customer who came in.

Rachel was relieved when five came and she left Sinful Retreat for the day. She gave Diane the responsibility to print all the reconciliation reports, including the ecommerce ones from the weekend, and she disappeared upstairs with her laptop to work on the fiduciary reports she hadn't been able to touch all day.

"Can I go to Kasey's to work on our science project?" Aspen asked as Rachel worked from the kitchen.

Rachel looked up from her work on the computer. "What is your science project?"

"It's so stupid. Mr. Crawford is making us build a gear system and then we have to test it. First without lubrication and then with lubrication. Then we have to report what we find in a paper. Kasey and I are partners. Her mom said it was okay if I came over so we could start planning how we would build it."

"Umm, sure. But I want you home by eight. Do you need a ride or anything?" she asked.

Aspen shook her head. "No, Kasey's brother Austin has his license. He said he'd pick me up."

"Her brother? How old is he?" Rachel asked.

"Eighteen."

"Eighteen. You really think I should let you, a twelve-year-old in a car with an eighteen-year-old?" Rachel asked.

"Mom, stop being so spastic. She's got older brothers, who cares? It's not a big deal. He's going out of his way to help out. Just be thankful. Man, chill out."

"Aspen, I really hate when you talk to me like that. You don't need to go anywhere if that's the kind of attitude you're going to have."

"Ugh," she groaned. "Mom, this is for school. You're always telling me how I have to keep my grades up and now you're getting on my case because my schoolwork has to do with a friend. I can't win with you."

"No," Rachel said firmly, "I'm getting on your case because you need a reality check. Now drop the attitude or you'll be figuring out how to do this science project solo. I can talk to Mr. Crawford. And I'm sure I will have no problem convincing him of why you suddenly didn't need a partner for you project."

Aspen put her hands on her hips. "You can be so mean sometimes."

Rachel looked back to her computer. "Yeah, well, it's in my job description."

"Really? Under *Mom*, it says to be mean to your children?"

"When necessary, it does. You'll understand someday."

"Whatever. I don't think so."

Rachel rolled her eyes as Aspen went back into her room to get her things before her ride got there. And after she left, the apartment went very quiet. Rachel worked for the next couple hours nonstop on work. She finished her reports, the new paperwork for Darlene to start work later that week and was able to submit book orders. She made a reminder note to herself of the books she needed to pull from the shelves in the morning that were not selling and that needed to be returned to the vendors.

She glanced at the clock, her stomach rumbling. It was getting late. She thought about calling Ethan. Quickly she pulled up her email and saw she had a new one from Dana.

> Got your forward from your friend, Rose. How cool that someone in your family was a Rabbi? And now you certainly have confirmation about the Judaism in your family. I did find a birth certificate for Alter Schneider. Although it didn't yield much information, I learned a few things we didn't know before. I attached the image of it, even though it's in German. He was born 10 Feb 1863 in Saxony, Germany to Okef and Hodel. All I could find on them was on Okef and that he was from Lithuania. I didn't find a maiden name for Hodel. I did find a marriage certificate, also attached and also in German, for Alter Schneider and Ahuva Regenbogen in 1888. And the last thing I found was a POW record for your Great Grandfather Otto Schulz in World War I. It appeared he was captured by France but escaped twenty-one days later and made his way to German-annexed Lorraine, France. After digging deeper into his WWI military records, I made another discovery. He was the commanding officer over Isak Schneider. I'm assuming this has something to do with how Isak met and later married Otto's daughter. Did you have any luck with the National Archives?
> -Dana Albrecht

As if Rachel's head hadn't been spinning before, it was definitely in a whirlwind now. How peculiar, she thought, that Isak, coming from a Jewish family, married Rachel Schulz and then during WWII, his own father-in-law was a Nazi. The dynamic seemed impossible. But then she was reminded of the things she had read about the Civil War in her own country; brothers fighting against brothers. Maybe it wasn't so impossible after all. How tragic for Rachel Schulz to be married to a man that her father would be later conditioned to despise.

Amid everything going on with her own father, Rachel had completely forgotten to look up the passenger manifest for the *Rochester*, the ship that sailed from Le Havre, France to New York City with Abarron on board.

She wasn't sure where to look or what exactly to search for. But after trying a few different options, something interesting was yielded in her results and she clicked on it. *Manifest of Alien Arrivals at Buffalo, Lewiston, Niagara Falls, and Rochester, New York, 1902-1954.*

Before she even had a chance to realize what she was looking at, she had found it: the Form 657 Record of Registry for Abarron Schneider, age 11, male, occupation: student. The registry even included a small photograph of Aaron. Rachel's stomach tightened and she tried just the last name in the search field. It returned fourteen results; two of the names, she recognized immediately: Ephraim Schneider and Hanna Schneider. Ephraim was fifteen and Hanna was ten. It appeared there were no adults, at least under the last names of Schneider or Schulz, that had made the trans-Atlantic journey with the children. From there, their trail was cold. Rachel didn't know where the children went or who, if anyone, was waiting for them in the United States.

She rose to her feet and slowly crossed the now darkened apartment toward the sofa where she lay down on her side. Her body went numb. As a mother, it was both a horrific and sickening thought to put her children aboard a ship alone and send them halfway across the world. She couldn't begin to fathom the pain that Rachel Schneider had felt in the moment when she said goodbye to her children. Did she think she would ever see them again? Did she try to be strong? What compelled her to actually let go of their hands and let them board that ship?

She thought about Aspen, only miles away and working on a science project. She had this overwhelming need to see her. But she knew her daughter would only laugh at her. Instead, Rachel went into Aspen's room and crawled into her bed. It smelled so overwhelmingly of her daughter, and she buried her face in the pillow, taking it in. She pulled the blanket up to her chin and began to weep. Her heart broke for the mother who faced no better option than to ship away her own children. The thought left Rachel feeling empty and hollow and cold; she shivered, pulling the blankets tighter around her.

She found it so tragic. A part of her began to despise mankind for having it in them to do such awful things to their own people. She'd learned about World War II and the Holocaust at a young age, certainly from grade school on, but she had never connected with it until now. And now she felt it ran so deeply through her veins that she didn't know how to separate herself from it.

She wondered where she should go from here. Where could she find the answers that would fill in the blanks of what happened to Aaron when he arrived in New York in October 1935 to when she picked up the trail in 1949 when he married Elaine Thompson?

Tuesday evening, after the day at Sinful Retreat, Rachel stopped at Stater Bros. and perused the selection of wine. She selected two bottles of Cabernet and headed out to her car. With Aspen at her dad's for the night, she was on no one's schedule but her own and she headed out to AJ's.

"Oh good, you brought sustenance," AJ said when she answered her door and saw the bottles in Rachel's hands.

Rachel laughed. "Umm, yeah, if that's what you call these. Anyone else joining us?"

"Both Kristin and Tiff, but they're both feeding their families first. Then they'll be here," she said as they made their way into AJ's apartment. It was small and old but had character and AJ had decorated it well.

The two kicked back on the sofa, enjoying the quiet relaxation until the others arrived. And later, after Tiff and Kristin came, Rachel shared with them the latest discoveries in her search on Aaron.

Tiff shook her head in amazement. "That story is unbelievable, Rach," she said, clasping her hand over her chest.

"No kidding. My heart just aches after hearing it. No wonder he tried to leave all of that behind," Kristin said.

"Where do I go from here? I feel like I hit another brick wall. And now I know all this stuff, but I don't have any resolution," Rachel said.

"But it's not a movie. Maybe there won't be any resolution," AJ said.

The other three turned to look at her.

"Not to be the pessimist here, but this is real life. The truth is you may never learn the truth. You may never know the entire story and you may never find the resolution you're looking for."

Tiff looked from AJ to Rachel. "She might be right. The Nazis destroyed a lot of things. If there were further documentation about Otto or Isak, it could've been destroyed."

"Or it's out there but not digitized. It's fractured information that you'd have to hunt for in person. How do you plan on navigating a search like that?" AJ asked.

Rachel hadn't considered any of that. When Dana asked her to see it through, in her head, she imagined literally seeing it through. She thought she'd find closure. But the scenarios her friends were posing suddenly seemed more realistic than any closure seemed. She felt disheartened.

"Sorry Rach, I know that's not what you wanted to hear," AJ said, moving closer to her.

Rachel looked up, a sober look on her face. She shrugged her shoulders. "It's not. But you're right, though. Why hadn't I considered this?" She rose to her feet and began pacing AJ's small, rectangular living room. "Why did I get my hopes up? How did I let myself get so vested in this? I mean, I looked at those people in those photographs and even though I never knew them, it's like I thought to myself that if I could just uncover the truth that it would somehow redeem their tragedy. How stupid is that? How stupid am I?" She got louder with every question as she paced faster and faster, back and forth and back again.

"Rachel," Kristin said, "it's okay. Anyone would have gotten emotionally wrapped up in it. It's impossible not to."

She turned to look at them. "Who killed Rachel Schneider? Was she really killed by a Jewish man or was that person just trying to help? That place was so messed up at the time. It was so fucked up!" She spun on her heel and headed to the kitchen. She grabbed a wine glass from AJ's cupboard and poured herself a glass, larger than normal. She took a large drink. It was a pleasant combination of dry and sweet in her mouth as she swallowed and took another. When she looked up, she saw AJ, Tiff and Kristin standing in the doorway and watching her carefully.

"I have an idea," Kristin said. "Abarron's brother and sister—"

"Ephraim and Hanna," Rachel said.

"Have you tried looking them up?"

"How so?" Rachel asked.

"You know, like a phone number? There is a chance they're alive today. They'd be old, but there is still a chance," she said.

"She's right," Tiff said.

Rachel shook her head. "No. I didn't think of that." She pushed through the other three and headed toward AJ's computer. Her first stop was Ancestry where she put in Ephraim's name first. To her chagrin a death certificate was produced in the search results. She opened the file to view it. He had died in 2001 in Staten Island, NY. With a sigh, she searched for Hanna Schneider.

Hanna, she knew, could prove to be more difficult to search for. As a female, it was likely that she had married and taken her husband's name. This wouldn't make things impossible; however, it could make things more challenging.

When Rachel typed Hanna's name into the search field, she was shocked with the result it yielded. It wasn't a death record. Instead, the 1940 census appeared. She clicked on it and a summary of Hanna Schneider appeared before her:

Birth Year: 1924
Age: 15
Birthplace: Germany
Residence: New York, New York, USA
Race: White
Gender: Female
Relation to Head of Household: Niece
Marital Status: Single
Father's Birthplace: Germany
Mother's Birthplace: Germany
Household Members:
Avi Schneider   Age 40
Anne Schneider   Age 39
Max Schneider   Age 20
Ephraim Schneider Age 20
Levana Schneider   Age 17
Hanna Schneider   Age 15
Samuel Schneider   Age 14
Ruth Schneider   Age 13

"This is her," she said with excitement. "This is Hanna, Aaron's sister." The other three gathered around the computer for a closer look.

"When is this?" Tiff asked.

"1940 U.S. Federal Census," Rachel said.

"Aaron's not listed in the household members," AJ said.

Rachel shook her head. "He would've only been sixteen at the time. It says Hanna's relation to the head of household was niece. Looks like she was sent to her uncle's."

"At least they had someone to send the kids to," Kristin said.

Rachel continued her search but found nothing else on Hanna Schneider. At first she felt discouraged, but AJ quickly reminded her that it might mean good news. It might suggest she was still alive somewhere.

Leaving Ancestry behind, Rachel began searching online phonebooks for Hanna Schneider. She knew it was a long shot, but she had to start somewhere. She began her search parameters in New York State for Hanna Schneider.

Six forms of Hanna Schneider appeared before her eyes. There was Hanna Schneider, Anna Schneider, Hannah Schneider, Hanna Schneider-Davis, Hanna Snyder and Hannah Hollis-Snyder. Rachel was glad there were only six. She wrote down all six numbers, it was too late to call anyone on the east coast at that hour, and closed the computer, feeling a bit rejuvenated.

"Do you see what I'm seeing AJ?" Kristin asked as Rachel made her way back to the living room.

"I am seeing what you're seeing Kristin," she said with a giggle as they watched her from behind.

"That woman's got a little spring in her step."

AJ nodded. "It would appear so." They laughed as they followed her back into the living room.

"Rach, your phone's going off. Looks like Matt's calling you," Tiff called from the kitchen.

"Answer it," she called back as she made her way to the kitchen. Tiff handed her the phone.

"What's up?"

"Who are these boys Aspen has been hanging out with?" he asked.

"What boys?" Rachel asked as she grabbed her jacket and slipped out AJ's back door.

"She said she had to work on a science project with one of her friends—"

"Kasey Hetherington," Rachel added.

"Anyway, she told me her older brother would pick her up and drop her off. I said she had to be home by eight. By ten after, I sat outside to wait for her. She wasn't answering her cell. Finally, at 8:30 she pulled in with a car full of kids. It was her, one other girl, and the rest were all boys. I want to know who these boys are that she's hanging out with. She's twelve."

"Did you ask her who they were?" she asked.

"Of course I did. This isn't my first day as a dad. She shrugged her shoulders at me and said they were no big deal. She said they were Kaleb and Kevin's friends. Who the hell are Kaleb and Kevin?"

She sighed. "They are Kasey's brothers."

"Who?"

"Her science partner. Matt, I know you meant well, but don't you think if you were going to let her go with her science partner you should've found out who the science partner was? And if the partner's brother was driving, maybe you should've found out who that was as well," Rachel said.

"Oh, now you're going to jump down my throat? I know just where she gets it from. She's too young to be hanging out with kids like that."

"I agree. But who's to say she was even hanging out with them? They may have just all been in the same car while she was getting a ride home. If that's the case, then you need to have a conversation with her and be willing to go pick her up if a situation like that presents itself again. Listen, I'm sick of being your parenting tutor. You two need to work this out. You're the adult. Get her to talk to you. And that doesn't mean using force or threats. I've got to go. Good luck," she added before hanging up, not giving him any more opportunity to interject anything into the conversation.

"Sorry guys, always drama between Matt and Aspen," Rachel said, taking a seat on chair in the living room.

"Shocker," Tiff said, taking a drink of wine.

"What're we talking about?" she asked, grabbing her glass from the end table. "I like your new little round tables," Rachel said, observing the one she took her wine glass from.

"Well, continuing what you've brought to the conversation, we've been talking about what we know of our genealogy."

"I just told them how Jack's great-great-grandfather served in the Czarist Army," AJ said to Rachel. "I kind of filled him in a little on your journey."

"Russia, huh? That's cool. Not something you hear every day," Rachel said.

"Yeah, and both mine and Darren's families come from England. Well, England to Canada for Darren," Kristin said.

"Ah, well we know my spice comes from my dad's side from his Cuban roots," Tiff said with a little shimmy. "And my mom's side is German."

"You know," Rachel said, pausing to rack her brain, "I think I remember Ethan telling me something about having Nazis in his family. Yeah, on our first date."

"Wow, that seems like a bit of a mood killer," AJ said. "Hey, I think you're gorgeous. By the way my ancestors were Nazis. Let's do this again some time."

"No really," she said. "I think he said something about that. I can't believe I didn't think of that until now. I can't remember what it was though. I'll have to ask him about it. But I got the impression that they were some pretty serious Nazis."

"Just what you need to learn right when you discover you had Jewish family in Nazi Germany," AJ said.

Rachel's eyes met hers, suddenly unsure of what to think.

FIFTEEN

While Mark reviewed procedure with Darlene, Rachel sat in her office, the door slightly ajar, thumbing the piece of paper that held the numbers of all the listed Hanna Schneiders in New York. Her stomach was in a profound ball of knots and at any given moment, she felt she could throw up.

She glanced at the phone on her desk, and it seemed to beckon to her. Her hands drumming on the desk, she reached for the receiver and dialed the first number on the list.

The phone rang seven times before Rachel hung it up.

She tried the next number on the list. A man answered and she asked for Anna Schneider.

"She's working. Can I take a message?" he asked.

"Umm, could you tell me if Anna has ever gone by the name Hanna before?"

"That's a weird question. No. She's always been Anna. Who are you?"

"I'm sorry to bother you. I'm just looking for Hanna Schneider. Thank you for your time." She hung up the phone and drew a line through that one on her list.

Next on her list was Hannah Schneider. Again, there was no answer, but a machine picked up. The voice was an elderly woman, which was a hopeful sign for Rachel. She marked beside the name and moved to the next name on the list.

No answer, no machine.

The last two were completely different spellings of the name entirely and she wasn't confident they would be the person she was looking for. But it was worth a shot anyway. She didn't come this far to give up now.

A woman answered after the second ring. "Hi, I'm calling for Hanna Schneider," Rachel said.

"This is her," the woman on the other line said.

"My name is Rachel Taylor. I'm sorry to bother you, but I'm wondering, are the sister of Abarron Schneider?"

"I'm sorry dear, I never had any brothers. I'm not the person you're looking for."

Rachel felt her heart drop slightly. "Thank you for your time."

"Best of luck to you."

Rachel tried the last number on her list. A man answered that phone, but when she asked for Hanna Schneider, he told her to hold while he went to get her.

"Hello?" a woman's voice asked. She didn't sound much older than Rachel.

"Hanna Schneider?" Rachel asked.

"Yes. Who's this?"

"I'm Rachel Taylor. And I'm looking for Hanna Schneider, the sister of Abarron Schneider. That wouldn't by any chance be you, would it?"

"Ah, sorry, you've got the wrong woman. Besides, Schneider is just my married name."

"Okay. Thank you for your time," Rachel said, but couldn't finish before the woman hung up the phone. She scratched the last two names of the list, not knowing if she should feel disappointed or pleased that she was narrowing down the six names.

"Hey Rach, sorry to interrupt, but we could really use you out here. We're getting slammed," Mark said, sticking his head in through the open doorway.

Rachel sighed as she pushed herself away from her desk and stood up. Stepping out of her office, she was surprised to see as many customers as there were around the store for a Wednesday afternoon. Her heart dropped when she saw Tom sitting near the Christmas tree reading a book. She quickly bypassed him and went for a customer.

"What're you looking for today?" she asked a shorter woman who looked completely clueless as she wandered the aisles, looking the shelves up and down, studying the spines of the books carefully.

"Oh, my granddaughter is really into books. It's pretty much all she put on her Christmas list this year. And I just hate giving gift cards. They're so impersonal. You know what I mean?" she asked, looking at Rachel and pushing her glasses up the bridge of her nose.

Rachel nodded her head. "Absolutely. Do you know what she is into?"

The woman grabbed a list out of her bag and handed it to Rachel. She looked down at it and caught her breath. There was a list of nearly a dozen Holocaust books typed out before her, title and author included. Rachel felt her heart grow heavy.

"Yes," she said solemnly, "I know these books. Let me help you." She led the woman to the historical fiction section of the bookstore and pulled a few from the list. "How old is your granddaughter?"

"Twenty," the woman replied proudly. "She's studying history in college and I think that's why she's into this so much," she said with a nod toward the book in Rachel's hand.

"Well," Rachel said, nodding toward the book she held, "*Rachel's Key* is an exceptional, powerful story that she would probably like, *Those Who Save Us* is quite intense and powerful as well, and *The Lost Wife* is an incredibly wonderful book and definitely leaves its readers inspired. So here are three from that list that I would recommend. I think she would enjoy any of them. Hope this helps you out," Rachel said.

"Oh it does, very much," the woman said, a pleased look on her face.

Rachel offered a weak smile before moving on to another customer in the store. She was relieved when her next customer was looking for a specific sci-fi trilogy that was far less connected to her own life at the moment.

By the end of the day, she was relieved to head home, and even more relieved to see Aspen vegetating on the couch, watching television. Rachel collapsed beside her, trying to be inconspicuous that she simply wanted to just be near her daughter.

"What's up, Mom?"

"Long day."

"Did you hear Dad and I got into a fight?" Aspen asked, a sharp tone in her voice.

"He called me. How did it all pan out?"

"Ugh," she grunted. "He doesn't even give me a chance to explain anything. He just freaks out on me and then sends me to my room."

"Who were all the boys you were with?" Rachel asked, making sure to avoid eye contact so Aspen wouldn't feel like their conversation was turning into an interrogation.

"They were just friends of Kasey's brothers. I don't know them. Kaleb was giving me a ride home because Dad said I had to be home by eight, and it was already after that when Kaleb picked me up. I knew Dad was going to freak out about that but there was nothing I could do about it, and when he got there, both of her brothers had friends in the car. What was I supposed to do about it?" Aspen folded her arms across her chest.

"Did you tell your dad that?"

"I tried. He wouldn't listen. He just yelled at me for a while and then sent me to my room."

"What was he saying?"

"He said I was too young to have boyfriends. And then he wanted to talk about sex and I was like, eww, I already talked to Mom about this, I was not going to talk to him about it. And then he got even madder at me. He threw his hands up in the air and kept saying he gives up. He told me he didn't care if I got pregnant. As if I'm having sex."

Rachel sighed as she sat up on the couch. "He said that?"

"Yeah. Great dad I have."

"What else did you say?" Rachel asked.

"Nothing. I didn't want to keep getting yelled at. So I waited until he was done because I knew I would eventually get sent to my room."

"I've got to go call him. I'll be right back," Rachel said, standing and stepping into her room.

"Matt," she said, skipping the hello when he answered. "Did you seriously tell her you didn't care if she got pregnant?"

"Well I don't. She didn't want to listen to me when I tried talking to her. I am so done with that kid and her attitude," he said.

"Would you listen to yourself? You sound ridiculous. A sex talk is an incredibly uncomfortable and awkward conversation that you don't just have in the middle of an argument with someone that you barely have a relationship with."

"Barely have a relationship with? I'm her dad!"

"I hate to break it to you, but relationships with our kids aren't an automatic. And you're not there with her. That's why she doesn't come to you with anything yet. Just because you're here, suddenly, doesn't mean that she knows you're actually here for her. You have to prove yourself to her. You don't wake up one day and suddenly have the relationship and connection with her that I do. It took me twelve years to build and create that. And let me tell you, it won't come by forcing it, either. And that's exactly what you're trying to do. You've got to give her space. You need to show her that you respect her and support her and in time your relationship will become what you want. But not now and not like this. You're pushing her away like this. I guarantee it."

"Who are you to tell me how to parent?" Matt asked.

"I'm her mom, that's who. And if you can't figure this crap out, then we will use your method and go to court. Because she's old enough to speak on her own behalf. And what do you think she'll say?"

Matt was suddenly quiet on the other end.

"Are you still there?" she asked.

He sighed. "Yeah, I'm here." He had calmed down significantly. "Please don't do that. Take me to court."

"I don't want to. But if things don't change, I'm not sure what else to do," she said.

"When I decided to quit my job and come here, I just pictured this all happening so differently. I pictured my daughter being happy and excited about this. Running into my arms. I pictured you and I working things out. I don't know, this just, it isn't how I imagined it would be. It's harder than I thought," he said somberly.

"You're about six years too late for that picture. But you know what, you're here. And that's what matters. And believe it or not, it matters to her. I can guarantee that despite all the attitude, she is so much happier since you showed up. She has her dad. She's testing you. She's testing her boundaries. That's what kids do. It's just harder to start learning the ropes when they're teenagers."

He laughed. "You can say that again. I'll try to cool it. I really do want to figure this out."

"Then you've definitely gotta cool it," she said.

"Rach? You home?" Ethan called from the living room.

"Listen," she said, "I've got to go. But she'll see you tomorrow."

"Sounds good."

Rachel stepped back into the living room to see Ethan sitting on the couch beside Aspen. He looked like he had gone home after work to shower and shave and change clothes before coming over. He glanced over the back of the couch.

"Hey, you," he said, a smile on his face.

"Hey," she said. Looking at him, all she could think about was their conversation from their first date, when he mentioned that he had family members who were Nazis. But she couldn't remember anything else from that conversation. What else did he tell her?

"You okay?" he asked.

She nodded. "How was work?"

"Fine. Why don't you come sit down instead of standing in that doorway?" he said, a peculiar look on his face as he studied her.

"Actually, I've got some calls to make for work. Mind if I step back in my room to make them?"

"Sure," he said, still trying to read her face. He could tell something was off.

She grabbed the slip of paper from the table and went back into her room. She locked the bedroom door.

Picking up her phone, she tried the first number again. This time someone answered. It was a young voice, too young to discern between boy and girl.

"Hi, I'm looking for Hanna Schneider. Does she live there?"

"Umm, yes. Can I ask who's calling, please?" the child asked.

"This is Rachel Taylor."

"Please hold," the child enunciated carefully, taught specifically what to say when answering the phone. Rachel smiled to herself, recalling when she taught Aspen the same thing.

"Grammmmmy!" the child's voice yelled. Rachel had to pull the phone from her ear. The child hadn't learned to move the phone away from their mouth before calling for someone.

A couple of minutes went by with mumbling on the other end of the line. Rachel wondered if she had been forgotten about and debated hanging up the phone and calling again later. Then she heard some scratching, like the receiver was being moved around and finally a voice spoke on the other line.

"Hello?" There was a slight accent in the voice when she spoke.

"Umm, yes, hi," Rachel said, excitement building inside her. "My name is Rachel Taylor. I'm sorry to bother you ma'am. I'm looking for a specific Hanna Schneider."

"Well my name is Hanna Schneider. But I'm not sure if I'm the specific one you're looking for."

"Are you related to Abarron Schneider?" she asked, holding her breath after putting the question out there.

"Abarron? I'm afraid I'm not. Guess I'm not the Hanna Schneider you're looking for. Sorry."

"Thank you anyway."

Rachel was disappointed when she drew a line through that name on her list. Only two more left. And that was provided the Hanna she was looking for was even on her list. What were the chances, though, that in the entire county, in the entire world, that of the six names she wrote down, the one woman she was actually in search of was on that list? After all, Aaron had changed, his name, hadn't he? Who's to say Hanna wouldn't have done the same? They were family. They lived the same tragedies. And whatever horrors had influenced Aaron to run from his life maybe influenced Hanna as well. It was most likely a hopeless search.

She tried the next number on the list, the one she had put a mark beside earlier because the voice on the answering machine sounded elderly. Once again, the answering machine picked up. Rachel sighed and hung up the phone. How many times, she wondered, should she try calling?

She tried the next number, the last one, still uncrossed, on her list. There had been no answer at this number earlier and no machine either. It rang several times. Rachel was feeling discouraged and about to hang up. As she pulled the phone away from her ear, she heard a voice. Quickly she brought the receiver back to her ear.

"Hello?" she said, wondering if she was simply losing her mind and hearing things now.

"Yes? Is someone there?" a soft voice asked from the other line.

"Yes, hi. I'm sorry about that," Rachel said. "I'm looking for Hanna Schneider."

"I'm Hanna Schneider. Well, Hanna Schneider-Davis."

Rachel shrugged. "Maybe you can help me. My name is Rachel Taylor and I'm looking for a specific Hanna Schneider."

"Oh, I do hope she isn't in any trouble," the woman's soft voice was sweet and slightly squeaky when it spoke.

"No, no, nothing like that. I'm actually a relative of hers. You wouldn't, by chance, happen to know an Abarron Schneider, would you?" Rachel asked.

There was no response from the woman. Rachel looked to make sure her phone hadn't disconnected.

"Hello? Are you there?" she asked.

"How do you know my brother?" the woman finally asked.

SIXTEEN

"It's you. You're Hanna Schneider, his sister. Your other brother is Ephraim."

"Who are you?" Hanna asked. She sounded baffled and completely taken back.

Rachel was overcome with emotion. She wanted to jump, scream, laugh. Tears filled her eyes and her heart raced in her chest. She paced her bedroom, with no place to go and willed herself to stay calm.

"I'm sorry. Like I said before, my name is Rachel Taylor, my father is Joseph Taylor. He is Abarron's son."

"You're his granddaughter. I… I never thought I would hear from my brother ever again. Is he there? Does he know you've contacted me?"

Rachel felt her breath catch. "I'm sorry, he… he passed away thirteen years ago. I actually didn't even know you existed until a few days ago."

"Oh," she said with a heavy breath.

Rachel felt a pit open inside of her.

"Was he happy?" Hanna asked.

Rachel could hear the emotion in the woman's voice when she asked about her brother.

"I always thought he was. I didn't know him as anything other than happy. He was the best grandfather ever when I was growing up," Rachel said, swallowing her rising emotion. She knew she needed to be strong for the woman on the phone.

"I'm so glad to hear that. Although I'm not surprised. Abarron loved children. He always said, God willing, he would someday have a big family. If you didn't know about me, how did you find me?" she asked.

"I live in the home that he and my grandma raised their family in. And I found an old trunk in the attic—"

"He kept it," Hanna whispered.

"It took a lot of piecing together because he had changed his name, but I was finally able to figure out who his family was and then I called all the Hanna Schneiders in New York."

"You're persistent. He changed his name? To what?" she asked.

"Aaron Alter Taylor."

"Hmm, interesting," she said. "And let me guess. You discovered more than a new name when you found that trunk."

"That's an understatement," Rachel said.

Hanna was silent for a moment, but Rachel could hear her heavy breathing. "Did he at least continue to honor the teachings of the Torah?"

"He didn't really practice any religion," she said hesitantly.

"Rachel, I am an old woman. And I remember the day my brother left like it was yesterday. I remember the look in his eyes. I could never forget it because I knew it would be the last time I would ever see him. There are many moments in my life that I look back on that make me happy and make me smile, but today, child, you bring more joy to me than you will ever know. And I thank you for calling me and giving me back a piece of my family."

Rachel's tears flowed freely down her face. She wasn't sure what to expect by calling Hanna. She hadn't thought a moment past finding the right woman. And in one phone call she knew her life was completely different. Everything was forever changed. She knew she had to meet her.

"I'm just so glad I found you," she said, trying desperately to compose herself.

When Rachel emerged from her room, emotion was undeniably all over her face. It was in her body movement and in her posture. Ethan rose in an instant from the couch and crossed the room to her aid.

"What's wrong?"

Her cloudy eyes met his and for the first time since knowing him, she felt uncertainty. "I found Aaron's sister," she whispered so that Aspen wouldn't hear.

Ethan took her by the wrist, and they stepped back into her bedroom and closed the door.

"I didn't realize you were looking for her. Or that she was alive," he said in clear disbelief.

Rachel nodded. "I wasn't sure if she was alive either. Kristin, AJ, and Tiff helped me track down all the Hanna Schneiders living in the New York City area. I called all of them today and found the right one."

"Rachel, how do you know this woman is for real? She could be a fraud," he said.

She shook her head adamantly. "She's for real. I never told her the relationship, but she knew. She knew the connection, that he was her brother."

"This is great news, then," he said, his excitement growing. "Why don't you look happy?"

She bit the bottom corner of her lip while she lowered her body to the bed.

"Rach?"

She studied him for a moment. She had always believed that what she had felt for Matt all those years was true love. She was foolish. True love looked nothing like what she and Matt had. But Ethan, that was real. And rare.

"I need to ask you about something," she said. Her hands began to shake in her lap.

"Anything," he said, a look of concern on his face.

"The first time we went out, I told you about this project. That I was tracing my lineage. It was just the beginning, and I didn't know anything."

He nodded his head in recollection.

"You told me something that night. Something about your family lineage. About Nazis in your family?" she asked.

Ethan swallowed as he crossed his arms over his chest and gave a nod. "Yeah, on my dad's side. Why? What does that have to do with anything?"

"Can you tell me about them?" she asked.

"Umm, why?" he asked with a strange look on his face. "I mean, it's not really something that's fun to talk about."

She nodded, understanding his reluctance. "I just… I just want to hear the story."

He took a deep breath. "Okaaay," he said, drawing out the word. "Off the top of my head? They were my grandpa's brothers and my great grandfather. I don't know really. I guess they were tried and convicted as war criminals. They were executed. That's about all I know. It's not something we discuss much in my family, if you know what I mean?"

"I understand. They were executed? Not imprisoned?" she asked.

"Maybe they were imprisoned, I don't know. I'd have to ask my Aunt Maggie. She's the one who has all the information on it," he said. He was getting flustered. "I don't see how this has any relevance to anything going on."

"I just want to know."

"You want to know about your family. Why do you suddenly need to know about mine?" he asked getting defensive.

"Because my family were the victims."

"I get it," he said with a nod. "And my family members were the persecutors. And that's my fault, somehow? Is that what this is about?" His voice was rising.

She shook her head. "No. I mean, I guess I don't even know how my family connects to all of this. But if your family was executed for war crimes, clearly someone was their victim."

"You know," he said throwing his hands down, "I don't need this. And I really don't need your judgment on things about my family. I think I'm going to stay at my own place tonight. Glad you found Aaron's sister," he said opening the door and storming through the living room toward the front door. He didn't even glance over his shoulder before he stepped out into the darkness.

Thursday morning, Rachel woke to a layer of snow on Lake Arrowhead Village. She made sure to head down to the store early to give herself enough time to shovel the front sidewalk for her customers.

She got a nice fire roaring in the fireplace and Sinful Retreat smelled of rich chocolate as Kristin pulled a batch of sinful Truffle Tarts from the oven that she would later adorn with raspberries after they had cooled.

Rachel slipped into her wool coat and mittens, stepped outside and began shoveling the snow on the sidewalk. Still angry from the night before, she found it easier to move the heavy whiteness aside for her customers than usual. Fifteen minutes later, a clearing was made, and she was back inside thawing her hands.

She opened the store and customers began filtering in, mostly for the bakery, but a few wandered into the bookstore. She took the quiet time to place orders and to rearrange a few shelves with promotional items. This time of year, she liked to keep things in constant rotation.

With both Mark and Darlene working, Rachel had more time to do the things that she needed to do to run the store. She stepped into her office to finish the bookkeeping so that everyone would get a paycheck on time, and then contacted her EDI Provider about some ordering discrepancies. While sitting on hold, Rachel opened the browser on her laptop and did a search for an airline ticket to New York City. The results appeared before her while she was still on hold and suddenly, she found herself staring at prices and dates. Why not spend a weekend in New York City? Hanna wasn't getting any younger. She had lost the opportunity with Grandpa Aaron. This might be her only chance with Hanna.

Before she had time to think about it any longer, she grabbed her wallet from her desk drawer and within a few minutes had completed the transaction. She was going to New York City, leaving a week from tomorrow and she didn't have an ounce of regret.

"Rachel, are you still there?" a voice asked on the other line. She almost forgot she was still on the phone.

After her phone call, she stepped out of her office and headed eagerly over to the bakery counter. She grabbed Kristin's arm and led her desk in the far corner of the kitchen. "You're never going to believe what I did," she said.

Kristin had a look of concern on her face.

"I found her. I found Hanna Schneider."

"Aaron's sister?" Kristin asked, her eyes growing wider.

Rachel nodded. "And I just booked a ticket to go see her."

Kristin's shoulders dropped. "You did what? Please tell me that ticket is for January."

Rachel winced. "It's next weekend."

"Rachel! You can't leave! Do you know what time of year it is? I can't run this place without you. You know we don't get vacations this time of year."

Rachel knew Kristin had every right to be angry with her. "I know, I know. But this is a once in a lifetime opportunity. She's almost ninety, Kristin. And I lost my chance with Grandpa and I can't lose this chance with her. I'm so sorry to do this to you."

Kristin looked stressed out. She sighed. "You're so lucky you're one of my best friends and I know the situation. But you so owe me for this."

"I know. I know, and I will make it up to you. I promise I will."

"Oh, I'm holding you to that. You will make it up to me. I can't believe I'm letting you get away with this."

Rachel stood in her kitchen, trying to decide what to make for dinner. Aspen was with her dad and she still hadn't seen or talked with Ethan. She felt badly for making Ethan think she was judging him because of his family. She knew it wasn't fair. She had been completely overwhelmed with emotion from her conversation with Hanna and everything she'd discovered over the last few weeks, and she'd taken it out on him.

There was a knock on her door, and she went to answer it. She was surprised and relieved to see Ethan standing on the other side.

"I'm sorry," he said.

"No. I'm sorry. I don't know why I pushed things like I did. It wasn't fair," she said.

He stepped inside her house, and she wrapped her arms around him. She felt better when he reciprocated and wrapped his around her.

"All of this has affected me so much more than I thought it could," she admitted.

"It's heavy stuff. It's an awful part of our world's history. How could it not affect you?"

She nodded. "I'm just sorry I took it out on you."

He gave her a smile and leaned in to kiss her. She kissed him back. His lips were soft and smooth, and she felt at peace with him. In an instant she forgot all about food and she pulled his body closer to hers and kissed him harder.

They made their way to her bedroom, and she was thankful Aspen was with her dad for the night. Ethan's hands roamed her body, caressing and massaging her as her went along. His lips followed and she let out tiny groans of pleasure.

They made love, and after a short break, they made love again. Afterward, she lay naked in the crook of his body and smelled the sweetness of his sweat. Her heart swelled with joy as she turned to look up at him and his lips met hers.

"I love you," he whispered in the quiet darkness of her bedroom.

"And I so love you," she whispered back as she settled back down into him.

After a while he stirred. "I'm hungry," he said as he rolled out of bed and slipped on his underwear. He made his way through the darkness and into the kitchen, and she saw a light come on somewhere in the distance.

Rachel grabbed her underwear and a t-shirt from her dresser and followed him to the kitchen where she found him in the middle of making a sandwich.

"You want one?" he asked.

"Sure," she said as she took a seat on a barstool.

He nodded and went to work on a second one for her.

"I called my Aunt Maggie today," he said, not looking up from the sandwich. "The one who did all the research on my family. I have the information you asked about, if you still want it," he said stoically.

At first Rachel didn't say anything. She wasn't sure if this was information she really wanted or not.

Ethan looked over his shoulder with a sober face. "Did you hear me?"

She nodded. "I'm not sure. I mean, what do you think? It's your family."

"I didn't really know much of the facts of any of it. There is just the common knowledge of having war criminals in our family. But no one liked to talk much about it. However, my aunt wanted to know the details. She is the one who went digging for the truth."

He took a deep breath and let it out slowly. "It's certainly interesting, if that's what you're looking for. And I'm not really sure how I feel about all of it. Or how I feel about knowing about it. These were awful people who affected the lives of so many people. I know I had nothing to do with any of it. I never met them. But I still can't help but feel shameful for it all," he said.

She winced. "That bad?"

He nodded as he grabbed the sandwiches and brought them to the counter. "Yeah."

They ate in silence beside each other, Ethan deep in thought. When they were done, she took his hand in hers. "Only if you want to talk about it," she said.

He looked up at her, his eyes meeting hers. "They were fucking bastards, Rach. Some of the worst of mankind," he blurted out.

She gave his hand a squeeze. "My grandfather was the middle of three boys. All the boys in his family, his father, Finn, included, were radical Germans. And they were hit hard by the depression after World War I. Finn was an early recruit in the Third Reich. My Grandpa Kurt, however, left Germany in the late twenties for a shipping yard job in the U.S. He was basically laughed at on the way out of the country by his dad and brothers. His younger brother was Heinrich. Maggie said that he joined the *Schutzstaffel* early on and served as a guard at a labor camp in Lublin, Poland in 1939 on Lipowa Street. He was mostly known for being an executioner. And then in January 1940, he was one of the German guards who oversaw the death march of 627 of the camp prisoners over eighty miles, through snowstorms, in temperatures below zero degrees. And in the end, only 287 survived. To make matters worse, on November 3, in 1943, all the remaining Jewish prisoners in the labor camp were slain by the German guards. Heinrich Kuhn was one of them."

Rachel felt her stomach churn as her body went cold. She pulled Ethan into her and hugged him tightly. She knew there was nothing she could say. No words could mask the horrors that he spoke of.

Ethan sat up and his eyes met hers. There was a look of anger in them. "Heinrich had an older brother. Fritz. He was an SS guard for the prisoner barracks at the Neuengamme Concentration Camp near Hamburg. Apparently in a position like that, brutality was rewarded because really, they were just handling enemies of the state. He was just sentenced to life in prison during the Nuremberg Trials. He died during a prison fight sometime in the 1950s. And then there's Great Grandpa Finn Kuhn. Mr. Aryan himself. I had to write this one down because I couldn't even pronounce it," he said as he walked to his coat near the door. He reached in his pocket and pulled out a folded piece of paper and walked back over to Rachel, setting the paper down in front of her.

Schutzstaffel Totenkopfverbande.

"He was the leader of Neuengamme's Death's Head unit, responsible for administering Nazi concentration camps," he said with fury in his eyes. He slammed his fist against the counter and Rachel jumped in her chair. "This son-of-a-bitch actually managed to evade authorities after the war. He changed his name and went into hiding for a few years until someone recognized him. When authorities came to arrest him, instead of facing what he'd done, the coward committed suicide."

His fist punched the palm of his other hand, and he headed back toward Rachel's bedroom. She followed after him.

"Where are you going?" she asked when she saw him dressing quickly.

"For a walk. Will you come?" he asked.

"Yeah," she said, heading to her dresser to grab jeans and socks.

She bundled up for the cold and was glad she had. The wind was chilly as it blew through the night air. A light snow was falling on them as they walked through the vacant village, the lake a black abyss in the darkness.

"I'm sorry, I couldn't stay in the apartment anymore," he said, taking her hand in his, despite her thick mittens.

"I understand. Trust me, I understand," she said with a nod.

"I just don't understand mankind. How is it that we have it in us to be so cruel? We're the only creature that tortures for pleasure," he said.

"I don't understand it either. And we don't learn from it. Genocide didn't stop with the Holocaust."

He took a breath as he turned to look at her. "You're right. I just can't decide if it's better knowing the truth or not."

"I struggle with that every day. There's that old saying 'ignorance is bliss', but I keep thinking that ignorance is what put us in these situations in the first place. So maybe, as hard as it is to take, it's still better to know."

He nodded his head. "You're probably right. But right now, I'm just too pissed off. I wish I could meet these guys. Just so I could beat the crap out of them."

She laughed. "And what would that accomplish?"

He shrugged. "It would get out some of this rage I feel right now."

It began to snow a little harder. The white snowflakes contrasted the dark night sky that encompassed them. Rachel looked up at the streetlight and watched as the tiny flakes danced with abandonment in the light. "Let's just be happy. And grateful for the choices that our direct ancestors made, which allow you and I to be here, right now, at this moment," she said, looking up at him, snowflakes catching on her eyelashes.

Ethan looked down at her and smiled. "You're right," he said with a nod. "You're so right." He leaned down and kissed her.

The store was incredibly busy all weekend as shoppers prepared for a mountain storm moving in that was projected to hit the Lake Arrowhead area sometime late Saturday afternoon. Rachel tried working double-time in anticipation for the couple days that she would be gone to New York City, but the busy crowds of people were making that difficult for her.

Aspen and Matt stopped in around lunch time on Saturday and Rachel was relieved to see that they had been getting along for the weekend. Maybe Matt had taken her advice to heart. Then again, she had thought that several times about him over the years and he, more times than not, tended to disappoint her. She decided not to read too much into it and just smiled instead.

"What kind of science books do you have, Mom?" Aspen asked.

"What kind are you looking for?"

"Ones about gears."

"I don't think I have anything that would help you with that. We could look in our online catalogs though," she said.

"Why wouldn't you have science books? You're a bookstore."

"Yes, that's true. However, I tend to get more people interested in animals, insects, trees, things like that around here rather than gears. I just don't really see it being a big seller."

"Well I would buy it," Aspen said.

"With my money."

"Technicality," she said with the wave of her hand.

"Anyway. Did you guys try the library?" Rachel asked.

"I didn't think of that," Matt said.

"No, Mom. I hate going there. Only the nerds go in there. It would be like social suicide."

"Well, then you better wear a disguise, because that's where you're headed next."

Matt laughed. "I might have a paper bag in my car."

Aspen groaned. "You guys are so unfair. What are you trying to do to me?"

"Get you to pass science," Matt said as he ushered her toward the door. "Thanks, Rach. See you later."

"Bye guys," she said with a wave.

As Matt and Aspen stepped out of the store, AJ came in, a very straight look on her face.

"Someone die?" Rachel asked.

"This is serious," she said. "Where's Kristin?" She spotted her and waved her over.

"What's up?"

"Jack called me. He wants to go to Cancun in January."

"Ah, nice," Rachel said with a nod.

"With his family."

"Not nice," Rachel added.

"Are you kidding?" Kristin said. "What family?"

"His daughter. His parents. His sister and her family. Oh, and the family dog."

Kristin giggled. "Wow. Congratulations. You just got married."

"I know, right?" AJ said, her mouth falling open. "I called Tiff on my way here and she said I shouldn't go."

"I'm with her," Kristin said. "You don't do commitment too soon very well. And family, well, that certainly means commitment. In a big sort of way."

"I don't know. I think it might be kind of nice," Rachel said.

Both AJ and Kristin looked at her with cocked eyebrows.

"Oh come on. It's not like you haven't been spending every day that you can with him. And he's even a couple of hours away. So clearly you like him. And he likes you. And you're in your thirties; I don't see the big deal. Besides, it's freaking Cancun," Rachel said.

"Are you just telling me this because all of a sudden you're happy and in love?" AJ asked.

"She drank the Kool Aid," Kristin said.

AJ nodded.

"Whatever. You came to get our opinion, I'm giving you mine. I think you should go."

"I think AJ's right. You really are out of sorts. First you bought a ticket to New York and now you're encouraging this. I'm not sure what's happened to you. Maybe it's the sex. Is this what you're like when you have sex?" Kristin said.

"What are you going to New York for?" AJ asked.

"Oh, I didn't tell you! I found Hanna Schneider."

"You did? From the numbers we found at my place?"

Rachel nodded.

"And you talked to her? Obviously, you talked to her. So you're going to see her? That's incredible."

"Yeah, and she's leaving me high and dry in the middle of holiday season," Kristin added.

"I'll come help you out," AJ said.

"For some reason I still don't feel better about this," Kristin said.

"Watch yourself or I'll buy my coffee elsewhere."

Kristin laughed. "That would require you to *buy* your coffee. Try a threat you might actually follow through on."

"We're not anywhere near a solution to my problem," AJ said, sticking her hand in Kristin's face to cover it. Kristin slapped it away.

"What do you want to do?" Rachel asked.

"It doesn't matter what I want to do," AJ said.

"Sure, it does," Kristin said.

AJ's eyes flitted back and forth between them, but she didn't say anything.

"You want to go!" Kristin said. She turned to face Rachel. "She wants to go."

Rachel nodded fervently. "She does. You do," she said looking back at AJ. "So go. Why are you asking us?"

She sighed loudly. "Because you guys, I'm nervous. I like this guy. What if this doesn't work out?"

"I'd hardly believe he'd invite you to something like this if he wasn't thinking along the same lines," Kristin said.

"Yeah, I'm with Kristin on this one."

"Okay. But if he breaks my heart, I'm breaking your…ffff…fingers," she said.

"Good one," Kristin said. "I've got to get back to work."

"Me too," Rachel said.

"And I'd better call Tiff and tell her I caved like a mine."

In the evening, Ethan picked up an order of food from Papagayos in the village. He and Rachel sat at the table eating their dinner.

"When were you going to tell me you were going to New York?" he asked.

Her body went still mid-bite. She looked up from her food. "A few days ago," she said, her eyes meeting his. "I'm so sorry. I was going to tell you. Things have been so crazy around here," she said, knowing that wasn't good enough. "How did you even find out?"

"I ran into AJ in Stater Bros. today. She mentioned it. Imagine my shock when I was completely clueless to what she was talking about."

Rachel winced. "Ethan, I'm so sorry. I didn't mean for you to find out that way. Really, I didn't."

He seemed mostly indifferent. "Well, can't change anything now."

She felt guilty and they finished their dinner with menial conversation.

Afterwards he pulled up his email on her laptop. "My Aunt Maggie sent me a photo she got from a curator at a Holocaust Museum on the east coast. I don't know what it's a picture of," he said.

Rachel hovered behind him as he opened the photo file.

It was a black and white photo of military men. The caption read: SS guards from Neuengamme concentration camp, camp march 9 Nov 1942. Ethan enlarged the photograph. Men, four wide and deeper than the photo was able to capture, marched down a street, a two-story building in the background. They wore long, buttoned trench-coats secured with belts around the waist, hardened helmets on their heads, and supported rifles on their left sides.

Maggie made a note in the email.

Fritz Kuhn is the only face looking directly at the camera. He marched on the far-right flank. – Aunt Maggie

Rachel felt a chill run through her as she read the line. Ethan pulled the image of the photo back up and together they scanned the faces. Then she spotted it. And in an instant her heart stopped. It was like Fritz Kuhn was looking right at her, his eyes boring into her as she looked back at him in the photograph. She shuddered.

"I'm not even sure what to do with this," Ethan admitted as he looked away. "It's a face I could've lived my entire life never having seen."

Rachel gently rubbed her hand over his shoulder blades. "He's dead. Just remember that."

"That's the only justice in this, that he's rotting in a grave right now."

"Come on. Let's not think about this anymore tonight. Want to watch a movie or something?" she asked.

He nodded. "Sure."

The week passed by in slow motion for Rachel as she prepared for New York. But when Friday finally came, she could hardly contain her excitement. Kristin, on the other hand, was not thrilled to see her go. She knew the next three days were going to be stressful trying to run and manage Sinful Retreat without her. But she vowed she would do it. And Kristin was determined.

She tried to sleep during her flights, but it was completely useless. Her nerves prohibited an ounce of sleep. It's like she was strung out on coffee, which she'd had none of in days.

When she landed, she eagerly retrieved her luggage and hailed a cab. She had written down the address that Hanna had given her over the phone so she could mail her photos of her family. Excitement and nerves jumbled inside her as she told the driver where to go. Hanna wasn't expecting her. But she hoped the old woman would be as excited to meet her as Rachel was.

As she rode through the busy streets of New York, Rachel gawked out the window. All of the Christmas decorations gave the city a magical feel. Everyone appeared to be unaffected by the cold as the sidewalks were filled with crowds. Holiday decorations and lights adorned buildings, streetlamps, parks, doorways, archways and fountains. She couldn't take it all in on a single cab ride.

Before she knew it, they had arrived at the Gershwin Towers, their destination. Rachel paid her driver and with her bags in tow, stepped onto the streets of New York City. She looked up at the building before her, the home of Hanna Schneider-Davis. Taking a deep breath, she opened the front door and stepped inside.

At the front counter she signed in and was pointed in the direction she needed to go. She went up sixteen floors, took two right turns and then a left. And then she found it. On the door hung a welcome sign and a simple mat laid at the floor.

She closed her eyes for a moment to gather all the inner strength she could muster. And then, before she could talk herself out of it, she reached out and knocked on the door.

SEVENTEEN

It took a while for the door to be answered. But Rachel knew someone was inside the assisted living apartment. She could hear the sound of a television and other muffled noises after she knocked.

She waited patiently, nervously outside the door. A few nurses and other residents of Gershwin Towers passed her, but no one seemed to notice her presence. She knocked again.

There were more sounds from inside the apartment, and finally the door opened. A thin woman, yellow tinted skin, thin lips, and bright eyes answered the door. It was surreal to Rachel how she was standing in front of a complete stranger, yet her eyes, the same eyes she had studied in those old photographs, could be so familiar.

"Can I help you?" the sweet voice asked.

"Hanna?" she asked.

She nodded. "Yes. And you are?"

"I'm Rachel."

Hanna caught her breath and took an unsteady step backward as she began muttering in another language, whispering under her breath.

"I'm sorry, I probably should've called. At least when I got to New York. I…I wanted to meet you and—"

Hanna reached out her hand and silenced Rachel. "Come in. Let me see you," she said amid watery eyes.

Rachel swallowed hard. Grabbing her bag, she stepped inside.

Hanna looked her up and down, clasping her hands over her mouth. "You are so beautiful," she said. "You remind me so much of my mother. Her name was Rachel, too." Hanna smiled as her eyes met Rachel's.

Rachel nodded. "I know. I found her on Ancestry.com. And her parents, Otto and Lena, too."

Hanna looked shocked. "Amazing the things that are out there just waiting to be discovered. Please, take a seat," she said, offering a chair to her as she sat in a recliner with a throw blanket across the back. "Unfortunately, all those details are black and white. And life is all gray area."

The door to Hanna's small apartment opened and a nurse came in with a look of concern. "*Savta*, what's going on?" the woman asked.

"Ahh, Cindy," Hanna said, lighting up with joy. "I have someone I want you to meet," she said with a nod of her head. "This is Rachel. She's here from California."

Cindy looked confused as her head swiveled between Hanna and Rachel. "I'm sorry, who are you?" Cindy asked.

"Rachel is Abarron's granddaughter," Hanna continued.

Cindy's head shot quickly back to Hanna. "Your brother? His granddaughter?"

Hanna nodded with excitement. "Isn't it wonderful? After all these years…"

"*Savta*," she said. "Would you excuse us," Cindy said, looking toward Rachel as she squared herself between Hanna and Rachel and began whispering, even though Rachel could still hear her. "What are you thinking letting a stranger in here? You don't know her. She could be making all of this up."

"Why would she do that? To rob me?" Hanna asked, not nearly as concerned about whispering as Cindy was. "Shall I put my mini menorahs and the artwork from your kids in my safe, just in case?"

"Why are you so stubborn?" Cindy asked.

"Because not everyone is out to get me. It's going to be fine. I assure you. Now go on. I'm sure someone somewhere in the building has rolled onto their oxygen cord and is in need of your attention," she said with a wave of her hand.

Cindy sighed as she rose to her feet. "I'll be back later to check on you."

"Oh har har. I'll be just fine."

Cindy smiled at Rachel. "Welcome to New York," she said. "Have fun with my grandma."

Rachel smiled back. "Thanks. I will." She was relieved when Cindy left the room.

"Forgive her, she's a bit overprotective of me. She's a good kid. Well, not really a kid anymore, but she will always be a kid to me. All that," she motioned toward the rows of finger paintings and colorful drawings that lined the wall near the television, "that's all from her children. She has three kids."

"Wow," Rachel said. "My one keeps me busy."

Hanna laughed. "They have a way of doing that. Now, I'm sure you didn't come all this way just to talk about that."

"Actually, I brought a few things that I thought you might want to take a look at." Rachel opened her carry-on bag and pulled out a folder. Tucked safely inside were some of the photographs she had found in the trunk. She first grabbed the photo from the beach and handed it to Hanna.

Hanna inhaled loudly with a quiver when she took it gently into her hands. "I don't think I've ever seen this one before," she said. She turned it over in her hands and read the scribble on the back. "We used to vacation to the Baltic for two weeks every summer. This," she said with a heavy sigh, "was the last vacation we ever took as a family. My brothers and I left for America only a few months after this. That right there," she said pointing to the oldest man in the photo, "is my grandfather, Otto. He was my mother's dad. And beside him is my grandmother, Lena. They were wonderful people and they loved to spoil us. They always gave us candies, which my father hated. He said one was okay, but more than that was bad for our teeth."

Rachel smiled as she tried to picture Isak fathering his children, trying to manage the amount of candy they ate while their grandfather slipped them more.

"Even my mother is in her bathing suit," Hanna noted, studying the photo. "She rarely went in the water. It was always cold. It was the Baltic after all," she said, looking up at Rachel. She handed back the photo and Rachel handed her another one. This one had no caption on it. She knew it was the children. That much she could tell. But the other two adults in the picture she had never learned the identity of.

"Ah, this is *Zeyda* and *Bubbe*. That's what we called my grandparents on my father's side because they were Jewish. It's Yiddish. *Zeyda* Schneider died not long after this photo was taken. He had a heart condition. I think he'd had it his whole life. And then *Bubbe* moved to Prague to live with my dad's youngest brother, Ismael, who was a surgeon there."

"In Prague?" Rachel asked.

Hanna nodded. "My father's family was very divided. In the end, it's what saved some of us. My father was a middle child of six boys. My poor *Bubbe*. All those sons. And they all did well for themselves. Eli was a dentist in Philadelphia. He left Germany first. And Johan was a bank manager in Berlin. Etan was a family doctor in Paris. It was Etan who sent us to Avi in America. Avi was a lawyer here, in New York City."

"What happened to everyone? I mean, can I ask that?" Rachel asked hesitantly.

Hanna nodded. "They are your family, too. Eli and Avi and their families were of course safe, being in America. Etan and his family managed to get to England, but his youngest son died in one of the German bombings. Eventually they went back to Paris and my nieces and nephews and their families still live there. Johan, Ismael and *Bubbe* were all killed during the war."

Rachel felt her chest tighten.

"Sometime in late 1941, *Bubbe* and Ismael were arrested and imprisoned in the Theresienstadt Ghetto in Terezin, Czechoslovakia. After the war, I tried hard to find everyone and put the pieces of what had been my family back together. I found record of Ahuva Schneider, that was *Bubbe's* name, being processed into the ghetto but never anything after that. There was a camp census taken in 1943 and Ahuva was not listed on it. I can only assume that she died there sometime before that date. As for Ismael, he was on that census. He was also included on a manifest in December 1944 in a list of people sent east to Treblinka. After that there is no record of him. Treblinka was an extermination camp and that was during the time of Operation Reinhard, so I'm fairly certain he was gassed." Hanna's eyes looked lost in thought as she sat nearly motionless in her chair.

"I'm sorry, Hanna. If this is too difficult to talk about, we don't—"

"I know difficult," she interrupted with the shake of her head. "For some people, they lock their stories away. My brothers were those kinds of people. But talking is therapeutic for me. Talking is not difficult."

Rachel swallowed hard. "Do you know if Aaron, I mean, Abarron ever knew the fate of these people? Of your family?"

Hanna shrugged. "I'm not sure. It took me a lot of years of digging to find all of this. Everything was displaced for so many years. Even now we are still making discoveries and finally putting together broken pieces. The Nazis destroyed so many records that we will never know what happened to everyone."

"Do you know what happened to Johan?" she asked, readjusting in her chair. She was scared to ask about the people she really came for.

Johan was in Berlin, one of the worst places, when it all began. And he insisted that it could never get as bad as it eventually did. Even when my parents sent us away, he told them they were crazy. He was a proud German and even after being denied his citizenship, he refused to accept it. My Grandfather Otto, who was a Nazi, told me that when Johan was arrested by the SS for refusing to wear his yellow star, he was beaten in the streets of Berlin and then shot in the head in an alleyway. And they left his body there to just rot."

Rachel shuddered at the image in her head. "I am actually confused about Otto. So he was a Nazi?"

Hanna nodded. "Yes. But not a very good one."

"What do you mean?"

"Grandfather had served during World War I as a platoon leader. This was before my parents had ever met. And my father served under him in his platoon. Otto liked Isak. My father even earned himself a medal serving in the war. But to this day I don't know what it was for."

"Do you know if it was a cross?" Rachel asked.

"Hmm, it may have been. Actually, I think so," she said nodding her head.

"I found one in my grandpa's trunk. I actually thought it was Otto's when I found all the military records. I didn't realize that Isak served as well."

"Otto had awards, too, but he would've held onto them himself. Shortly before our vacation to the Baltic, he was recalled into the Wehrmacht. He tried everything he could to avoid it because he wasn't a much of a supporter of the Reich. But he started to feel their pressure and that's why my grandparents were with us on that vacation. I remember them telling us that Grandfather was going back into the army. And that people might start to talk, and we might hear things but that we shouldn't listen to anything we heard. I couldn't understand, at the time, why Grandfather being in the army would make people call my family Jew-haters. *I* was a Jew. And grandfather certainly didn't hate me. And then I realized it was because of the black spider. That's what I thought the swastika looked like. Everyone was nervous around it. It changed people when that symbol was around. People who had been friends our entire lives suddenly pretended not to know us. Kids called us names. I wasn't sure what to make of any of it."

Rachel tried to imagine the life Hanna was describing. It must have been such a confusing time for a young child. She thought about Aspen, who wasn't much older now than Hanna would've been then. Her heart broke as she tried to imagine how she would explain why people who had been her friends suddenly wanted nothing to do with her.

"When we returned home from the Baltic, someone had defaced our home. *Jude umkommen.* Perish Jew. My parents tried to hide it from us, but there was no hiding that. I saw it quite plainly. I think even before they did. But it was the Nuremberg Laws that sealed the fate for our family. Suddenly my parents' marriage was void in the eyes of our country. And in an instant my father, who was a literature professor, which was a civil position, was now unemployed. That's what motivated our parents to send us to America. The plan was temporary; just until things had time to calm down. At least that was my understanding. But looking back, it's odd that we were made to pack nearly all of our most precious valuables. We even had to take some of the things our parents treasured most."

"So that was it? You just said goodbye and never saw them again?" Rachel asked. She felt a pull at her heart, unable to comprehend the thought of sending her children away.

Hanna nodded somberly and avoided eye contact with Rachel. "I can remember that day like it was yesterday. My parents ushered us along like it was just another day, just another thing to do. They wouldn't let us get caught up in an emotional display because it would draw too much attention to us. Abarron held my hand the entire time and wouldn't let go, even after we were seated on the train. It was noisy and busy. People were coming and going. No one paid much attention to us. There were more police around than I usually remembered at the train station, but my grandfather made sure to come along and he was dressed in uniform so no one suspected anything when they saw him with us. Our goodbye was short. But I couldn't let go of my mother. I gripped her so hard, and I slipped my hands into her pockets. When my father had to pry me away, with Grandfather trying to block me from the SS guards nearby, I ripped Mother's dress. My bottom lip quivered so hard that I could barely tell her I loved her. But she nodded that she understood. And it took both Ephraim and Abarron to get me on the train."

"Inside I was just a little girl who had lost her mother and father. But on the outside, I was big enough and old enough to have to carry on the façade that it was just another day for my family. I had been carefully instructed to not show emotion and to not draw attention to myself. I buried my face between my brothers and didn't even look up until we were out of Germany."

Rachel watched as tears fell from Hanna's eyes. The old woman gingerly reached for a tissue from the nearby table and dabbed at her eyes, beneath her glasses. She took a deep breath and turned to look out the window. The room was quiet. Rachel sat in her chair, afraid to move, afraid to even breathe. She watched Hanna carefully, studied her. On the outside she looked like a frail old woman, approaching the end of a long life. But she was resilient and had stood the test of time.

"I supposed next you'll want to know about Isak," Hanna said, breaking the silence in the room.

"Only if you want to share. I can't imagine it's a story you like to tell," Rachel said.

Hanna looked back to Rachel from the window, a disheartened grin on her face. "No. It's not a story I like to tell. But it's one you should know. He is, after all, your Great Grandfather. And he has a chance to live on through you and your family."

Rachel felt an overwhelming sadness come over her. It was a moment she had been searching for and now it was upon her and a part of her wanted to flee. Everything leading up to this had been so tragic, why would this be any less? She took a deep breath, wondering if there was really a way to prepare herself.

"For a short time in 1936, there was talk of sending my brothers and I back home. The Olympics were going on in Germany and although no laws had changed in the country, things were at least given the illusion of improving. My uncle Avi, however, was quite insistent, along with my grandfather, that we wait out the Olympics. And it was a good thing we did."

"So you were still corresponding with your parents?" Rachel asked.

"Oh yes. As much as possible," Hanna said with a nod. "During the summer of 1937, there was a significant increase in the enforcement of the Law for the Protection of German Blood and German Honor. That was the law that nullified my parents' marriage. Anyone suspected of breaking that law or any German citizen suspected of engaging in sexual relations with a Jew was facing fines and jail time. And the Jewish person was facing deportation to Buchenwald. So my parents moved from Dresden to Leipzig, into my grandparents' home. That officially put my father into hiding."

"Otto, a Nazi officer, was hiding Isak in his home?" Rachel asked in disbelief.

Hanna nodded. "See, he wasn't a very good Nazi." She smiled. "And this allowed us to still correspond with our parents. Grandfather mailed all of our letters, and no one thought twice about what he was sending."

"I can't believe Isak was living in Otto's home. What would they do if people came over? Didn't people know his daughter had been married before?"

"Oh yes. They didn't hide my mother, Rachel. Isak would go to the basement when people, even other officers, would come to the house. They used my mother to show that they had followed the Nuremberg Laws, that they were upstanding Germans. No one questioned anything they did then," Hanna said. "But in reality, my mother and father were so in love. To this day it's one of my favorite memories about them. They were one of those couples that never got past the honeymoon stage. I don't recall them fighting, and rarely bickering. And there were just always these small gestures of love: glances, winks, touches, lingers. Always sweet, always there."

"I just can't imagine going to the basement every time someone would come to the house. Didn't that kill his pride?" Rachel asked feeling badly as she thought of Isak being put downstairs like a wet dog.

Hanna nodded. "I'm sure it did. But by fall of 1937, they began to notice their friends were disappearing. Yes, some of them fled, but others had been arrested. Some more publicly than others. And others just silently disappeared altogether. It was growing more and more imperative that no one know my father's whereabouts."

"How long did all of this go on?"

Hanna took a long sigh and glanced at the clock on her wall. "I'm hungry. Are you hungry?"

Rachel thought it was an odd time to think about her stomach, but it was dark outside now. "Umm, sure. I've probably caused you to miss your dinner. I'm so sorry."

"Ah, that's just fine. I'm always looking for an excuse to get out of this building," she said with a wave of her hand. "Let's make a reservation somewhere. There's a great little Italian place down the street. Do you like Italian?"

"Of course, who doesn't?" Rachel said.

They were on their way out the door when Rachel spotted Cindy walking toward them.

"*Savta*, where are you going?" she asked, walking briskly to cover the distance between them.

"Ahh, there you are. Are you done for the day?" Hanna asked, leaning on her cane as she turned to lock her door.

"Yeah. I was coming to check on you."

"We're headed to dinner. Join us, won't you?" she said as she began down the hallway toward the elevators.

"Why didn't you just eat here?" Cindy asked, walking with them.

"We got to talking. Imagine that, I talked myself right through a meal," she said with a giggle.

Cindy rolled her eyes. "She's got a few stories, huh?" she said, looking at Rachel.

Rachel laughed. "That's an understatement." She didn't want to take a break, but after getting out of the small apartment she realized how badly she was in need of one. When they finally reached the lobby on the main floor, she marveled at the all the lights outside on the street.

"I'll go ahead and get us a cab," Cindy said, stepping ahead.

Rachel walked alongside Hanna, who took her time getting to the doorway. "If I don't get a chance to say this at some point," Hanna said, "I'm so glad you came."

Rachel's heart swelled. "Me too."

Sitting down at the table for dinner, despite all the bustling noise around her, Rachel was quiet. In the cab on the way over, she had felt her phone vibrating in her handbag, and when she glanced down at it she saw her father's name on the screen. A knot had formed in the pit of her stomach. He was clueless, back in California, that she was here, in New York City, with his aunt. And Rachel wondered how he might react.

"Tell me about your family," Hanna said. "Tell me about your daughter."

Rachel smiled and her heart warmed at the thought of Aspen. "She's wonderful," she said. "She keeps me on my toes. That's for sure."

Hanna laughed. "They always do," she said. "She's twelve?"

Rachel nodded. "She'll be thirteen in February. I have a picture," she said, reaching into her bag and pulling out a photo. She reached across the table and handed it to Hanna.

"You said you aren't married. Is Aspen's dad in the picture at all?" Hanna asked, looking at the photo in admiration.

"He's in the picture, but only as dad."

"You're not together?" Cindy asked.

Rachel shook her head. "It didn't work out."

"Is there someone else it's working out with?" Hanna asked with a grin as she looked up from the photo and handed it back across the table.

"Kind of," Rachel said with a shrug.

"And does he have a name?" she asked with a smirk.

Rachel felt her cheeks redden. "Course he does. Ethan. Ethan Kuhn."

"Ahh, it sounds like he's got some German in him," Hanna said.

She sighed as she gave a weak smile and was relieved when the waiter appeared to take their order.

Rachel let Hanna and Cindy do most of the talking through dinner. They shared stories of living in New York and about Cindy's children, who were young, and loved to visit *Savta* Hanna. Rachel marveled at the fact that Cindy's children knew their Great Grandmother while her father Joseph had spent his entire life never knowing even the names of his grandparents. The world was unfair. But if there were anything that digging into the realities of the Holocaust had shown her, it was that the world was never a fair place. Her heart began to ache as she thought of the story that the woman sitting across from her had shared. But they weren't just stories, they were peoples' lives. She wanted to know more but wasn't sure how to ask. She wasn't sure how much Hanna was able to tell in one day. And at that moment the old woman seemed to be happy and at peace. Rachel didn't want to be the one to disrupt that.

Sitting there, Hanna wasn't the little girl clutching her mother's dress at the train station, she wasn't orphaned in a new country, she wasn't searching for the whereabouts of her family members, dead or alive. She was just a woman in a pizzeria with her granddaughter and great niece, enjoying a weekend in December.

"Well ladies, what do you say we head back to the tower?" Hanna suggested as she glanced at the time.

Rachel knew it was getting late. Even she was exhausted and it was three hours earlier back home. She could only imagine that Hanna had to be completely drained.

When the three of them arrived at the Gershwin Towers, Cindy remained in the cab and continued home to her family. Rachel got out and helped Hanna back upstairs to her small apartment.

It was brisk outside and the warm air inside the lobby felt nice when they stepped inside. As they headed up in the elevator, Rachel felt Hanna's eyes on her and she glanced her way.

"I really love having you here," Hanna said.

Rachel smiled.

They walked in silence the rest of the way back to her door but when Hanna opened it, she motioned for Rachel to come inside.

Rachel stepped into the small, one room apartment and took a seat in the chair that she had spent the afternoon in. Hanna crossed the room and flipped on a light and a soft glow lit up the room.

Rachel felt compelled to talk. The silence felt awkward between them. "How long ago did your husband pass away?" she asked.

"Michael died seven years ago. Lung cancer. There's a picture of him on the dresser over there," she said with a nod as she took her pills.

Rachel rose from the chair and made her way to the dresser. She didn't have to ask who Michael was. Hanna still had a wedding photo framed, and a few family pictures from over the years. It was almost as though Michael were still here today.

"How did you two meet?"

"A family friend introduced us. He lost family during the war, too. So we had that in common," Hanna said casually as she took a seat in her chair.

Startled, Rachel looked over her shoulder. "He did?"

"We pretty much all lost someone. Back then, he was Michal Davidovic. When he came through Ellis Island, they made him change his surname to Davis. It was easier. And by the time I met him, he had made a change to his first name, as well," she said as Rachel made her way back to the chair. "He was young when he came here. Was by himself and had a couple of brothers already here, working in America. Times were tough for his family. They were in the southern Czech, now Slovakia and northern Hungary, and they were poor. Mostly farmers. His youngest brother, Adalbert stayed behind though, to take care of their parents Adolf and Helena. He was much younger than the others. He was sixteen years younger than Michael," Hanna said. She took a drink of water and rested her head against the back of her chair.

Rachel could tell she was tired. "We don't have to—"

"Michael carried the guilt with him for years. His parents had both died before the war. There was no need for Adalbert to have even stayed, but he insisted on staying on the farm. And even Michael was broke. He had no money. He skirted from job to job back then just to make ends meet."

Hanna took a breath. "It was a long, long time before we ever found out anything about what happened to his brother. It was just a few years before Michael found out he had cancer. And it was what we had dreaded all along."

"What happened to him?" Rachel asked. Her throat had gone dry and her voice was barely a whisper.

"Auschwitz happened to him."

A chill ran through Rachel.

"He was arrested in September of forty-two and five days later he was processed as a forced laborer at Auschwitz. He never came out alive. And there's no record of him after he was processed into the camp. 6. 5. 0. 8. 5." Hanna closed her eyes and recited the numbers quietly to herself over and over and over again. The hair on Rachel's arms slowly began to rise as Hanna whispered each number, her breath catching with the sound of Hanna's voice.

Slowly her eyes opened but they looked to a fixed, far-off place, a cold, lost expression in them. "I will remember those numbers until the day I die. My husband would repeat them in his sleep."

"What are they?"

Hanna turned and her eyes met Rachel's. "It's the serial number that was tattooed on Adalbert's forearm."

At the hotel, Rachel checked into her room and changed into pajamas. It was dark outside, but the city lights kept it from actually getting dark outside her window. The sounds of traffic, car horns and sirens played outside her room, but she didn't notice. Instead, she lay on the bed, numb to the world around her.

Hanna wanted her to come back the next day so she could finish telling their family's story, but Rachel wasn't sure she could hear anymore. Her chest felt so heavy already. She was overwhelmed with everything she had learned in one day. Hanna had years to come to terms with everything, but Rachel was learning it all right then. She wasn't sure she would be able to go back in the morning. How could she finish?

She thought about Aaron, the goofy, crooked, closed-lipped smile and playful eyes that she remembered. The coffee drip that was in the middle of every shirt, caught by his belly because he wasn't capable or willing to use enough caution when drinking his daily coffee to not spill it.

Her heart grew full when she recalled all the games of Yahtzee that they played with her brother and the late nights they spent at the car races. Suddenly she yearned to hear the sound of the chimes from the grandfather clock that stood in her parents' home. It was the clock he handcrafted for them for their wedding day, having made a similar one for his bride that also stood in Sinful Retreat, but no longer chimed. Rachel made a silent vow to hire someone to get it working again.

Tears rolled down the side of her face as anger took over her insides. When she took the very first step on this journey, she thought it would bring her closer to the grandfather she missed she much, but the truth bore a hole so deep inside of her that she wasn't sure she would ever be able to fill. She wanted to close it up tight, lock it away and make it disappear.

With everything inside of her, she now understood the choices that Aaron had made so long ago.

Rachel felt her phone begin to vibrate alongside her leg. She reached down to look at who was calling her. Ethan's photo flashed across the screen and her eyes lingered on the image of him smiling at her for a moment before she dismissed the call. She set the phone on the nightstand beside the bed, reached for the lamp and turned off the light.

When Rachel stepped onto the street outside her hotel on Saturday morning, she was surprised to see a layer of snow covering the ground. Snow was still falling all around her. The cold air filled her lungs and refreshed her, and she felt rejuvenated. Thankfully the hotel was getting her a cab. Despite her rest and rejuvenation, she wasn't confident in her abilities to hail one amid all the New Yorkers, especially in the snow.

Hanna was up and eagerly waiting for Rachel when she arrived. Cindy popped in to greet her and brought them both a morning coffee. They made small talk for a few minutes before Cindy slipped out of the room and went back to work.

"Well, are you ready to jump back into things?" Hanna asked before taking a drink of the coffee.

"I guess so," Rachel said, feeling less sure of herself now that she was here.

Hanna grabbed a folder from the top drawer of the dresser and made her way across the room to her recliner. "Now, where did we leave off yesterday?" she asked.

"Uh…" Rachel wracked her brain. "We were talking about Otto hiding Isak."

"Ahh, yes. Thank you. Some of my short-term memory isn't too good these days. But this other stuff, I assure you, I don't think I'll ever forget," she said with a nod. "So that would have been 1937."

"Yeah, that's right," Rachel said, recalling their conversation yesterday.

"My mother, Rachel," Hanna said solemnly, "died in December that year."

"I actually found an article in a German newspaper about her death," Rachel said reluctantly.

Hanna sat up straight in her chair. "You did? How were you able to read it?"

"A friend of mine translated it."

"And you were certain it was my mother?"

Rachel nodded. She bent over and reached for her bag. She had printed off the article and brought a copy of it along with her and gave it to Hanna.

Hanna read through it, her face draining of color as she did so. When she finally looked up at Rachel, Rachel could tell she was holding back her anger.

"Just figures this is how it would be written," she said bitterly. Hanna took a breath.

"I'm sorry. I know it's incredibly biased, but I don't follow. I'm confused."

Hanna looked to the ground for a moment and Rachel stopped talking. They sat in silence for a few minutes while Hanna gained her composure and Rachel wished she hadn't shown her the article.

When Hanna looked up again, she seemed to be the Hanna that Rachel knew, calm and collected. "My mother got pregnant that fall."

Rachel felt her heart drop.

"It was of course my father's baby. And the Jewish man the article refers to is my father," Hanna said.

"It was Isak?" Rachel asked.

Hanna nodded. "That was how he was captured."

"How did Rachel die?" she asked.

Hanna opened the folder she was clutching in her hands. "I translated this many years ago so that my children would someday be able to read it. About a month after my mother died, when my Grandmother Lena wrote to us and told us the fate of our parents, she included a journal entry that my mother had written. I think it was meant to give my brothers and I some insight into what our mother was thinking when she had made the choice that she made."

Rachel began to feel uneasy as she listened to Hanna speak.

"I'll let you read it," Hanna said as she reached forward and gave Rachel two pieces of paper with her handwriting on them.

Rachel took them into her lap and looked down at Hanna's delicate handwriting.

December 4th, 1937

It's been a colder winter than I remember growing up here in Leipzig. But maybe it's the chill of this new Germany. It has gone straight to my bones. I don't know my home anymore. I don't recognize it. Even Vater says this is un-German. The Fuhrer says our lives are to go on as before. He says they are to be better but I don't see how it is going to be. It is because of him and his policies that my children are gone, that it is not safe to be in my own home, that Isak has lost his job and now hides shamefully in the home of my vater.

I felt the movement in my belly for the first time last week. I was getting flour and it stopped me in my tracks. I got strange looks from all around and I tried not to draw attention to myself. I ducked into an alleyway and stuck my hand inside my coat to get a better feel. It was amazing. I felt that life fluttering inside of me and pure joy came over me. In that moment I had forgotten where I was. The only thing that could have made it more special would have been to have Isak there, to put his hand on my belly with mine, to let him feel the life we had created together. But then I remembered where I was. In an alleyway, hiding. My husband hiding, as well. I was not even allowed to be pregnant with his child.

I was not surprised, when I figured it out, that I was pregnant. And it was strange but I was happy for the news. With all this folly going on around us I would think it would be bad news for me, but I miss my children. They are so far away, and it was my chance to have motherhood back again. It did not take long for truth to settle in and I knew that this baby would mean very bad things. It broke my heart instantly. And for a long time I said nothing about the baby I had growing inside of me. Even to Isak. Which was very hard because we never keep secrets. At night when he is next to me I feel most guilty. I keep thinking this will all be over soon, someone will come and stop this. But no one comes. The *Wehrmacht* keeps moving and is getting stronger. And I know I cannot keep my baby. I told *Mami* about the baby and *Vater* overheard. He knew right away the dangers and told me I must have the baby taken care of. *Mami* would not hear of it but I knew it had to be. I prepared myself for this before I spoke to *Mami*. But *Vater*, being military, knows the gravity of this. He told *Mami* he could only protect me so much, but that if the *Schutzstaffel* had me, there was not much he could do and that there would be nothing he could do for Isak. He would be taken away. He would certainly be punished and possibly killed. And that is something I just cannot live with. Even if we get separated, I could never live with myself if I am the reason Isak is killed.

I know the risks I am taking are equal by aborting my baby. And I know my heart will die alongside this precious *life inside me. But death comes with every choice I make in this matter. How do I choose what life is more important? Right now I think of my husband and I think of our other three children across the sea and I hope that someday we can be a family again. And I hope that the choice I make now will allow that to happen. Vater says he will find someone in secret who will help me with my problem. I worry for him, as he is a highly respected man, but I know he is capable and smart. I am scared but I must be strong for my family because they are all facing things that I cannot understand. I pray for my children. All four of them.*

Rachel looked up from the papers in her hands with tears flooding her eyes. She could barely make out the figure of Hanna the short distance from her in the recliner. She blinked to focus, water dripping down her face. "It was the abortion that killed her, wasn't it?" she asked.

Hanna nodded somberly. "They were illegal and highly risky. No one knew what they were really doing. It was an infection that killed her."

Rachel struggled to breathe, as if all the air had been suctioned from the room. "Did she really have no other option? I mean, did she really think that was it? That some dirty coat hanger somewhere was the answer?" she began pacing the room. Feeling constricted she tugged at the collar around her neck.

"Rachel, honey," Hanna offered from her chair.

Rachel ignored her and she continued to pace. "I…I need some fresh air." Without a glance, she reached for her coat and headed for the doorway. Before she was fully aware of anything she was doing, she was sitting in the backseat of a cab and headed for Central Park.

She paid her driver and stepping into the snow, a strange serenity washed over her.

As she stepped into the park, the white snowflakes landing onto the wool of her sleeves, she let her feet begin to wander. As she willed her mind to pause, she let her feet take her where they wanted to go. They guided her through the park, past hibernating fountains, bridges, trees, fences, and benches all blanketed in fresh powder.

Rachel wandered past people, all uninterested in her as she walked farther into the park. The cold air served like a brace for her cracked and brittle heart, and coming to a pond, she stopped along a vacant fence. Leaning against it she knocked snow loose, the chunks crumbling down the front of her and into her shoe and around her ankle. It was icy cold as it melted instantly around her ankle, soaking her sock.

Tears sprung to her eyes, and she looked out over the open water, the New York skyline in the distance. Overwhelmed she let her tears fall. In that moment she wasn't sure who she was crying for. Maybe it was Rachel Schulz Schneider, the baby she aborted and the life she lost as a result. Maybe it was Rachel and Isak and the three children they had to send away. Maybe it was the girl who clung so tightly to her mother at the train station that she ripped her dress while saying goodbye. Maybe it was the man who fled from all of it, changed his name and hid the truth so he wouldn't have to face any of it.

Maybe it was all of it.

She dropped her head into hands and cried harder. She wasn't sure if anyone was looking at her. She wasn't sure if anyone was even around. She didn't care. She cried harder. And harder yet. Pressure built in her chest and more tears flowed down her face and still she cried harder.

How long she stood there, clutching that fence, crying the life out of her, she didn't know. But when she was done, Rachel felt weak. She felt exhausted and drained. She felt broken.

Looking around her she was uncertain of where she was. It was still snowing; a thin layer had accumulated on her jacket and was beginning to ice over. She was alone.

Turning around, she watched as people carried on with their lives, passing her as though she wasn't there. She was thankful no one glanced her way. Instead, she took pleasure in just watching them. It had a tranquil effect on her.

A man sat on a bench and fed the pigeons who eagerly accepted his graciousness. A couple that reminded Rachel of her parents, bundled up to bear the cold, walked arm in arm beneath a large umbrella, and shortly behind them were a mother and her children walking their dog, although it was the dog that seemed to be walking them. A few moments later a jogger interrupted her vision of the family walking the dog. He whizzed past Rachel, a puff of steam coming out of his mouth and in a moment, he was gone.

Some people passed her in conversation, others were quiet and some were laughing. But none paid any attention to Rachel. And she liked it that way.

All of these people, she knew, had a story. She wondered what theirs were. She wondered how Hanna managed to keep going after all these years, with all the tragedy and loss in her life. What was it that made Aaron bottle it all up while Hanna laid it all bare?

Burying her hands deep into her pockets, Rachel headed back in the direction from which she had come. It was time, she knew, to finish this. It was time. Time to learn the rest of the story.

"You were gone for a long time. I wasn't sure if I should get worried about you or not," Hanna said when Rachel knocked on her door.

"I needed to clear my head."

"I understand. It's heavy stuff. And you're like your grandfather. His pain cut deep," she said.

"But I'm here. And I want you to tell me the rest," she said.

"Are you sure?" Hanna asked.

Rachel nodded. "For Aaron."

Hanna reached forward and took Rachel's hand in hers. It was soft, like baby's skin, and warm against her icy cold fingers. "Then let's finish this."

"In Jewish tradition," Hanna said after they had both taken their seats, "when someone dies, we try to have their funeral as quickly as possible. Obviously, it's a few days to give people time to travel and make arrangements to come, but since that wasn't necessary for my mother, my father wanted to bury her immediately. My grandfather had warned him that he couldn't do that, but that night, he left with her body anyway. He was grieving and it was his way of saying goodbye. He wanted to bury his wife. And he was nearly successful. But, as you read in the newspaper, the *SS* discovered him, and they misread the entire situation and arrested him. It took my grandfather almost three weeks to tracks down my father's whereabouts after he was arrested. He found him near Hamburg at the Neuengamme concentration camp."

Rachel felt her heart stop.

EIGHTEEN

"You're pretty quiet," AJ said as they made their way up the San Bernardino Mountains, Rachel sitting in the front seat of the car.

She shrugged. "I'm exhausted."

"I bet. How's Hanna?"

"Amazing. I've never met anyone like her in my life. She's just unreal."

"When are you planning on telling your dad about all of this?" AJ asked, making hairpin turns along the highway up the mountain.

Rachel sighed. "That's a good question. I wish I knew. I don't know when, and I don't know how to tell him, either."

AJ sighed. "You are going to tell him, though. Right?"

Rachel was silent for a moment. She had had this exact conversation with herself on the entire flight back to California. And the entire flight, she had been back and forth, back and forth. So where did she stand now?

"Rach?"

"I'm going to tell him."

"I think you should. It's not up to you to hold back this story."

AJ was right. It was up to Aaron. And he had chosen to hold it back. So shouldn't she? But then again, it wasn't just his story. And these people weren't just his family, they were also her family, and Joseph's too. She took a deep breath. "Yeah, I'm going to tell him," she said once again.

Her apartment was chilly, but it was nice to be home. She had just enough time to unpack before Matt dropped Aspen off. And Rachel had never been so relieved to see Aspen before. She hugged her tightly when she came through the door.

"Geez, Mom, what's gotten into you? You were gone for like three days. Not three months."

Rachel didn't care. She hugged her daughter anyway and felt the tears sting her eyes. "I love you. You know that, right?" she asked as Aspen stepped back.

"Course I know that. Are you okay?" Aspen asked when she saw her mom's reddening eyes.

Rachel nodded.

"You're not dying or anything, are you?"

She laughed. "No. I'm not dying. How was your weekend with your dad?"

Aspen shrugged. "Meh. We got in a big fight, so I spent Friday night at Grandma Linda's."

"Why didn't you call me?"

"I knew you were busy. I didn't want to bug you," Aspen said.

"What did you get in a fight about?"

"Thong underwear."

"Where did you get thong underwear?" Rachel asked.

"Target," Aspen said proudly. "Me, Breanne, Kasey and Olivia all got a pair."

Rachel rolled her eyes. "And why did you and your dad get in a fight?"

"Why do you think? Because Dad thinks I'm still six years old. So of course he freaked out on me. Even Grandma was on my side. Which is why I slept at her house. I think he would just be happy if I became a nun or something."

"Give him a break. I mean, yeah, it's a stupid thing to freak out over. But he's adjusting to fatherhood. He'll come around. He's not quite as square as you think he is," Rachel said.

"Yeah, I think you're just delusional about that. Anyway, I've got a ton of homework to do that I didn't finish because Dad's computer got a virus, so I've got to finish it. I'll be in my room if you need me."

"I'll go call your dad about the underwear," Rachel said.

"Thanks, Mom!"

"Yes, I freaked out," Matt said on the phone. "Those are sexy underwear. I don't want to know my twelve-year-old is wearing sexy underwear."

Rachel laughed. "At some point you need to just consider them underwear. Because your daughter is going to wear them. And eventually much worse."

"Why? Why did you have to go and say that?" he said with a laugh.

"Because it's true."

"Why are you always right? I really hate that, you know?" he said.

"I can imagine you do. But I'm the woman. I'll always be the right one. It's just a fact of life."

He sighed. "How was your trip?"

"Good doesn't really seem like the right word for the kind of trip this was," she said.

"So I'm guessing you learned some pretty horrific things, huh?"

"Matt, it's so awful. I don't even know how to begin to wrap my head around it. I just… I don't understand how humanity has it in them to do these kinds of things to each other," she said, her heart feeling heavy.

"I know. And you're right. But maybe, instead of hanging on to all that terrible, try to remember that people got out. There were survivors. And despite all the tragedy, you're here today because of the choices someone in your family made back then. Yeah, some really evil people tried to get rid of all these people. But they failed. You're here because they failed.

Not everybody was evil. Not everybody believed in what the German's were doing. Not even all the Germans believed in it. And there were people who risked everything so that others could live. If you're going to hang on to something, hang on to that. The other stuff will just tear you down and you're too good of a person to let that stuff win."

Rachel was silent. Matt was the last person in the world she thought would be comforting her in the moment, yet she felt her heart grow still.

"Are you there?" he asked.

"Yeah. I'm here," she whispered into the phone. "Thank you for that."

An hour later, while getting ready for bed, there was a light knock on her door. Rachel gave a heavy sigh as she headed to answer it. She was expecting this for a while now.

Ethan greeted her with a welcoming smile as he scooped her into a hug. "I've been thinking about you all weekend. How was New York?" he asked, coming into the house and taking off his shoes.

"It was good," she said.

"I was shocked when I didn't hear from you," he said.

"I know. I'm sorry. Things were so busy while I was there. I felt like I just landed and barely had a chance to really get to know her before I was leaving already. How was the weekend at the fire station?"

He shrugged. "Just fine. Tell me about your weekend."

"I'm actually so tired. Do you care if we talk later? I'm sorry to do this right now. I was just about to head to bed," she said, motioning toward her pajamas.

"Oh. I see that. Uh, yeah," he said, taken back.

"You don't have to come to bed. Aspen's still doing homework. The television is all yours if you want it. No girls to fight with over the remote," she said.

"Oh. Well, I guess I'll do that then," he said taking a step closer to her.

She gave him a gentle smile. "Good night, then," she said and spun on one foot toward her bedroom door.

Inside the confines of her bedroom, Rachel lay in her bed in the dark. She rolled onto her side and curled into a ball and thought about what Matt had said to her. Maybe it was those kinds of things that had gotten the survivors through. But not every survivor had made it through quite so well. She thought about Aaron and how coping for him meant locking it away. She wondered if it had really worked, or instead if it meant that he suffered silently and alone. She would never know that truth.

Instead, she clung to the happier times with Grandpa Aaron: the homemade ice cream, the backyard tree house, fishing in Lake Arrowhead. The fishing was Ben's favorite part. Rachel's favorite part was swimming afterward. But she hated the weeds in the lake, so Grandpa Aaron would drop anchor and be the first to jump in the water. Then he would carefully swim around the perimeter of the boat making sure that he never touched a single weed just so that Rachel could swim in peace. She smiled at the memory, and she realized that this would be what he would want her to hang onto as she tried to let the joy she felt inside of her fill the emptiness deeper inside.

Rachel was glad to get back to work on Monday morning. She was thankful to have a routine back and was even relieved to see the pile of work that had accumulated over the weekend for her.

Kristin was overjoyed to have her back. Even though she had managed Sinful Retreat quite successfully in Rachel's absence, she said she would never again do it under those circumstances. Rachel smiled and hugged her and thanked her.

"You've really given me a gift that I'll never be able to repay you for," she said.

Kristin smiled back at her. "Well, when you say it like that, then I feel guilty for making such a big deal about you leaving. But really, never do it again. Not like that anyway."

Rachel laughed.

Mark came in at opening while Rachel stepped into her office and immediately began typing up invoices. No one would get paid at the store if the store didn't get paid by their customers. Rachel was making it a priority to get all the invoices done as soon as she could.

Ethan came in shortly after nine with flowers for her, but Rachel told Mark to deal with him. "Tell him I am so swamped. I will talk to him after work. But I will be home late because I need to do all the fiduciary reports from the weekend."

"Umm, you don't want to just tell him yourself? He's right out by the register," Mark said.

"Please just take care of it," she said not glancing away from her computer screen.

A few minutes later Mark returned to her office. "Okay, well, your boyfriend is gone and here are the flowers he left for you," he said, putting them on her desk.

"Actually, I don't have room in here. After I get this done, I need to go through those boxes there. Kristin said the orders are all messed up and I need to make some calls to our vendors and I'm going to need all the desk space I can handle. Just put them near the register or something. The customers will like them," she said.

"Sure thing," he said.

Rachel emerged from her office only when she had to all day. Otherwise, she remained behind her desk, buried in the workload, her eyes glued to the computer. Aspen had stopped in to say hello, but since Rachel didn't have time even for her, she agreed to let her spend the evening with friends, as long as she was home by eight.

Around 6:30, Kristin stopped back into the store with a bowl of hot soup and some rolls for Rachel. "Thought you might get hungry," she said, setting the food on her desk.

"Aww, you're the best."

"I know," Kristin said with a smile. "Figured I had to feed my family, might as well feed you, too. Does Aspen need food?"

"No. She's at her friend's house for a few more hours."

"Okay. Well, call if you need anything."

"Will do," Rachel said, grabbing the bowl and lifting the lid. The smell of Kristin's potato and bacon chowder filled her senses and her stomach growled. "Mmm, this smells so good."

Kristin laughed. "You enjoy. And I'll see you later."

At five after eight, Aspen poked her head in the doorway of Rachel's office. The store had been locked up for an hour and Rachel was enjoying the quiet and Aspen startled her.

"Whoa, didn't mean to scare you," she said with a laugh. "Dang, Mom, you're still working?"

Rachel sighed. "I've got so much to do. And Diane made a huge mistake on one of our daily reports, so I've been going through that for the last half hour trying to figure out where we're off by forty-seven dollars." Rachel looked up from the papers and receipts in front of her. "How was Olivia's?"

"Fun. Ethan's upstairs. He said he'll have dinner ready in a little bit."

"Oh. Tell him Kristin stopped by and brought me dinner already."

Aspen winced. "Uh oh. I think he's been working on dinner for you two for a little while."

"Well he never said anything to me. How am I supposed to know? It's after eight."

Aspen threw her hands up. "Don't shoot the messenger."

"Just tell him, please? And if he wants to talk, tell him I'll be up in a little while."

She nodded. "Will do. I've got a little more studying to do and then I'm going to bed. Night, Mom."

"Love you," Rachel called out her door as she heard Aspen tromp up the stairs on the other side of the wall behind her office.

"You too!" she hollered back.

By twenty after ten, Rachel made her way up to her apartment. It was quiet when she opened the door. All the lights were off as she stepped inside.

She rubbed her tired eyes as she locked the door and headed toward her bedroom, but something stirred on the couch and made her jump. It was Ethan.

"You scared me," she said through the darkness.

"I thought you told Aspen you were going to be up soon," he said. His voice was flat.

"I told her I was going to be up in a little while. You knew where I was. If you needed something, you could've come down," she said.

"And get warded off like I did earlier today? No thanks."

"That's not fair. I was swamped with work. Obviously, I have been working for thirteen hours," she said.

"Yes, I realize that. And I'm not trying to trivialize your workload, but will you just be straight with me?"

"Straight with you about what?" she asked.

"About what's going on," he said folding his arms across his chest. "You ignored my calls all weekend, you got home last night, didn't tell me a thing about your trip, you haven't kissed me once, you went right to bed and suggested I just sit up and watch TV, you wouldn't let me see you at work and now this. What's going on?"

"Ethan, I'm tired. It was a long weekend. It was draining and exhausting and… and… and it was heavy. And last night I was tired and I wanted to go to bed and today I have been buried in work and now I want to go to bed," she said nodding toward her bedroom.

"Yeah, that may all be true, but those are just excuses that you're hiding behind."

"What are you talking about?"

"There's more going on here than you're admitting to. Something happened. Something changed."

Rachel sighed loudly as she shook her head. "You know what, I'm tired. I don't want to do this with you right now. I'm going to bed. You can either come with me, you can sleep on my couch, or you can go to your place. I don't care. But I am going to bed," she said walking past him into her room.

A moment later Ethan stepped in behind her. "Okay, so if we're not going to talk about this tonight, then when? When are we going to talk about this? Tomorrow? Aspen's with her dad tomorrow. Tomorrow will be the perfect time to talk about it."

"Tomorrow I'm heading to Newport to my parents to tell my dad everything that I know."

"Great. Let me come with you. Kill two birds with one stone. Only have to tell the story once," he said.

She looked up at him. "I can't do this with you. I'm sorry. I… I don't know how my dad is going to take any of this and it's just something I've got to do."

"Fine. I can understand that. But when Rachel? When do we get to be a priority? I go back to work on Thursday already," he said.

"We'll see what Wednesday looks like. Maybe we can have some time, just you and I," she said.

He gave her a half smile as he crossed the room toward her and pulled her into him. He wrapped his arms around her body, and she lightly patted his shoulder blade before slipping out of his grip and into the bathroom to wash up for bed. She could feel his eyes on her as she washed her face in the sink, but she didn't look his direction. After she changed in her pajamas and stepped back into the bedroom, Ethan had undressed and slipped beneath the blankets on the opposite side of the bed. Without exchanging another word, Rachel crawled into her side of bed, turned off the lamp and went to sleep.

By Tuesday afternoon, Rachel's head was spinning. Nothing was going right. She still hadn't been able to figure out how they were missing forty-seven dollars. Their vendor's computer system was down so she wasn't able to finalize any ordering corrections. And if that wasn't enough, the credit card machine wasn't working in Sinful Retreat and Rachel had a splitting headache.

Ethan stopped in after lunch to tell her he was going to grab some food and hang out with some guys from his crew that night and so he would see her whenever she got back from Newport. He wished her luck, but she was distracted with everything else going on and barely noticed when he left the store.

A customer, tired of waiting for the credit card machine to get back up and running, gave Rachel and earful, left her selection of books on the counter and stormed out of the store. Rachel sighed, took an Excedrin and stepped into her office. A few minutes later there came a light knock on the door.

"Yes?" she asked with some reluctance.

"Your mom is on line two," Darlene said through the closed door.

Rachel sat up in her chair. "Thanks," she called back through the door and picked up the phone.

"Hey Mom," she said.

"Hi Rachel. I was looking at my phone a little bit ago and just realized that your dad and I have plans tonight with Roger and Kathy. We have tickets to the piano bar. We were wondering if we could have you come down tomorrow night instead? I know it's last minute. But I feel terrible cancelling on Kathy," Jenn said.

Rachel sighed. "Tickets, huh?"

"Yeah. And I completely forgot about it," she said. "No Dee-o-jee, down please," Jenn said to the dog.

"That's fine. I mean, if you have tickets, there's not much I can do about it. Hope you have fun. The piano bar sounds fun," Rachel said. She wasn't sure if she was relieved or not that she could postpone telling her dad everything she knew for one more day.

"Oh good. I'm glad you're okay with it. All right, well, I've gotta let the dog out. So I'm going to let you go. But I'll see you tomorrow then."

"Okay. Bye, Mom." Rachel sighed as she hung up the phone.

After work, sitting on her couch, she reveled in the quiet around her. Her eyes were heavy as her stomach growled and she laid her body down on the sofa. It felt good to relax, to close her eyes and just breathe.

The jiggling of the doorknob startled her, and she opened her eyes as Aspen walked into the apartment, Matt following behind her.

"What're you guys doing here?" she asked, sitting up.

"I thought you were going to Newport," Aspen said, as shocked to see her mom as Rachel was to see her.

"That got changed to tomorrow. What are you doing here?"

"I had to get a book for class," she said.

"You look tired," Matt said, standing awkwardly near the door, his hands thrust into the pockets of his jeans.

"Long day. Long week," Rachel said.

"It's only Tuesday, Rach," he said.

She sighed. "Don't remind me."

"Aspen and I are headed to get some pizza. Why don't you come with us?"

"Nah," she said with a wave of her hand. "I'm lame company tonight."

"No, really, come with us. It's on me and this way you don't have to worry about dinner," he said.

"Really?" she asked, looking up, her eyes meeting his.

He laughed. "Really. Now get up."

"Got it," Aspen said as she emerged from her bedroom.

"Your mom is going to join us for pizza," Matt said.

"Sweet. Let's go before all the good tables are gone," she said, heading toward the door, her parents following behind her.

Sitting down at the pizzeria, Rachel couldn't help but feel the situation was surreal. It was the first time in years that the three of them had gone to dinner as a family.

"Did you tell your mom?" Matt asked Aspen.

"Tell me what?" Rachel asked, her eyes looking back and forth between him and Aspen.

"Tell her," he said with a nod and a large smile.

Aspen's face went red. "It's about my science project. The one Dad helped me with that one weekend."

"The one with the gears? That he took you to the library for?" Rachel asked.

Aspen nodded. "I got 100% on it."

"And…" Matt added.

"And, Mr. Crawford has it featured in one of the glass cabinets in the entrance foyer at school," she said.

"No way," Rachel said, her eyes growing wide. "Aspen, that's awesome news! I'm so proud of you!"

Aspen smiled, her face turning a deep shade of red.

Rachel looked at Matt, their eyes meeting. "Way to go, Dad. I could've never helped with a project like that."

"Well, you know, me, science, kind of a good pairing," he said with a coy smile.

Rachel reached across the table and slipped her hand over Aspen's. "I'm very proud of you."

"Thanks, Mom."

"Now, what does everybody want?" Matt asked, glancing at the menu.

"I want chicken on mine," Aspen said.

"And I'd like—"

"Sausage, pepper and onion, no mushroom," Matt added for Rachel.

"Wow," she said, taken back.

"Wow what?" he asked.

"Nothing," she said with a smile. "I'm just shocked that you remember that."

"Give me some credit," he said with a smile. "You've never strayed from those pizza toppings in over fifteen years. Some things never change."

"It's true, Mom," Aspen said with a nod.

Rachel smiled at both of them.

They carried on conversation through dinner, told stories, and made each other laugh. Rachel was amazed with the ease that they went about being together. When, she wondered, did they get past the bickering? Even Aspen and her father were on more than amicable terms for the night. Rachel found herself enjoying the idea of family brought to her, the wholesomeness she felt.

"I'm glad you decided to come with us," Matt said, as they made their way through the parking lot to his car.

She nodded. "Me too. This was nice."

"Better not tell anyone that the three of us didn't fight for two whole hours. It might jinx us," he said.

Rachel laughed. "You're right. We better keep it secret," she whispered.

Matt laughed along with her.

"What are you two giggling about?" Aspen asked.

"Nothing," Rachel said.

"Ugh, now I've got homework to do. Anyone want to do it for me?"

"No thanks, I passed seventh grade already," Matt said as they got into the car.

Outside Sinful Retreat, Matt came to a stop. "Thanks for dinner. Aspen, you better get all that homework done or you won't be coming to Newport with me tomorrow night."

Aspen sighed from the backseat. "Way to ruin a perfectly good night."

Rachel smiled. "Yeah, I love you, too. Bye," she said, glancing up at Matt before closing the car door and heading up to her apartment. She was surprised to see Ethan standing on the deck in front of her door.

"Hey," she said when she reached the top. "What're you doing here?"

"I just got home and was headed over here when I saw Matt's car pull up. I thought you were going to your parents tonight," he said, bitterness in his tone.

Rachel walked past him to her door and unlocked it. She stepped inside, the warmth greeting her skin, and turned on a light. Ethan was just behind her. "My mom called and had to change our plans to tomorrow night. She forgot they had tickets to something tonight."

"Tomorrow night? *Our* night?" he said.

"We said we would see what Wednesday brought," she said as she set her handbag down in the kitchen.

"I told you I go back to work on Thursday. Are we going to wait until after my next shift to talk?" he asked, his voice getting louder.

"What do you want me to do, Ethan?"

"You could've called me when you found out your plans changed for tonight."

"You were going out with your friends," she said.

"Oh, so you would rather be with Matt."

"What? Where is this coming from?" she said, her voice elevating to match his.

"What the hell happened in New York? Something happened and you're avoiding me. What is it?" His voice had never before taken on such a demanding tone.

Rachel's eyes met his and immediately swelled with tears. She broke eye contact and went to her bedroom. He followed after.

"Rachel, what is it? You can talk to me," he said. He took a seat beside her on the bed. Gently, he slid his hand over her back.

"Please, don't touch me," she whispered.

"Rach?" he said, clearly taken back.

She lifted her head and turned to face him, her eyes once again meeting his. "I don't think we should be together anymore."

Ethan's face went white. "What? Why? I don't understand. What happened? Why can't we be together?"

She swallowed hard. "Because your family killed mine."

His body lurched from the bed. "Rachel, what are you talking about?"

The awful churning in her stomach, the feeling that she was going to vomit, had returned in an instant, like it did that day in New York when Hanna told her where Isak had ended up. Rachel felt a wrenching pain in her stomach when she learned how he had died.

And in that moment, her already broken heart had shattered because she knew what she had to do, what she had to give up.

"He went to Neuengamme," she said, nearly catatonic.

"Who did? Who went there?"

"Isak."

"Who's Isak?"

Only Rachel's eyes moved and they met Ethan's as he bent over to her level as she sat on the bed. "Aaron's father. Isak Schneider was arrested and imprisoned in Neuengamme in January 1938. He was a forced laborer in the camp. And on April 26, 1945, the officers that ran the camp loaded nearly ten thousand surviving prisoners onto four ships. Isak was put on the *SS Thielbek* as a prisoner in the ship's hold, without food or water. It was anchored in the Bay of Lubeck in the Baltic for seven days before it was attacked by the Royal Air Force, who mistakenly thought there were *SS* officers aboard who were attempting to flee Germany. Thirty-two rockets were fired at the *Thielbek* and when it caught fire; it was simply left to burn. It took only twenty minutes to sink. Only fifty people managed to get out alive. Fifty out of almost three thousand prisoners. Isak's body was one that washed up on shore a few days later. Fortunately, they were able to identify him before he was buried in a mass grave."

Ethan's eyes were wide as he stared in shock back at Rachel.

"They were together. Don't you get it? Fritz was a barracks guard. Do you really think they never crossed paths?" Rachel stood, her anger seething. "You don't think Finn, one of the leaders of the Death's Head Unit skipped out on his chance to kill those ten thousand Jews, do you? Hell no!"

"Rachel this isn't me!" he yelled.

"But it's your family! I know it wasn't you, but I'd be betraying my family. I'd be dishonoring them and everything they went through by being with you, by being with the man who comes directly from that line."

"Don't do this..." His voice grew quiet.

She felt her chest tighten. "I'm sorry—"

"No Rachel," he said, clasping her hands between his. He kissed her thumbs and then looked up at her, tears gathering in his eyes. "Don't do this. I love you. We can figure this out."

She took a deep breath as she shook her head. "I'm sorry."

He stood there, holding her hands between his, feeling the warmth radiate between them, his eyes locked on hers for as long as he could. Rachel didn't move.

Taking a heavy breath, he released her hands and left her apartment.

NINETEEN

Kristin stepped into Sinful Retreat and was surprised to see the fire roaring in the fireplace. The lights were on, the registers lit up, holiday music playing softly. All of the display shelves had been recently turned over, new merchandise put out, everything neatly and freshly organized.

Her kids took off their jackets and headed to the children's nook and she popped her head into Rachel's office. "Did the bookstore fairy pay us a visit?"

Rachel laughed as she swiveled around on her chair. "Hardly. I was up early so I came down here and was fairly productive."

Kristin's eyes scanned the store. "I think that's an understatement. Why were you up so early?"

Rachel shrugged. "Couldn't sleep."

"Bad night?"

"I ended things with Ethan," she said.

"What?" Kristin said. "Why?"

She sighed. "It's complicated. But it has to be this way. Besides, now I can get back on track. I can focus on things again. I've been distracted the last few months."

"Distracted? From what? Rachel, life isn't this bookstore," Kristin said.

"I know that."

"I don't think you do. You're always telling Matt that life isn't his job. But I don't think you realize that it also applies to you. You use this place as your scapegoat."

"That's not why I ended things with Ethan," she said, rising from her chair. "It's more complicated than that."

"Then what is it? Tell me. I can handle complicated. We've been friends for a long time," she said.

Rachel sighed. "Our lives collided long before we ever met."

"You're talking about your families?"

She nodded. "His ancestors ran the very concentration camp that my great grandfather was imprisoned and tortured in."

"Rachel—"

"Right now, I don't know how to be with him. It hurts, it physically hurts me to be in love with someone knowing these things," she said.

Kristin reached out her hand and pulled Rachel closer to her. Rachel leaned her head onto her shoulder. "I'm sorry," Kristin said as she smoothed her hand over the edge of the hair that hung past Rachel's shoulders. "I'm just sorry that you have to go through this."

Rachel let her job consume her that day. She refused to let her mind wander and she forced herself to engage with every customer that she could. The interaction with so many people helped her get out of her own head and distance herself from the heavy and burdening emotions she was carrying around.

The ninety-mile drive to Newport, however, wound her back up, even with Aspen in the passenger seat. In the box in the backseat were the remnants of the lives she had set out to preserve. And she reminded herself that this was why she was facing her dad. But it didn't make anything easier. As she drove down the 15 Freeway, weaving around other vehicles, she could feel the pain she knew he was going to feel. She was still feeling it all herself.

Dee-o-jee was thrilled to see Aspen, as usual, when they first arrived at her parents' place. Rachel was relieved to see that Aunt Sarah was also there. She grabbed the box from the back seat and headed into the house behind Aspen.

"It's kind of cool to be sitting out on the patio. Is it okay if we just stay inside today?" her mom asked after they exchanged hugs.

Rachel nodded. "I'm fine with that."

"Anyone want anything to drink?"

"I'll take some wine," Rachel said bluntly, following her mom to the kitchen.

Jenn gave her a peculiar look as she glanced over her shoulder.

"It's been a long day," Rachel said.

"Okay," she said. "Sure thing. Red or white?"

"Whatever."

"So what's this big news you want to tell us?" Joseph said as he came into the room. "Are you pregnant? Getting married? Where's the groom? I figured he'd be coming with you."

"She broke up with him," Aspen said, making her dissatisfaction clear from the living room as Dee-o-jee cuddled up next to her on the couch.

"Another baby by yourself?" Joseph said, a worried look on his face.

"I'm not pregnant. And yes, we broke up. It's…complicated," she said. She took the glass of wine her mom slid in front of her and in three swallows the glass was empty.

Everyone in the room silently exchanged glances with one another.

"Oh lighten up. It's not like I just did a line of coke or something," Rachel said with a roll of her eyes. Rachel reached for the bottle of wine, popped the cork and refilled her glass. Grabbing it and the box, she nodded toward the study. "Well, shall we?"

The other adults silently followed suit behind Rachel as she led the way down the hall as Aspen and Dee-o-jee got comfortable in front of the television.

Inside the study, Rachel took the spot behind the desk. She set the box down beside her glass of wine as her parents and Sarah found seats on the sofa and the chaise.

"It's about my dad, isn't it?" Sarah asked, breaking the silence first.

Joseph looked at his sister and Rachel nodded her head. "Yeah. It is."

"So what, more conjecture? Or do you have real information?" he asked.

Jenn reached over and squeezed his thigh. "Just listen."

Rachel stood in front of the desk, leaning her backside against it. "I've learned a lot over the last few weeks. Some of it, a lot of it, is heavy. And I'm telling you right now that this information will change you. And I'm not saying this to freak you out, but just as a general warning. So you can either choose to stay and hear what I have found, or you can walk away. It's your choice." Rachel waited a moment before continuing. She silently hoped her dad would choose the latter. It would be easier if he decided to just live in the dark. But, despite her wishes, he stayed seated on the sofa.

"I also want to say that I'm not telling you all this to change your opinion of Grandpa Aaron. Of your dad. I'm just trying to give you the full picture."

Joseph crossed his arms and leaned back against the sofa. "Okay. So, enough with the prelude. Out with it already."

Rachel took a breath and then reached for the box. She decided to start with the WWI medal. Taking it out she handed it first to her dad. "This medal belonged to Isak Schneider, Aaron's dad." Sarah and Joseph's eye's shot up to Rachel in an instant. "He earned this while serving on behalf of Germany during WWI under platoon leader Otto Schulz."

Sarah moved from the chaise to the sofa, beside her brother. Rachel watched as they turned the Friedrich-August Cross over in their hands. She felt a surge of pride in Isak, the young man who had gone off to serve and fight for his country. Despite the fact that he would later be betrayed by that same country, serving for them changed the course of his life forever. It was while serving for Germany that he met Otto, who ultimately allowed him to meet Lena. And it was he and Lena that had created the entire legacy that was in that very room marveling at his military award.

Rachel went on to explain how Otto became Isak's father-in-law and about the three children, Ephraim, Abarron, and Hanna, that they had together.

"So Aaron was born Abarron?" Sarah asked. "You had said that before."

Rachel nodded. "Yes. He was born Abarron Alter. Alter was the name of Isak's father, who died of heart condition. I have photos of all of these people." Rachel reached back into the box and pulled out the photos. First, she pulled out the photo of the children with *Zeyda* and *Bubbe* and she explained to them who Alter and Ahuva were. But she was careful not yet to explain how Ahuva died. She did, however, mention the five brothers Isak had: Eli, Johan, Etan, Avi and Ismael.

Joseph, Sarah, and Jenn marveled in what Rachel had uncovered. And when they started finding features in their ancestors that reminded them of living relatives today, Rachel couldn't help but feel the tears sting at the back of her eyes.

The next photo she handed to them was the one at the Baltic Sea, and introduced them to Otto and Lena Schulz, as well as to what Isak and Rachel Schneider looked like.

"I love that you have the same name as Isak's wife," Jenn said.

Rachel gave a weak smile as she nodded her head. She did find it bittersweet but was honored to be named after such a brave woman. And she wasn't sure she had ever done a thing in her life to warrant such an honor, unintentional or otherwise.

Joseph's smile gently faded away as he looked up from the photos to Rachel. "They were Jewish, weren't they? Alter has quite the beard on him."

Rachel smiled and gave a nod. "Yes, Dad. They were Jewish. The Schneiders were. Otto and Lena and Rachel weren't. They were Protestant."

"Really?" Sarah said, looking up from the photos as well. "The note on the back of this picture," she said, nodding toward to photo along the Baltic, "is this a date?"

"Yes. That picture was taken the summer of 1935."

"But," Sarah said with a pause, "but that would have been Nazi Germany."

"That's right," Rachel said.

"Oh my God…" Sarah said, her voice fading.

"Rachel, did my dad's family get caught in the Holocaust?" Joseph asked soberly as he reached for his wife's hand.

Rachel saw the look of pain already in his eyes. She gave them all a nod. "Some of them did."

Sarah gasped.

"So this was the reason for the prelude. All the warning in the beginning," he said.

Rachel bit her bottom lip.

"Hey, calm down," Jenn whispered to him. "Obviously your dad was just fine."

"What happened?" he asked.

Rachel took a seat on chaise, the others listening intensely from the sofa as she spoke.

"First let me tell you that I met Grandpa's sister."

"You what?" Joseph said, his eyes growing wide.

She nodded. "I just got back from New York on Sunday night. I spent the weekend there with her. She lives in an assisted living apartment. I also met her granddaughter."

"Oh my goodness," Sarah said in shock, her hand on her chest. "I… I'm not even sure what to say to all of this. She's alive? How did you find her?"

Rachel gave a slight laugh. "That's kind of a long story, but yes. She's alive. She's quite an amazing woman. And she hasn't seen her brother in almost seventy years."

"This…this," Joseph searched for words, his head in his hands. "This is surreal," he said looking up.

"She was able to tell me the most incredible stories. And she had letters and journals and pictures."

"Okay, so go on. Tell us. What happened to the family?" Sarah said.

Rachel began the story with the end of their family vacation along the Baltic. First she told them about the defacement of their family home. And how the real upheaval came with the instatement of the Nuremberg Laws. She told them of their family goodbyes at the train station and bit back the tears as she repeated Hanna's story. As she told them about how little Hanna had ripped her mother's dress, tears streamed down Sarah's face and Rachel made a point to avoid looking at her. Joseph was in awe with the passport that was found in the trunk.

She told them how Otto had taken them into his home and hidden Isak while being conscripted into the *Wehrmacht*. Then came the hard part, when she had to tell them all about Rachel Schneider's pregnancy and subsequent abortion and how it had killed her. She found the raw emotion even from her dad to be shocking and it took every ounce of strength she had to continue. She read to them the translated journal entry that Hanna had given her.

The devastation in her father and Sarah was written plainly all over them. They hunched over one another and Sarah wept in the arms of her brother. "She died trying to protect her family," she mumbled between tears.

Jenn, in shock, was nearly unresponsive to Rachel when she asked if she was okay. "I… I'm going to go check on Aspen," she said blankly. In a swift movement she rose from the sofa and left the room. Concerned, Rachel watched her walk down the hallway, but she disappeared around the corner, and she lost sight of her.

"Keep going, Rachel. What happened next," Joseph said.

"Umm, well," she said, glancing down the hallway.

"She'll be fine. What happened?" he said.

"Isak tried to bury Rachel's body. When he took her out to the woods that night, he was caught and arrested. Otto found him a few weeks later in the Neuengamme concentration camp."

"So that was it for him," Joseph said. "Was that where he died?"

"Sort of." She took a breath, gathering her thoughts. "He managed to survive for six years there."

"For six years?" Jenn said, coming back into the room.

Rachel nodded.

"That's incredible," Sarah said in disbelief.

"He had children to get back to," Jenn said.

"But…" Joseph said.

Rachel told them about the Nazis and their heinous plan to gather surviving prisoners from the concentration camps of Neuengamme, Stutthof and Mittelbau-Dora and scuttle them at sea with no food or water.

"I don't get why Allied forces attacked the ships," Sarah said.

"Because the Royal Air Force had information that the ships were really German forces attempting to retreat across the Baltic to German-controlled Norway. So they attacked," Rachel said.

"And he made it as long as he did," Joseph said, a devastated look on his face.

Rachel sat down between her parents and her dad slipped his hands around her. They were thick and strong, and she felt safe wrapped inside them. Her mom rested her head on her shoulder and Rachel closed her eyes.

The feeling that came over her surprised her. She felt, for the first time in weeks, relief. Not only had she told her family the story, but she lived through telling it. Not that she really thought she would fall down dead by retelling the story, but a part of her thought it might just be too hard to do. That somehow she wouldn't manage to do it. But she did. And it was over. The truth was out. And she no longer had to grieve alone.

"I really don't get why I have to spend the weekend with you. I mean, technically it's my weekend to be at Dad's because you went to New York on your weekend with me," Aspen complained on Saturday after Rachel was done with work for the day.

"Wow, okay, so you're still pissed at me," she said as she set her computer down on the counter and slipped her shoes off.

"Whatever. I don't get how you get to punish me for making stupid decisions but I just have to deal with yours," she said from the couch as she flipped incessantly through the channels.

"Just because I didn't give you the details of why Ethan and I aren't together doesn't mean it's stupid," Rachel said as she stepped into the kitchen and opened the fridge to survey the options for dinner.

The front door opened, and AJ came in, a large tote in her hand. "Hey punk," she said to Aspen when she saw her on the couch.

"And I suppose you're here to comfort my mom for her stupid decision," Aspen said.

"That's enough from you," Rachel said. "You've made your point. Hey AJ."

"I figured since this was a special occasion, I'd make an exception to my rule," AJ said as she took of her jacket and shoes.

"Huh?" Rachel said.

"I brought tequila."

Rachel's eyes lit up. "Wow, this really is an exception."

"Well, it was either this or ice cream. But ice cream is just going to make me fat. And I told Jack I couldn't come down to Carlsbad this weekend because it was a best-friend-broken-heart kind of situation. Oh, and I also brought Excedrin for the headache tomorrow."

Rachel laughed. "Any thoughts for dinner tonight?"

"I already ordered pizza. It should be here in about twenty minutes," AJ said as she tossed her bag beside the couch.

"I love it when you stay here," Aspen called over the back of the couch.

"Yeah, well, you better shape up or you'll be eating sandwiches while your mom and I get the pizza. Enough giving her a hard time. Someday, mark my words, you're going to have a broken heart and you're going to need her."

"Ugh. Whatever," she said, turning back around.

Rachel gave AJ a smile.

Long after Aspen disappeared into her room, Rachel and AJ sat around the coffee table in the living room, a shot glass in front of each of them, the saltshaker and a bowl of sliced limes also on the table.

"So you haven't seen him since he left your apartment?"

Rachel shook her head, and the room took an extra few seconds to come in to focus. "Gosh. I miss him so much. I'm actually not sure what hurts more, saying goodbye, or not seeing him," she said.

"Oh. That deserves another shot," AJ said. She reached for the bottle and refilled the glasses.

They quickly threw back the clear liquid; Rachel coughed slightly and then she shoved the lime wedge into her mouth.

"He's working now. So unless I start a fire or something, I won't see him. He's holed up at the station," Rachel said. "I could start a fire."

"That's the tequila talking. And maybe a little bit of the broken heart. If you miss him that much, just call him, Rach."

"I can't do that. Nothing has changed. I think about the faces in those pictures and all I can think is that they would be so disappointed in me. How can I be in love with the great grandson of one of their persecutors? Ugh, just saying it makes me want to throw up."

"That might also be the tequila. But just because you're not with him doesn't mean you're not in love with him. I saw you two together. No amount of time will ever change that. I guarantee it," AJ said with a nod.

"What?"

"He's just that one. The one you'll love forever. So maybe you never get back together. It won't change what you feel in your heart."

"Ughhh," she groaned as she threw her head back. "Okay. One more shot and then I've got to go to bed. Before my head explodes."

AJ laughed as she poured another shot. They chinked their glasses and shot back the alcohol. Rachel felt the burn down the back of her throat as she wedged the lime in her mouth. A moment later she rose to her feet, stabilizing herself with her furniture. Wobbly, she made her way to be bedroom. Foregoing pajamas and her bedtime routine, she crawled into her bed. Grabbing the pillow beside her, which still had the faint scent of Ethan, she wrapped her arms around it, buried her face into it and passed out.

On Sunday morning, Rachel felt a pain soar through her head and slowly she opened one eye. A gray light came in through her window and she was afraid to move, afraid more pain would follow the first.

"Ahh look, it's my alcoholic role models," Aspen said in the living room to AJ.

Rachel winced at the sound through her open bedroom door.

"Make yourself useful, punk, and bring me that bottle of Excedrin and some water," AJ called to her.

"Seriously, you can't get it yourself?"

"Seriously, don't be a brat."

"Ugh. Fine," Aspen said.

Rachel still hadn't moved. Her second eye had yet to open.

"Bring two of these to your mom. And water. Please," AJ said.

"Oh, you do have manners."

Rachel had been awake for less than five minutes and already she wanted to sell her daughter.

"Mom, are you alive?" Aspen asked from the doorway.

"I think so," Rachel mumbled from the bed.

"Maybe you should go to rehab or something," she said with a laugh.

"Aspen, I swear to you…"

"Oh chill out, it was just a joke. Here's some stuff for your head," she said handing the pills to her as Rachel rolled over. She had been right to fear the movement. Pain seared through her head. She took the pills and swallowed them quickly. "Do you care if I go to Kasey's? Her brother said he would pick me up."

"Fine, whatever. I want you home by seven tonight."

Rachel spent the day on the couch, nursing her hangover, with AJ alongside her. Tiff stopped by for a while with food from the Malt Shop in Cedar Glen, and that seemed to help settle their stomachs.

She laughed at both of them for acting like they were twenty-one again.

"Hey, she needed a distraction," AJ said, defending herself.

"Well, then get her a stripper. They won't hurt the next day. And trust me, they work just as well for distraction."

Rachel laughed and then cursed Tiff for making her laugh.

"I should get going. I told Jake I would be home to give the girls a bath and help with bedtime," Tiff said.

Rachel sat up. "What time is it?"

"About twenty after seven," AJ said.

Rachel groaned. "I told Aspen to be home by seven. She's late." She reached for her cell and called her daughter. The phone rang five times and went to voicemail. "Aspen, it's Mom. Wondering where you're at. Please call me and let me know what's going on. I'll come get you if your need a ride."

"Wow, you sounded nice," AJ said.

"That's because if she yells right away, Aspen will just delay coming home or calling back," Tiff said.

Rachel nodded. "It's true. The yelling will come. Trust me." Rachel rose from the couch and went to the window to see if she could see

Kaleb's car. She tried calling again and after the fifth ring, the phone went to voicemail.

"Now what?" Tiff asked.

"She's got until 7:30. Then I'm calling Kasey," Rachel said. "Tiff, you don't have to stay. Go home to your girls."

"Are you sure? I can help you look for her."

"I'm sure. She's just in a mood. She's mad at me because of Ethan. Nothing happened to her. I'll find her and she'll be grounded," she said.

"All right. Text me when you find her," Tiff said before leaving.

"Has she done this before?" AJ asked.

"She's done it with her dad. Not with me." Rachel tried calling her again. Still no answer. She left her another message.

Finally, at 7:30, Rachel called Kasey's house. "Hi Karen, it's Rachel. I'm looking for Aspen. Is she still at your house?"

"Yeah. The girls are upstairs. Want me to go get her?" Karen asked.

Rachel felt her anger rising. "No thanks. I'm going to come get her. I'll be there in ten minutes."

"You found her?" AJ asked after Rachel hung up the phone.

"She's still at Kasey's. I'll be right back."

"Oh boy. I'm just going to wait here. Maybe I'll head downstairs and check out the store. Find a book to read. The entire thing," she said.

"Wish me luck," Rachel said before stepping out into the cold night.

Rachel parked the car in front of Kasey's house and headed for the front door. Karen was waiting for her. "I wasn't sure if you wanted me to tell her you were coming or not. I didn't say anything."

"Perfect," Rachel said. "Where are they?"

"Upstairs. With my son, Kevin, and his friends," Karen said.

Rachel headed up the stairs. It sounded like a teenage party was taking place. She rounded the corner to see a room full of girls and boys. She recognized some of them. Aspen was in the corner, wedged on a chair with a boy next to her, his arm around her, their legs twisted together. Aspen's eyes went instantly wide when she saw her mom in the doorway.

"Mom!"

"Let's go," Rachel said, not wanting to make a scene. She didn't know the boy Aspen was sitting with but had seen him around with Kevin before, who was four years older than Aspen.

Aspen jumped from the chair and scrambled to find her things. She didn't bother with goodbyes as she fled from the room and followed her mom down the stairs and out the door.

"What are you doing here? You said I could be here until seven!"

"Too bad it's almost eight."

"What?" Aspen reached for her phone in her bag. "Shit."

"What did you say?" Rachel asked as she spun around on her heel. She grabbed the phone from her daughter's hands. "Oh look at that. Four missed calls from Mom."

"Mom, I didn't realize what time it was."

Rachel laughed. "Yeah well, I didn't realize what you were really up to. So let's just call this whole thing a blessing in disguise. Now get in the car."

Without another word Aspen got into the front seat of the car.

"Who is he and tell me how old he is. And I swear to you if you lie to me, I'm shipping you off to some military school."

"His name is Adam. And he's not that old."

"That wasn't what I asked you," Rachel said.

"He's fifteen."

"When does he turn sixteen?"

Aspen was silent.

"Aspen?"

"In February. I know what you're going to say. But I'm not too young. Mom, I like him. I really like him," she pleaded.

"I don't care how much you like him. You are too young. You are not having a boyfriend."

"I hate to break it to you, but you can't be around me all the time. I will still see him at school. You can't stop me."

Rachel turned to look at her. "When did you get so bold? Who do you think you are to talk to me like that?"

Aspen folded her arms. "It's true and you know it."

"You better drop the attitude. Now."

They pulled into Sinful Retreat alongside another vehicle. "You called Dad?"

"You bet I called your dad," Rachel said. "He's sitting upstairs right now."

"Great. Just hang me now."

"Cut it out. And get up there. You need to face the music."

Aspen walked through the door with reluctance. Matt was sitting on the couch when they got back. Rachel was surprised, however, that he didn't immediately begin yelling when they walked through the door.

"Come sit," he said as he nodded toward the vacant spot beside him.

Leery, Aspen did as she was told.

"So you think you're old enough for a boyfriend?" he asked.

She shrugged. "Well, yeah. I'm almost thirteen. All my friends have one."

Matt's eyes briefly met Rachel's. "So when you're almost thirteen, what does dating look like?"

"I don't know. Hanging out, I guess."

"Do you kiss?" he asked.

"Dad!" Aspen's face turned instantly red.

"If you think you're mature enough to be dating," Rachel said, cringing at the word, "then you should be mature enough to talk with us about it."

"Ugh. Fine. Yes."

Rachel saw Matt swallow hard. She knew he wanted to stand up and start yelling.

"Do you do other things?" Rachel asked.

"Eww. No."

She felt instant relief.

"Although I think you're too young to have a boyfriend, I also can't stop you," Matt admitted.

Aspen seemed pleased with herself.

"However, there will be rules. And I will expect those rules to be followed," he said sternly.

"Public places, always groups," Rachel said.

"I agree," he said. "And you need to disclose whenever he is going to be somewhere that you're going. If you're going out with friends and he will be there, I want to know about it."

Rachel nodded. "In the meantime, you are grounded for this stunt."

"What?" she gasped. "I lost track of the time!"

"You deliberately manipulated me into thinking you were doing something different than you really were," Rachel said. "And until we can trust you, you won't be doing anything with friends, boys or girls."

"You guys are so unfair!"

"Aspy, you brought this on yourself," Matt said.

After forfeiting her digital devices and retiring to her room to finish homework, Matt and Rachel stayed on the couch.

"A boyfriend, I can't believe it," she said.

"Honestly, I want to punch a wall right now," he said.

She laughed. "You handled it very well. I'm impressed." Rachel nodded with approval.

"Really? I've been trying to take what you've been saying into account."

"Well I think it's working. I was waiting for you to freak out tonight. And it never happened."

"Oh I was freaking out. I just had to swallow it."

She laughed. "I was freaking out, too."

"Good," he said, laughing. "Do you have any beer? I could really use one after that."

"Uh, there might be one or two in the fridge. You'll have to look."

Matt rose from the couch and walked into the kitchen. "You've got three. Want one?"

"No thanks. AJ and I had our fill of tequila last night. I've met my quota for a while now," she said.

He laughed as he cracked it open and made his way back into the living room and took a seat beside her on the couch.

"You know, I was only thirteen and you were fourteen when we had our first kiss," she said.

"Yeah, but that was Spin the Bottle."

"I guarantee you would be freaking out just as badly if you found out she was playing Spin the Bottle with a group of friends," Rachel said with a laugh.

"Oh man, you're right. When did I become this person?"

"When you became a dad."

He took a swallow of the beer. "Maybe it was easier on me when I was everywhere else in the country and I just let you handle all this."

"Easier for you."

"Ah, so the truth comes out," he said.

She smiled. "Tonight, would not have gone this way without you here, that's for sure."

"Wow."

"Wow what?" she asked.

"I'm just shocked that I did something right for a change."

"Don't be so hard on yourself," she said.

He exhaled. "You want to know why I took that job? Why I left?"

Rachel furrowed her brow. "What do you mean? You took the job because that's where your heart was. It was always there. I knew that."

He shook his head. "No. You're wrong. My heart was with you. I loved you so much. You and our new baby."

"What?" she said. She had never heard him talk like this before.

"I looked around at what I had to offer you both and I was ashamed of myself. I had nothing. The only thing I had was that job offer, so I took it because it was all I could think of to make something of myself for you two."

"Matt, I never knew that."

"The kicker was, after I was finally in a place that I felt good enough, you guys didn't need me anymore. And then I just didn't come back because, well, you didn't need me and I was needed there."

"So what changed?" She asked.

"I got tired of missing you guys." He slid his hand along the side of her face. It was warm and soft as it stroked her cheekbone. "It just didn't matter where I was headed anymore, the only place I wanted to be was here, with my family."

Rachel was paralyzed listening to him speak. She had never heard him talk like this ever before. Words she had wanted to hear so badly thirteen years earlier were finally playing in her ears.

Matt leaned forward, his lips brushing gently along hers. Rachel closed her eyes for a moment and breathed him in and in an instant she knew.

"Matt, I'm sorry. I am so glad that you are here and that we have the chance to raise Aspen together. Because she deserves both of her parents. But I am not in love with you. And I'm sorry because I know that hurts you. But I just can't tell you that I am. You and I are not meant to be together."

"Rach—"

"I'm sorry," she said as she stood and walked away.

TWENTY

"**W**hat is that heavenly smell?" Rachel asked as she stepped into Sinful Retreat on Tuesday morning. Kristin was already there, her kids watching cartoons in the children's nook.

"You like that?" Kristin said, popping her head out of the kitchen and stepping behind the bakery counter.

"Like it? I think I might melt into a puddle right here," she said as she powered up the register and credit card machine.

"I made red velvet cheesecake, peppermint brownie pie, café latte turtle cake, and what you're smelling is the pudding filling I'm making for the four-layer poppy-seed torte."

"You get better every year," Rachel said.

Kristin smiled and waved her hand. "I know."

With Christmas a week away, Sinful Retreat stayed busy all day. Customers were in and out in steady rhythm and Rachel worked between her office and the floor, helping customers, making orders, and processing paperwork. She was more than thankful when the end of the day came around and it was time to retire upstairs, even if she had reports to do from home.

She welcomed the change of scenery, and with Aspen at her dad's for the night, she welcomed the peace and quiet.

She opened a bottle of wine and poured herself a small glass, then she sat down on the couch and watched a little television before opening the computer back up for a couple of hours.

Thirty minutes later, she was back at it, inputting numbers and transferring data. By nine, she was more than exhausted and decided to just go to bed early. She headed into her bedroom and changed. It was snowy outside, partly sleeting, so she chose a warm, cozy pair of jammies to snuggle into. Rachel washed her face and a few minutes later she crawled beneath her blankets.

She thought briefly about reading but decided just to sleep instead. She rarely went to bed early anymore. She flipped off the light and closed her eyes.

Rachel awoke with a startle to a rapid banging on her door. Confused, she flipped on her light and glanced at the clock. It was almost midnight. She must have been sleeping hard because she struggled to gain her footing as she left her bedroom and headed for her door.

She flipped on the front light and glanced out the window. She was surprised to see Ethan banging on her door. She opened it.

"What are—"

"Rachel, there's been an accident," he said. His voice was rushed and panicky,

"What?"

"It's Aspen."

She instantly felt her heart stop and her stomach drop.

"She's being taken to Arrowhead Regional in Colton. Get dressed. I'll drive you. We can get Matt on the way."

The next several minutes were a blur to Rachel as she ran back into her apartment. She changed her clothes while Ethan used her phone to call Matt. There was no answer.

"What happened? How was she in an accident? How does Matt not know? She's supposed to with him."

"She was in a car full of kids."

Rachel was frantic. "I…I… I don't know what I need."

"Shoes, Rachel. You need shoes," he said.

Ethan grabbed socks for her from her dresser and sneakers from her closet. Rachel was unable to focus.

"Did you get a hold of Matt?" she asked.

"No. But we'll get him," he said.

"How did you know about the accident?"

He took a breath as he looked her in the eyes. "I was a first responder on the scene."

"Ohhh," Rachel's knees buckled, and she collapsed into Ethan. He grabbed her and pulled her body up. "Is it bad? Tell me the truth."

"I don't know, Rach. She was talking to me. She was conscious."

"That's good, right?" Rachel pleaded.

Ethan swallowed. "Let's get Matt and get to the hospital."

She nodded as she let him escort her out of the apartment.

When Rachel stepped outside, she was greeted with cold, wet sleet. It was wet and heavy and coated her eyelashes as she carefully made her way down the slippery stairs to Ethan's car.

Inside, despite the heat that was blowing full blast on her, Rachel felt numb. The world went by around her in a blur as they drove to Matt's; Ethan repeatedly called him to no avail.

"Damnit. Why won't he answer?" He threw his phone down as he sped around a sharp corner. Rachel grabbed the door instinctively but didn't react otherwise. A moment later, Matt's small house appeared through the sleet. Ethan pulled into the shallow driveway and before the car had come to a halt, Rachel was out the door and headed toward the house.

Ethan quickly caught up with her as she pounded restlessly on the door. Finally, Matt answered in a t-shirt and boxer shorts.

"What the hell?"

"It's Aspen. She's been in an accident," Rachel said, stepping around him into the house.

"What? She's sleeping," he said.

"No. She was in an accident, Matt," she said, feeling her emotion rising. "We've got to go. Get your stuff."

Matt looked at Ethan who gave him a sober nod.

"Aspen!" he yelled as he turned and ran down the hall. He barged through the closed door of her bedroom, the curtains of her open window fluttering in the icy breeze.

Tearing through the blankets on her bed, Matt called her name. He went to her closet next, tearing through the clothes on hangers. "Aspen!" he called, over and over again.

"Matt, we've got to go," Rachel said from the doorway.

He stopped and turned, looking up from his bare feet as they stood on the slushy, partially frozen carpeting. "How did she… when did she…" he asked, emotion flooding his face.

"I'll drive you guys," Ethan said.

Matt pushed past both of them as he headed toward his bedroom. Barely two minutes later, he reemerged in jeans, a sweatshirt and baseball cap and with socks now on his feet. "Where are they taking her?" he asked Ethan.

"Arrowhead Regional."

"Then let's go."

On the road, Rachel sat in the front seat, staring blankly at the road ahead, while Matt took the back. For the longest time the three of them were silent. Matt broke it first.

"Were you there? Were you a first responder?"

Ethan glanced at him through the rearview mirror. He nodded.

"Tell me what happened," Matt said.

Ethan hesitated as he focused on the road. Rim of the World Highway was windy and it was dark and visibility was low. The further they descended in elevation the more the sleet turned into rain.

"Tell me! I need to know. I want the truth."

Rachel looked at Ethan as his eyes met hers in the dark car.

"They took out a guardrail. A witness said they were going too fast around the corner, and it looked like they hit the gravel and lost control," Ethan said, avoiding eye contact with Rachel. "I'm not sure how many times the car rolled, more than once. It fell at least a hundred feet down a steep embankment, taking out small trees and brush along the way. It finally stopped upside-down when it collided with a massive pine."

"Is everyone okay?" Rachel asked.

"The driver wasn't seat belted. He was thrown from the car and we pronounced him dead at the scene," he said softly.

Rachel gasped.

"He?" Matt asked.

Ethan nodded. "It was four boys and one other girl with Aspen."

Rachel reached for Ethan's hand, and he laced his fingers through hers. "What happened to Aspen?" he asked.

He sighed heavily. "She was on the side of the car that hit the tree."

Rachel and Matt gasped together.

"Her head was pretty beat up, but she was conscious. She talked to me."

"She talked to you?" she asked, tears welling in her eyes.

He nodded reassuringly at her. "Yeah, we… we talked for a while. I held her hand while paramedics secured her and cut her out of her seat belt. I told her I was going to get you guys."

Rachel heard Matt sit back as he sighed with relief. "And everyone else?"

"Everyone was taken to the hospital," Ethan said.

Rachel buried her face in her hands as they reached the bottom of the mountains. "Just get me to her, Ethan. Just get me to her."

At the hospital, Rachel, Matt and Ethan were put in a large waiting room while Aspen was undergoing tests. They were given no information on her status which sent Rachel reeling. She had wanted to crawl across the counter and claw the woman's eyes out, but Ethan took her by the hand and gently led her away.

"I need to make some calls," she said, unable to sit and wait. She knew it was the middle of the night, well after one by now, but it wouldn't matter. There were people who would want to know. She called her parents first, who immediately set out to meet her at the hospital. Then she called her friends.

Afterward, she returned to the waiting room, where Ethan and Matt were still waiting. She took a seat, but sitting simply made her imagination run wild. She stood and began to pace. She was relieved when her parents finally arrived. There were two more people to help distract her.

It felt like hours had gone by. And just after two thirty, a tall black man with glasses emerged from double doors in a long white coat. "Are you Aspen's parents?" he asked, eyeing Rachel and Matt as they sat beside each other.

Rachel jumped to her feet. "I'm her mother. Please, how is she? Tell me what's going on."

"I'm Dr. Donahue. Your daughter has a broken right arm and collar bone."

"That's not bad," Matt said with relief.

"She also," the doctor continued, "I'm afraid, has a broken neck."

Rachel felt Ethan's arms tighten around her as she flinched. "What?"

The doctor nodded. "The C2 vertebra in her neck is broken. We call it a Hangman's Type III bilateral fracture."

"Is she paralyzed?" Matt asked.

"The extent of damage to her spinal cord is unknown at this point," Dr. Donahue said. "These kinds of fractures are rare and due to the delicate nature of them, we will be transferring Aspen to Loma Linda University Medical Center. They're a level 1 trauma center and there she will see their neurosurgeon Dr. Allen Cohen. I've been consulting with him, and he is up to speed on Aspen's situation. He's expecting you yet tonight."

Rachel swallowed hard as she felt the life drain from her body.

"Also," Dr. Donahue said, "as a result of Aspen's head injury, she has developed neurogenic pulmonary edema, which is a rare form of swelling around her lungs. It's caused by an increase of fluids that can develop after a head injury. In an effort to combat the low oxygen levels from the edema, we currently have Aspen on a ventilator and in a medically induced coma. But you are welcome to see her before her transport to Murrieta arrives."

Feeling the room begin to close in on her, Rachel closed her eyes and braced herself on Ethan's arm. In an instant her world was falling apart.

She swallowed hard when she saw a brace stabilizing Aspen's neck, the tube feeding into her mouth, and one into her nose, and she grabbed for Matt's hand as he stood beside her.

He clutched it firmly and together they approached the bed.

"Aspen, it's Mom. I'm here," she said as she stroked her hand through her daughter's blonde hair as it fanned across the white pillow.

"I'm here, too, kiddo," Matt said as he reached forward with his other hand and clasped it around Aspen's. "You've got to be strong, okay? You hang in there and we're going to do whatever we can for you."

Rachel licked her finger and wiped as the dried blood along the side of Aspen's face. It was useless.

A nurse came in the room. "I'm sorry, but her ambulance is here and we need to finish prepping her for the transport," she said sympathetically.

Rachel nodded before leaning down and kissing Aspen on the forehead. "I love you so much. I'll see you soon."

At Loma Linda University Medical Center, Ethan made himself comfortable in the waiting room outside the ICU with Jenn and Joseph. He was also on the lookout for AJ, Kristin and Tiff who were all on their way to the hospital. Rachel and Matt sat in a smaller, private waiting room, waiting for Dr. Cohen.

He entered the room with longer, chin-length hair, black, thick rimmed glasses and a serious nod of his head as he introduced himself, shaking their hands.

"Aspen is here. She's being set up in a room now. I've been looking at both the radiographs and CT scan that Dr. Donahue sent over and I think we need to establish if there has been any spinal cord damage. That will make a difference from here on out on how we treat Aspen's fracture."

Matt reached for Rachel's hand as they nodded their head.

"The procedure to do that sounds worse than it is, but let me emphasize that it is non-surgical. Which good. We'll do a closed reduction. It's a form of traction that involves inserting tongs into the skull, attaching a pulley to the tongs, and attaching small weights to the opposite end of that pulley. The weight then pulls the head away from the shoulders just enough to enable the soft tissue that's around the spine to push the fractured bone back into place. We'll then inject a dye into the damaged area and x-ray it and evaluate what is really going on with the spinal cord."

Rachel cringed. "That sounds awful!"

He nodded. "I know. It sounds much worse than it really is. But Aspen won't be aware of any of it. And it's quite simple."

She swallowed.

"And this will be able to determine if she's paralyzed?" Matt asked, squeezing Rachel's hand harder.

"It's a crucial step in determining that, yes."

Matt nodded. "Then do it."

Rachel took in a deep breath as she closed her eyes.

"If you guys go back to the main waiting room just outside the ICU doors, I will come find you as soon as the procedure is over and I have any information for you," the doctor said with a nod.

Back in the waiting room, Rachel was relieved to see AJ had made it down. She was as white as a ghost as Ethan was explaining to her what happened. As soon as Matt and Rachel emerged from the ICU doors, everyone immediately wanted an update. Matt filled them in about their conversation with the doctor as Rachel took a seat in the corner of the waiting room.

Her mind raced with fear and panic as she thought about her daughter, her baby, somewhere behind closed doors, in the hands of strangers. She thought of Rachel Schneider, the mother who had sent her children halfway across the world because she thought it was the better option for her. In that moment she realized what it had taken for Rachel Schneider to do what she did. It took love. So much love that her own pain and worry had to be set aside because it was no longer about her; it had become solely about protecting Aspen and doing for her what needed to be done, despite how much it made her cringe or scared or worried. It also took faith. Faith that the decision she was making based on the information she had and the situation she was in, was the best decision she could make. Faith that something greater was meant for Aspen, faith that she was in the best hands possible.

"How're you doing?"

Rachel looked up through watery eyes at Matt as he towered above her.

"I wonder what the last word I said to her was," she said.

"Don't talk like that," he said, sitting down beside her. "You'll have more conversations with her. You'll laugh and fight with her for years to come."

"And how do you know that?" she asked.

"It's just something I have to believe right now," he said, his eye meeting hers.

She inhaled deeply, her gaze not dropping from his.

"So tell me something, why're you avoiding the group? They're here just as much for you as they are for Aspen, you know?"

"I know. I just wanted to be alone. To be with my thoughts," she said.

He nodded. "You know," and if you ever repeat this, I'll probably deny it, "that Ethan's not such a bad guy."

She gave a weak laugh.

Matt dropped his playful look. "Rachel, he saved her. I'm sure of it. He saved Aspen."

She swallowed hard as she felt a tightening in her chest. She felt tears stinging in her eyes.

"Do you still love him?" he asked.

She was startled by his question. "What?"

"Oh, come on. I'm not blind. He's in love with you," he said.

She sighed as she looked across the waiting room. He was sitting beside Tiff and AJ and looked as restless as the others.

"I hurt him," she said quietly.

"How so?" he asked.

Rachel turned to face him. "Since when do you want to give me advice on my relationships?"

He sighed and shrugged. "I've got nothing better to do right now. Tell me, what happened?"

Rachel wasn't sure why, but she did. She opened up and shared the complicated story of how her and Ethan's lives had overlapped generations earlier and how she'd pushed him away when she'd discovered it.

"And you did this because—"

"I spent my whole life never knowing I had any connection to these people. My dad spent his entire life never knowing his connection to them, and I feel like it's my obligation to honor them. But how can I do that when I'm in love with a man who comes from the very family who tortured them?"

"Rach," he said with a sigh, "I know you mean well and all, but Ethan's not family to these people so much as he is a descendant of them. I mean, he can't help where he comes from any more than you can. And he doesn't just come from that line; that's not all that he is. Genetics isn't everything. We have choices in life. His grandpa made the choice to leave Germany. That's the line that he comes from. Not the people that stayed and committed all those murderous acts."

Rachel thought about that for a moment.

"And I'm probably crazy for giving you this advice, considering how I feel about you, but if you let this stand in your way, I think you're foolish."

She looked at him and raised an eyebrow. "I'm sorry, what?"

"These people, the Jews, had their lives sacrificed in the name of ignorance and hatred. That is the worst thing to sacrifice anything for. But they had no control over it. They were powerless to stop it. But in a small way, you're letting it happen all over again."

"How am I let—"

"Let me finish," he said bluntly. "Are you really going to give up on this, on him, because seventy years ago some ignorant, racist bastards decided who they thought were racially superior? You're still giving them what they wanted all these years later. They wanted to divide. It's coming together that defies them, that rejects the entire intention and movement of the Holocaust. I mean, maybe I'm wrong, but it was your ancestors who knew what it meant to give up everything. You've got a chance here that few people ever get. And trust me when I say that few people even realize when that opportunity is there for them to seize. So take it. Go after it. And in their honor, spend your life being happy, not fighting your heart because you think it's honoring them."

"You're a good man, Matt," she said, her heart swelling with a mixture of emotions: gratefulness for Matt, love and confusion for Ethan.

"Unfortunately, it's the good guys who never win," he said. Matt sighed.

"That's where you're wrong. You did win. The girl behind those doors is your grand prize," she said.

He gave her a weak smile. "You're right. I just hope she pulls through this."

The double doors to the ICU opened and Dr. Cohen stepped into the waiting room. Rachel and Matt rose to their feet instantly and the group followed behind them.

"Good news. There didn't appear to be any damage to the spinal cord. Of course we'll learn more when Aspen wakes up, but for now, this is a good sign. It also allowed me to prepare a plan to move forward with her treatment. I'm anticipating her edema to reduce and dissipate in the next twenty-four to seventy-two hours. We should see significant improvements in her breathing in that time and I'm hoping to take her off the ventilator. Although there is significant angulation in the fracture line in the vertebra, the good news is that there is no displacement, meaning it didn't move. I won't need to do surgery on her neck. Instead, we will use a halo brace until the fracture heals."

"I'm sorry, what is a halo brace?" Rachel asked, listening as intently as she could.

"It's a good question. It's a brace that will completely immobilize her head and neck while her bone and ligaments heal. But it allows her to still get out of bed and move about. It's a metal frame that goes around her head with a ring that will screw into her skull. The frame extends down into a vest that she'll wear around her chest."

"And how long will she wear that?" she asked, trying to picture the contraption.

"I'm going to do another CT scan on her at eight weeks," he said.

Rachel took in a deep breath as she realized the uphill battle ahead of them but was also relieved knowing it could have been much worse.

"We are going to put the brace on her now and as soon as we're done with that, you'll be able to see her. We'll let you know," he said with a positive smile and a shake of their hands.

"Thank you, Dr. Cohen," Matt said before turning to hug Rachel. "This is such good news. Oh this is such good news."

Rachel joined the others in the waiting room as they waited for clearance to see Aspen. When it finally came, joy flooded her body like she had never felt before.

"Please, only two people at a time. Please keep it to a minimum of a few minutes for each person and immediate family only," the nurse said as the group gathered near the door.

Rachel looked over her shoulder, her eyes meeting Ethan's. They lingered for a moment before he nodded for her to go on. She felt Matt pulling her along and before she knew it the doors to the ICU closed and she could no longer see his face.

Summoning her strength, she turned, and together she and Matt headed toward their daughter's room. It was dark and quiet, except for the low hum of the ventilators and the soft beep of the heart monitor attached to Aspen. She lay peacefully on the bed, covered neatly in blankets. Aside from the disrupting tubes and metal framing around her face and head, anyone could have thought she was simply sleeping of her own accord.

Rachel took a heavy breath as she approached the bed and slipped her hand into Aspen's. She found comfort in finding it was warm to the touch. She surveyed the new brace. A ring was screwed in in two places to Aspen's forehead and it circled her head. It was suspended by four bars, parallel with her neck, extending down and attaching to the vest hidden beneath her hospital gown.

Rachel felt her stomach tighten but she knew that this too would make them stronger, and she gave Aspen's hand a gentle squeeze. "We'll get through this. Whatever it takes," she whispered, afraid to talk any louder in the quiet room.

"I'll be right back," Matt whispered into her ear before stepping out of the room.

Rachel stayed by Aspen's bedside, gripping her hand firmly until she felt Matt return. She knew the nurse would come back any minute and tell her that her time was up, but she wasn't moving from that bedside until that moment.

She felt his hand on her shoulder and she looked up. She was surprised to see Ethan standing beside her. "Matt said I should come in."

Rachel reached up with her free hand and slid it over his and tears welled in her eyes. She wondered what she had ever done to deserve him. She rose to her feet and turned to face him.

"I haven't had a chance to thank you," she began.

"I was doing my job," he said.

"It was more than that."

He paused and nodded his head. "I couldn't leave her side. The car was so smashed up, you could barely recognize it. And everyone kept yelling at me to get out of the car, that it was unstable on the side of the embankment. It was too steep. It could go at any second. And I knew that. Everything in my training told me it wasn't safe. But I just held her hand and I looked at her like she was my own and I couldn't leave her. And they finally got the seatbelt cut loose and I swear to you, Rach, I'd never been so relieved and so scared in my life," he said, his voice shaking when he spoke.

She pulled him into her, wrapping her arms firmly around him. "She's going to be okay. It's because of you that she's going to be okay," she said.

He buried his face in her hair and they stood there in silence until the nurse came.

"I'm sorry," she said, "but we need to let her rest."

Rachel looked up toward the nurse who had a pitying looking on her face. "We'll be right out," she said. She glanced up at Ethan and then turned back to Aspen. Leaning over her bed she kissed the top of her hand. "I'll be back soon. Get some rest."

By morning, Rachel's body ached from stress, sleep deprivation and the uncomfortable furniture that filled the waiting room outside the ICU at Loma Linda. Ethan handed both her and Matt a cup of coffee, along with cheap toothbrushes wrapped in cellophane with the gift shop logo on them.

"Thought you might want them," he said with a nod.

Matt yawned as he took them. "Thanks, man," he said as he stood. "I've got to stretch my legs."

Ethan made his way back down the hall to get more coffee and Tiff filled the spot Matt had had vacated.

"How are you holding up?" she asked.

"About the same I was an hour ago," Rachel said, glancing toward the wall on the clock.

Tiff nodded. "Sorry. It's lame, I know. But I don't know what else to ask."

Rachel laughed and shrugged her shoulders. "I kind of like the routine we've established. Gives me something to look forward to at twenty past every hour."

Tiff smiled. "Oh, well, glad I could help. Where did Kristin go?"

"To call Darren. He's going to put a sign in Sinful Retreat saying we're closed today," she said.

"Wow. I don't think that's ever happened," Tiff said.

Rachel shook her head. "It hasn't."

"Miss Taylor?" the nurse said, opening the ICU doors. "Your daughter just opened her eyes."

Rachel jumped to her feet and bound across the floor of the waiting room. "Someone find Matt," she called over her shoulder. Her heart began racing as she entered the ICU, willing herself to calm down as she rounded the corner, Aspen's room coming into sight.

Stepping inside the room, she gently approached the bed. Aspen was lying beneath the blankets and looked just as she did when Rachel saw her before. Then her nose wrinkled and her eyelashes fluttered and her eyes slowly opened. Rachel's face lit up in a smile and her eyes welled with tears as she reached for her hand.

"Hi baby," she said, and she leaned over the bed. "You're going to be okay. It's going to be okay."

A moment later, Matt appeared in the room, followed by Dr. Cohen.

"Welcome back, Aspen," Dr. Cohen said, a smile on his face. "I'm Dr. Cohen. You were in a car accident. I know you can't talk right now because of the ventilator, but I want you to blink. Once for yes and twice for no. Can you do that?" he asked.

Aspen blinked once.

"Good."

Rachel smiled.

"Do you remember the car accident?" Dr. Cohen asked.

One blink. Yes.

"Are you in pain right now?"

One blink.

"Is it a lot of pain?" he asked.

Two blinks. No.

Rachel felt relief.

"Do you recognize your mom and dad here with me?" Dr. Cohen asked.

One blink.

Dr. Cohen rounded the bed and lifted up the blankets at the foot of the bed, exposing her bare foot. "I'm going to touch this to your foot. You let me know if you can feel what I'm doing," he said.

One blink.

One blink.

One blink.

"Great," he said. He covered her foot back up and moved to her hands and arms and repeated the procedure. Once again she blinked yes. "This is great, Aspen." He approached the side of her bed and carefully explained to her what was going on. Panic rose in her eyes when he told her that her neck was broke. "Calm down. It's okay. There doesn't appear to be any paralysis, which is a good sign. And we have the brace on to stabilize your head and neck and we have no reason to think you won't make a full recovery. Aspen you are young and healthy; this is the best time to make recoveries like this."

Aspen's eyes moved to her mom's and Rachel nodded in assurance.

"We're going to take really good care of you here. I promise. And as soon as we get your edema under control, we'll be able to send you home, okay?" he said.

Aspen's eye flitted back to the doctor. Slowly they began to fill with tears. Rachel grabbed a tissue from a nearby box and rushed to her side to blot the tears before running down her side.

"Asp, it's going to be okay. We'll get through this. I promise we'll get through this."

"Why don't you guys take some time," Dr. Cohen said with a nod before saying his goodbyes and slipping out of the room.

"Aspen, we love you, so much," Matt said as he approached the other side of her bed.

Her eyes glanced toward him, and she blinked twice.

"No? Why wouldn't we?" he asked.

"Because you snuck out?" Rachel asked.

One blink.

"Aspen," Matt said, "so you made a mistake. That doesn't mean we don't love you. We have done nothing but worry about you the last day."

"Oh honey," Rachel said, "I'm just glad that you're okay. You will be okay. We'll get through this and one day, I promise, you will look back and this will just be a bad memory."

"Hey Mom," Aspen called from her bed. She had been home from the hospital for two days.

"Yeah?" Rachel asked, poking her head into her bedroom. "Everything okay? Do you need something?"

"What're you doing?" she asked, pulling the blankets up to her chest, her head in the brace as she rested back on a stack of pillows.

"Just wrapping some last-minute gifts. I can't believe it's Christmas tomorrow."

Aspen laughed. "I just wanted to give you a heads up, Ethan texted me, he was going to stop by. He has to work tomorrow but has a gift for me and wanted to see how I was doing since I got home."

"Ethan?" Rachel said, feeling her stomach tighten. "Oh, yeah. Okay." She bypassed the pile of wrapping paper and the last few gifts that needed to be wrapped and headed for her bedroom. Quickly she slipped out of her sweatpants and into a pair of jeans. She exchanged the sweatshirt for a long sleeve Henley and ran a brush through her hair.

There was a knock at the door.

With no time to brush her teeth, she quickly popped a tic-tac, spritzed herself with body spray and headed toward the door as another knock came.

"Mom, are you going to get that?" Aspen yelled from her room.

"I'm coming," she yelled.

She felt nervous when she opened the door, the cold breeze blowing the scent of him into her apartment and making her heart beat faster. "Come in on. I mean, come on in," she said, feeling her cheeks go red.

He smiled as he stepped inside. "You look nice," he said as he bypassed her and took off her jacket.

"Oh," she said with the wave of her hand. "I've just been wrapping presents all day."

He glanced at the pile of holiday papers and gifts on the floor and nodded. "I see that. How's Aspen doing?"

"She's good. Her spirits seem to be better since she's been home."

"I'm glad to hear that. I got her a Christmas present. I hope that's okay," he said.

"Of course. Yes, Ethan. She's right in her room. Go on in," she said with a nod.

She felt relief when he disappeared from sight. It felt awkward to talk to him. Why was it awkward to talk to him? She inched closer to the door to listen to them.

"You look like you're doing good," he said.

"As long as I don't go through airport security any time soon," she said with a laugh.

He laughed too.

"Have your friends stopped by?"

"Yeah. I mean, Kasey can't. Her arm was broken in three places and she has two broken legs. She's not really going anywhere. But my other friends have been by. And I've been getting lots of cards and stuff from other kids in my class," she said.

"That's good. How's your mom doing?"

Rachel felt a pull inside of her.

"You know, you should just ask her. She missed you, too," Aspen said.

Ethan laughed.

"She does, I can tell."

"I got you a Christmas present," he said.

"Way to change the subject. What is it?" Aspen was quiet for a moment. "Ooh, that's a box that jewelry comes in," she said.

There was another quiet moment between them.

"Oh, it's beautiful," she said, losing her sarcastic tone.

"The Jewish pendant is for your newly discovered roots, the Christian pendant is for your deeply established roots, the amethyst is your birthstone and finally the tanzanite is the stone for the month that you said that you 'would not go gentle into that good night.' You were a brave soul that night, Aspen, braver than you'll ever know," he said. "Can I put the necklace on you?"

Rachel caught her breath. Knowing her emotions would be written across her face, she quietly made her way back to the couch and sat down to wait for Ethan to emerge from the room. She heard more mumbling but couldn't make it out and a minute later he came into the living room.

"How long were you listening?" he asked.

She feigned shock. "I don't know what you're talking about. I've been sitting here the entire time."

He laughed as he crossed the room and sat in the chair beside the couch.

"I'm actually glad that you came by," she said, feeling nerves take over her body as her pulse quickened. "There's something I've been thinking a lot about. Something I didn't know how to talk to you about, really."

"Rachel," he said, leaning forward on the chair. "We don't have to rehash all of this. I get where you're coming from. And it's your decision."

"Just," she put her hands out to stop him, "just hear me out. When I learned everything that I did, about what I'm made of and where I come from, I wasn't sure what to do with all of it. I'm still not sure. But of everything that I'm not sure of, there are a few things that I am quite certain of. One of those things being that I've never loved anyone like I love you. And I'm also sure, that somehow, with you by my side, if you'll still have me, that somehow, we'll figure out how to get past this. That we will figure out how to make this work and honor those innocent people who were murdered and that in the end, we'll be better off together than we ever were apart. Please tell me you want these things, that you want to be with me, too," she said. She took a breath.

Ethan looked up from his hands, his eyes meeting hers.

EPILOGUE

It was a partly cloudy day and the spring breeze blowing off the sea was cool. Rachel shuddered as she pulled her hands further into the sleeves of her jacket, thankful she had put on her sweatshirt instead of leaving it in the car.

"I've never seen waves this big back in California," Aspen shouted from up ahead.

The beach was deserted, which Rachel liked. It was more peaceful that way.

"You know, I don't mind the beach on a gloomy day here. It sort of fits, you know?" Sarah said, coming up behind Rachel, Jenn alongside her, and Joseph next to her, pushing the wheelchair through the sand with some difficulty.

"I told you to just let me walk," Hanna said with authority. "I would've done just fine."

"And I told you there was absolutely no way I was letting that happen. Now sit back and enjoy the view," Joseph said.

Hanna sighed heavily as they finally caught up to Rachel and came to a stop. She turned and gazed out over the vast Baltic before her.

"*Hallo alter Freund.* Hello old friend," she whispered to the crashing waves.

They stood silent around Hanna as she sat in her chair and gazed over the open sea. Rachel felt Ethan slide his arm around her waist and pull her in closer. She turned to lightly kiss his lips before returning her gaze to the sea.

Later that afternoon they made their way down a paved pathway, Joseph once again pushing Hanna's chair. They reached a small clearing in the trees, and before them appeared a white stone monument: three rectangular pillars, the largest in the middle, connected by two smaller squares that displayed crosses across the front. The largest pillar, the middle one, was inscribed with the number seven thousand, the letters K-Z, and the date, 3 April 1945. The smaller outer pillars listed the twenty-four nationalities of people murdered during the bombings of the *SS Thielbek* and *Cap Arcona.*

Finally, the bottom slab that supported the monument wore the dates 1933 and 1945.

Hanna moved first. Bracing herself with the arms of her chair, she rose from the wheelchair, waving off assistance as it was offered. Standing on two feet she made her way to the stone monument. With an unsteady hand, she set down a candle on the slab and lit it, weeping as she did so.

"*Isak, alav ha-shalom,*" she said between tears as she set a rock onto the slab and slowly returned to the wheelchair.

Joseph gave her a gentle squeeze on the shoulder as she sat down, and Jenn handed her a tissue to wipe her tears. Somberly, he made his way toward the marker that memorialized the grandfather he never knew. When he reached it he carefully lowered himself to his knees. Placing one hand on the stone memorial, he dropped his head.

Aspen hugged Rachel firmly at the sight of her grandfather and tears streamed down her face. Rachel gently smoothed her hand through her daughter's hair, careful not to take her eyes off her dad.

After several minutes he stirred. When he emerged from his position, he placed a stone beside Hanna's and returned to Hanna's side with swollen, red eyes.

Rachel went next. She was keenly aware that everyone was watching her, but as soon as she arrived at the memorial it no longer seemed to matter. She lowered herself to her knees like her father, but instead of bowing, she stared straight ahead, her eyes piercing into the K-Z carved into the stone.

"When I started this journey, I had no idea what I would find. It certainly wasn't this. What I discovered were lives and people who were all too soon forgotten. And I'm here to change that." She reached out and touched the stone with her hand; it was hard and cold beneath her skin and sent a chill up her arm. "Your legacy will live on. And I just want to thank you for being a part of who I am."

Rachel set her stone beside her dad's, and giving the memorial another look, she rose to her feet and returned to Ethan's side.

Once they had all taken turns at the memorial, each putting a stone on the slab in honor of Isak, they observed a moment of silence in honor of those they lost.

As they turned to make their way back down the path toward the German town of Neustad, Rachel slowed her pace. She watched as her family pulled ahead, her daughter side-by-side with Ethan, her parents alongside each other as her dad pushed her Great Aunt Hanna in her chair and on the other side of her was Aunt Sarah.

Glancing over her shoulder, back at the memorial, she couldn't help but see Isak's face. He was smiling at them. After all, they were all his legacy. And even though it took them seventy years to get there, they had made it.

Tilting her head back, her face exposed to the sky, she suddenly felt the warm rays of sunshine on her skin, and in an instant, she felt peace wash over her. She looked back at her family and smiled.

"Wait up," she called, jogging ahead.

Ethan looked over his shoulder and smiled back at her.

She reached for him and took his hand in hers, their fingers lacing together as they walked on.

Acknowledgments

This book was made possible by many individuals. And my appreciation for them is unending. Firstly, there are my wonderful girlfriends, Teriann Mayfield, Kristin Elswood, and Ashley Janssen. Thank you for providing me with so much inspiration in my writing. Thank you, Kristin and Ashley for reading my very first draft as I wrote it, letting me bounce ideas off the both of you, and for giving me your honest feedback. Kristin, I couldn't have done so much of this without our late-night taco runs to clear my head. Ashley, you are worth more than a million thanks for giving me all of your honesty, even when it is completely brutal. Thank you for helping me to clean up my drafts.

I want to thank Shoshannah Cobb. You were such a crucial component of the successful outcome of this novel, and I am forever indebted to you. Thank you for all of your help in teaching me about the beautiful Jewish culture and opening my eyes to a world I've never before known. Thank you for helping me with my Yiddish and Hebrew. It is your passion and fervor that kept me going.

An enormous thank you goes to the Seymour family for sharing with me the untold story of dear Adalbert and the tragic end to his life at the hands of the Nazis. Although so much is unknown about his imprisonment in Auschwitz, I only hope I was able to translate what is known of his story in a way that honors him.

Thank you, Patrick Sinner for your keen eye and editing skills. Mom, thank you for being so inspiring, and persistent, about the dog names you like.

And thank you to my amazing husband, Tim. I could have never made this possible without all of your love, patience and support. You were such a rock for me during the entire process of making this book a reality, and I love you to the ends of the earth for it.

About the Author

Originally from small-town Minnesota, Nicole currently lives in the Greater Salt Lake City, Utah area with her husband, two kids, and a very fluffy dog. She is a graduate of the University of Minnesota, Morris. In addition to having an addiction to writing, she is an avid reader, a baseball enthusiast, and has an affinity for novelty coffee mugs.

Find on social media:

Facebook.com/AuthorNicoleAhles

Instagram: NicoleA_Books

www.NicoleAhles.com

Also By Nicole M. Ahles

Convergence

Resurgence

The Cape House

What I Am Made Of

www.ingramcontent.com/pod-product-compliance
Lightning Source LLC
Chambersburg PA
CBHW010307100726
47905CB00011B/3241